The dream was forever the same

When he first awakened in the shadowy gloom, he thought it was all a dream—the same terrible nightmare that had haunted his sleep and hounded him out of bed for more years than he cared to remember.

In his sleep, his nightmare prison was just like this real one, measuring eight feet in diameter by thirty feet deep. Rocks and other things— foul things he didn't want to think about—littered the dank, rain-puddled floor.

But this waking nightmare was no dream.

Then the rocks began to fall in a horrifyingly accurate barrage. At first, only small pebbles rained down on him, but the sizes grew steadily larger and their weights heavier. He tried dodging out of the way, but he couldn't.

There was no point in calling out for help. No one would hear him.

There was no place to hide.

TOMBSTONE COURAGE

A JOANNA BRADY MYSTERY

AVON BOOKS
An Imprint of HarperCollinsPublishers

AVON BOOKS
An Imprint of HarperCollins*Publishers*
10 East 53rd Street
New York, New York 10022-5299

Prologue

Rocks rained down on him in a steady, deadly barrage, small ones at first; then, gradually, larger. In the beginning, he managed to crawl out of the way, dodging this way and that, scrabbling on his belly with his hands and arms wrapped around his head, protecting it.

"Stop," he begged, his voice strangely muffled by the dirt and rocks beneath him. "Please stop. I swear I'll never do it again. Never."

But still the brutal rocks kept falling. They smashed into his legs, his arms, the small of his back. He screamed in pain, in agony, but there was no escape, no place to hide.

The attack couldn't have lasted more than five minutes from beginning to end, but for him—the target—it seemed like forever. And it was, because when it was over, he lay partially buried and lifeless on the rock-strewn floor of the hole, with a ten-pound boulder crushing part of his skull.

One

HAROLD LAMM Patterson squinted through the rain-blurred windshield. Checking for traffic, he pulled his rattletrap International Scout through the gate of the Rocking P Ranch and onto the highway. Pouring rain made it hard to see. Part of the problem was his eyes. Ivy, his daughter, was constantly nagging him about that, and she was probably right. Thank God his ears still worked all right.

At eighty-four, even with his new, thick trifocals, the old peepers weren't nearly as good as they used to be. But Harold figured the real problem was the damn wiper blades. The rubber was old, cracked, and frayed. The blades squawked across the windshield, barely making contact and leaving trails of muddy water on the dusty, bug-splattered glass.

In southern Arizona, it seemed like you never noticed that the wipers weren't working until you needed them, and when you noticed, you were too busy driving blind to remember. The next time he went into A & A Auto Parts to drink coffee and shoot the breeze with the counterman, Gene Radovich, Harold still wouldn't remember, not if

3

it wasn't raining at the time. It reminded him of the words in that old-time song "Mañana." No need to fix a leaky roof on such a sunny day? Same difference.

But that particular day—an unseasonably cold early-November morning—it was raining like hell. A pelting winter storm had rolled into the Sonoran Desert from the Pacific, filling the normally dry creek beds and swathing the Mule Mountains in a dank gray blanket that was almost as chill as the pall around Harold Patterson's stubborn old heart.

His daughter's personal-injury trial was due to start in Cochise County Superior Court first thing tomorrow morning—Wednesday at nine o'clock. Unless he could figure out a way to stop it. Unless he could somehow bluff Holly into agreeing to talk to him. Unless he could work a deal and convince her to call it off.

He had tried to talk to her about it several times since she arrived in town. That ploy hadn't worked. That damn hotshot lawyer of hers had insisted that until Harold came to see her with his hat in his hand—to say nothing of a settlement— it was a straight-out no go. His own daughter refused to see him, wouldn't even tell him where she was staying.

His own daughter. Just thinking about it caused Harold's gnarled, arthritic hands—hands that had wrung the necks of countless Sunday-dinner chickens—to tighten into a similar death grip on the smooth surface of the worn steering wheel. Harold thought about Holly and her damn lawsuit the whole time he guided the wheezing yellow

Scout over the rain-swept pavement of Highway 80, up the mountain pass locals called the Divide and then down the winding trail of Tombstone Canyon into Old Bisbee.

Holly had been a Fourth of July baby. He had wanted to call her Linda—Indy for short in honor of Independence Day, but Emily wouldn't hear of it. She insisted that if she had daughters, they would be named after their grandmother's favorite Christmas carol, "The Holly and the Ivy," regardless of whether or not they arrived any time near December 25. And Holly it was. Would she have been less prickly, Harold sometimes wondered, had she been given a different name?

Holly Patterson had entered the world sandwiched neatly between Bisbee's traditional Independence Day Coaster Races and the annual Fourth of July parade down Tombstone Canyon. She was born in the Old Copper Queen Hospital— the brick one up in Old Bisbee, not the new apricot-colored one down in Warren. It had been a hot, miserable morning. On that pre-air-conditioning summer day, the nurses had left the delivery-room windows wide open in hopes of capturing some faint hint of breeze. Emily had screamed her fool head off. For several hours running. To a poor, anxious, prospective father waiting outside, that's how it had seemed.

Harold remembered the whole morning as vividly as if it were yesterday. Left to his own devices in the waiting room, he had been propelled out of the hospital by his wife's agonized cries. But with the windows open, there was no escape from Emily's frantic shrieks. No one else in the downtown area—onlookers watching the races or waiting for the parade—could escape them, either. The relentless screams echoed off nearby hillsides and reverberated up and down the canyons. People lined up on the sidewalks kept asking each other what in the world were they doing to that poor woman, killing her or what?

Pacing up and down in the small patch of grassy park between the hospital and the building that housed the Phelps Dodge General Office, Harold had wondered the same thing himself. What were they doing to her? And when old Doc Winters finally slipped Emily the spinal that shut her up, Harold had despaired completely. As soon as she grew quiet, he was convinced it was over, that his wife was dead.

Of course, that wasn't the case at all. Emily was fine, and so was the baby. Men don't forget that kind of agony. Women do. Had it been up to him, one child was all they would have had. Ever.

Afterward, holding the beautiful baby in her arms, nursing her, Emily had smiled at him and told him Holly was worth it. Harold wasn't so sure. Not then, not ten years later when Ivy was born, and certainly not now.

Things change. The delivery room where both Holly and Ivy had been born now housed a Sunday-school classroom for the Presbyterian church across the street. A law firm—the biggest one in town—now occupied the lower floor space where the old dispensary and pharmacy had been located. In fact, Burton Kimball, who was Harold's nephew as well as his attorney, kept his offices there. And as for the waspish Holly? Harold shook his head and clenched his jaw. Once more the powerful fingers tightened their viselike grip on the Scout's loosey-goosey steering wheel.

Holly was Holly. Had it been in Harold's power to make her life different, certainly he would have. She had grown up tough, headstrong, and hard to handle—a runaway while she was still in high school. Well, she was back in Bisbee now, staying God knows where. He had heard rumors about Holly and that friend of hers tooling around town in somebody's bright red Allanté, lording it over whoever saw her. Harold wondered about the car. It might possibly be hers, but Harold doubted it.

If Holly had enough money to buy a car like that, why was she back home, trying to take his ranch away from him? No, if she wasn't dead broke, she had to be close to it. After thirty-four years with no letters, no phone calls, why else would she suddenly come back home to a place she despised? As a precocious sixteen-year-old, Holly had found life on the Rocking P worse than prison. What else but abject poverty could bring her home as a fifty-year-old demanding her fair share of the family fortunes?

Holly was Harold's firstborn daughter. If she had needed help and asked for it, he would have given it to her gladly, regardless of the heartaches and disagreements that might have gone before. But Holly's reappearance had come in the form of a legal attack, mounted by some big-time California attorney who expected Harold to just lie down and play dead. And the attack had been aimed, with pinpoint accuracy, at the one place in Harold's life where he was most vulnerable. And guilty.

Of course, he had denied Holly's allegations. And when the *People* magazine reporter had shown up at the Rocking P and told him she was doing an article on "forgotten memories," Harold had tried to throw her off track without having to tell his side of the story. But the woman was one of those sharp-eyed, sharp-tongued little city women. He couldn't remember now exactly how it was she had phrased the critical question.

He may have mentally misplaced the exact text, but he recalled the reporter's meaning well enough. He had wondered if that particular line of questioning had come directly from Holly or from that so-called hypnotherapist of hers, Amy Baxter. The assumption behind the question was the idea that since one daughter had been forced to run away from home in order to avoid sexual abuse, what about the daughter who didn't leave? Was Ivy—the stay-at-home, old-maid daughter—a willing participant?

The reporter had made a big deal about the fact that Harold and Ivy lived alone together on the Rocking P, as though that in itself was enough to raise suspicions. Harold had exercised incredible restraint in not throwing the woman bodily out of his house. It was no surprise that the resulting article had made Harold sound like some kind of sex-crazed monster whose incestuous relations

with his daughters had no doubt ruined both
their lives.

The usually even-tempered Ivy had been livid
when the article came out, and she had blamed
Holly for it. Ivy had wanted Harold to sue, wanted
him to have Burton Kimball go after the magazine
for defamation of character. Harold had his own
good reasons for refusing, but when he did, there
had been a huge blowup between him and Ivy.
For weeks now, they had barely spoken, doing
their chores together around the ranch, but with
none of their customary camaraderie. By attempting not to fight with one daughter, Harold
had inevitably quarreled with the other.

Determined to solve the problem with the least
additional damage to everyone concerned, Harold
had put all his hopes in what would happen once
Holly came home for the trial. He had thought
that somehow he would be able to get his two
daughters together in the same room where he
would finally, once and for all, put the past to rest.
But that hadn't happened.

For the entire week since Holly had been back
home in Bisbee, she had insisted that all contact
be conducted on a lawyer-to-lawyer basis. Harold
hadn't been allowed access to her by telephone,
and no one would tell him where she was staying.
Well, that was changing today. He had figured out
a way to make it happen, a way to bring her
around.

Harold was coming to town with what, on the
surface, would appear to be an enticing carrot. He
was prepared to offer Holly the ultimate prize—

total capitulation. Everything she wanted. For someone like Holly, that should prove irresistible, but there was a stick as well. And when it came to those two things, both carrot and stick, what he had to say would not be discussed on a lawyer-to-lawyer basis. Those were private—to be discussed with his daughters alone. No one else. Once and for all time, he would finally tell both of them the truth.

Surely, once they both knew the truth, he might be able to find some common ground, some avenue for reconciliation. Once he came up with the plan, he had allowed himself to hope it would work. Perhaps if Holly knew all of it, she'd call off the trial and her hired attack dogs. Harold Patterson could imagine nothing worse than having to endure the humiliation of a public trial. He could imagine how it would feel to sit in one of those overheated Cochise County courtrooms. The place would be packed with friends and neighbors, people who had known him all his life. He would have to sit there and be stripped bare; would be forced to listen while his daughter recounted the exact nature of his alleged crimes and the horrible things he had supposedly done to her.

The possibility that Holly might really remember caused Harold to squirm on the Scout's sway-backed front seat. Just thinking about it set off a severe ache that started in Harold's breastbone, spread across both shoulders, and arched down his tense forearms. What if she really did remember? What then?

Harold remembered hearing someone say that

the truth would set you free. Could it do that for him? Harold doubted it. In this case, truth seemed like some kind of evil genie. Harold worried that once he rubbed the bottled past and set the genie loose in the world, things would never be the same. Telling the truth meant that long-made promises would have to be broken, that the lives of innocent people would be forever changed. But then, innocent people were always being hurt. That was the way the world worked.

Two

WEARING ONLY her bathrobe and with a towel wrapped around her wet hair, Joanna Brady stood in the kitchen doorway observing her daughter, Jenny. The nine-year-old was halfheartedly trailing a spoon through the cold, partially eaten contents of her cereal bowl.

"I thought you said you wanted oatmeal," Joanna snapped irritably. "If you don't, fine. Give it to the dogs, but stop playing with it."

The words were barely out of her mouth before Joanna wished she could take them back. Jennifer was eating next to nothing these days, giving her mother yet another cause for worry, something else to add to Joanna's own considerable pain.

"I'm sorry," Joanna apologized quickly, trying to make light of it. "I sound just like Grandma Lathrop, don't I?"

And it was true. Those were exactly the kinds of things Eleanor Lathrop would have said—*had* said, in fact, especially when she herself was hurting. Criticism had always been Eleanor's trump card, but why did Joanna have to replay those old tapes now, with her own daughter, when all she really wanted to do was take Jenny in her arms, hold her, and comfort her? Instead of harping, Joanna needed to share her own hurt with Jenny. After all, Joanna Lathrop Brady understood all too well how it felt for a daughter to lose a father. The very same thing had happened to her.

But the pain of being a newly made widow somehow got in the way of consoling her daughter, the newly made orphan.

Joanna had always prided herself on the special relationship she shared with Jenny, but in the six short weeks since a drug-cartel hit man had gunned down Joanna's husband, Cochise County sheriff's deputy Andrew Brady, an unfamiliar wall of silence and misunderstanding seemed to have grown up in the Brady household. The once open give-and-take between mother and daughter was now full of uneasy silences punctuated by angry words and occasional bouts of tears.

Without glancing at Joanna, Jenny took her bowl and slipped wordlessly out of the breakfast nook, heading for the back porch. Always interested in a handout, both dogs—the recently adopted Tigger, a comical-looking golden retriever/pit bull mix, and Sadie, a rangy bluetick hound—sprang from their usual resting places near the door and rushed to follow.

Joanna removed the towel and shook her red hair loose. She was pouring herself a cup of coffee when Jenny returned to the kitchen sink to rinse her bowl. The child's troubled blue eyes were downcast; she seemed near tears. Long after all trace of food was gone, Jenny continued to rinse her dish. Joanna resisted the urge to tell her to turn off the faucet and not waste water. Once again she attempted to put things right.

"I'm sorry to be so impatient," she said. "The election is today. I guess I'm nervous and in a hurry. We need to leave here early enough so I can vote on the way to work."

Jenny turned from the sink to face her mother. "Are you going to vote for yourself?" she asked.

"Vote for myself? Of course. Why do you ask?"

Jenny dropped her eyes and shrugged. "I dunno. I guess I thought a good sport always votes for the other guy. In games and stuff."

Joanna stepped over to Jenny, held her by the shoulders for a moment, then lifted the child's chin and looked directly into her eyes.

"This is something I have to do, Jenny," Joanna said. "For us and for your dad. It isn't a game. What if I didn't vote for myself and then ended up losing by a single vote? It wouldn't make sense for me to vote for one of my opponents, now would it?"

"I guess not," Jenny mumbled, then dodged out of her mother's grasp. "I've got to go get dressed."

As Jenny darted away, Joanna blinked back tears of her own. How could it still be less than two months since Andy died? It seemed much longer, more like a lifetime. How could her entire world have been turned so upside down in so short a time? Ostensibly, not that much had changed. They still lived in the same home, the same cozy Sears bungalow she and Andy had purchased from his parents years earlier. But the house was no longer the same place. Without

Andy's presence, it was far too quiet, and so was Jenny.

The cheerful, laughing, loving child who had eagerly marched off to tackle third grade the first of September . . . was no more. Two months later she had been transformed into a subdued, pale husk of her former self. She had turned into a somber miniature adult, living her life inside a hard, brittle shell.

Joanna's heart ached with sympathy. She understood what was happening with her daughter, but why did their mutual grief separate them rather than draw them together?

Shaking her head, Joanna retreated to her own room to dress. She stood dispiritedly in front of the closet door—a closet from which she had not yet found the heart to banish all trace of Andy's clothes. With Andy's scent still lingering around her, she tried to decide what she should wear. What was the proper mode of dress for her today? There was no manual of suitable behavior for a sheriff's candidate who was also a recent widow. Not only that, the question of what to wear touched on all the deeper questions as well. Why was she running for office in the first place? Why was she putting herself through all this? Why was she putting Jenny through this?

It had seemed like a good idea at the time, back during and just after Andy's funeral when people's feelings were running high. Friends, neighbors, and even complete strangers from all over the county had urged her to run, encouraged her to take Andy's place on the ballot. Back then, even

Jennifer had wanted her to do it. And when Joanna had reluctantly agreed, one of the reasons she had done so was the belief that running for office would be something she and Jenny would do together—would work toward together—a shared goal that would unite them and help occupy both their time and energy. She had thought it would give them a needed focus and would keep their lives from being constantly centered on Andy's death.

But it hadn't worked out that way. Not at all. In fact, as the campaign had heated up, it had become a bone of contention. Jenny had lost interest in the election process almost immediately. She had dragged her feet every step of the way, constantly creating logistical roadblocks of childish whimpering and whining rather than helping.

As for Joanna, even though she had worked hard on both her father's and Andy's separate campaigns for sheriff, in both cases she had been part of the campaign—a cog in the wheel, a member of the team—not the candidate. Doing it all on her own, without Andy there to backstop her, she had found overwhelming.

As the candidate, she had been forced to juggle all the time commitments of electioneering—the civic meetings, speeches, and doorbelling—that couldn't be delegated to anyone else. Nor could she delegate the complexities of her life as a newly single parent or the demands of a job that was now a sole source of income rather than a shared one. The only good thing about all this was that sometimes when she fell into bed at night, she was too worn out to toss and turn.

At last Joanna chose two hangers and pulled them down from the clothes rod. One hanger held a winter-gray blazer made of a medium-weight wool. On the other was a pearl-gray blouse. She was in the process of laying out the clothes on the bed when the phone rang. Dropping what she was doing, Joanna hurried to answer.

"Hello," Eleanor Lathrop said to her daughter. "How are we holding up this morning?"

Not very well, Joanna thought. She said, "Fine, Mother. How are you?"

"What are you going to wear today?"

"Funny you should ask," Joanna answered. "I was standing here in my underwear wondering that very thing."

"Well, wear something nice," Eleanor ordered. "I was just watching the news from Tucson. They were talking about you, about how you're the only woman candidate for sheriff in the whole state. They said that if you're elected, you'll be breaking new ground. They plan on sending a television crew down here to cover it live."

At the word "television," Joanna sank onto the bed. "To cover me?" she managed.

"What about that new gray blazer of yours and that light gray blouse?" Eleanor continued. "Those would be good. And speaking of which, what are you doing after work?"

"After work?"

"I already checked with Helen Barco at Helene's. She could do you right at four."

"Mother . . ." Joanna began, but Eleanor rolled over the abortive objection.

"Now, Joanna, I know you don't believe in going to the beauty shop all that much, but this is television. People all over the state are going to see you. It's important for you to look your very best. Besides, I told Helen it's my treat. It isn't every day your daughter gets elected sheriff, you know."

Eleanor's initial opposition to Joanna's candidacy had gradually changed—first to grudging acceptance and later to highly committed partisan support. It was one thing for Joanna to tell her mother to go jump in the lake. It was another thing entirely to insult a loyal campaign worker. Only Marianne Maculyea, Joanna's campaign coordinator and best friend, had logged more hours on Joanna's run for office than her mother, Eleanor Lathrop.

"All right," Joanna relented. "Four o'clock?"

"Right. Shampoo, blow dry, makeup, and manicure."

"Manicure, too?"

"It won't hurt," Eleanor told her. "You might even like it. Now what about Jenny? Is she going to come to the polls-closing party at the convention center or not?"

"I haven't asked her. It's a school night. If she comes at all, she shouldn't stay very late."

"Well, I'm sure the Bradys would be glad to take her back home with them if she gets too tired. Mark my words, Jim Bob and Eva Lou Brady won't hang around celebrating for very long. They're not much on socializing."

That was something of an understatement. Joanna's in-laws' idea of social intercourse was limited to staying after church long enough for a post-sermon coffee hour once or twice a month or going to a church-sponsored evening potluck.

"I'll check on that," Joanna said. She glanced at her watch. Time was flying. "I've gotta go, Mother," she said.

"Okay," Eleanor replied, "but don't forget to vote. I'm on my way to the Get-Out-the-Vote phone bank as soon as I get off the phone here."

When talking on the telephone, Eleanor Lathrop was in her natural element—a situation Joanna's campaign manager had wisely utilized to the campaign's very best advantage.

"I won't forget," Joanna assured her mother. "And thanks for the appointment with Helen. That was very thoughtful of you."

After putting down the phone, Joanna returned to the closet. The gray blazer and blouse were promptly returned to their respective positions on the clothes rod. Out came a navy-blue coatdress, double-breasted with two rows of large gold buttons. She would have preferred the gray blazer, but since that was her mother's first choice, she'd be damned if she'd wear it.

Joanna was finishing drying her hair when Jenny tapped on the bedroom door. Jenny, already fully dressed and followed by the two dogs, flopped dejectedly on her mother's bed, while the dogs settled on the floor nearby.

"That was Grandma Lathrop on the phone," Joanna said. "She wanted to know if you're coming to the party tonight, the one uptown."

"Do I have to?"

Looking past the reflection of her own blue dress in the mirror, Joanna saw that Jenny resembled her blond, blue-eyed father in looks, but in the personality department she definitely took after her mother.

"Of course you don't *have* to," Joanna returned. "But you are my daughter, and I'd like you to be there."

"Even if you lose?"

Joanna sat down on the bed to put on her shoes. "I don't think we'll lose," she said, trying to sound far more confident than she felt. Her two opponents, Frank Montoya, the Willcox city marshal, and Al Freeman, the assistant chief of police from Sierra Vista, hadn't cut her any slack. The results of the election were by no means guaranteed.

"And even if we do lose," she continued, "we have to go to the party anyway. No matter what, we should go there to thank our supporters."

But then, in the brief silence that followed, something from Jenny's voice—perhaps a quaver of doubt in the way she spoke—registered tardily on Joanna's brain. She turned to her daughter.

"You do want us to win, don't you, Jenny?"

"I guess," Jenny whispered.

"Good."

Joanna rose to her feet, pulling the child along with her. For a long moment, they stood there next to the bed in Joanna's small bedroom, clinging together in a fierce and mutually protective hug.

Eleanor Lathrop had always claimed to have eyes in the back of her head. Her daughter made no such assertions, so while she and Jenny hugged each other, Joanna didn't see that, behind the child's back, Jennifer Ann Brady's fingers were tightly crossed.

On both hands.

Three

Traveling down Tombstone Canyon, Harold was tempted to drive right by the Canyon Methodist Church. At the last minute he swung into the parking lot. This was, after all, Election Day. From the time he first became eligible, Harold's voting record had been absolutely perfect. He had never missed a single election.

Now, though, with the trial due to start the next day and with Bisbee's gossip mills churning out stories about his family troubles on an overtime basis, Harold actually wanted to skip it, to let this relatively unimportant election pass by without his vote. But that would have been perceived as cowardly. Harold Lamm Patterson was no coward.

He doffed his rain-stained Stetson and shook the water off it as he stepped inside the basement social hall of Canyon Methodist Church, the place where his precinct had voted for the last thirty-two years. He had hoped the hall would be fairly empty except for the usual band of election-board workers, but that wasn't the case.

Handed the potential clientele of possibly hungry voters, the enterprising ladies of the United Christian Women's Prayer Fellowship were hold-

ing a bake sale. Several of the town's leading female citizens were clustered around a huge coffee
urn, chatting and laughing.

None of the women were strangers to Harold,
and he did his best to stay out of their way. One
in particular, Tottie Galbraith, had cut him dead
the last time Harold had encountered her in the
post-office lobby. That had been right after the *People*
article. Tottie had almost broken her neck,
crashing into the revolving door in her haste to
avoid him.

This time, her behavior was somewhat more
subtle but no less disapproving. Although she
must have glimpsed him out of the corner of her
eye, she gave no hint of recognition. Instead, she
raised one eyebrow and shifted her position so she
could continue standing with her back turned in
his direction. Meanwhile, the previously energetic
hum of the women's voices dropped to the merest
of whispers.

Harold didn't have to hear what they were saying to know they were talking about him. His ears
flamed red, but he didn't cut and run. In fact, he
thought wryly, anything that kept him from having to speak to Tottie Galbraith couldn't be all bad.

Harold was almost safely past the group when,
at the last moment, Marliss Shackleford broke free
from the others and came after him, hand extended, lips arranged in a phony but welcoming
smile.

"Why, Harold Patterson!" she exclaimed. "How
are you managing to hold up through all this, you
poor thing?"

Fifty years after leaving high school, Marliss had yet to outgrow the gushiness she had learned as a local cheerleader. She had devoted twenty-five years to her life's work—writing "Bisbee Buzzings," a weekly piece that passed for a society column in the *Bisbee Bee*, the town's barely extant daily newspaper. Marliss Shackleford's enthusiasm at being a large fish in a very small pond remained undimmed.

"Fine, Marliss," Harold reassured her. If he couldn't avoid her altogether the best tactic was to get Marliss talking about something else. "I'm doing just fine," he said. "How are the grandkids?"

"Oh, the twins are just fine." She beamed. "So nice of you to ask. Care for some coffee?"

"No, thanks. I only stopped by to vote. You know how it is—too much to do and not enough time."

Marliss nodded as she fell in step beside him. "Isn't that the truth? Hardly enough time to turn around. But I wanted to talk to you all the same, Harold, just to let you know that a lot of us here in town think it's a crying shame what Holly is doing. And to her own father yet. It's a crime, if you ask me."

"Thank you, Marliss," Harold said, still hoping to shut her up. "I surely do appreciate that." But Marliss continued undeterred, without even acknowledging the interruption.

"For her to go away all those years and come back now just to raise all kinds of fuss, I don't understand it at all. Not for a minute! Do you?"

"No, ma'am," Harold agreed, edging away, trying to reach the relative safety of the table where a stern-faced Barbara Wentworth presided over the list of registered voters. Marliss stuck to him like glue.

"I read that whole article in *People* magazine," she continued. "I surely did. I don't see how they can get away with printing such terrible stuff. We used to call it yellow journalism in my day, and that's exactly what it is. After all that wild publicity, where in the world is Judge Moore going to find an impartial jury? I mean, doesn't everybody read *People*? And as for all the awful things they said about Bisbee in that article ... My goodness, if I were Judge Moore, I'd give that girl a swift spanking and send her right back home to California where she belongs."

Marliss seemed able to talk without ever having to pause long enough to draw breath. About the time Harold decided there would be no escape, that he was destined to stand there trapped forever, the Reverend Marianne Maculyea, pastor of Canyon Methodist Church, came to his rescue. Deftly insinuating herself between Marliss and her hapless victim, Marianne took Harold's hand and shook it firmly.

"Why, hello there, Harold," Marianne said with a polite, dismissive nod in Marliss Shackleford's direction. "Is Ivy here, too?"

For a moment, Harold seemed unable to answer. "N-no," he stammered finally. "I came by myself. I don't know where she is."

And he didn't, either, not for sure. Most likely

she was still at the house, but the usually steady Ivy had become unpredictable of late. In fact, she had left the house the night before right after chores, and she hadn't returned until just before sunup. That was something else that was bugging Harold, another bone of contention, and something she had never done before.

Since the big blowup over Holly, Ivy had suddenly taken to coming and going without bothering to tell him where she was going or when she'd be back. Of course, since they weren't speaking, how could she? This new situation with Ivy reminded Harold of Holly, back when she'd been an errant teenager. But Ivy was no teenager. At forty years of age, she hardly needed to ask her father's permission to do any damn-fool thing she pleased. He saw this latest incident as one more thing to lay at Holly's door.

"I see," Marianne said.

Harold's mind had wandered briefly. When he came back to himself, Marianne Maculyea was examining his face so closely that he wondered what she saw there. And when she said, "I see," what exactly did she mean? Did this Reverend Maculyea somehow know more about what was really going on out at the Rocking P than Harold wanted her to?

"All this trial business must be almost as hard on her as it is on you," Marianne continued. Her voice was kind: sincere and caring where Marliss Shackleford's had been sharp and self-serving.

Harold dropped his gaze and examined his

mud-spattered boots. "Yes," he allowed reluctantly. "I reckon it is."

Marianne reached out and took the old man's hand. "You take care of yourself now, Harold." She turned to Marliss and engaged her in some kind of small talk that finally set Harold free to go vote. He quickly planted himself in front of Barbara Wentworth's table and gratefully dived into the election process.

In other times, he and Barb Wentworth would have shot the breeze while she found his name in the voter-registration list, showed him where to sign, and gave him his ballot. This time, Barbara seemed disinclined to talk. Did even the no-nonsense Barbara Wentworth read *People*? he wondered.

Minutes later, breathing a sigh of relief, Harold escaped to the relative privacy of a voting booth. He read each page of the ballot carefully. It wasn't a very exciting election. The usual people were running for the usual offices, and no one would be particularly surprised when the incumbents were reelected to their traditional positions in the state legislature or on the board of supervisors. As far as county races were concerned, the only one of any special interest to Harold Patterson was the wide-open contest for the office of sheriff.

Two months earlier, right after the primary and when the general-election ballots had already been printed, all hell had broken loose in Cochise County. Both candidates for sheriff, the two men whose names even now were listed on the pre-printed ballots, had perished the previous September in a series of harrowing events that had stunned the entire state. The previous sheriff, Walter V. McFadden, and his opponent, Deputy Andrew Brady, had succumbed to gunshot wounds within days of one another.

In the ensuing investigation, the community had been shocked to learn that several long-term members of the Sheriff's Department had been deeply involved in drug-trafficking. By the time the smoke cleared, Joanna Brady—widow of one of the dead men—had agreed to run for sheriff in her husband's stead. For the past two months, the murders, the investigation, and the subsequent campaign for sheriff had been front-page news. Only Holly Patterson's forthcoming legal battle with her father had finally displaced the Sheriff's Department from top position on the front pages of the *Bisbee Bee*.

Joanna Brady was someone Harold Patterson remembered as the feisty daughter of yet another Cochise County sheriff, the long-dead D. H. "Big Hank" Lathrop. Big Hank had once played poker with Harold on a fairly regular basis. The other two current candidates—one from Willcox and the other from Sierra Vista—weren't people Harold knew personally. In fact, standing in the voting booth, he barely remembered their names.

What he remembered best about Joanna Lathrop Brady was seeing her as a sprightly little red-haired imp in a freshly pressed Brownie uniform standing outside one or the other of the Phelps Dodge Company stores. She had been a capable businesswoman even way back then, selling him

Girl Scout cookies and carefully counting back the change. That long-ago child with her two missing front teeth deserved far better cards than the tough ones life had dealt her with disturbing frequency.

When she was a high school sophomore, Joanna's father had died in a tragic automobile accident. Now, somewhere under thirty years of age, she was already the widow of a gunned-down police officer, but she wasn't ready to give up and quit. By agreeing to run in her husband's place, she showed plenty of grit and determination, qualities Harold Patterson both possessed himself and admired in others.

To Harold's way of thinking, a vote for Joanna Brady was a vote for continuity, for the way things ought to be.

In the space provided for write-in candidates, Harold used a stubby pencil to write in Joanna Brady's name. Then, squaring his shoulders, he emerged from the voting booth and dropped his ballot into the box. Voting for Joanna Brady felt good. It almost made the stop at the church worthwhile; almost balanced the scales for his having to put up with the likes of Tottie Galbraith and Marliss Shackleford.

Almost, but not quite.

Harold left the church before anyone else could corner him into a conversation. He certainly didn't want to hang around long enough to risk running into Ivy when she came in to vote.

After all, it was bad enough that Harold was forced to undergo public attacks from one of his two daughters. He worried that if Ivy saw him there in the church and simply cut him dead, that would be almost as bad or worse than a noisy row with Holly. That would give the ladies of the United Christian Prayer Fellowship so much to talk about that they wouldn't shut up for a week.

Harold Lamm Patterson, one tough old bird, could handle just about anything, but the prospect of having Ivy—his favorite—spurn him in public was more than he could endure.

Four

BISBEE AS it is known now was created in the fifties when several different hamlets, including Old Bisbee, incorporated into a single entity. Forty years later, the old lines of demarcation still persist.

That election morning, seven miles down the road in the Warren business district, not much work was being conducted at the Davis Insurance Agency on Arizona Street. When Joanna arrived, she found two baskets of "good wishes" flowers from clients waiting on her desk. A box of glazed doughnuts and a percolator of coffee covered most of the surface of the receptionist's desk. The receptionist herself, a young woman named Lisa Connors, fielded an occasional business phone call between serving coffee and doughnuts to the steady parade of drop-by well-wishers.

Milo Davis himself, flushing with good humor from the tip of the resin-imprisoned scorpion on his bolo tie to the top of his shiny bald pate, grinned, shook hands, and told people he wasn't losing an office manager, he was gaining a sheriff. Milo's shoulder-whacking jest was made with the best of intentions, but it bothered Joanna all the same.

From high school on, this building with its single, three-office suite was the only workplace she had ever known, and Milo Davis had been her only boss. If she won the election, all that would change. Joanna felt like a reluctant and uncertain fledgling about to be shoved from the nest, regardless of whether or not she could fly. And yet she did want to win, didn't she?

At nine, Milo left for a nine-thirty appointment. Moments after he left the office a call came in from a newspaper reporter from the *Arizona Sun* in Tucson. When Lisa put the call through to Joanna, the woman explained she was calling for an Election Day comment from the woman who might possibly be Arizona's first female county sheriff. The reporter's questions were the sort Joanna had come to dread during the course of the campaign.

As far as the media were concerned, the election of the Cochise County sheriff was newsworthy primarily because Joanna Brady, one of the three candidates, was a woman. And no matter how she answered the questions, the way the articles were written generally made Joanna sound like a wild-eyed, gun-toting feminist—an unlikely cross between Dirty Harry and Gloria Steinem.

Finished with the call, Joanna was sorting through a stack of home-office underwriting requirements and correspondence when Harold Lamm Patterson appeared at Lisa's desk. Standing politely with a damp and battered Stetson in hand, he asked to see Milo right away. Joanna heard

Lisa tell Harold that Milo was out for most of the morning, and she saw the look of grave disappointment that washed across the old man's leathery features. Like everyone else in town, Joanna knew Harold Patterson had his hands full with his ring-tailed bitch of a daughter back home and making trouble. There was no reason to add to the old man's woes.

Getting up, Joanna wandered to the outer office and stopped beside Lisa's desk. "If it's something urgent, Mr. Patterson," Joanna suggested, "perhaps I could be of help."

"I would appreciate it, ma'am," Harold Patterson said sincerely. "I surely would."

When ushered into Joanna's office, Harold took the seat she motioned him into. Like a wary old bird poised for sudden flight, he perched uneasily on the chair with his hat balanced precariously on one knobby knee. He squinted at her through narrow, lidded eyes.

"You're Hank Lathrop's little girl, aren't you? The one who's running for sheriff?"

Joanna nodded without comment. Little girl? Hardly, but compared to Harold's eighty-odd years, she must seem improbably young for that kind of responsibility.

"I reckon your daddy would be real proud of you if he could see you today," Harold continued. "I voted for you, by the way. Stopped off on my way into town."

Joanna felt a flush creep up her neck. "Thank you, Mr. Patterson. I appreciate that. But tell me, what can I do for you today?"

"I'm used to dealing with Milo," Harold Patterson hedged. "And with Milo's father before that . . ."

"It's all right, Mr. Patterson. If you don't want me to take care of whatever it is, that'll be fine. The problem is, I have no idea how long Milo will be gone. It could be after lunch before he comes back. I do have access to all of the files, and . . ."

Harold leaned forward in his chair and lowered his voice. "It's personal, ma'am," he whispered so Lisa couldn't hear. "Personal and confidential."

Joanna took the hint, got up, and firmly closed the connecting door between her office and Lisa's. "There," she said, sitting back down. "Is that better?"

Harold nodded. "What do I have to do to change the beneficiaries on my policies?" he asked. "Do I have to bring the policies into the office, or what? I think they're over at the bank. . . ."

"Oh, no. If that's all you want, I can do it in a minute. All you have to do is fill out a change-of-beneficiary form."

"Just one form for all the policies?"

"No. You use a separate form for each one, but I will need the policy numbers."

"Dang. I don't have them along."

Joanna smiled. "No problem, Mr. Patterson. Give me your date of birth."

"November the twelfth, 1910."

Joanna switched on her desktop computer and booted it up. Once she had entered Harold Patterson's name and birth date into the database, the screen showed her a listing of his set of several policies. Harold Patterson had come into the world when automobiles were still a rarity. He watched the computer operation with some interest.

"You have five policies in all with us, Mr. Patterson," Joanna said a moment later. "Would you care to have a printout on each one?"

"You can do that?"

"Certainly."

Joanna typed in a series of commands, and moments later the dot-matrix printer behind her whined out a stream of printed paper. Tearing off the tractor-feed holes and separating the printouts into individual sheets, she handed them over to Harold. He sat there for some time, squinting at each one in turn.

"Is everything in order?" Joanna asked.

He looked up at her as if startled at the sound of her voice. "Oh, yes. They seem to be fine."

Joanna reached into her bottom drawer, thumbed through a series of files, and came up with a fistful of change-of-beneficiary forms. "You don't have to complete them here, but they do have to be properly witnessed at the time of signing. Did you want to change the beneficiary designation on all of the policies?"

Harold first nodded, then shook his head. "Yes. Well, no. I'm not sure." Finally, he tossed the stack of papers back onto Joanna's desk.

"How can I tell?" he demanded in disgust. "Eyes are so damn bad, I can't hardly read the dang things."

Joanna picked them up and glanced through

them. "Your daughter Ivy is the sole beneficiary on all of them," she explained. "If she's not then living, the proceeds are to be divided equally between your nephew, Burton Kimball, and your daughter Holly. If you'd like to make a change in those arrangements, Mr. Patterson, I'd be happy to complete the forms for you."

To Joanna's surprise, Harold Patterson's eyes filled with a sudden pool of tears that threatened to overflow his eyes despite the old man's valiant attempt to blink them back.

"Always thought of myself as sort of a caretaker," he mumbled hoarsely. "Thought I'd take care of what my pa gave me and pass it along to my children and to their children's children. As it turns out, my girls are the end of the line. Instead of valuing the Rocking P and what I've worked for all my life, they're fighting over it."

He shook his head sadly. "Reminds me of a pair of dogs I had once, years ago, an older one and a pup. The old dog had this blanket, an old, woreout horse blanket, that he slept on out in the barn. The pup took a liking to that blanket and tried to make off with it. There was plenty of blanket to go around. They could have both used it, but they each pulled and tugged on it until there was nothing left but pieces. Turned out neither one of them had the good of it."

Harold paused and looked at Joanna. "You see what I mean, don't you?"

Joanna nodded. "I think so, yes. Your daughters?"

He nodded wearily. "And the Rocking P is the

blanket. Or maybe I am. You want your children to grow up to like each other or at least get along, but it seems like that's not how things work out most of the time."

"Mr. Patterson," Joanna said kindly, "I can see that you're under a good deal of stress today. Understandably so. Why don't you take the printouts and the change-of-beneficiary forms with you and give yourself some time to think things over and sort them out."

As she talked, Joanna folded the two separate stacks of paper together into a single letter-sized sheaf and placed them in a blank manila envelope.

"Talk to your daughters and your nephew if you think it will help. Or wait until tomorrow or the next day and speak to Milo himself about this. In other words, don't rush into anything. And if you do change the beneficiary and later on you think better of it, then all you have to do is sign another set of forms." She smiled. "We're bureaucrats here, Mr. Patterson. We like doing paperwork. It gives our lives meaning."

For the first time since Harold Patterson entered her office, Joanna noticed the ghost of an answering smile playing at the corners of his mouth.

"Thank you," he said, taking the envelope and putting it in his pocket. "Thank you kindly. Sounds like real good advice."

He used the arm of the chair for support and awkwardly raised himself up. "I'm so stiff," he said, "I must be getting old. And I ought to be ashamed of myself, acting like such a dang fool in public. I hate to be so much trouble."

"It's no trouble at all," Joanna assured him.

Harold Patterson held out his gnarled hand, and Joanna shook it warmly, hoping her outward appearance camouflaged the lump in her throat. She didn't want him to see how much his distress affected her.

Standing before her, he seemed shrunken somehow, as though the very act of talking with her about his problems had robbed him of some of his vitality. He seemed far more frail than when he'd first walked into her office a short time earlier. It hurt Joanna to see this proud old man reduced to near tears, awkwardly mumbling apologies and thanks.

There was much Joanna Lathrop Brady should have thanked him for. Buying all those Girl Scout cookies was only the barest beginning. Although she hadn't learned the truth of the matter until much later, Harold Patterson's behind-the-scenes lobbying had resulted in Joanna's being nominated for Girl's State the year after her father died. And when she graduated from Bisbee High School the year after that, Harold had delivered an inspiring if homespun commencement address.

As they shook hands now in Joanna's office, she remembered that other long-ago handshake on a warm May night under the lights of the baseball stadium. The principal had called out Joanna's name, and she had marched across the stage to the place where Harold Patterson, as president of the school board, was dispensing the coveted red-and-gray diplomas. Every graduate in line both before and after Joanna Lathrop received a straightforward handshake, and so did Joanna.

But after that, and before she could continue across the stage, Harold had grasped her by both shoulders and held her for a moment. Looking her straight in the eye, he said, "Your daddy would have been very proud." Then he had winked at her, given her a gentle shove, and sent her on her way.

Other people had said much the same thing to her that night, but Harold's words were the only ones she remembered specifically. The timely encouragement and comical wink, both from her father's old poker-playing buddy, had given her a much-needed boost. His kindness had helped propel her across the stage and somehow granted her permission to toss her red cap with its gray tassel high in the air along with everybody else's when the long ceremony was finally over.

Now, with the tables suddenly reversed, what comfort could she offer him in his time of need?

"We're here to help, Mr. Patterson," she said softly. "Anytime. It's no trouble at all."

Harold Lamm Patterson nodded and started toward the door, where he paused with one hand on the knob. "What's Milo Davis going to do without you if you go and get yourself elected?" he asked.

Joanna had been wondering that herself, but it wasn't a subject she had broached aloud, not with Lisa and certainly not with Milo. It seemed as though talking about what might happen if she won could bring her bad luck, sort of like stepping on a crack and breaking your mother's back.

She laughed. "Nobody's indispensable, Mr. Patterson. I'm sure Milo and Lisa would get along without me just fine."

"Well," Harold Patterson said, "they may just have to."

When he finally limped out of her office, Joanna followed him as far as the office window. His mud-splattered Scout was parked out front in the place usually reserved for one of Milo Davis' several Buicks. To Joanna's surprise, the old man bypassed the Scout. And instead of utilizing the crosswalk, he marched across Arizona Street on a long, jaywalking diagonal, making straight for the bank.

"That poor man," Lisa said, as she and Joanna watched him cross the street.

"You mean because of his daughters?" Joanna asked.

Lisa nodded. "What a mess. How old is he?"

"Eighty-four?"

"Jeez. And here he is with his whole life blowing up in public before his very eyes. How can he stand what they're doing? How could anybody?"

Lisa was twenty-three years old. Recently engaged, she and her fiancé were busy planning a big, spare-no-expense wedding that was scheduled for sometime the following summer. Both of Lisa's parents were still alive and well. Listening to her, Joanna was startled by how young Lisa seemed— how young and inexperienced.

"Most of the time," Joanna said quietly, "you

do it because you have to, because God doesn't give you a choice."

And, she added silently to herself, because you never know how much the people you love are going to hurt you until it's far too late.

Five

ALL HIS life, Harold Patterson had been the kind of man who, when faced with a particularly onerous task, would lay out the entire job in a very orderly fashion. Then he would set about doing each separate part of the chore, carrying each one through to completion before going on to the next.

Today was like that. He had mentally organized each separate part of his scheme before ever coming to town. Having gathered insurance forms, he headed straight for the bank.

When Sandra Rose Henning had graduated from high school, her scholastic standing should have made her a shoo-in to receive scholarship help. She was offered some, but not enough to make a difference. Faced with the grim reality of two disabled parents to support, she had chucked the idea of going on to college. In June, while her classmates were busily planning their fall school wardrobes, Sandy hustled down to the local First Merchant's Bank and wangled herself a job as a teller.

Thirty-two years and fifty-five pounds later, she was still there, only now she was the manager of the Warren Branch. First Merchant's had changed some over the years, and rumor had it that the bank was about to be gobbled up by an out-of-state conglomerate.

Local scuttlebutt said that all of Bisbee's neighborhood branches, strung like so many pop-beads along what had formerly been a ten-mile bus route, would soon be consolidated into a single large branch at the new shopping center in Don Luis. That rundown area, once a primarily Mexican enclave, was now the unlikely location of a new shopping area that boasted the town's only Safeway, and soon, perhaps, the town's only bank.

Sandy Henning wasn't particularly worried about the coming merger. Regardless of what happened, she was sure she would still have a job. If it meant being demoted to "personal banker" or even going back on the teller line, that hardly mattered. Sandy liked people, and people liked her.

She was seated at her desk when Harold Patterson marched into the bank. She had been Harold's "personal banker" since long before a worried banking industry had invented the term. When she had been promoted and moved from the downtown branch to Warren, Harold's accounts and business had followed her, even though, from a geographical standpoint, the bank in Old Bisbee was seven miles closer to the Rocking P which should have made it more convenient. But the uptown branch didn't have Sandy.

Sandy's heart went out to Harold as soon as she saw him. Despite his advancing years, he had always stood ramrod straight. Now, though, his shoulders drooped, as if the weight he carried on them was more than even his tough old spine could bear. And his step, while certainly not faltering, seemed somewhat slower, more hesitant.

Sandy rose to greet him. "Good morning, Mr. Patterson. How are you today?"

"Fair to middling," he answered. "Can't complain."

Although he could have complained, Sandy thought, and probably should have.

She and Holly Patterson would have graduated from high school the same year—if Holly had stayed around long enough to bother, that is. During their junior year, Holly had eloped with some high-flying, fast-talking real-estate developer from California. The marriage hadn't lasted more than three months, but when it was over, Holly Patterson didn't come home to what she had often called "backward Bisbee." Sandy Henning had always considered Holly's abrupt departure a case of good riddance. A week after Holly's much-publicized return, a single glance at Harold Patterson's haggard face did nothing to change the banker's mind.

"What can I do for you today, Mr. Patterson?" she asked.

He fumbled in his pocket for a key ring and removed a small key. "I'd like to take a look at my box," he said. "There are some items in there that I need to go over."

Settling himself at a partially screened table, he removed his glasses and rubbed his bleary eyes while he waited for Sandy to bring his safety deposit box from the vault.

Holly's demands were so outrageous that they should have been laughable. She wanted a full public confession of Harold Patterson's alleged misdeeds. In addition, she demanded as damages title to half the Rocking P. That was what bothered him most, rumors that with this so-called therapist as a partner, Holly expected to build a recovery center, a place for people who realized late in life that they too had been abused by members of their own families.

Those were the terms of settlement. If the case went to trial, her lawyer had told Burton that he intended to go for blood—for everything they could get, for title to the whole shooting match if they could get it.

That wouldn't happen because the case wasn't going to trial. Because Harold Patterson himself was going to see to it.

It was easy for Ivy and Burton Kimball to tell him what to do. They weren't caught between a rock and a hard place, and they didn't know the whole story. In addition, they didn't have Harold's two prime pieces of motivation, either. For one, he wanted to live long enough to see his daughters together and reconciled for once in their lives.

And the other? With one major exception, he had lived his whole life as an honest, upright, law-abiding man. Before Norm Higgins planted him down in Evergreen Cemetery, Harold Patterson wanted his reputation back.

He had weighed all the risks. If he fought Holly in court and lost, he risked losing everything. If he settled, he handed over half the ranch to Holly—to the prodigal daughter who had turned her back on all of them for thirty-some-odd years—while dispossessing Ivy, the nonprodigal daughter, who had stayed home to help him with the ranch, who had cared for her invalid mother through years of steady decline that led inevitably into helpless insanity, who had always put other people's needs and wants before her own.

What would happen to Ivy if the Rocking P was cut in half or disappeared altogether? Like the baby King Solomon threatened to divide in the Bible, a ranch the size of the Patterson spread was of no more use cut in half than half a child would be. It took the whole ranch to make a living, to make a life.

Returning to the table with the box, Sandra Henning easily turned her key in the lock. Harold's hand trembled as he attempted to insert his own. It took three separate tries before the key clicked home. The long metal drawer flipped open, and the old man slumped back into his chair.

By eleven o'clock, Harold had sorted through all the papers in the drawer. In one stack, he put the papers that would stay in the safety-deposit box—the insurance policies he didn't need in order to change the beneficiaries, the few ribbon-wrapped letters he and Emily had exchanged during those rare times when he was actually away from home. In the other stack were the things Harold would need to take with him to Burton Kimball's office—his will and the deed to the Rocking P.

At the very bottom of the drawer, Harold found

the last item, the single yellowed envelope that he and Emily had together solemnly sealed away years earlier. Emily was the one who had insisted on a greasy candle-wax seal that now allowed some of the loopy, old-fashioned writing from the letter itself to bleed through onto the outside surface of the envelope. It was almost as if the words themselves were eager to escape their paper-bound prison.

Harold could have broken the seal and opened it, but he didn't. There was no need. The faded pencil-written words were committed to memory, seared into his heart even more clearly than they were into his brain. He remembered them all; was incapable of forgetting even one.

He sat holding the envelope and wondering what he should do with it now. He had kept it all these years because he had promised Emily he would; because she had begged him to, and because he had been afraid he might someday need it. Now, though, if his gamble paid off, if he could go to Holly and get her to listen to reason, maybe he could finally destroy the letter and be done with it. Maybe he could go to his grave taking the letter's ugly secret with him.

Finally, after many agonizing moments of indecision, he placed the fragile, unopened envelope in the stack with the insurance policies and placed the whole pile back in the drawer. If Holly and Ivy didn't take his word for it, didn't accept his version of what had happened, then it would be time to remove the letter from the safety of its hiding place. By then he would know if he was taking the letter out to show it to his daughters or to burn it once and for all.

Pushing back his chair, Harold stood and signaled to Sandy Henning. "I'm ready to go now," he said.

When she came to retrieve Harold's safety-deposit box, Sandy peered closely at Harold through her red-framed bifocals. "Are you sure you're all right, Mr. Patterson? Your color's not all that good."

Harold stood and picked up his hat. "I'm fine, Miz Henning," he said, carefully replacing the tiny key in the narrow pocket of his jeans. "I'm just a little wore out is all. Don't go getting all pistol-sprung about me."

Leaving the bank, Harold drove straight to Evergreen Cemetery. For a long time, Evergreen had been the only burial game in town. During the first half of the twentieth century, it had been a lush, green, and well-tended place, irrigated for free with the mineral-rich effluent pumped from the underground mines. Then, in the late fifties, when Phelps Dodge started a leaching operation on the new open-pit tailings dump, the circulation of free mine water was removed from the community and returned to industrial use.

Bisbee's would-be gardeners had been left literally high and dry. They could use the city's drinking water pumped from a deep underground well down near Naco. But the clear well water, although fine for drinking, didn't do a thing for the garden growers, because it came with two distinct disadvantages. Not only was it outrageously expensive, it also lacked the abundant minerals that had once made Bisbee's lawns, trees, and gardens flourish. And cemeteries, too, for that matter.

During the next decades, Evergreen Cemetery fell into such a dusty or muddy deterioration that the name "Evergreen" seemed little more than a cruel joke. When Emily Patterson had died five years earlier, the place was in such disrepair, Harold had been ashamed to bury her there, but the other cemetery in town, a relatively new one dating from the sixties, wasn't much better. So Harold had bitten the bullet, bought a double plot in Evergreen—he got a better deal that way—and a double headstone as well.

Driving to Emily's plot, Harold was surprised to see that the place appeared to be in somewhat better shape. The thinly paved drive still had potholes here and there, but the grounds themselves were much improved. Maybe a new manager was on the job, a person who actually cared about the families of the people who were buried there.

Harold parked the Scout. The rain finally was letting up as he climbed stiffly down out of the truck and hiked over to the familiar plot. He took off his Stetson and stood bareheaded, staring down at the red granite headstone. Both his and Emily's names and birth dates were already chiseled into the stone in elegant, graceful letters and numbers. Emily's date of death was there as well. The only date left to be filled in was that of Harold's own death, whenever that might be.

Looking at the stone always made the hairs stand up on the back of his neck. Not because he was afraid of dying, but because seeing the two names linked together like that made him feel that he was still married to the old Emily; as though the woman he loved had just gone on ahead. With any kind of luck, he'd have a chance to catch up with her sooner rather than later, and things between them would finally be set right as well.

"The shit's really hit the fan on this one, Em," he said, addressing her aloud as he usually did when he came to visit.

Years earlier, he might have looked around to make sure no one was watching or listening when he spoke to her like that. He no longer bothered. After all, he was an old man. If people saw him talking to himself or acting funny, they'd think he was crazy, or senile, or both, and let it go at that.

"We still may be able to make it through," he continued. "You know I've kept my promise all these years, but the price keeps going up, getting higher all the time. Maybe we were wrong trying to keep it a secret in the first place. Maybe that's why God seems to have it in for me now. I've got this one last chance to do something about it, one more wild card to turn up. I hope to God that one'll do the trick. If not, I figure it's time I stood up and took my punishment like a man. I just wanted you to know about it in advance. That's all."

He closed his eyes tightly and bowed his head for a moment, murmuring a silent prayer. Afterward, he slammed the battered Stetson back on his head, turned on his heel, and hobbled back to the Scout with a real sense of purpose. Talking things over with Emily always gave him comfort and direction.

At the cemetery's gate, he paused long enough for old Norm Higgins from Higgins Funeral Chapel and Mortuary to make a left-hand turn through the entrance. No doubt Norm was on an errand to scope out the location of some soon-to-be-used burial site. Harold supposed Norm and his boys had some poor old coot stashed in the cooler up at their place, waiting long enough for the deceased's far-flung, out-of-town relatives to arrive on the scene before setting about the grim ceremonies of putting him in the ground.

Well, Harold thought, as Norm's shiny gray Cadillac limo squeezed past the disreputable Scout on Evergreen Cemetery's narrow main track, at least it isn't me they're burying. He had his casket all picked out and paid for, same as his plot, but it wasn't time to use it. Not yet.

Norm Higgins and Harold Lamm Patterson had known each other for sixty-some-odd years. In passing, they exchanged the kind of casual half-wave/half-salute with which men of long acquaintance greet one another if they want to say hello but don't want to make much of an issue of it. Both men waved and nodded and went on by.

Harold headed uptown, past the Lowell Traffic Circle and on up to Old Bisbee. Talking it over with Em really had helped prepare him for what he knew would be a knock-down, drag-out confrontation with Burton Kimball—his nephew as well as his attorney.

Some people around town discounted Burtie;

thought of him as your basic pushover. But not Harold Patterson. The man who had raised Burton Kimball from a baby—the kind uncle who had taken an orphaned pup to raise—knew better than to dismiss either the younger man's abilities or his tenacity.

Harold might use Burtie to further his own purposes, yes. But underestimate him? No. The coward's way, of course, would have been for Harold to go ahead and do what he was planning to do without mentioning a word of it to Burtie. But Harold Lamm Patterson had never walked away from a fight in his whole life.

At eighty-four, he decided, it was too damn late to start.

Six

As PREDICTED, Burton Kimball's reaction was nothing short of astonished disbelief. "You're going to do what?"

"You heard me. I'm gonna offer Holly whatever the hell she wants. But she's gotta agree to see me. Alone. No lawyers on either side. Including you."

Kimball shook his head in disgust. "Uncle Harold, let me point out that you've already paid me a bundle of money on retainer to handle this case for you. Why would you suddenly want to go it alone at the very last minute? And why on earth would you suddenly agree to settle with that unmitigated bitch?

"Let's go to court, Uncle Harold. Please. We'll have the home-court advantage. People in this county know you. How many times have you served on the school board? Five? Six? You've lived here all your life, while Holly left town thirty years ago and only came back now to make trouble. Given a choice, who do you think the jury will believe?"

"That's what I'm trying to tell you," Harold said. "I don't want a jury."

But Burton Kimball continued undeterred. "No

one from around here is going to fall for this woo-woo 'Forgotten Memories' bullshit. It's all going to boil down to her word against yours, and she's not going to win. People like Holly Patterson may be big news in *People* magazine and in New York and California, but Bisbee's a part of the real world. I tell you, Uncle Harold, it isn't going to wash here.

"If you settle, Holly gets whatever you give her, but if you win—if the jury finds in your favor—you won't have to pay that woman one thin dime. Which one of those sounds like the better deal?"

"I still mean it," Harold said. "You call her up and tell her I want to see her. You know where she is, don't you?"

"I know," Burton answered, "but as you know, I'm under a court order not to tell. Anyway, my advice still stands. Take your chances in court."

"You're not very old to be going stone-cold deaf, Burtie," Harold put in mildly. "You'd better have those ears of yours checked. I told you once, and I'll say it again. I'm not going to court tomorrow, and neither are you. We're going to settle this thing now. Today!"

Burton Kimball prided himself on being a patient, reasonable man. In fact, Linda, his wife, insisted he was far too patient for his own good. She blamed her husband's overly forebearing nature for the fact that their two children, a boy of ten and a girl eleven, were spoiled rotten. Now, though, faced with his uncle's unyielding bull-headedness, Kimball's much-touted patience was beginning to fray.

"Call her attorney. Tell him to have her meet me tonight," Harold repeated. He paused and frowned. "Wait. Where should we go? I can't have her coming to the house."

"You could always do it here in my office, I suppose," Burton allowed grudgingly, pulling out a pen and making a few quick notes on a yellow pad.

But Harold shook his head. "No. That won't do. It should be someplace else, someplace neutral."

Burton Kimball sighed. "All right then, how about the hotel dining room over here at the Copper Queen? That won't be all that private, though. But what makes you think she'll agree to come, especially on my say-so?"

"I know Holly," Harold said. "Once she realizes she is going to win, she won't be able to resist. Tell her to meet me there at six."

Now it was Burton Kimball's turn to shake his head. "Six is too late. If you're serious about settling out of court, then do it early enough in the afternoon so Judge Moore can remove the case from tomorrow's docket."

"I am serious," Harold Patterson returned resolutely. The two men's eyes met and held across the younger man's paper-strewn desk. Burton looked away first.

"Okay, okay," he said. "So you're serious. But you'd better give me some idea of what you have in mind. That way, when I call Holly's attorney, he can decide whether or not it's even worthwhile to get together."

"I already told you. Everything she asked for. Tell the lawyer that."

"Uncle Harold," Burt objected, "you're a better businessman than that. You never start negotiating by giving somebody everything they want. Besides, she's demanding half the ranch."

Harold Patterson seemed suddenly very interested in the cleanliness of his fingernails. "So?" he asked innocently.

"So what about Ivy?" Burton demanded suddenly, his eyes alight with sparks of anger. "What about the daughter who didn't run away from home? What about the one who stayed on and helped you look after the ranch? The one who took good care of her mother? Is this the thanks she gets?"

Angered, Burton let his voice rise in volume. "And what the hell good is half a damn cattle ranch the size of the Rocking P? Half isn't going to be enough for both of you to make a living or even for Ivy by herself, for that matter. And which half does she get? The part with the house and the well so she'll still have a damn roof over her head? Or does Holly expect her sister to pitch a damn tent somewhere up on Juniper Flats?"

One of the few pleasures Harold Patterson found in being old was the ability to abandon an unpleasant current of conversation in favor of drifting back over the years. When the lines of the present became too harsh and glaring, when he tired of the bright colors and loud noises, he sometimes immersed himself in the cool, dim shadows of the past.

He did it again in that moment. When he looked across Burton's desk, he didn't see an angry forty-five-year-old professional lawyer with a loosened silk tie knotted halfheartedly around his neck or the monogrammed cuffs of the stiffly starched white shirt. What he saw instead was a shirtless, towheaded seven-year-old boy—a barefoot child wearing nothing but a pair of Oshkosh coveralls cut off just above the boy's scrawny knees.

Both of those bare knees were scraped raw and bleeding, as was the boy's nose. There was a deep gouge on his chin, a cut Harold suspected was serious enough to require stitches, one that was likely to result in a permanent scar.

It was summer. The boy and his uncle stood in the cool, gloomy barn. They faced each other in silence while a cloud of sunlit dust motes danced gaily around them. Dangling from the man's hand was a thick, supple leather strap. The boy's fists were clenched. His chin trembled, and tears glistened in his eyes, but his head was unbowed.

"Burtie, your aunt Emily says you won't tell Holly you're sorry you hit her with the rock."

"That's 'cause I'm not," Burton Kimball declared fiercely, sniffing and wiping away the trickle of blood that had dribbled over the lump of his swollen upper lip. "If she ever does it again, I'll hit her harder next time."

Harold Patterson took a deep breath. He wanted desperately to impart this needed lesson to the boy, to make it stick. As his Christian duty, he had taken in his dead sister's orphaned and abandoned son, had taken him to raise, but Harold was determined Burton not grow up to be like his no-good, worthless father.

"Look, son," Harold explained patiently. "This is important. It's something you got to learn and understand once and for all. Men don't go around hitting women. Ever. No matter what."

"Holly was tickling Ivy," Burtie countered. "She was tickling her, and she wouldn't stop, not even when I asked her nice."

"Tickling's not bad," Harold said. "She didn't mean anything by it."

"Yes, she did, too," Burton insisted. "Holly did it until it hurt, until Ivy cried, until she peed her pants."

He blushed then, embarrassed that he knew about Ivy wetting her pants, humiliated by having to talk about it to Uncle Harold, and outraged that Holly had laughed at Ivy, pointing at her muddied garments and calling her a stupid crybaby.

Burton sniffed again, but he straightened his shoulders. "Give me my licking, Uncle Harold," he said, swallowing hard. "But please don't make me say I'm sorry."

"Ol' Doc Winters sure did a good job of sewing up your chin that time," Harold said suddenly, shifting with a time-warping jolt back to the present. "Scar hardly shows at all. Looks more like a dimple. Who's that movie actor? The good-looking one with the dimple?"

"Kirk Douglas," Burton answered mechanically. "But don't change the subject, Uncle Harold. I want to hear you tell me exactly what you think will happen to Ivy if you go through with this fruitcake idea."

"Remember that time I had to give you a licking in the barn after you chucked Holly over the head with a rock?"

"I remember," Burton Kimball answered grimly.

"You were right back then, you know," Harold said. "Holly was the one who should have had her butt whupped over that one. I used the strap on you because your aunt Emily insisted, but I didn't hit you all that hard, not as hard as I could've. And here you are, all these years later, still sticking up for Ivy."

"It seems to me," said Burton Kimball, "that I shouldn't have to. Her father should be the one looking after her instead of her cousin."

There was another momentary lull in the conversation.

"I reckon this means I'll have to change my will," Harold ventured. "I already talked to Milo Davis's girl about changing the beneficiary agreements on my life insurance."

Maybe, in the interim, Burton Kimball, too, had been caught up in a remembered glimpse of that long-ago scene in the barn; of that determined and unrepentant little boy standing his ground in a swirl of spinning dust motes.

"You're changing the life insurance, too? Dear God in heaven. I don't believe it. What's gotten into you?"

"I've got two daughters," Harold said. "The way it was set up wasn't fair. One was in; one was out. I've thought about it all week. I'm going to talk to Holly about settling this thing with the understanding that she'll have half the ranch, and Ivy will have the rest. Beyond that, I'm going to treat 'em fifty-fifty. That's fair."

Rolling his chair away from the desk, Burton Kimball got up and stalked over to the window. He stared silently out through the glass, studying a sudden burst of sunshine that glinted, blinding and silver, off the still-damp pavement of Main Street.

The relationship between Harold Patterson and Burton Kimball was far more complicated than simply nephew and uncle, lawyer and client. Harold was the only father Burton had ever known. He had been raised and put through school by the unwavering kindness of this stubborn old man. Without Harold's financial support, neither college nor law school would have been possible. Everything Burton Kimball was or owned, he owed to the generosity of this supposedly tough and hard-bitten character.

Burton Kimball had spent most of his forty-five years as Ivy Patterson's champion and protector. The Pattersons had raised all three children in a manner that made them more like brother and sisters than cousins. Burton was five years younger than Holly, and Ivy was ten, but the dynamics of their childhood had always been the same. The two younger children had banded together as small but determined allies, united in their mutual resistance to Holly's constant bullying and torment.

From Burton Kimball's earliest memory, Holly

Patterson had been mean as a snake. Now, some forty years later, the bitch was doing it again, in spades.

And so Burton Kimball found himself standing in front of the window, torn by a lifetime's worth of conflicting loyalties, rocked by disappointment and betrayal. How could he condone a father turning on his own daughter? How could he help Harold Patterson rob Ivy of her birthright?

The plain answer for Burton was that he couldn't. He gave it one last try. "There's nothing fair about it," he said. "Don't do it. Don't cut Ivy out like this. Holly wants the Rocking P. She doesn't need it. She's got her career. Ivy's different. She's spent her whole life working like a dog on the ranch, and you know it. She's never held a regular job, and I know for a fact that you've never paid a dime's worth of wages or Social Security on her."

"Holly's broke," Harold Patterson asserted.

Burton stopped in mid-harangue. "You know that for a fact?"

"She hated Bisbee," the old man answered. "The only reason she'd come back was if she had to."

"Uncle Harold," Burton said evenly. "Are you saying I'm supposed to feel sorry for Holly?"

"You don't know what happened to her," Harold answered softly. "You don't know any of it."

"No," Burton agreed. "You're right. I don't know because you haven't told me, even though I'm your attorney. If anyone ought to know, I should. What *did* happen to Holly, Uncle Harold?"

Burton asked, his voice once more controlled. "Tell me the truth. Let me help you."

But Harold said nothing. For more than a minute no further word passed between them.

"You won't tell me?" Burton said at last.

"There's nothing to tell."

Burton swung away from the window then, turned and stared down at the old man who continued to examine the backs of his mottled, liver-spotted hands with the utmost concentration and studied unconcern. And as Burton looked down at his uncle, a slow dawning—an awful realization—washed across him. The younger man's face blanched.

"That's not true, is it," he said coldly.

"What's not true?" Harold asked.

"That there's nothing to tell."

Harold looked up at Burton. On his face was an expression of feigned innocence, one that even the most inept juror would have seen right through.

"My God!" Burton whispered. "It did happen, didn't it. Holly's telling the truth! That's why you don't want to go to court. That's why you're suddenly willing to settle. You're afraid people around here—your friends and neighbors, the folks who think Harold Patterson is the salt of the earth—will finally see you for what you are."

With no warning, Harold Patterson's eyes betrayed him. Once again, as they had several times that day, they brimmed over with unexpected and unwelcome tears. He tried to brush the telling dampness away, but he wasn't able to, not before Burtie saw the tears and surmised what they meant. With a clutch in his gut, Burton Kimball stumbled into the realization that Holly Patterson was telling the truth.

"If that's the case," the lawyer said carefully, "then maybe you'd better go ahead and settle. But I won't help you. I won't have any part of it. Because you disgust me, Uncle Harold. I can't even stand to be in the same room with you."

He started toward the door.

"Does that mean you quit?" Harold asked.

Burton paused at the door. He answered without looking back or raising his voice. "Yes, that's what it means," he answered slowly. "Given the way I feel at this moment, I don't think I could adequately represent you. You'll be better off with someone else, maybe with one of my partners."

"Please, Burtie," Harold begged. "Your partners don't know anything at all about this case. Don't walk out on me now, not when I need you to help me get in touch with Holly or with her attorney. Nobody else could do that. Only you."

Burton felt the wave of cold fury begin to rise in his chest, threatening to drown him, to rob him of breath and speech both. It was all he could do to summon what could pass for a normal voice, but with a supreme act of self-control, he managed.

"Holly's staying at *Casa Vieja*," he said, "court order be damned! You'll have to do your own dirty work, Uncle Harold, because I'm a son of a bitch if I'll help you!"

With that Burton Kimball stalked out of the room, slamming the door behind him. Harold sat for several minutes, alone in the empty room, regaining his composure; coming to terms with the idea that he now had what he wanted, but not the way he wanted, not at this high a price. He had never thought he'd lose Burtie as well. Never.

Shriveled by this latest penalty, it took some time for Harold to gather his strength and make his way out of Burtie's private office. In the reception area, he paused in front of the desk that belonged to Maxine Smith, Burton's secretary.

"When Burtie gets back," Harold said, "give him a message for me, would you? Tell him I'm sorry, and tell him thank you."

"Why certainly, Mr. Patterson," Maxine said, jotting a quick note on a message pad. "Anything else?"

"No," Harold Patterson said, shaking his head. "That's all."

Seven

HOLLY PATTERSON sat in the back upstairs bedroom at *Casa Vieja* and stared out the window at the tawny wall of rock and tailings that rose two hundred feet in the air. Nothing green grew on the dump. It was dead, empty earth that reminded Holly of the moon. And of herself.

The Stickley rocker with its stiff leather back and broad, flat arms groaned each time it arced across the hardwood floor. The sound reminded her of a door creaking shut. The door to her heart.

She rocked and rocked. A cheerful fire crackled in the little stone fireplace, but nothing warmed her. Not the fire and not the two layers of woolen sweaters she was wearing, either. She was cold, and she was frightened. She had warned Rex Rogers, her lawyer, that it would be bad for her to come here, but Amy had insisted that they had to do it on her father's home turf, and Rex had backed her up. They said there'd be a much better settlement if they bearded the lion in his own den.

Amy Baxter, her hypnotherapist, had told Holly that coming back to Bisbee wouldn't be that big a deal, had assured her that she'd be perfectly fine.

Maybe for publicity and legal reasons, Rex and

Amy were right, and Bisbee *was* the correct place to be. After all, they were the experts who had handled similar cases in towns and cities all over the country. But for Holly, being here was wrong. Bisbee and all the people in it were what she had spent thirty years trying to drink and drug out of her memory. Now that she was back, so were all the old bad feelings.

No one here gave a damn that she had gone out into the world and made a success of her life for a while. If anyone in Bisbee knew or cared that she had a screenwriting Oscar sitting in her storage unit back in Studio City, no one mentioned it. And if anyone knew that she had reached the pinnacle of success only to fall off and land in a series of mental and drug-rehab institutions, no one mentioned that, either. They didn't care if she was a success or a failure. That didn't matter. The people of Bisbee hated her anyway. They hated her because she was Holly Patterson. That was reason enough.

Holly pulled the sweater tighter across her chest and looked down toward the base of the house. Amy, dressed in sweats, was down on the terrace working out on a trampoline. Catching sight of Holly peering out the window, Amy smiled and waved. Holly didn't wave back. Now that the rain was gone and a fitful November sun was peeking through the cloud cover, Amy Baxter was far too energetic for Holly to tolerate. Too energetic and too positive.

Holly, on the other hand, was more like that gaunt, brown-needled pine tree thirsting to death at the top of the once-lush gardens, remnants of which still lingered on the grounds of *Casa Vieja*. Holly knew about the gardens because she and Billy Corbett had ditched school there once during sixth grade. They had taken off their clothes and lain naked in the ivy until they were both itchy and covered with aphids.

Billy had bragged to classmates at school that he had already done it. Twice. Holly had called him a liar and had dared him to prove he wasn't. They agreed to meet in the covered garden behind *Casa Vieja*, a wonderful turn-of-the-century mansion at the top of Vista Park. In an earlier life and under a different name, the brown stuccoed mansion, with its mission-style and molded-plaster details, was a place one of Bisbee's original copper barons had once proudly called home.

By the late fifties, the mansion had been renamed *Casa Vieja* and the huge dump was already inching slowly across the desert toward the lush backyard, although the tailings weren't nearly as close then as they were now, nor as tall. Fueled by grumbling trucks and noisy ore trains, the dump grew larger day by day. And the steady round-the-clock barrage of dust and noise began having serious detrimental repercussions on the fine old house.

The wealthy widow lady who owned it and had lived there for twenty years sold out to a sharp-eyed investor who carved it up into low-cost apartments for oversexed newlyweds who didn't mind being awakened at all hours of the day and night by the roar of heavily laden trucks and the thunder of cascading boulders.

At the new landlord's direction, the gardens out back that had long been nurtured by a loving full-time gardener were ignored. Left to their own devices, the covered arbors dried up and went to seed. For a while, without human intervention, only the ivy and one tall tree were tough enough to hold out against the dry realities of the arid Southwest. Now Jaime Gonzales, the new gardener, was starting the slow process of reclaiming the gardens and the upper terraces, but on that far lower level, all that remained was that one old tree, brown-needled and dying.

Holly remembered how tall and alive it had been, green against a warm blue sky that spring afternoon. The precocious eleven-year-old Holly Patterson had been flat on her naked back, waiting for poor, hapless Billy Corbett to figure out how to make his dinky, useless "thing" stand up. It finally did, after Holly showed him how to rub her stiff little nipples with his groping fingers, but even then it didn't work. When Holly had taunted him, laughed at him because he didn't even know where to put it, Billy had slapped her hard across the face. His blow had left a bright red handprint on her cheek, one she had been hard-pressed to explain to Mama that afternoon when she came home from school.

Remembering that time, Holly rocked even harder and pulled the sweater closer around her body. Billy Corbett had died in Vietnam. His was one of the first names on the memorial plaque over by the new high school.

It served him right, Holly Patterson thought, thirty-nine years after that jewel-clear spring afternoon. Whatever Billy Corbett got, it served him right.

There was a knock on the door. Holly jumped, surprised by her own nervousness. She would have to remember to tell Amy how she was feeling and ask her what it meant. Ask her to put her under and calm her, make the bad feelings go away. Maybe, later on, they could go for a ride in Rex Rogers' bright red Allanté. Maybe Amy would even let Holly drive.

She had read in the paper that Marliss Somebody, the old battle-ax who wrote a weekly column for the *Bisbee Bee*, actually thought the car belonged to Holly. That was a laugh. When she was evicted from her last roach-plagued apartment, Holly Patterson had scarcely anything left to call her own. Amy had helped her salvage the few paltry possessions that remained in storage back in California. And what she had she could keep only so long as she continued to pay the month-to-month storage rental.

The knock came again, and Holly realized she hadn't answered. "Who is it?"

"It's me. Isobel."

"Come in."

Isobel Gonzales, the gardener's wife who served as both cook and housekeeper, bustled into the room. She stopped short when she saw Holly's untouched lunch tray.

"You don't like what I cook for you?"

"I'm not hungry."

Isobel shook her head and clucked her tongue. "Not eating is bad for you. It will make you sick."

This place is making me sick, Holly thought. And it wasn't just Billy Corbett, either, although at first she had thought it was, hoped it was. No, it was something else, something much more than that, something about the dump itself, perhaps. Whatever it was, it remained just out of reach, beyond the grasp of her conscious mind.

She had felt it the first day, as soon as she had set foot in the house. Of course, it was nice of Paul Enders—Pauli to his friends—to lend his "cabin by the lake" to his friends when he found out they were going to Bisbee on business. Of course, there was no lake anywhere near Bisbee. But for someone who lived in the high-pressure world of Hollywood costume design, it was important to have a hideaway where he could go to let the creative juices flow. Besides, *Casa Vieja* had been such a wonderful period-piece bargain that he simply couldn't afford to turn it down.

Paul Enders was only the latest in the long series of *Casa Vieja*'s would-be rescuers. The exodus of miners in the late seventies along with a real estate glut had left even low-cost rentals sitting empty and in even worse decay. Into that economic slump came an unexpected sum of remodeling money that most likely had its source somewhere in Colombia's drug cartel. Cocaine paid the bills for returning *Casa Vieja* to a single-family residence.

Alleged drug money repaired the dry rot, renewed the plumbing, fixed the wiring, and cleaned up and replanted a few of the gardens. The job was only partially finished, however, when the feds moved in to take over. That was how Pauli Enders had picked the place up in the late eighties at a bargain-basement price.

Paul Enders said he found *Casa Vieja* to be a homey place where he could work on a project and not have his creative bursts interrupted by unexpected visitors. He claimed that working in a room that overlooked that wild brown dump made him feel that he was perched somewhere just below the rim of the Grand Canyon. But what was good for Pauli was bad for Holly, although why it was bad for her she couldn't quite fathom. What was it about the dump? Why did it call to her so? Why did its looming nearness keep her from sleeping or eating or thinking?

"Well," Isobel was saying, "are you coming or not?" She sounded impatient, as though she'd said much more than that, only Holly had heard none of it.

"Coming?" Holly repeated stupidly. "Coming where?"

"Downstairs. To see your father. He's waiting to see you."

"My father? Here?" She quailed and pulled back into the chair, rocking desperately. "I don't want to see him. I can't."

"Mrs. Baxter says you should come on down."

"No. Tell her I won't come."

"All right," Isobel said. She went out and closed

the door. Moments later the door opened, and Amy bounded in. "What do you mean you won't come?"

"I don't want to see him. I can't."

Amy came over to Holly's rocker and knelt in front of it. "Yes, you can, Holly. You've got to. He wants to settle. He's willing to make a deal, but you have to talk to him in person."

"No. Please."

"Come on, Holly, after all this, don't back down now."

"Why not?"

"Because you've already come this far and done so damned much hard work to get here," Amy insisted. "This is the one last thing you have to do to regain your self-respect and take control of your life. Now's your chance to hold your father's feet to the fire. He's managed to get away with what he did to you all these years. Don't let him do it again. He owes you. And you owe it to yourself."

"Can't Rex talk to him?"

"Rex is in California today, remember? He'll be back tonight, in time to be in court tomorrow if he has to. It's up to you, Holly. I know you can do it. Take a deep breath now. Relax."

Holly nodded, then distractedly ran her fingers through her sweat-matted hair. "But I'm a mess," she said. "I can't see him like this. I've got to shower, wash my hair, put on makeup."

"Oh, for heaven's sake!"

"Please."

At last Amy relented. "All right," she said with

a smile. "Get in the shower. I'll tell him to come back a little later."

"You're sure I can do it?"

Amy came over to Holly's rocker and knelt in front of it.

"Do you remember what I told you when you first came to me for help? After we met at that screening?"

Holly nodded. Her spoken answer was almost like a recited catechism. "That I'd have to trust you, but that the only way to learn to trust others was to trust myself."

"Think how far you've come since then, Holly. Think how much you've accomplished. Child molesters are basically cowards, and you've called his bluff. That's why he's here. That's why he's come to offer you a settlement. You don't have to be scared of him anymore. The tables are turned. Now he's scared of you."

"That doesn't seem possible."

"But it is. Go get in the shower. I'll tell him to come back in an hour."

"Not an hour," Holly said flatly. "That's too soon. It makes me sound too eager. Tell him to come back at four."

"All right," Amy said. "Four it is."

Long after the door closed, Holly lingered in the chair without moving. If this was what she wanted; if this was what was supposed to happen; how come she felt so awful? If this was victory, why was she shivering and sweating at the same time? Why was the prospect of seeing her father again after all these years so terrifying?

Finally, though, after half an hour or so, she managed to pull herself together enough to rise up out of the chair and head for the shower. If Amy still believed in her, maybe Holly Patterson could somehow find a way to believe in herself.

She had to. Amy had said it was the only way she was going to win. And winning was supposed to be worth it.

Eight

IN THE relative pre-lunch quiet of Bisbee's Blue Moon Saloon, Angie Kellogg was studying her Arizona state driver's license manual as though her very life depended on it. Studying—serious studying—was something she had done so seldom in her short life that it came as a surprise. Even to her.

On the run from her drug-cartel, hit-man boyfriend, Angie was an ex-L.A. hooker who had landed in Bisbee two months earlier. Under circumstances that still amazed her, she had been taken under the protective wing of an unlikely trio of rescuers made up of Joanna Brady, Reverend Marianne Maculyea, and Bobo Jenkins, one of Bisbee's few African Americans. As the enterprising owner/operator of the Blue Moon, he had offered Angie Kellogg her first legitimate employment.

Determined to be out of "the life," Angie was walking the straight and narrow for the first time in her short existence. She had purposefully changed her lifestyle, but not necessarily her clothing. Her trademark skintight jeans, platform heels, and voluptuous figure continually provoked comment and notice in the post office and Safeway.

They also made her by far the best-looking relief bartender in town. Bobo, a sharp businessman with one eye on Angie's figure and the other on the daily receipts, was quick to notice a distinct upswing in business whenever Angie Kellogg pulled a shift.

He joked that she was his most valuable employee. Since she was also his only employee, Angie didn't take that compliment very seriously. But in a place as small as Bisbee, where a severely limited population also limited the number of drinkers, anything that improved the bottom line of a marginally profitable business was an addition to be welcomed with open arms.

At first Angie Kellogg didn't pay that much attention to the well-dressed man who crashed through the swinging door of the Blue Moon Saloon and Lounge and slouched over to the farthest booth. It was a little before eleven-thirty when he ducked into the bench seat with his back to the entrance.

Annoyed to have her quiet study time interrupted prior to the normal lunch-hour rush, Angie put down her driver's license manual and hurried over to take his order. "What'll you have?" she asked.

"A Bloody Mary," he answered. "A double."

Angie guessed the stranger might be an attorney right away, although of a far better caliber than the ones her various L.A. pimps used to hire to bail their girls out of the slammer.

"Hot or not?" she asked.

Bobo had directed Angie to ask the question in

just that way, carefully explaining that some customers liked mild Bloody Marys while others
wanted the drink so fired with Tabasco sauce that
they required a water chaser. When Bobo, an ath-
letically built black man, asked that particular
question, no one gave him any crap. When Angie
did, things usually went from bad to worse in a
hurry.

The dweeb lawyer answered her with a disturbingly blank stare, and Angie braced herself for
the inevitably rude comment that was bound to
follow. If it was bad enough, she was fully prepared to tell him what he could do with the piece
of celery she was supposed to put in the drink to
stir it.

"I beg your pardon?" he said finally. "What was
it you asked me?"

"The drink," she prodded. "How spicy? Hot
or not?"

"Not very," he said.

Angie flounced away from him, tossing her
blond hair. Maybe he didn't go to bars much. He
acted like he didn't even speak the language, like
he was from a foreign country or something. But
at least he hadn't propositioned her. Bobo had
made it clear that if Angie wanted to keep her
part-time job as relief daytime bartender, "frater-
nizing with the customers," which Angie trans-
lated to mean screwing around, was absolutely
forbidden. To be honest, there weren't that many
men who looked remotely interesting to her these
days, and certainly not for free. As far as *that* job

was concerned, Angie Kellogg was permanently on vacation.

By the time she delivered the lawyer's drink and collected his money, the first of her noontime regulars had wandered in from outside. Archie McBride and Willy Haskins were already arguing when they sauntered into the bar and settled into their usual places at the far end of the counter nearest the door. Angie brought two vodkas along with Coors draft chasers without bothering to ask. They always ordered the same thing anyway, and it was too hard waiting for them to stop yammering long enough to get a word in edgewise.

The two old guys, both former underground miners, had been retired from Phelps Dodge for at least twenty years. They were relatively harmless maintenance drunks who had to keep a certain amount of liquor in their systems to keep from dipping into DTs. Their ongoing arguments never caused much trouble, although Angie always hoped the conversations would steer clear of politics or religion.

If it had been just the two of them, Angie might have tried to grab a few more minutes' worth of study time, but they were joined by another noontime imbiber, Don Frost, who meandered in out of the Gulch and settled onto his usual barstool.

Don, part of Bisbee's arts community, was a sculptor specializing in what he called "Mixed Media Dreg Art." Frost's pieces consisted of hunks of discarded junk, glued and/or welded together. Sometimes, on a good day, they were even painted. Although Don Frost's work was prominently displayed in galleries around town, they seldom ever sold. He subsisted on monthly checks from some kind of trust fund that allowed him to drink and eat as long as he lived in a $150-a-month apartment above an abandoned Mom-and-Pop grocery store up Tombstone Canyon.

Sometimes, toward the end of the month and toward the end of that month's money, Don Frost would come into the Blue Moon and hit up Bobo for a loan to tide him over. Bobo was always careful to ask for an accounting at the beginning of the next month.

"It's good business," Bobo told Angie with a sly grin. "Sure I lend him money, and he always pays me back from the next check. And that keeps it all in the family—he borrows here and drinks here too."

Twenty-three-year-old Angie liked working as Bobo's relief bartender, her first-ever nonhooking employment. It was honest work that enabled her to keep up the payments on a modest two-bedroom house that had once served as company housing. It allowed her to indulge in her new-found hobby of bird feeding while still maintaining most of the cash nest egg Joanna Brady had helped her finesse away from Adam York and the Drug Enforcement Agency.

Most of the time Angie enjoyed her job, but some of the customers got to her—Don Frost most of all. An obnoxious loudmouth and self-appointed expert in everything, Frost freely shared with Angie his encyclopedic knowledge of mixology and was forever offering her unsolicited advice as she struggled with learning the intricacies of her new job.

Don Frost fancied himself quite a catch, always hinting that there was a whole lot more money where the trust funds came from, and whatever woman was lucky enough to land him would be in for quite a ride. Since Angie was literally the "new girl in town," Frost maintained a constant barrage of what he regarded as flirtatious banter. He had even gone so far as to bring in one of his recently completed works of art for her approval.

Angie Kellogg's taste in art was fairly unsophisticated. When Don assured her this was a five-thousand-dollar piece, she couldn't imagine why anyone would want to pay that much money for a chunk of painted garbage. Had Angie still been working the streets, one dose of Don Frost would have been more than enough. But here he was one of Bobo's regulars, someone whose daily presence contributed to both paychecks and tips. So she made the best of it.

With a sigh, Angie plucked the driver's training manual off the counter. As she slipped it into her purse and stowed it under the bar, Don noticed.

"So when do you take the exam?" he asked. "How long before the streets stop being safe for humanity?"

"Thursday," Angie answered. "What'll you have?"

Frost grinned. "A nooner?" he asked hopefully.

The stranger in the booth caught Angie's eye and waved to her. "I'll have another," he called.

Angie left Don Frost sitting at the bar and went

to mix the Bloody Mary. "When you make up your mind," she said over her shoulder, "let me know."

When she came back from delivering that drink, Frost was ready to order his early-in-the-month Kahlúa and coffee. By the end of the month, he'd be down to beer spiked with occasional shots of tequila.

"Why do you suppose Mr. Burton Kimball is out slumming?" Frost demanded morosely, nodding toward the stranger in the booth as Angie put the chipped coffee mug down in front of him. "I've never known him to set foot in the Gulch."

"Who's Burton Kimball?"

"If Bisbee had a *Mayflower*, Burton Kimball's family would have been on it. It's his uncle's case that's supposed to start in Judge Moore's court tomorrow. You've probably heard about it. The daughter claims her old man liked to play hide-the-salami with her when she was little. Now she's hired herself a lawyer, and she's taking his ass to court, suing him for damages."

"Good for her," Angie said, and hurried down the bar to bring Willy and Archie another pair of beers.

"You got something against men?" Don Frost asked, when she came back past him.

"Only ones who mess with their daughters," she replied.

"You're not one of those feminazis, are you?"

"A what?"

"Don't you ever listen to Rush Limbaugh?"

"Who?"

81

"That jerk on the radio. I don't listen to him, either," Don Frost said, pushing his cup away. "He makes me sick. Give me another."

Angie poured herself a cup of coffee at the same time she made Don Frost's drink. "Let me give you some advice about when you take the driving part of your test," Frost said. "Signal for everything. And keep checking the rearview mirror. They mark you off if you don't check that enough. Do you know the manual forward and backward?"

Angie shook her head. "I should have spent more time studying over the weekend, but I was busy with the phone bank."

"Fun bank?" a puzzled Archie McBride called from down the bar. Years of setting off dynamite blasts and loading ore cars underground had left Archie very hard of hearing. His twenty-six-year-old hearing aid had finally given up the ghost, and he refused to buy another.

"How the hell does a fun bank work?" he demanded loudly. "And where do we sign up? Right, Willy?"

The two old men collapsed against each other in gales of raucous laughter while Angie frowned and shook her head. "Phone bank," she repeated, more loudly. "For Joanna Brady. For the election."

"Oh," Archie said. "That's right. The election. Isn't that today? You voted yet?"

Everyone in the room shook their heads. For the first time in her life, Angie Kellogg had actually wanted to vote—had even found a candidate she wanted to vote for—but she had come to town too late to register for this election.

The guy at the booth waved to her again. She went over to him, expecting him to order another drink. "Would it be possible to use the phone?" he asked.

Angie Kellogg studied the man Don Frost had called Burton Kimball. She was gratified to realize her first impression had been right. The man really was a lawyer. At first glance, she had assumed he must be better than the lawyers she had known, the ones who had plied their trade by bailing whores out of jail, their retainers paid by pimps or drug dealers. But she had been wrong. If Burton Kimball was defending a child molester, a man who screwed his own daughter, then he was no better than the lawyers she had known before. In fact, maybe he was worse.

"Local?" she asked.

"Yes," he said.

Bobo didn't generally allow customers to use the house phone. Outgoing calls could be made only from the phone in the back room. And Angie's first instinct was to tell this pervert-loving bastard to take a hike and go make his precious phone call from a pay phone, preferably one in the middle of a busy street.

But then another thought came to her. Hadn't Don Frost just told her that the attorney's big-deal trial was due in court the next day? What would happen if the attorney for the defense was too damn hung over to hold his head up? Keeping him out of court probably wasn't realistic, Angie decided, but she could maybe make him wish he'd stayed home. Even a novice bartender was capable of inflicting that much damage.

"You can use the phone in the back room," she told him with a beguiling smile. "The number's on it in case someone needs to call you back. By the way, what's your name?" she asked, even though she already knew the answer. "I don't think I've seen you in here before."

"Burton Kimball," he said, but he dropped his voice as though he really didn't relish the idea of other people hearing him.

Angie held out her hand. "I'm Angie. Glad to meet you, Burton. Welcome to the Blue Moon. Care for another drink? It's on the house. Sort of an introductory offer."

"Sure," Kimball said. "As soon as I make this call."

When he came back, the new Bloody Mary was waiting in his booth. It seemed quite a bit stronger than the previous ones, and hotter.

Angie Kellogg watched with satisfaction as Burton Kimball stirred the new drink with the stalk of celery and swilled some of it down. His eyebrows shot up and down and he made a face, as though he was surprised by the extra jolt of Tabasco. But instead of complaining about the extra heat or the extra booze—a triple instead of a double—he nodded his thanks.

Angie smiled in return and returned to looking after her other customers, anticipating with some pleasure the moment when, because he was so drunk, she would be justified in throwing Burton Kimball out into the street.

With any kind of luck, he'd have to crawl back down Brewery Gulch on his hands and knees.

Nine

As HE drove home to the Rocking P, Harold Patterson found himself in a state of hopefulness that verged on euphoria. It was going to work. Holly would see him. The woman named Amy, who was Holly's therapist or nurse or whatever, had been genuinely helpful. That was something he had never anticipated. He had built her up in his mind, expecting her to be some kind of monster. Rather than throwing him out of the house as soon as she learned who he was, Amy Baxter had been almost cordial.

He had sat nervously in *Casa Vieja*'s long, box-beamed living room, waiting for Amy to return from upstairs to tell him whether or not Holly would see him. When she first said Holly wouldn't be down right away, he had been crushed. Then, after learning she would see him later on in the afternoon, he was almost ecstatic.

Talking to Amy had given him some clues as to what he might expect of Holly's current state of mind. "Don't be surprised if she acts a little odd," Amy had said. "She has these little spells. They come and go. Sometimes she's better, sometimes worse."

No doubt, had the lawyer been there—had *either* one of the two lawyers been there—Harold was sure things would have gone in a far different fashion. He had been right to go on his own.

But now, with the prospect of finally confronting Holly only an hour away, he had to break the news to Ivy as well. He had two daughters, and if they were going to be neighbors on the Rocking P, if they were going to live in such close proximity, then one couldn't be privy to the terrible secret without the other knowing as well.

Harold pulled into the yard and was relieved to see Ivy's faded red four-by-four Luv pickup parked near the front gate. She was home. The only question now was would she listen to him? Would she give him a chance to talk?

Moving stiffly, slowly, Harold climbed out of the Scout just as the front screen door slammed open. A man named Yuri Malakov came out of the house, his arms stacked high with boxes.

"Hey," Harold said. "What's going on? What are you doing?"

Harold knew the man to be a newly arrived Russian immigrant and a friend of Ivy's. Marianne Maculyea, the pastor up at Canyon Methodist Church, had hooked Ivy up with some kind of literacy program. For the past few weeks, the huge Russian and his stack of books had become a constant evening fixture at the Patterson kitchen table. By day, Malakov worked as a hired hand over at the Robertson place a few miles closer to Tombstone on Highway 80. By night, he and Ivy studied grammar and vocabulary.

Yuri stopped short when he encountered Harold standing on the porch. A few seconds later, the door opened again, and Ivy pushed her way out, a loaded suitcase in each hand.

"What are you doing?" Harold asked again.

Ivy shouldered past him. "Come on, Yuri. Those boxes should go in first. There's another stack in the kitchen that's all ready to go. Bring them, too."

Obediently, Yuri shoved the boxes into a spot left in the back of the already loaded pickup. Then, without a word to Harold, he turned and headed back into the house.

Ivy was short, stocky, and solidly built—an exact duplicate of her mother. After years of hard physical labor, of digging fence-post holes and wrestling stock, Ivy Patterson was far stronger than she looked. She reached down and effortlessly tossed the suitcases into the bed of the truck.

"Are you leaving?" Harold asked, unwilling to believe the evidence offered by his own eyes.

"You could say that," Ivy answered. She didn't look at him as she hurried past to retrieve the next stack of boxes Yuri was in the process of depositing on the front porch.

"But what's happening? Where are you going?"

"I don't think that's any of your business."

"None of my business?" he echoed. "How can that be? I'm your father."

"Well, pin a rose on you!" The cold bitterness in Ivy's usually kind voice shocked Harold as much as if she had slapped his face.

"Ivy, please. I've got to talk to you."

"Don't bother. I already know. Burtie called and gave me the news."

"He shouldn't have done that."

"Well, he did. And if you think I'm going to live here and share my home with that woman, you're crazy."

"But, Ivy, she's your sister, and you have no idea what she's been through. She's had some bad luck, some really hard times."

"Haven't we all. Get the tarp, Yuri," Ivy said, turning her back on her father. "I doubt it's going to rain anymore, but we'll lash it down just in case. That way, nothing will fly out of the truck once we hit the highway."

Together they spread the tarp over the load. While Ivy began expertly tying it down, Harold limped over to the edge of the porch.

On either side of the top steps, framing the entrance to the porch, stood the knotted trunks of two huge wisteria vines. Harold had planted them himself when they were little more than twigs. Those two vines had been Emily's pride and joy, coming to the house with her when she first arrived as a bride. He had always teased Em by telling her that those vines with their generous summer shade and sweet-smelling flowers were the best part of her dowry. In actual fact, they had been Emily Whitaker Patterson's only dowry.

Slowly, struggling to steady his breath, Harold eased himself down against one of the trunks and looked up at the twining branches, leafless, now, and empty with the approach of winter. The twisted wood looked ancient, brittle, and lifeless—

as though a strong breeze would splinter it into a million pieces. Harold felt the same way.

"As soon as we unload this, we'll come back for the horses. Natasha Robertson said Bimbo and Sam can stay on their place until I make other arrangements. They sure can't stay with me at an apartment in town, and Yuri can look after them when I can't."

"Ivy, please listen to reason. You don't have to leave home. It isn't like that. You've got to understand."

Handing the rest of the lashing process over to Yuri, Ivy Patterson stalked over to the bottom of the step. "What do I have to understand?"

"Why I'm doing what I'm doing. I have to talk to you. In private. I can't say what I have to say in front of anyone else, anyone outside the family."

She eyed her father coldly. "Yuri is family," she answered. "We're going to be married as soon as we can make arrangements. Look."

Ivy held up her left hand. Harold was astonished to see a ring where there had never been one before.

"Don't you recognize it?" Ivy asked. "It's Mother's. The one she gave me before she died. On what little he makes, Yuri couldn't afford to buy me a ring. It's lucky I happened to have one."

Harold Patterson was dumbfounded. "How can this be? How come I didn't know anything about it?"

"Because you weren't interested," Ivy responded. "Because you were so wound up worrying about what was going to happen with Holly that you couldn't see the nose on your face."

Harold glanced at Yuri, who was standing by the truck. The Russian was looking up at them quizzically, his huge hands dangling awkwardly by his sides.

"But you haven't known him very long, have you?" Harold objected. "How can you be sure . . . ?"

"How long did you know Mother?" Ivy countered. "And I'm a lot older now than either of you were then. I'm forty years old. I've got a chance to grab some happiness before it's too late, and I am by God taking it."

"Does Burton know about this? Did you tell him anything about it?" Harold asked.

"No, I didn't tell Burton. Why should I? This isn't the old days, Pop. I don't have to ask permission from every male relative before I make a decision. It's my life. I've spent all these years putting other people first. Well, I've learned my lesson. I'm not going to do that anymore."

"But what about the ranch? What about the Rocking P?"

"What about it?" she raged back at him. "Have Holly come take care of it."

"She can't. She's sick. She's been sick for a long time."

"She's sick, all right," Ivy retorted. "Holly's a drug addict, Dad. Face it. She may have had talent once, but she's burned her brain up on booze and cocaine and God knows what else."

"A drug addict? Are you sure?"

"She's been in and out of treatment half a dozen different times. That's one of the reasons Burton doesn't want you to settle with her. If it comes down to your word against hers, who's going to believe her?"

Without answering, Harold leaned back against the wisteria trunk and closed his eyes.

"You went to see her, didn't you?" Ivy flared. "You've made arrangements to settle, haven't you?"

"Not yet," Harold murmured. "But I will. Later on today."

"Why?"

"Because she couldn't see me right then."

"I don't give a damn what time you go see her. What I want to know is why did you go at all? Burton told me what he thinks, but I want to hear it from you, from your own lips."

Yuri moved closer to Ivy. Towering over her by nearly two feet, he put one protective hand on her shoulder. For years Harold Patterson had longed for someone to come into his younger daughter's life, someone who would honor her and care for her the way she deserved. Yet now that Yuri had showed up on the scene, he seemed like more of an enemy than a friend.

Harold was glad the letter was still safely stashed in his box at the bank. After all those years, now that he was finally willing to share the awful secret with his two daughters, this one demanded unreasonable conditions. He couldn't see spilling his guts after all these years with some interloping stranger hanging on every word. Harold shook his head helplessly and didn't answer.

Ivy shrugged off Yuri's hand and moved closer, leaning forward until her face and her father's were only inches apart. "Is it true, then?" she demanded. "Is that it?"

"No," he protested, holding up his arm as if deflecting a physical blow. "It's not that at all. You've got to believe me."

"Well, I don't. And no one else will, either, not if you settle. If you were innocent, you'd go to court to prove it. In the meantime, don't bother splitting the ranch. Go back to Holly and tell her she can have the whole damn thing. I don't want any part of it. Let her come back home and take care of you the way I took care of Mother if it ever comes to that. She can be the one who keeps the doors locked so you don't wander outside without remembering to put your clothes on the way Mother did."

"Ivy, please . . ."

But Ivy wouldn't stop. "And when it gets to the point where you can't feed yourself anymore, let your precious Holly be the one to ladle the soup into your mouth and change the filthy sheets and empty the damn bedpans. Tell her I've already done it once. Tell her I've already served my time, and I'll be goddamned if I'll do it again! Come on, Yuri, let's go."

As afternoon sunlight warmed the wet yard, a few chickens, the peacock, and two peahens had ventured into the yard and were scratching for bugs in the damp dirt outside the fence. Harold sat without moving while the Luv roared away, sending startled fowl squawking in every direction.

Only after the Luv was entirely out of sight did he get up and wander into the house. With a despairing gaze, he stood in the middle of the room and looked at the things that were missing—the things Ivy had packed to take with her—pictures, books, knickknacks that were probably every bit as much hers as they were his.

He stumbled over to the armchair in front of the fireplace where a small fire still burned on the grate. It was too bad he hadn't brought the letter with him. He could just as well give up and burn the damned thing. The fire would have been only too happy to consume the old yellowed paper saturated with candle wax.

But giving up would have been too easy, and that wasn't Harold's style. Instead, he lurched to his feet and hurried through the house. In his bedroom, he leaned into his age-mottled mirror and combed his sparse hair. He was old and buttsprung all right but he could still take care of his ownself. So far, anyway.

After sprinkling on a dab of Old Spice, Harold Patterson clambered into the Scout and once more headed for *Casa Vieja*.

Ten

LATER ON, when Burton Kimball tried to recall the exact sequence of events, it was difficult for him to sort out that long, emotionally troubling afternoon. What he did know for sure was that it had been right about noon when he strode into the Blue Moon Saloon and Lounge, and all he could think about was Ivy, poor Ivy. What could he do to help her? What would become of her if she lost the Rocking P? Where, for instance, would Ivy go looking for a job?

Cattle ranching was all Ivy Patterson had ever known or cared to know. Working with her father on the ranch had been her whole life, but if cowboys were a dying breed, cowgirls were even more so. When Trigger, Roy Rogers' old horse, went to the great pasture in the sky, someone had gone to the trouble of calling in a taxidermist to stuff the carcass. But whatever happened to Dale Evans' horse? Burton wondered morosely. The way the world worked, Buttermilk probably turned into a horsehide sofa.

The bartender at the Blue Moon, a young slender blonde Burton Kimball never remembered seeing around town before, came out from behind the bar to take his order. Burton pulled himself out of the depressing morass of thought only long enough to order a Bloody Mary. As soon as the bartender walked away, he returned to his somber contemplation of Ivy Patterson's dismal future and Holly's treachery.

Because that's how Burton saw it—as treachery pure and simple. Holly's allegations of childhood sexual abuse at the hands of her father were too much a part of current pop-psychology myth—a belief system that tended to blame everything from ingrown toenails to snoring on the convenient bogeyman of childhood abuse. The presence of Amy Baxter, a supposedly internationally recognized hypnotherapist, was designed to lend legitimacy to Holly's claims.

But Burton Kimball wasn't about to fall for the phony visiting-expert-therapist gambit. Amy Baxter's professional attendance on Holly's team didn't impress him any more than Rex Rogers' out-of-town lawyer act did. Despite Rogers' pious claims to the contrary, the expected courtroom confrontation with her father had been played up as a necessary part of Holly's recovery.

They could all claim until the cows came home that Harold Patterson was Holly's only target, but Burton Kimball knew better. Harold's destruction was only a means to an end. Holly's real target was Ivy.

It had been that way from the beginning, almost from the moment Ivy was born. Long before the baby could talk or defend herself, Burton remembered Holly pinching her baby sister when she thought no one was looking just to hear Ivy cry. When Burton had tried to tell his Aunt Emily, he had been punished for being a tattletale; for making things up.

And if Holly had hated Ivy then, now she had far more cause. After all, Ivy was still "the baby," still the well-loved child—the easygoing, cooperative kid who never gave anyone a moment's trouble. For someone who was a born troublemaker, whose entire family had been only too happy to see her leave home at sixteen, it had to be galling for Holly Patterson to come face-to-face with a sister who had never been thrown out of the nest; one who, at age forty, was still living happily at home.

It hardly mattered that Holly had gone off into the world, finding success in life and losing same. As far as Burton could see, her favorite role had always been that of spoiler, of someone far more interested in destroying someone else's happiness than in creating her own. It stood to reason that if Ivy wouldn't leave her comfortable nest on the Rocking P, if Harold couldn't be prevailed upon to give his daughter the necessary shove, then Holly would simply demolish it, making the ranch untenable and useless for all concerned.

That seemingly had been her intention, and Burton Kimball's only interest was to stop her. In attempting to do so, he had discovered the reality of what Harold Patterson only now suspected. Holly's much-vaunted success was nothing but a sham. Yes, she had an Oscar—at least she had won one once. But she had slipped a long way from the pinnacle. In preparing Harold's defense, Burton had learned the truth about the extent of Holly's drinking and drugging; about her ongoing merry-go-round of treatment and relapse.

Burton could see now that he had been wrong to withhold that information from his client, but he had done so deliberately. He knew Harold too well. The old man was all wool and a yard wide. Burton had worried that if Harold had guessed how desperate Holly was, he'd simply give away the store. And now, despite Burton's scheming to the contrary, that's exactly what had happened. Burton had counted on going to court. Had banked on Harold's not caving in to Holly's demands; on his being able to demonstrate to the jury exactly what kind of person she was. Now the awful reality was slowly sinking into Burton's consciousness. He had been outmaneuvered.

Without paying much attention, he downed one drink and ordered another. The problem at the moment was finding a way to regain control. Harold had made up his mind to settle, and once Harold Patterson made up his mind about something, it would be a hell of a job to change it. The biggest difficulty with someone like Harold was the fact that his word was his bond, and so was his handshake. He'd do what he said he would do regardless of whether or not his name was on the dotted line. It was slimy bastards like Rex Rogers who never made a move until all contracts had been properly drawn, signed, and executed.

Suddenly, sitting there by himself in the booth, Burton Kimball wondered if Ivy knew she was about to be run over by a train; wondered if she had any idea what her father intended to do.

Ethically, Burton didn't have a leg to stand on, but it wasn't fair for her not to have some warning. Burton waved to the bartender. This time, when she approached the booth, he asked her if he could use the phone. At first, he thought she was going to turn him down, but then she relented. Directed to the phone in the back room, Burton dialed the Rocking P. The phone rang and rang, but no one answered.

Leaving the phone, a slightly tipsy Burton Kimball returned to the table, where a new Bloody Mary was waiting for him. Now that he'd decided to do it, now that he'd decided to tell Ivy, he could hardly contain himself. He gulped that drink and hardly noticed that this one was much hotter than the other two. And much stronger. When it was gone, he tried the phone once more and ordered yet another drink.

By the end of the fourth drink, Burton Kimball was well on his way to being drunk. He was also more than a little worried. He should never have told Harold he quit. That was dumb. How would he ever be able to lobby on Ivy's behalf if he was outside the case looking in? He should probably track Uncle Harold down and unresign. Was unresign a word? Disresign maybe? There had to be some kind of word that said what he meant, but he couldn't think of it.

There may have been more drinks after that. Burton seemed to remember singing show tunes with a toothless old miner at the end of the bar.

By the time he finally reached Ivy by phone, Burton could barely talk. Mumbling incoherently, he blurted out the news. The dead silence on the other end of the line sobered him instantly.

"Ivy," he said, when the silence persisted. "Say something. Are you all right?"

"I'm fine," she said. But she didn't sound fine.

"Do you want me to come out? Can I do something to help?"

"You've done enough," she said.

When he put down the phone, a subdued and surprisingly sober Burton Kimball paid his bill. The bartender had been very nice, so he left her a sizable tip. Unfortunately, as soon as he stepped outside, as soon as the bright sunlight hit him, he was drunk again.

Staggering, Burton managed to make it down the street without seeing anyone who knew him. He found his car and succeeded in inserting the key in the lock on the fifth try. Settling in the seat with his head against the backrest and telling himself that all he needed was a little nap, Burton Kimball passed out cold.

For a fleeting moment, when he first awakened in the shadowy gloom, Harold thought it was all a dream—the same one he always had, the terrible nightmare that had haunted his sleep and hounded him out of bed for more years than he cared to remember.

The dream was forever the same. Harold would find himself trapped in a glory hole, in one of those useless, abandoned exploratory shafts that riddled the stony pastures of the Rocking P. And it always took place in the very same glory hole—the deepest one, the one nearest the summit of the Mule Mountains, high up among the red rock-bound, scrub-oak-dotted cliffs called Juniper Flats.

In his sleep, Harold's nightmare prison was just like this real one, measuring eight feet in diameter by thirty feet deep. Uneven slide-prone sides rose in an almost perpendicular fashion from a dank, rain-puddled floor to the rounded lip at the top, left by a pile of excavated tailings. Rocks and other things—foul things he didn't want to think about—littered the floor and made footing uncertain.

In real life, a sturdy barbed-wire fence surrounded the tailings mound and separated it and others like it from the Rocking P's pastureland. The fence served as a lifesaving deterrent to thirsty desert-dwelling livestock that might otherwise be drawn to their deaths by the luring smell of water. In Harold's dream, the fence never did any good, because it never kept him from falling in and being trapped.

Each time the nightmare opened, Harold would find himself on his hands and knees, his desperate fingers groping and clawing along the steep wall, searching for some hold, some purchase, that would allow him to scramble up and out of his rocky cage. But each movement, each tentative touch, would jar loose stones and pebbles that would rain back down on his body, sending dirt and gravel spewing into his watering eyes and mewling mouth, battering him into the ground like some shamed biblical harlot.

In his terror, he always cried out to Emily. "Help me, Em. Please help."

Of course, Emily never answered his panic-stricken cries, and why would she? She'd been dead for five years now and marooned out of reach for many years before that. Emily Patterson was long dead but not forgotten.

On this day, though, once his brain cleared, Harold realized this waking nightmare was no dream. Instead of sopped, sweat-drenched bedsheets beneath him, when he came to himself there were rocks—real rocks—that were all too cold and sharp, especially the one that was biting painfully into his shoulder. This time he really was trapped in the dank depths of that very same glory hole, the one he had always avoided whenever possible.

He lay flat on his back and tried squinting up through the darkness at the distant blue far above him. That had to be sky, although he couldn't really tell for sure, couldn't actually see it. His glasses had somehow disappeared in what must have been a fall although Harold couldn't remember it. Without his trusty spectacles, Harold Patterson was as good as blind.

Blind, he thought grimly, but maybe not helpless. He tried to shift his weight then, to dislodge whatever it was that was digging into his shoulder. But even that slight motion was too much. A crushing wave of pain washed over him—a pain so intense that it flattened him, robbed him of breath, and rolled his eyes back into his head.

Ribs, he thought to himself when he struggled back to wavering consciousness. Shattered ribs. No telling what damage they might do if he tried to move again, if they poked into something vital—a lung perhaps, or maybe even his wildly pounding heart.

So he lay still and tried to think, tried to imagine what he could do to save himself. The glory hole that had for years tormented his sleep was miles from the house, so there was no point in calling out for help. No one would hear him. Unless someone came out there deliberately. Unless they came looking for him.

He tried then to remember how it was that he had come to be near the glory hole in the first place. Had he been out doing chores? Feeding cattle? Working fences? Try as he might, he couldn't corral his memory into any kind of order. Whatever had happened earlier in the day, before he fell into the hole, remained a total mystery, as did the days immediately preceding that. It was as though his memory of the last few days prior to this terrible awakening had been wiped out of existence.

Had he told anyone he'd be working this part of the ranch? Would anyone have an idea of where to start looking once he turned up missing? If he couldn't remember how or why he had come to be there, would anyone else? Would Ivy realize he was hurt and institute a search, or would she simply shrug her shoulders and forget it, annoyed that her father was once again late for dinner?

At first shock helped deaden the pain, but as

that natural analgesia disappeared, increasing clarity brought with it excruciating agony. Even lying perfectly still, the shattered ribs still stabbed and poked at him with each ragged breath. He was aware of shards of splintered bone pressing and piercing where no bone should have been.

In addition to the pain, he grew increasingly aware of a familiar but fetid smell. It was some time before recognition crystallized in his brain. The appalling stench—a combination of human excrement and urine—belonged to him. Both bowel and bladder must have let go at once. He had no control whatsoever.

Harold Lamm Patterson was an experienced stockman who understood the meaning of such things. If he was lying in a pool of his own bodily filth and waste with no muscle control and no sensory awareness from the bottom of his fractured ribs down, that meant his back was broken. It meant he was going to die.

That realization was too much for him. Mercifully, he again lost consciousness. For the time being, his physical pain eased, but not the mental torment, for soon the dream came again—the dream this time somehow layered in with nightmarish reality. The part of him that recognized it as a dream welcomed it, even though it was more vivid, more terrifying, than ever before.

The scene had barely opened—he was still crawling around, looking for a way out—when the rocks began to fall in a horrifyingly accurate barrage. At first, only small pebbles rained down on him, but the sizes of the rocks grew steadily larger and their weights heavier. He tried dodging out of the way, but he couldn't. There was no place to hide. No place to get away.

"Em, help me. Please . . . please."

Eleven

It TURNED out to be one of the longest days of Joanna Brady's existence. Once Harold Patterson left her office, the morning seemed to drag. At lunchtime, she drove from Warren up to Old Bisbee for a celebratory, end-of-campaign lunch with Jeff Daniels and Marianne Maculyea.

Jeff—a full-time, stay-at-home, minister's husband—had planned the event, weeks earlier—win, lose, or draw. With the election over, Jeff hoped life with his pastor-turned-campaign-manager wife would return to some semblance of normalcy. Their usually neat parsonage had deteriorated to a shambles while Marianne masterminded the whole campaign and Jeff handled the mass mailings out of the room that usually served as Marianne's study.

It was a great lunch, complete with an appropriate set of toasts. Later in the afternoon, however, the effects of the champagne kicked in, and it was all Joanna could do to keep from falling asleep at her desk. As much as she hated the prospect of going to a beauty salon, she was grateful when it was time to abandon the office in favor of Helene's Salon of Hair and Beauty.

Helene's looked exactly like what it was—an ill-disguised two-car garage that had been hammered-and-tonged into a beauty shop by virtue of some very creative do-it-yourself plumbing and electrical work provided by Helen Barco's retired handyman husband.

When Joanna sat down in the chair, Helen Barco took one look at her, shook her head, clicked her tongue sadly, and said, "Oh my, no. This will never do. Your mother tells me you're going to be on the TV news tonight. We don't want one of our girls looking like something the cat dragged in, now do we?"

We certainly don't! And an hour and a half later, Joanna didn't.

The remodel job on the building might have been amateurish, but the finished-product Joanna Brady who walked out the door of Helene's at five-thirty that afternoon was strictly professional—a classic makeover. Her red hair had been cropped off in a short but stylish cut. Her makeup had been professionally applied. Lipstick and unaccustomed nail polish matched perfectly. She'd have to remember to use the lip-liner Helen had insisted she take.

"Good luck," Helen Barco said as Joanna headed out the door. "I hope you win. Eleanor's very proud of you, you know."

The fact that Eleanor Lathrop might be proud of her for any reason at all was a notion Joanna found somewhat foreign. It didn't seem the least bit likely. In her whole life, she could count on one hand the other rare instances when Eleanor had been proud of her or had come out and said so.

Joanna sat in her Eagle, leaned back against the headrest, and closed her eyes. Her neighbor Clayton Rhodes was still handling the evening chores, so there was no need for her to rush home. It was a good thing, too. Working round the clock, she had driven herself to the very edge of exhaustion.

Cochise County measured eighty-five miles by eighty-five miles. In fighting to win the election, Joanna had covered damned near every inch of it. She had worked on the campaign tirelessly and with every ounce of her being. Yet even now, this close to the end, she still didn't know if she wanted to win. That was crazy, especially now when there was nothing to do but wait. The polls would close at six—in twenty-five more minutes. After that, it was simply a matter of time, of letting the election officials count the ballots and eventually certify a winner—whoever that might be.

Sometime later, Jim Bob Brady's knuckles rapped sharply against the window beside her head, jarring Joanna awake. Embarrassed, she sat up straight, pulled her coat around her, and rolled down the window.

"I just wanted to sit here and think for a while," she said. "I must have dozed off."

"You coulda fooled me," her father-in-law returned, standing with both hands on the windowsill. "You were dead to the world, snoring so loud, it's a wonder the glass didn't break. And sitting out here in the chill like this, you're liable to catch your death of cold."

Obligingly, Joanna reached over and switched on the engine, but the air that blew through the heater seemed colder than that outside the car. "What time is it?" she asked.

"Half-past six. Dinner's on the table and getting cold. That mother of yours is tearing her hair out."

"And so they sent you out looking for me. Sorry to cause so much trouble. Let's go then," Joanna said, but Jim Bob Brady refused to budge.

"You're still not sleeping so good, are you?" he said accusingly.

Joanna yawned and stretched. She was stiff with cold. "Only when I'm not supposed to," she returned with a disparaging smile. "I have a hard time closing my eyes and keeping them shut when I'm in bed at night, but I've spent a whole hour sitting out here in a freezing car, sleeping like a baby. Helen Barco's neighbors must think I've lost my mind."

"Helen Barco's neighbors are too damn nosy," Jim Bob Brady muttered under his breath, finally letting loose of the window and returning to his own vehicle.

Eleanor Lathrop met them at the front door of the Bradys' duplex apartment on Oliver Circle. "Where in the world have you been?" she demanded. "I tried calling Helen, but she was already closed. All I got was her answering machine."

"I'm sorry," Joanna said. "I fell asleep. In the car."

"In the car!" Eleanor echoed. "In this weather? And with dinner already on the table!"

Eva Lou Brady brushed aside the controversy. "Don't worry about it, Eleanor. No harm's done. Go wash up, Joanna. And see if you can drag Jenny away from that TV set long enough to come eat. It won't take but a minute to warm all this back up in the microwave."

The dinner was vintage Eva Lou Brady, what her husband called "old-fashioned comfort food"—meat loaf, mashed potatoes, canned-from-the-garden green beans, cherry Jell-O with bananas, and homemade pumpkin pie for dessert. Jim Bob and Eva Lou were still dealing with Andy's death—still grieving over their lost son—but helping with Joanna's survival seemed to give purpose to the elder Bradys' lives. Joanna was only too grateful for their unwavering support. Her own mother was another matter entirely.

While Eleanor sniffed disdainfully and picked at her food, Joanna ate with far more relish than she would have thought possible. Eating food Eleanor disapproved of was one way of continuing the Lathrop family mother/daughter grudge match that had been years in the making. Although hostilities between them boasted occasional periods of relative truce, none of those had ever blossomed into a lasting peace.

"I thought you were going to wear your winter gray," Eleanor said, holding tight to her fork while a piece of Jell-O quivered delicately on the tines.

"It had a spot on it," Joanna lied. She turned to her father-in-law. "Any word on the turnout?" she asked, daring at last to make some direct reference to the election.

"Better'n anybody figured," he replied. "It's turned into a real horse race."

Jennifer made a face. "Can't we talk about something else?"

"Why don't you want to talk about the election, Jenny, honey?" Eva Lou Brady asked mildly. "Don't you want your mama to win?"

"No!"

And there it was. The dining room grew quiet while Jennifer's blurted answer hung in the air like a dispirited balloon.

"That can't be true, Jenny," Jim Bob Brady said. "Of course you want her to win. She's doing it for all of us—because we need her. She's doing it for you."

Jennifer's eyes flashed with defiance. "She is not. She's doing it for her."

With that, Jennifer flung her crushed paper napkin into her plate, shoved her chair into the wall behind her, and crashed from the table.

"What in the world was that all about?" Eleanor Lathrop demanded. "Whatever's gotten into her?"

Joanna carefully folded her own napkin. "I'd better go talk to her," she said.

Jennifer had slammed the bedroom door shut behind her. Joanna knocked and waited.

"Come in," Jenny said finally, reluctantly.

Her grandparents had furnished the extra bedroom with Jenny specifically in mind, making it a home-away-from-home; a place where she was always welcome. A serviceable secondhand daybed sat in one corner of the room. The coverlet—a homemade quilt—was strewn with a collection of matching pillows. Jennifer lay on the bed sobbing, her head buried beneath the body of a huge brown teddy bear.

Joanna stood in the doorway, her hand on the doorknob, unsure whether or not she should enter the room. A yawning, treacherous gulf seemed to lie between her and her daughter. Had there been a time like this for her own mother? Joanna wondered. A time when Eleanor had stood frozen in a doorway wondering helplessly how to comfort her own grieving child?

Joanna noticed a shadow on the floor of the room. It looked like a tightrope stretching between the doorway and the bed, between her and her despairing, sobbing child.

Joanna's heart caught in her throat. What would happen if she made the wrong decision? What if she somehow failed to successfully negotiate the distance between them? Would Joanna be destroying whatever relationship had once existed between herself and her daughter? Was history bound to repeat itself?

"Could I talk to you, please?" Joanna asked.

Jenny pulled the teddy bear more tightly over her head and didn't answer.

"I need to know what's wrong," Joanna continued softly. "I need to know why you don't want me to win."

Jenny rolled over, flinging the teddy bear aside, allowing her mother a glimpse of her tear-stained, desolate face. "I'm afraid," she whispered.

Joanna resisted the temptation to close the distance between them. This was a turning point. She needed to hear Jennifer's answer, needed to listen to what the child had to say without smothering her in a word-strangling embrace.

"What are you afraid of?" Joanna asked.

Jennifer's chin quivered. "That you'll die, too," she whispered. "That somebody will kill you, too, just like they did Daddy. If that happens, I'll be all alone."

That was it. The answer when it came was so blindingly simple, so logical, that it took Joanna's breath away. Of course! Why hadn't she seen it coming? If she had been a better mother, a more perceptive parent, maybe she would have.

"Just because I'm elected sheriff doesn't mean someone's going to try to kill me."

"But Sheriff McFadden got killed," Jennifer returned with unwavering childish logic. "And Daddy. And Grampa."

"Grandpa Lathrop died because he was changing a tire in traffic—because he was helping someone—not because he was sheriff," Joanna pointed out.

But even as she said the words, Joanna knew they weren't the right ones. They didn't address Jennifer Brady's very real concern; didn't do justice to her heartfelt worry. D. H. Lathrop had died by legitimately accidental means—if drunk drivers can ever be considered truly accidental. But the other two hadn't.

Walter McFadden and Andrew Brady had both died violent deaths as soldiers in the ongoing warfare between good and evil, between wrong and right. And Jenny wasn't mistaken in her concern.

Winning the election would put Joanna Brady directly on the front lines of that exact same conflict.

As though negotiating a minefield, Joanna walked carefully to the side of the bed and settled on the edge of it with her hands folded in her lap. Still she made no attempt to touch her daughter. "Sometimes you have to take a stand," she said softly.

"What do you mean?"

"Your dad saw what terrible things drugs and drug dealers were doing to the people around him. He decided he had to try to stop it and . . ."

"And they killed him," Jenny finished.

The room grew quiet. From the dining room came the hushed murmur of muted conversation.

"Everyone must die sometime, Jenny," Joanna said at last. "Grandpa and Grandma Brady. Grandma Lathrop. You. Me."

"But Grandma and Grandpa are old," Jennifer objected. "Daddy wasn't."

Again the room grew still as Joanna struggled to find the right words. "Do you remember the night of Daddy's funeral?"

Jennifer nodded wordlessly.

"We made a decision that night, the two of us together, a decision for me to run in your father's place, right?"

"Yes."

"And when we said it, people believed we meant it—people like Jeff and Marianne, Angie Kellogg, your grandparents, and lots of other people, too. They've all worked hard to see that what we said that night comes true."

"But . . ."

"No. Wait a minute. Let me finish. You're not the only one who's scared, Jenny. That's the reason I was late coming to dinner. While I was sitting outside Helen Barco's shop and worrying about whether or not I wanted to win the election, I fell asleep."

Jenny's eyes widened. "You're worried, too?"

Joanna nodded. "And for the same reasons you are. If I win, what happens then? Maybe you're right. Maybe the bad people who came after Daddy will come after me as well. But I promised to run for sheriff. Promising to run means that if you win, you're also promising to do the job. Even if you're scared to death."

Jennifer moved slightly on the bed, cuddling closer, putting her head in her mother's lap. "I don't want to be alone," she whispered, grasping her mother's hand, squeezing it tight.

Joanna felt hot tears well in her eyes. "I know," she said. "I don't want you to be, either. I'll try to be careful."

"Promise?"

Not letting go with one hand, Joanna used the other to brush a strand of damp hair off Jennifer's still tear-stained cheeks. Unable to speak, she nodded.

"Girl Scout's honor?" Jennifer pressed.

"Girl Scout's honor," her mother whispered in return, while Helen Barco's mascara streamed unnoticed down her face.

Twelve

ONCE MORE Harold awakened, caught in a disorienting spin—the turbulence between real and dream, between known and unknown. He had no sense of how much time had passed, but the sky far overhead was dark now. Blackness surrounded him like some all-enveloping, evil shroud.

Harold was so desperately cold that he wondered for a moment if maybe he was already dead; already put away in that cut-rate casket he had taken off Norm Higgins' hands. Eventually, though, he sorted it out—remembered where he was if not how he'd come to be there. Remembered that his body was broken; that he was trapped and unable to move.

Harold was lying there trying to think of a rational way to escape his prison when he heard the familiar wheeze and thrum of his old Scout's much overhauled engine. He heard it laboring up the steep dirt track toward the basin, toward the glory hole. It must be Ivy, he thought at once. Had to be Ivy, come to search for him. Who else would bother? And who else would know to come here looking?

Sudden tears filled his eyes—not tears of self-pity but tears for his daughter, for Ivy. What would happen to her now? After taking care of her mother all those years, would she have to spend the next ones taking care of him as well?

He wished suddenly, fervently, that he had died in the fall. He upbraided himself for not trying harder to die. He should have concentrated on that rather than on trying to find some way out.

Now, with Ivy approaching ever nearer, Harold was filled with a desperate need to escape his broken body quickly—to do it now, before Ivy found him. Before she had a chance to call for help. Before she could turn him over to the care of doctors who would try valiantly to patch the shattered pieces back together.

He already knew that wouldn't work. Broken backs didn't magically heal themselves. Once the doctors finished screwing around with their casts and braces and astronomical bills, Ivy Patterson's worst nightmare would materialize and she would be handed yet another cripple to care for.

If Ivy calls to me, Harold thought wildly, I won't answer. I'll pretend I'm already dead. Maybe she'll go away and leave me alone. Overnight, he would simply will himself to die. He had seen his own father do it after he was hurt in the mining accident. He knew it was possible. And the cold would help.

But even as Harold toyed with the idea, the Scout's engine grumbled closer, climbing steadily, grinding up over the final incline. As the Scout came closer, a flash of light splashed across the small pile of wood-chip-sized rock that made up the mound of tailings around the mouth of the glory hole. Almost directly overhead, the engine coughed once and backfired as the ignition was switched off. Harold heard the driver's door creak open on familiar rusty hinges; heard leather shoe soles scrape across loose shale, pausing long enough to climb over or through the barbed-wire fence that surrounded the glory hole. Then there was another sound of something heavy, cardboard perhaps, scraping along the ground.

Harold pressed his lips together, and forced himself to keep quiet. He was determined not to answer, no matter what. He waited for Ivy to speak to him and was surprised when she didn't. Instead, a flashlight switched on. A powerful beam of yellow light slid down the darkened walls of the shaft, searching here and there, to the right and then the left, before finally settling on his body. Still nothing was said, nothing at all.

He was tempted to speak then, but abruptly the light switched off. In the sudden jet-black darkness, everything was still until the first five-pound river rock plunged toward Harold with accidental, but still deadly, accuracy.

Long before it hit him, he heard it bouncing off the walls and knew what it was. And in that split second, he remembered everything. But by then it was much too late.

The rock hit him full on the chest, sending a long splinter of broken rib deep into his heart. Harold Patterson died instantly, died in exactly the nightmarish way he had always dreamed he would, with the rocks of retribution raining down around him.

The barrage continued uninterrupted for some time as the rocks plunged through the darkness. Some of them hit him. Most didn't, careening harmlessly off the walls of the shaft. At last, when all the ammunition was gone, the flashlight came back on. This time, the hand that held it trembled violently, and the wavering beam jerked crazily as it zigzagged down the rocky walls, panning through the darkness in search of a body.

When the light finally settled on Harold's inert form, on his open and unblinking eyes, there was a single, sharp intake of breath, a sigh of relief. And then the flashlight fell, plunging—still lit—through the eerie, enveloping silence. It slammed into Harold's shattered chest, bounced once, then rolled off into the water.

Soon after that, the Scout's engine choked and coughed back to life. It shuddered once, then caught and kept on running. As the International rumbled away toward Juniper Flats and Bisbee beyond that, the flashlight—one of Harold's best—continued to cast a feeble, flickering light that lingered in the darkness of the glory hole. Even totally submerged, it still glowed through the murky water, long after the Scout had disappeared into the overcast night.

Thirteen

Jᴉᴍ Bᴏʙ and Eva Lou Brady weren't exactly social butterflies. It took some serious persuasion to convince them that they should attend the post-election party at all. They agreed, finally, only on the condition that Jenny ride with them. Joanna suspected it was a ploy giving them a convenient excuse to leave early, pleading the necessity of getting Jenny home and in bed because of school the next day.

Jenny opted to ride with the Bradys. Eleanor Lathrop went with friends. That meant Joanna Brady drove to the post-election party at the convention center alone.

Brave words to Jenny notwithstanding, Joanna was filled with grave misgivings as she made her way uptown. In her only previous attempt at elected office, she had run for student-body treasurer of Bisbee High School. She still remembered sitting in Miss Applewhite's biology room (which doubled as Joanna's homeroom) while Mr. Bailes, the principal, read the winners' names over the intercom. With the sharp smell of formaldehyde filling her nostrils, she had listened intently, holding her breath the whole while, as he droned through the congratulatory list.

After what seemed forever, when he finally reached the position of treasurer, the name he read wasn't Joanna Lathrop's.

Joanna no longer remembered which of her classmates actually did win. Someone else's victory wasn't nearly as important as her own personal loss. The memory of that defeat came to her as clearly and painfully now as if it had happened yesterday.

She remembered how her face had flushed hot with embarrassment, how she had fought back tears of disappointment while well-meaning classmates told her, sympathetically, "Better luck next time."

There'll never be a next time, Joanna had vowed back then. It turned out she was wrong about that. Here she was, twelve years later, running for office after all.

"Whatever you do, don't cry," she lectured herself sternly, repeating words Marianne had been telling her for weeks. "Win, lose, or draw—do not cry."

There were two readily available parking spaces directly across the street from the convention-center entrance, but Joanna ignored them both. Instead, she drove farther up the street, parking at the upper end of the lot near the post office. She locked the car and started toward the plaza, where she counted three different vans bearing the logos of Tucson television stations, as well as one more from a station in Phoenix.

Cochise County elections didn't usually garner that much interest from out of town, but this year's race for sheriff was different. The earlier deaths of both declared candidates had spurred uncommon statewide and national media attention. The fact that Joanna was both a candidate and the widow of one of the slain men had contributed to keeping the hotly contested election in the human-interest spotlight. Not only that, but pundits continued to dwell on the idea that if Joanna Brady won, she would be the first female county sheriff in the state of Arizona.

Rather than go directly to the convention center and into the glaring lights of the waiting cameras, Joanna delayed her entrance by crossing the street and approaching the building with the wary attention of a battle-weary scout reconnoitering enemy territory. Stopping in the park, she gazed at the pale green building that appeared a ghostly gray in the evening light.

And truly, the convention center was a ghost. The structure that now functioned as the Bisbee Convention Center had once housed Phelps Dodge Mercantile—a branch of the company store—in the days before most of the jobs in the domestic copper-mining industry literally went south—to Mexico and South America.

In their heyday, P.D. stores in a dozen separate mining communities had been true department stores—places where, by signing a chit, company employees could purchase everything from groceries to furniture, from washing machines to ladies' fine millinery, and have the cost automatically deducted from future paychecks.

Joanna didn't actually remember shopping in this particular store, although she must have accompanied her mother there on occasion when she was little. She did have a dim, lingering, and traumatic recollection of being lost on a store elevator once, of searching frantically for her mother, and of being found much later among the glass-walled showcases. Eleanor had been furious with Joanna for wandering away on her own. In the very best of times, Bisbee had boasted a grand total of only three elevators, so the chances were good that Joanna's vaguely remembered incident had actually occurred in the uptown P.D. store, especially since that had been Eleanor's favorite place to shop. Before the relatively upscale P.D. closed for good, Eleanor Lathrop wouldn't have been caught dead shopping at a J.C. Penney.

Since the store had been closed now for twenty-some years, Joanna's knowledge of the building's faded merchandizing glory came to her primarily secondhand, through her mother's steady harping back to the once-glorious good old days. Back then the P.D. store in Bisbee had been *the* place to shop. In its heyday the store had offered so much, much more than its withered successor—a humdrum, lowly grocery store that still clung stubbornly to life a few miles away in the Warren business district.

With modest renovation, the building's interior main floor had been redesigned into a meeting-hall configuration. The Bisbee Convention Center hosted each year's flurry of summer high-school reunions as well as other events. An echo of the store's retailing glory remained in the thin inner shell of shops that lined the edge of the marbled main floor. There, enterprising merchants hawked turquoise jewelry, curios, and knickknacks to any stray tourists who happened to wander inside. A modestly upscale restaurant occupied one corner of the building and usually catered whatever required catering.

Joanna Brady knew almost all those individual merchants on a first-name basis and had played on the tennis team with the woman who owned and operated the restaurant. All things considered, the Bisbee Convention Center should not have been a scary place for her, yet tonight it was. Impossibly so. Standing outside in the cold, watching others arrive and hurry inside, was far preferable to going inside herself.

"I see you're not all that eager to go inside, either," a familiar male voice teased from behind her.

Joanna turned to greet Frank Montoya, the Willcox city marshal, who was one of her two opponents in the race for sheriff. During a series of joint-candidate appearances in front of local civic groups, Joanna had come to like Frank—a tall, scrawny, crew-cut Mexican-American of thirty-five. Frank's ready wit and screwball sense of humor camouflaged real dedication to his work and a serious sense of purpose.

Frank Montoya was the son of once-migrant farmworkers who had, years before, settled in

Willcox on a permanent basis. He came to law enforcement through a hitch in the army as an MP and with an associate of arts degree in police science from Cochise College. In an area of the country where Mexican-Americans were still often deemed second-class citizens, voters in Willcox had surprised themselves and Frank, too, by electing him to serve as city marshal while he continued to commute back and forth to the university in Tucson to earn his B.A. in law enforcement.

"Hi, Frank," Joanna returned lightly. "You're right. I'm not looking forward to it. I'd much rather have a root canal."

"Me, too," Montoya agreed with a laugh. "The Big Guy showed up a few minutes ago. I watched him go inside. He was in seventh heaven with a television camera following his every move and with two microphones stuck in his face. It makes it easier for him to talk out of both sides of his mouth."

Joanna couldn't help laughing.

Al Freeman, the heavyset former chief of police in Sierra Vista, was the third candidate in the three-way race for sheriff. In campaign appearances and brochures, Freeman had self-importantly characterized himself as the "only law-enforcement professional" running for the office of sheriff. That tactic had effectively thrown Joanna and Frank Montoya together in an uneasy alliance, which, to their mutual wonder, had blossomed into an unlikely friendship.

With a lessening of tension, Joanna grinned back at Frank. "I don't know what's been worse—limping around with doorbelling blisters on both feet or having to sit through Al Freeman's endless redneck-and-proud-of-it speeches."

"No question in my book," Frank Montoya said. "Al Freeman's speeches win that contest handsdown."

They both laughed then, in unison. Frank held out his hand and smiled. "So may the best token win, Joanna," he said solemnly. "I hope to hell one of us beats the pants off that loudmouthed bastard." They shook hands. "By the way," Frank added, "I like the haircut. Your mother's doing?"

"How did you know?"

"Take one guess," Frank said, running one hand over his own freshly trimmed hair. "Joanna, our mothers may be from opposite sides of the tracks, but other than that, they must be twins."

Fourteen

THE USUALLY mild-mannered and easygoing Linda Kimball was on a tear. The Election Night bash in Bisbee's new convention center, a bipartisan effort where political enemies buried the hatchet and socialized, was also the primary fund-raiser for a prominent local arts group called the Bisbee Betterment Society.

As one of the movers and shakers behind the annual event, Linda was required to play hostess. Armed with a glass of plain fruit punch and an ironclad smile, she was doing her duty, but she was also looking for her husband. With some real fire in her eyes.

Three hours after he should have been home and two hours after they were due at the convention center, Burton still hadn't showed up or even called. Normally, that wouldn't have bothered her. Linda understood that the unexpected often happened in Burton's work life, especially the day before he was due in court with an important case. And if he had been working, she wouldn't have minded or said a word. After all, Burton's job was what made their comfortable lifestyle possible. They lived a far more affluent existence than Linda had ever dreamed possible growing up in Cotton-wood as the daughter of a school-cafeteria worker and a none-too-successful used-car salesman.

Burtie's tardiness had nothing to do with work. That was the problem. Linda already knew from several different sources that it had more to do with booze than the practice of law. Word had come back to Linda that Burton had spent a good part of the afternoon in the Blue Moon Saloon up Brewery Gulch. Of all places! If Burtie was going to go drinking, couldn't he at least do it someplace a little more respectable?

One of Linda's "friends" could barely contain her glee when she called with the news, which she had heard from someone else who'd heard it from a friend of Don Frost, who was a classic lush if ever there was one. To add insult to injury, not only had Burton been drinking in the bar, every-body in town evidently knew it.

The last time Burton Kimball had gotten himself really plastered was at his own bachelor's party twelve years earlier. He was still green around the gills by the time the wedding party got to the church the next afternoon. Linda Kimball had a whole wedding album of pictures as documented evidence to prove it. She had told Burtie then and there that if he wanted to be married and stay married, he'd better knock off the drinking. And he had. Until now.

Without Burton at the party to offer his technical assistance, Linda herself had been forced to over-see the placement of Harvey Dawson's paired tele-vision monitors, which would broadcast both local and statewide election results. Statewide results would come from Tucson stations, while local ones would be displayed on Bisbee's public-access channel. There typed messages listing local election results would be mixed in with civic and commercial announcements.

Linda had noodled her way through the television monitor confusion only to find herself caught in the middle of a last-minute run-in between Bisbee's two competing caterers. On this one night, they were forced to work together. And when a turf war broke out, Linda settled it. But as the evening wore on, as she was forced to handle one crisis after another, Linda's temper rose and Burton Kimball's rapidly tumbling husbandly stock fell that much further.

As Bisbee parties went, the Bisbee Betterment Society Election Night bash was not to be missed. Even early on, the center's main-floor meeting room was brightly lit and smoky. A local country-western band twanged away plaintively in the background. Busy circulating, Linda was near the door when Joanna Brady and Frank Montoya came in together. When Frank wasn't looking, Linda gave Joanna a discreet high sign.

Linda had grown up with a father addicted to Angie Dickinson's *Police Woman*. Linda Kimball— who baked her own bread, canned her own vegetables, and sewed her own clothes—would have been the last person to think of herself as one of those so-called "women's libbers." Still, it had done her heart good to vote for a woman for sheriff for a change, especially over that loudmouthed bigot named Al Freeman.

Linda started over to say hello, but Joanna was intercepted by one of the Tucson television reporters who was stationed just inside the main entrance. The reporter squeezed herself in between the two candidates, cutting Frank out of the picture and shoving a microphone in Joanna's direction.

"Mrs. Brady, are you excited about the possibility of becoming Arizona's first female sheriff?" she asked.

Linda thought she detected a hint of annoyance in Joanna's voice as she answered. "Being a female has nothing to do with it. Law enforcement is the only real issue here."

"I see," the reporter returned. "What about the campaign? Has it been difficult for you?"

Linda cringed inwardly at the crassness of the question. Everyone in town knew how devastated Joanna Brady had been over the death of her husband. Was this reporter some kind of idiot? Had she asked Linda Kimball that same question under similar circumstances, she could have expected to have her teeth rattled by someone shaking her by the fully padded shoulders of her fashionable wool blazer.

Joanna paused, as if gathering her resources. "Election campaigns are always difficult," she returned evenly. "Regardless of who wins, I'll be happy to have the election out of the way."

Linda wanted to cheer, "Good for you!" but she didn't.

"If you win tonight," the reporter continued, "when will you start work?"

"What do you mean, when will I start? Newly elected officials are all sworn into office early in January."

The reporter looked puzzled. "But I thought . . ."

"You thought what?"

"I was speaking to Mr. Freeman just a few minutes ago. He said that someone on the board of supervisors had told him they want to fill the sheriff vacancy immediately—right after the election, without waiting until January."

A deep red flush stole up Joanna Brady's face. "I wouldn't know anything about that," she returned coldly.

Behind Joanna the door opened, and Jim Bob and Eva Lou Brady came in with their granddaughter walking stoically between them.

"Isn't that your daughter?" the reporter asked, catching sight of them. "She's such a cute little thing. I wanted the camera to get a shot of the two of you together."

"You'll have to ask Jenny whether or not she wants to be on TV. It's up to her."

The reporter turned questioningly to Jenny, who shook her head emphatically. "That's that then," Joanna said. "Now, if you'll excuse me . . ."

As Joanna hurried past, Linda Kimball reached out and shook her hand. "Congratulations, Joanna. Good job," she said.

Linda could have been talking about just the election, but she actually meant far more than that.

In that brief exchange with the reporter, she had caught a glimpse of Joanna Brady's basic honesty and toughness.

Those were qualities Linda Kimball should have recognized. She had them in abundance herself.

Still steamed by her encounter with the reporter, Joanna took Jenny with her and set off across the room to where she had caught sight of Milo Davis standing visiting with Jeff Daniels and his wife, Reverend Marianne Maculyea.

"So," Jeff was saying to Milo, "we actually took back the study today. Cleaned out all the mass-mailing stuff, unburied Marianne's desk . . ."

"I even vacuumed," Marianne chirped proudly.

"You vacuumed?" Joanna teased, coming in on the tail end of the conversation. "I don't believe it. That only happens once in a blue moon, doesn't it, Jeff?" she asked.

"Mark your calendars then," he said, "because she did it, and we're not just talking her study, either. She vacuumed the whole house."

Marianne smiled good-naturedly at the ribbing. "Just don't expect it all the time. It's decompression. With all the campaign work over, I needed something to do with my hands."

Jenny naturally gravitated toward Jeff, who took her by the hand and led her toward the refreshment table. Meanwhile, Marianne examined Joanna's face. "What's the matter? You look upset."

Joanna glanced back over her shoulder toward the reporter, who was still stationed by the door.

"That reporter just told me that, according to Al Freeman, the board of supervisors wants to swear in the new sheriff right away. Is that possible?"

Milo, juggling a glass of wine and a plate of hors d'oeuvres, munched thoughtfully on a dip-covered carrot stick. "Are you just now hearing about that?"

Marianne frowned. "That creep," she said. As far as Al Freeman was concerned, Marianne's venture into political campaigning had divested Reverend Maculyea of some of her Christian charity. "He always did claim to have an inside track with county government."

"But it's not such a bad idea," Milo Davis said. "After all, the position is vacant. Swearing in the winner right away will give the new administration a head start on solving departmental problems. Dick Voland's been doing an okay job on an interim basis, but the board would be well within its authority to install the new sheriff immediately."

"But what if I win?" Joanna objected.

Milo looked at her with a shocked expression on his face. "What do you mean, what if? Are we having a crisis of confidence here? Of course you're going to win."

"But I couldn't just go off and leave you high and dry like that. Not without any notice."

"I've had plenty of notice," Milo said reasonably. "It's not going to be a problem. As soon as you said you'd run, I started looking for your replacement."

Trying to mask the flicker of hurt she felt, Joanna looked away. She had worked at the Davis Insurance Agency first as a receptionist, and later as office manager, from the moment she graduated from high school eleven years earlier. Before Andy's death, Milo had been grooming her to take over much of the selling end of the business as well. Was he really finding it so easy to replace her?

"You've found someone then?" she ventured tentatively, dreading his answer.

Milo's cheerful grin wounded her to the soul. "Yup," he said, sounding proud and almost gleeful. "Lisa took the last of her licensing exams just last week. The results came in today's mail. I won't be able to start taking her out on calls with me, though, until after we find a new receptionist. That could be a whole lot tougher proposition."

Joanna was dumbfounded. "I see," she mumbled.

Milo nodded. "Lisa's had her hands full, working on the licensing exams and trying to stay ahead of the regular workload as well."

Especially since she was doing it behind my back, Joanna thought bitterly. She said, "What happens if I don't win, Milo? Does this mean I'm out of a job?"

"Are you kidding? We'll still need to hire a new receptionist. If I have two full-time agents working for me, I'll finally start getting to take some time off. In fact, I wouldn't be at all surprised if my wife voted against you today for that very reason. She has her mouth all set for us to go on a two-week cruise in the Caribbean come January. If you win, she might not get to take it."

One of Milo's golf-playing buddies showed up then. Marianne took Joanna by the arm. "The candidate looks as though she could use some fresh air. Come on."

Linda Kimball caught sight of Burton the moment he stepped inside the door. He was green all right, the same shade as in the wedding pictures and in the video she'd taken of him and the kids when they got off the teacups ride at Disneyland. His hair was standing on end. His clothes looked as though he'd slept in them.

Linda was at his side before he was ten feet into the room. "Where the hell have you been?" she demanded in a tense whisper.

"I'm looking for Uncle Harold," Burton answered wanly. "Have you seen him? His Scout's out back in the lot. He must be here somewhere."

"Believe me," Linda returned coldly, "if Uncle Harold were here, I would have seen him. I've been watching this door like a hawk. Now how about telling me what you've been up to, mister. I've been hearing all kinds of rumors, and I don't like any of them. Come to think of it, I don't much like the way you smell, either."

"Linda, please," Burton said, glancing anxiously around the crowded room. "Do we have to talk about this here? Couldn't we have this discussion later?"

"We're discussing it now!" Linda answered, her voice rising in pitch. "Right this very minute!"

Burton took her arm and guided her back to the door. "Come on," he said. "People are listening."

"Listening isn't all they've been doing," Linda replied. "They've been talking a blue streak. Everybody in town knows you've been out drinking. How come you spent the afternoon at the Blue Moon up Brewery Gulch?"

Burton Kimball's shoulders sagged. "You know about that?"

"Damned right I know about it. You'd better tell me what's going on."

But something about Burton's careworn face, his desolate expression, muted the worst of Linda's anger. "What's wrong?" she asked more quietly, once they were outside.

Burton leaned against the wall of the building. "I quit Uncle Harold's case," Burton said. "He's going to settle with Holly out of court."

"Why on earth would he do a stupid thing like that?"

Burton shrugged hopelessly. "Who knows? He's going to split the ranch in half. When he gets done, there won't even be enough left for Ivy to make a living."

That was it. Ivy again! Linda might have known Ivy would be at the bottom of it. She had known her husband for fourteen years and had been married to him for twelve. She had never for one moment doubted that Burton loved her and their two children, but from the beginning she had always known that Ivy Patterson came first.

"And I did something awful," Burton continued. "If he wanted to, Uncle Harold could see to it that I was disbarred."

Linda felt a clutch of concern. "What did you do?"

"I told Ivy about Uncle Harold's decision," Burton said. "I got all tanked up, called Ivy, and breached my lawyer-client privilege. I can't believe I did it. That's why I'm looking for Uncle Harold. I've got to find him, try to make things right."

"You know Uncle Harold would never disbar you," Linda said confidently. "Not in a million years."

"He should," Burton Kimball replied grimly. "I certainly deserve it."

"No, you don't."

Linda reached out to hug him then, wrapping her comforting arms around his chest, ignoring the stench of booze that lingered around him like an ill-smelling cloud.

Gratitude flooded through Burton Kimball. Linda was steady and dependable. Like Uncle Harold, she, too, was salt of the earth. He was lucky to have a woman like her in his life. Leaning against her, he closed his eyes and inhaled the shampoo-clean fragrance of her hair.

He never saw the car coming, not until it was far too late. If it hadn't been for Joanna Brady, Burton and Linda Kimball both would have been smashed flat, just like that, embracing each other and resting against the building.

J. A. Jance

Without Joanna's timely intervention, not only would the speeding car have flattened Burton and Linda Kimball, it would have done exactly the same thing to Reverend Marianne Maculyea.

Fifteen

WHEN MARIANNE and Joanna stepped out of the building, the clear night air was a relief after the crowded, over-heated, and smoky convention-center floor. Still stung by what she regarded as Milo's underhanded actions, Joanna was eager to talk, but she wanted some privacy.

Just outside the entrance near the curb, they encountered an embracing man and woman who seemed in need of some privacy of their own. Joanna led Marianne across the street.

"Don't you think you're overreacting to all this?" Marianne asked after listening to what was on Joanna's mind. "It looks to me as though Milo thought you already had enough on your plate without adding in the complications of helping Lisa study for and pass her insurance exams."

But Joanna wasn't entirely mollified. "So you think he was being considerate instead of sneaky?"

"That's my opinion," Marianne replied. "Opinions are just exactly that—not worth the powder it would take to blow them up. But why not give him the benefit of the doubt?"

They had walked through the park as far as the

base of the steps leading up to the Copper Queen Hotel, then they had stood at the bottom of the steps to talk. Now, though, aware of the autumn chill, they started back toward the convention center.

The events of the last few months had instilled a new wariness in Joanna Brady. She observed things about her more; things that before would have passed unnoticed.

While they stood at the base of the steps, Marianne had been standing with her back to Main Street while Joanna faced it. Twice in five minutes' time, she had seen the same red car pass by on the street. Something about it had piqued her interest and attention. Maybe it was the speed, or rather the lack thereof. The car was going exceptionally slowly. Maybe it was the make and model. The Allanté would have been a standout car anywhere. Or maybe it was the color. Under the mercury-vapor halogen lights, the bright-red paint job glowed deep purple.

Chilled and ready to go back inside, Marianne and Joanna headed back toward the building. Marianne was talking, saying something neither of them could remember later. With her face turned toward Joanna, Marianne had just stepped out of the crosswalk and up onto the sidewalk when, with a squeal of tortured rubber, the accelerating car lurched half onto the sidewalk less than half a block away.

Joanna saw the whole thing at once—the oncoming car; the couple, still locked in their embrace and totally unaware of the danger;

Marianne, chatting away in lighthearted unconcern.

With only milliseconds in which to react, Joanna screamed, "Watch out!" Grabbing Marianne by the shoulder, she propelled her forward into the safety of the recessed entryway.

Startled by the warning, the man and woman straightened up and separated. The man stepped backward toward the safety of the building. The woman stayed where she was, directly in the path of the car. Joanna could see that the man was safe. But unless the car swerved back off the curb and into the street, the woman, transfixed by fear, was a goner.

Without even thinking about it, Joanna seized the woman's wrist as she leaped past. There was a whiplash jerk as the woman's arm was wrenched forward. Joanna heard the sickening pop of a dislocating shoulder, heard the shriek of pain, and then the two of them plowed forward into the entryway where a shaken Marianne was just scrambling to her feet. Joanna and the other woman landed on top of Marianne in a muddled heap of flailing arms and legs. Joanna's jawbone smashed into something hard in a skull-cracking explosion of stars.

It took seconds for Joanna's head and vision to clear. When they did, she was sandwiched between the other two women. Beneath her, Marianne's body was unnaturally still, while above someone moaned, "My arm, my arm! I think it's broken."

"Linda," Burton Kimball said, reaching for his

wife. "My God! Are you all right? They tried to kill us! Somebody call the cops."

By then people were trying to come out through the door, but Marianne and Joanna both blocked the way. With her head still spinning, Joanna managed to roll off. The door opened far enough for some of the people inside to squeeze out onto the sidewalk. Not surprisingly, one of the first people out the door was Jeff Daniels. Right behind him was the television cameraman.

Jeff was kneeling beside his stricken wife when Marianne's eyes fluttered open. "What happened?" she whispered.

Someone, the cameraman most likely, hurried to help Joanna to her feet. Her dress was torn, and three of the four gold buttons were missing.

Undersheriff Richard Voland appeared out of nowhere. "What's going on here?" he asked, turning to Joanna.

"There was a car," she stammered, pointing in the direction where the speeding vehicle had plunged off the steps at the end of the sidewalk and disappeared. "A red Cadillac. On the sidewalk. It tried to run us down."

Voland looked where she pointed, but by then no car was visible. "A car on the sidewalk?" he asked disgustedly, as though the story was too farfetched to be given the slightest credence. "Whatever would a car be doing on the sidewalk?"

"Trying to kill us," Burton Kimball answered. "Somebody call an ambulance. There are people hurt here."

The sound of Burton Kimball's voice galvanized Dick Voland into action. While he started issuing orders, Joanna knelt beside Jeff. "Is Marianne all right?"

Jeff shook his head. His wife was struggling to sit up, but he forced her back down to the sidewalk and covered her with a jacket someone handed him. "Lie still, Marianne," he whispered urgently. "You stay right where you are."

Unable to help Marianne, Joanna turned to Linda and Burton Kimball. Linda sat shivering on the curb, resting her injured arm on her lap while tears streamed down her face. She was trying not to cry, but the pain was too much. Burton attempted to put his jacket across her shoulders, but she ducked away.

"Don't," she said. "Don't put anything on me. It hurts too much."

Joanna's stomach turned. The car hadn't hurt Linda Kimball; Joanna Brady had.

"I'm sorry," she apologized, feeling sick. "I didn't mean ..."

Linda Kimball looked up at her through anguished, tear-filled eyes. "My God, Joanna, don't apologize. My arm hurts like hell, but if it weren't for you, we'd all be dead."

And then something funny happened. Linda Kimball started to laugh. "Did you hear that, Burtie?" she gasped. "Here's Joanna, trying to ... apologize ... for hurting ... for hurting my arm. My God! That's the funniest thing ... I ever heard of."

The laughter was high-pitched and hysterical,

and it echoed eerily in the street even as the canyon walls began to reverberate with the sounds of approaching sirens.

"Be quiet," Burton Kimball urged. "You'll hurt yourself more."

But Linda only giggled harder. "I know . . ." she managed. "It only hurts . . . when I laugh!"

Jenny somehow pushed her way through the milling throng of adults and threw her arms tightly around Joanna's waist. "Mommy," she wailed in a small, frightened voice. "Are you okay? You're bleeding."

Dazed, Joanna reached up and touched a finger to her face. There was a cut on her face where Marianne's head had smacked into her cheekbone—a cut, but not much blood. "It's no big thing," Joanna assured Jenny. "I'm shook up but okay."

Looking down at the top of her daughter's head, Joanna was suddenly aware that her double-breasted navy-blue dress, missing three critical buttons from the front, was gaping open to reveal an expanse of white bra to any and all who cared to see. With one hand still on Jenny's shoulder, she tried to hold the dress shut with the other.

People milled around them. Even though inside the city limits it wasn't the county's jurisdiction, Dick Voland had placed himself in charge, issuing orders to the city cops who answered the call, helping direct the arriving ambulance.

Joanna was well aware that Dick Voland had been all over the county campaigning on Al Freeman's behalf. Andrew Brady and the undersheriff had never seen eye-to-eye. There was even less love lost between him and Joanna. It annoyed her that his very first reaction to something she said had been outright disbelief. When Burton Kimball had said the exact same thing, he had automatically accepted it at face value. If that was the way he acted, what would happen if they ended up having to work together?

Despite Marianne's plaintive insistence that she was perfectly fine, the attendants and Jeff quietly overruled her and loaded her onto a gurney. With the city's single ambulance loaded and headed for the hospital, the ambulatory Linda Kimball and her husband climbed into the back of a waiting police car.

"Joanna," Eleanor Lathrop hissed from the sidelines, gesturing desperately. "Come here. Hurry."

The look on Eleanor's face was so pained that for a moment Joanna feared that her mother had been somewhere near the melee and that she, too, had been hurt in the scuffle.

"What's the matter?" Joanna asked worriedly as she and Jenny hurried to her mother's side. "You're not hurt, are you?"

Eleanor Lathrop shook her head. "For heaven's sake, Joanna. Can't you see those cameras are running?"

Joanna glanced back over her shoulder. Sure enough, three television cameramen were lined up, shoulder to shoulder, with their video cams humming away. "What about them?"

"Your dress, for one thing!" Eleanor wailed tearfully. "Your bra is sticking out. I've looked all over for your buttons, and I can't find them anywhere. The only thing I have in my purse is this. Now go in the rest room and use it."

Desperately Eleanor pressed a huge safety pin into Joanna's hand. Looking down at it, Joanna was tempted to burst into her own storm of semi-hysterical laughter. But she didn't.

Because it really wasn't a laughing matter. That safety pin encapsulated the difference between Joanna and her mother: between the active participant and the bystander. With the car screaming down on them, Joanna's prime concern had been to keep people from harm. Eleanor's prime consideration, on the other hand, was always and forever the maintaining of appearances.

With a sudden flash of insight, Joanna realized that same difference had always separated her parents from one another as well. That was why her father was dead. He had been physically incapable of driving past a stranded woman and her worn-out tire, and changing that tire had killed him.

D. H. Lathrop had offered to help because that was the kind of man he was. It was his nature—a part of him he was helpless to change. And when he died as a direct result of his own kindness, people had called Big Hank Lathrop a hero. No one tried to change him or make him anything other than what he was.

To be fair, if it was all right for someone to be a doer and a hero, wasn't it equally all right to be a bystander? Yes, Eleanor was concerned about appearances, but was that wrong? And if it was wrong, was it more or less wrong than changing a tire and being killed for it?

Slowly, Joanna closed her cupped hand around the safety pin. She looked at Eleanor, whose eyes were still scanning the nearby sidewalk in search of the missing buttons. Joanna's heart squeezed tight with a sudden quickening of understanding, like the first sensed movement of a baby within her womb.

At twenty-nine years of age, with emergency lights pulsing all around her, with video cameras rolling, and with only incomplete election results starting to trickle in, Joanna Brady had just learned something important about her mother. She had also learned something important about herself. She was a chip off the old block. She was definitely her father's daughter. But she was also her mother's.

"Jenny," she said, looking down at her own daughter and holding her torn dress shut at the same time. "Would you please see if you can help Grandma find my buttons?"

"Where are you going?" Jenny asked.

"Into the women's rest room to try to fix my dress. As soon as you find a button, bring it in there. And bring along a sewing kit as well. Ask Grandma Brady. I'm sure she has one in her purse."

As soon as Joanna started into the building, Dick Voland came charging after her. "Just a minute. Where do you think you're going?"

"To the rest room," Joanna answered evenly.

"Everybody else went to the hospital. I need

someone to give a preliminary statement to one of the officers here, to explain exactly what went on."

"I can do that," Joanna said, "but it'll have to wait."

Dick Voland was old school—male, stubborn, and used to having people snap to whenever he gave an order. "Wait for what?" he demanded.

"For me to fix my dress," Joanna replied. Then she turned her back on him and walked into the rest room where no old-school male in his right mind would dare to follow.

Sixteen

"The scratches don't show all that much," was Eva Lou Brady's practical and unperturbed assessment of her daughter-in-law's appearance after viewing the videotaped version of Joanna's late-night victory speech. "Your eye looks real funny, though."

"It doesn't feel very funny," Joanna returned.

The previous night's fall had taken its toll. Gulping ibuprofen for her sore and stiffened muscles, Joanna had limped over to her in-laws' house that morning and gratefully accepted Eva Lou Brady's pampering breakfast that included eggs and bacon, mashed-potato patties, and hot homemade buttermilk biscuits. There was no hurry. Milo had ordered her to take the whole day off. With pay.

Using all the makeup tricks at her disposal, Joanna had done her best to camouflage the damage done to her face, but not even Helen Barco's considerable skill with foundation and blush could have successfully masked the purplish bruise that blossomed garishly beneath Joanna's right eye.

Carrying coat and schoolbooks, Jennifer stopped in front of her mother and studied her face with an unsmiling and reproachful gaze. "You promised you'd be careful," she said. "Scout's honor, you said."

Those accusatory words were the first ones Jennifer had spoken to her mother that morning. "People were in danger," Joanna answered. "I was afraid someone might get hurt."

"It could of been you," Jennifer shot back.

"Could *have*," Joanna corrected reflexively.

"Have," Jennifer repeated woodenly, scowling.

"Jenny, are you ready?" her grandfather called from the front door. "I don't want to be late."

"Where's he going?" Joanna asked.

"Search and Rescue called this morning," said Eva Lou. "Harold Patterson's turned up missing. With all the excitement last night, it took awhile for someone to figure out that his car was there in the convention-center lot, but he was nowhere to be found. He wasn't at home, either, so they're talking about organizing a search. Jim Bob wants to go to the meeting, since he's a whole lot better at talking these days than he is at searching."

"Where are they going to look?"

"Out on the ranch, I guess, although since his car was in town, seems to me like that would be the first place they'd look." Eva Lou sipped her coffee. "Those Pattersons do seem to be having their troubles, don't they?"

"They do that," Eva Lou's daughter-in-law agreed.

Joanna had only seen the car as it careened toward them. Burton Kimball, standing off to the side, had insisted in his statement that the vehicle in question belonged to Rex Rogers, his cousin's out-of-town attorney, and that the driver of the Allanté was none other than Holly herself. Joanna was more than mildly curious about what was going on, but she had no real official recourse, and she wasn't about to call up Dick Voland to ask him.

While Joanna scarfed down her breakfast, Eva Lou Brady poured two more cups of coffee and then sat down across the table. "What's Jenny so bent out of shape about?" she asked.

"Remember last night when Jenny said she didn't want me to win the election?"

"Yes."

"Well, she's worried about me, afraid something bad will happen to me, just like it did to Andy."

"Makes sense," Eva Lou said. "And with your face all tore up the way it is, I can see why she might have some cause."

"Eva Lou," Joanna objected, "what happened last night could have happened to anyone. When there's an emergency like that, you do what you have to do because you're a person, because you care what happens to other people. It has nothing whatever to do with whether or not you've been elected sheriff."

"True enough, I suppose," Eva Lou agreed. "I mean, if a Methodist minister can end up in the hospital with a concussion, I guess it really could happen to anybody. How is Marianne, by the way?"

"They only kept her for observation. Jeff says they'll most likely let her out sometime today."

After that, an awkward and unusual silence

seemed to spring up between the two women. Eva Lou Brady was the one who finally broke it.

"Lord knows I don't mean to pry, Joanna, but I have to ask. Have you made any kind of arrangements for Jenny? I mean, with this new job and all, what if something awful *did* happen? Jim Bob and I could take Jenny in if we had to, but we shouldn't. It wouldn't be good for her in the long run. She needs somebody younger, someone more your age."

Joanna dropped her gaze and didn't answer. That in itself was answer enough. She hadn't made any such arrangements, although she understood all too well the ramifications of not doing so. Rewriting her will and appointing potential guardians to care for Jennifer were two of the nagging loose ends of her life. In the awful aftermath of Andy's death, those were two distasteful yet essential tasks she had not yet found courage enough to face.

"Maybe," Eva Lou continued, not unkindly, "once you do get all those details straightened out, you should talk them over with Jenny. She's a smart little girl. I think just knowing you've handled things and prepared for the worst would make her feel better, less alone. After all, both of your lives had been put through a wringer. I don't blame her for being scared."

"No," Joanna said, with a rueful shake of her head. "I don't blame her, either."

The phone rang, and Eva Lou hurried to answer it. The caller was none other than Marianne Maculyea looking for Joanna. "When there wasn't any answer out at the house, I figured I'd find you at the Bradys'. How's the candidate . . . ? Excuse me, how's the sheriff doing this morning?"

"The sheriff-elect is stiff as a board," Joanna returned. "Rolling around on sidewalks isn't good for me. I hurt in places I didn't know I owned. And I've got a shiner where you clipped me under the eye. How are you?"

Marianne laughed, sounding far more chipper than she should have. "Bored stiff. Ready to be out of here. If it comes down to a contest of who's more hardheaded, it's a toss-up. You've only got a black eye. They thought I had a concussion."

"Let's call it even," Joanna said, laughing into the phone herself, and starting to feel a little better. Maybe the painkillers were finally starting to do their stuff—the painkillers and, of course, a great breakfast. "What's on your agenda today?" she asked.

"The doctor says I'll be out by noon. It's time for me to get out of the campaign-manager business and go back to being just plain Pastor Maculyea," Marianne replied. "But I wouldn't have missed this election for the world. It's been fun, hasn't it?"

"I'm not sure 'fun' is the word that applies. How's Linda Kimball doing?"

"Fine. They didn't even keep her overnight. Just put her arm in a brace and a sling and sent her home," Marianne answered. "By the way," she added after a pause, "speaking of the Patterson clan, have you heard anything more about Harold?"

"Just that they still haven't found him. Grandpa Brady left here a little while ago to go work on organizing a search."

"He's dead, isn't he?" Marianne asserted quietly.

Joanna had been too preoccupied with her own concerns to give Harold Patterson's unexplained disappearance that much thought. Marianne's blunt pronouncement brought it home.

"Why do you say that?"

"I talked to Ivy just a little while ago. She wasn't home last night, either. I'm not sure what's going on, because she mentioned something about moving into an apartment. But she also said she went by the Rocking P early this morning. The city cops were getting ready to ticket Harold's Scout, so she drove it home and discovered that no one had done the chores. Based on that alone, Burton Kimball talked Judge Moore into granting a continuance."

"Oh," Joanna said.

Farmers and ranchers are among the last of the world's day-trippers. Their lives are like yo-yos with strings that stretch only as far as they can travel between morning and evening chores. If Harold Patterson had now missed both evening and morning chores, that was serious.

"You're right," Joanna agreed. "Either he's dead or he's badly hurt. He's a tough old coot. It would take something serious to get that man down."

"Heart attack, maybe?" Marianne suggested.

"I saw him yesterday morning," Joanna said,

"at the office. Now that you mention it, he did seem awfully upset."

"I guess we'll just have to hope for the best," Marianne said. "Now, what about you? What are your plans?"

"Milo gave me the day off. I don't think he wants someone who looks this awful beautifying his office. I'm due to go see Dick Voland a little later. One of the deputies took my statement last night. They're supposed to have it typed up by this morning so I can sign it."

"Why one of the deputies instead of one of the city cops?" Marianne asked. "After all, it happened inside the city limits."

"I think it was so hectic, they just passed out numbers, and whoever drew yours, that was it. Some people got city cops; some ended up with deputies."

"Speaking of deputies, did you talk to Dick Voland after the final election results came in?" Marianne asked. "You won by such a landslide that he's probably not a very happy camper this morning."

"I haven't seen him since the party. He and Al ducked out as soon as they saw the way the vote was going and that there was no way for Freeman to catch up. Frank Montoya stayed around long enough to concede and shake my hand."

"I wish I could have seen the look on Dick Voland's face when he finally figured out you were going to win. Do you think he'll quit before you take office, or will you have to fire him?"

"Fire him? Why would I do that?"

"Joanna," Marianne said severely, "haven't you been listening to all the things that man has been saying about you out on the campaign trail? I have. I'm afraid he'll try to undermine you every step of the way."

Joanna had been listening, but most of what Chief Deputy Voland had said in the previous six weeks Joanna had chalked up to campaign rhetoric. Voland had spent years working for the previous administration, much of that as second in command. So far, independent investigators had turned up no connections between Voland and any of the departmental drug-related skulduggery. He had been clean enough for the county board of supervisors to appoint him acting sheriff until a new one could be elected.

Personally, Joanna wouldn't have given Richard Voland the time of day. Around the department and directly to his face, the chief deputy was referred to by his official title. Behind his back, in unofficial circles, he was dubbed "Chief Redneck." Voland's "good ol' boy" mindset, one that had worked with Walter V. McFadden and would have been compatible with Al Freeman, wasn't nearly as good a fit with Joanna Brady.

"Dick will be fine," Joanna answered confidently, glossing over Marianne's concern as well as her own. "He's been around the department since my father was there. We'll wait and see if he's a problem."

Joanna and Marianne might have talked longer if one of the nurses hadn't showed up with a thermometer and a blood-pressure cuff. Marianne got off the line with only a hint of ill grace. Hospitals were like that.

When Joanna put down the phone, Eva Lou once more refilled their coffee cups. "I get such a kick out of your mother," Eva Lou said thoughtfully. "Eleanor was on the phone here bright and early this morning, excited as a little kid and wondering what kind of outfit I thought you should wear to your swearing-in."

Joanna laughed. "That's my mother for you," she said, but a moment later all trace of laughter was gone.

"Between now and January, there should be plenty of time for us to figure out what I should wear. Not that getting a new outfit will help. Mother had a fit yesterday because she wanted me to look great for the election-night television cameras. But even after she went to all the trouble of sending me to Helen Barco for the full, deluxe treatment, I still managed to show up on the news looking like the tail end of disaster. You'd think she'd finally just give up on me, wouldn't you?"

Eva Lou Brady shook her head. "No, Joanna, mothers don't give up," she said. "Haven't you figured that out yet? No matter what, we never, ever, quite give up."

Seventeen

STILL FEELING spoiled by Eva Lou's breakfast, Joanna drove down the Warren Cutoff and past the huge Lavender Pit tailings dump on her way to the new Cochise County Justice Complex two miles east of town on Highway 80. Built and furnished with the county's share of confiscated drug moneys, the pink and tan stuccoed buildings nestled in a cleft in red iron-tinted hills, while a line of stark limestone gray cliffs marched across the horizon forming a backdrop.

Andy had been working as a deputy when the new complex opened, and the new jail's ongoing difficulties had been one of the hottest campaign issues. Still, in Joanna's mind's eye, the words "sheriff's office" still meant her father's cramped and shabby digs in the old Art Deco–style county courthouse uptown.

There, seated at a scarred wooden desk, her father had ruled supreme, running a much smaller but seemingly more effective Cochise County Sheriff's Department. In terms of crime statistics, Hank Lathrop's administration put all succeeding administrations to shame.

Just for curiosity's sake, once Joanna turned off

the highway into the County Justice Complex, she played tourist and drove all the way around the whole facility—past the jail with its razor-ribbon-lined exercise yards and auto-impound lot, past the building housing the county justice courts, and around to the back parking area where a large posted sign said EMPLOYEES ONLY. The parking lot was only partially full, but directly behind the building the reserved spaces with a shaded canopy over them were 100 percent occupied.

The county Blazer Dick Voland usually drove was parked in the spot marked CHIEF DEPUTY. His personal car—a late-model Buick Regal—sat squarely in the spot reserved for SHERIFF. From that space, a separate and seemingly private walkway led to a door that entered directly into the far back corner of the office complex.

Finding Dick Voland's car parked territorially in the sheriff's spot was probably fair enough, Joanna reasoned. He was, after all, the officially desig-nated acting sheriff. But still, something about the way the car was parked there niggled at her, both-ered her in a way she couldn't quite pin down.

Shrugging off that fleeting shadow of doubt, Jo-anna drove back to the designated visitor parking area at the front of the building. When she went inside and gave her name to the young woman behind the counter, the clerk didn't seem to make a connection or attach any particular significance to it. Certainly, no one in the outside office had been told to expect a possible visit from the incom-ing sheriff. For all the courtesy and attention lav-ished on her, Joanna Brady might just as well have been a traveling ballpoint-pen salesman, with no advance appointment, wandering in off the highway for a cold call.

The clerk suggested Joanna take a seat, telling her that Mr. Voland was busy on the phone at the moment but that he would be with her as soon as possible. How soon was that? she wondered as she waited first five minutes, then ten, then fifteen.

While Joanna stewed in her own juices, the people behind the counters, apparently intent on their jobs, continued working, barely acknowledging her presence. It was almost as though she were invisible. After a while, impatient and unable to sit still any longer, Joanna got up and roamed the lobby, pacing over to the long lighted display case that decorated the spacious room's back wall.

There, among a collection of photos dating back to Arizona's territorial days, Joanna found the official portrait of her late father, Sheriff D. H. "Big Hank" Lathrop. She had seen the display before, but seeing her father's picture there among the others caught her by surprise and made Joanna wonder what her father's reaction would be if he could see her now. Would he be proud of her for running and ultimately winning the election? Would he understand why she did it, or would he be puzzled or upset or even disappointed? Without having the opportunity to know him as an adult, there was no way for his daughter to guess at his possible reactions.

Afraid to return to her seat for fear her tumbling emotions might betray her, Joanna examined the entire display, carefully reading through an encapsulated and officially photographed history of the Cochise County Sheriff's Department. The last photo in the group, the one on the far right, was also the newest one—a portrait of Walter V. McFadden. Next to his was a blank spot.

With a lump in her throat, Joanna realized that, had things been different, Andy's picture most likely would have hung there eventually. Now that spot would be hers instead, filled no doubt by the picture she'd used for her campaign brochure.

Realizing that eventually her picture would be there with her father's did something to her—stiffened her spine and strengthened her resolve. Most of those previous sheriffs of Cochise County had been fine, upright citizens, doing the best job they could under whatever difficult circumstances had been handed them.

Her father, Big Hank Lathrop, had been a straight shooter in every sense of the word. In his book of sherifflike behavior, scheduled appointments always came first, taking precedence over everything else—including the always unscheduled demands of a ringing telephone.

And thinking about that reminded her of stories Andy had related to her from time to time, stories about how Dick Voland was prone to throwing his considerable weight around. He had sometimes bragged about leaving people with appointments cooling their heels in the lobby for as long as he wanted. For the fun of it. Because he felt like it. Because he could.

By the time Joanna turned away from the display case, twenty minutes had passed, and her temper was on the rise. More than 140 people were employed by the Cochise County Sheriff's Department. Once she was sworn into office—whether in one week or after the standard two months—she would be those employees' chief administrator. Their boss. And whether they liked it or not, some things about the Sheriff's Department were about to change.

Joanna hit the wall at exactly twenty-three minutes and counting. She left off pacing in front of the display case and started for the outside door just as Dick Voland sauntered into the waiting room carrying an unsightly brown-stained mug filled with newly poured black coffee.

"Sorry to keep you waiting," he drawled casually. "Got tied up on the phone and just couldn't get away."

"That's all right," Joanna returned coolly. "I'm sure you're very busy."

Noisily sipping away, Dick Voland nodded sagely, making no move to invite Joanna away from the public part of the building.

"What with everything that went on overnight, I'm afraid we're a little behind on our paper," he said. "I just checked with the transcription clerk. She hasn't had a chance to get cracking on any of last night's work yet. She says it'll probably be another fifteen or twenty minutes, if you don't mind waiting that long."

Joanna was taller than Dick Voland expected, and she caught sight of the supposedly well-concealed smirk that leaked out over the top rim of his coffee mug. Seeing the look, Joanna Brady knew intuitively that Marianne Maculyea was right, and she was wrong.

Dick Voland's being a professional law-enforcement officer made not the slightest difference. His car being parked in the sheriff's space outside and not in the chief deputy's was in fact, an open declaration of war. He knew it, she knew it, and so did all the people toiling away in the outer office. The same thing went for being kept waiting.

"That's unfortunate," she said without raising her voice. "I didn't really have a spare half hour when I arrived here twenty-four minutes ago. I have even less now. I came here as a courtesy to sign that statement. If I still happen to be here when it's ready, I'll be happy to sign it. Otherwise, you'll have to have someone from here bring it to me."

Her curt response wasn't quite what Dick Voland expected. The self-satisfied smirk faded.

"I do have another minute or so, however," Joanna continued without giving him an opportunity to respond. "If you don't mind, I'd like to get an advance look at my office."

Dick Voland might have read the election results in the newspaper. He might have seen them on television. But Joanna Brady saw the man's face at the moment her words hit home, when the reality of the election outcome finally sank in.

His jaw stiffened. "You mean right now?"

A moment before, no one else in the public area had showed the slightest interest in Joanna Brady, but now an almost electric charge seemed to crackle through the room. Every eye and ear was aimed in their direction, hanging breathlessly on every gesture, every word. It was a test of wills, a critical first step that Joanna Brady could ill afford to fail.

She smiled. "Of course I mean now."

Without moving, Dick Voland stared back at her. Joanna stood still and waited.

"Oh, all right," he grumbled irritably, reaching for the hefty key ring that dangled from his belt. "This way." Frowning, Voland unlocked the door, opened it, and then stepped back, holding it open for Joanna to enter. "After you," he said with a slightly exaggerated and too-polite bow.

Joanna recognized the implications at once. It was a none-too-subtle issue of control, of who was in charge and who wasn't. Someone who hadn't grown up as the daughter of a sheriff might not have paid any attention, might not have caught it, but Joanna did.

In the world of law enforcement, prisoners walk in front; guards follow. Suspects walk in front; police officers follow. The person in the back is the one in charge, the one calling the shots. Nobody ever forgets that, not for a moment.

"No," she said, still smiling and stepping aside. "You lead the way."

Seconds passed—it might have been eons—while neither of them moved and while the whole office waited to see the outcome. Finally, with a disgusted shake of his head, Dick Voland gave in and lumbered off ahead of her.

Not daring to let down her guard, Joanna kept her shoulders ramrod straight as she followed him down the hall. She might have won the first minor skirmish. No doubt, the people in the front office would be talking about it for days to come. But it was a damn long way from winning a single battle to winning the war.

And it was another long way from winning the election to winning your stripes.

Joanna followed Dick Voland down a hallway to the far back corner of the building, where he led her into a suite of comfortable offices built around a common reception area. The upholstered furnishings—a couch and several side chairs— were from the *nouvelle* Southwest school of design—dusty roses and browns and turquoises. Brass-and-glass coffee and end tables created the atmosphere of an upscale attorney's office.

Everything about the place was a far cry from what Joanna remembered of D. H. Lathrop's old industrially furnished courthouse days. Back then, scarred wooden chairs and battered gray metal desks had been the order of the day.

A slim blonde sat at a spacious desk in the common reception room, busily typing on a computer terminal. As she typed, she leaned forward and frowned nearsightedly at the screen. Joanna suspected that she needed glasses but was too vain to wear them. D. H. Lathrop's four-by-four secretary—Miss Imogene Wyatt of the Coke-bottle glasses—had been every bit as industrial strength and no-nonsense as the serviceable old courthouse furniture.

Sensing that someone had entered the room, the young woman glanced up from her screen. Seeing

Dick Voland, she grinned at him knowingly as soon as he walked through the doorway. "Well?" she said with a coyly raised eyebrow. "How'd it go with the dragon lady?"

Joanna managed to glimpse the almost imperceptible movement of Dick Voland's head. The warning shake may well have been accompanied by a cautioning wink. If so, it was outside Joanna's sight line. Obviously, the secretary had missed it as well.

"Kristin," Dick Voland said hurriedly, "I'd like you to meet Joanna Brady. The new sheriff. At least she will be."

Instantly, the grin disappeared from Kristin's impeccably made-up face. "Oh," she said, scrambling uncertainly to her feet as Joanna came into view. "Glad to meet you."

I'll bet, Joanna thought.

When the long-legged young woman stood up, the hem of her eye-popping leather miniskirt barely skimmed the surface of her desk. Joanna sometimes wore short-shorts that were longer than that almost nonexistent skirt.

Pointedly leaving the staring to Dick Voland, Joanna held out her hand. For a moment, a look of utter confusion washed over the younger woman's startled features. Obviously, the "dragon lady" hadn't been expected to venture uninvited down the hall. When Kristin finally came to her senses, she had presence of mind enough to offer her own hand.

After the weeks she'd spent practicing on the campaign trail, Joanna's handshaking skills were considerable. She took no small pleasure in firmly grasping Kristin's limp, flaccid fingers. Smiling cheerfully, Joanna thoroughly ground Kristin's knuckles into one another. She pretended not to hear the satisfying crunch of bone on bone and seemed not to notice the surprised wince of pain that darted across the younger woman's petulant features.

"What did you say your name was?" Joanna asked.

"Kristin Marsten."

"And how long have you been working here, Miss Marsten?" Joanna inquired formally.

"I started out as a clerk/intern last summer," Kristin answered. "The old secretary/receptionist quit a few weeks ago. Mr. Voland asked me to work in here for a while, to fill in on a temporary basis."

"I see," Joanna said. And she did, too.

She glanced around the room, assimilating all the details at once. Several separate doors opened off the reception area. A light was on in the far corner office, the one with the private walkway and private door leading in from the sheriff's designated parking place. Without having to be told, Joanna knew that was the office she was looking for, but she asked anyway, just for form's sake.

"Which office is mine?"

"This way," Dick Voland muttered, heading off in that direction.

The northwest corner office was spacious and bright, with a pair of spotlessly clean windows set in each outside wall. Those windows afforded a

spectacular and unobstructed view of the surrounding desert. Joanna noticed that the furnishings in the room carried Walter McFadden's
distinctly masculine stamp. A long leather couch
occupied one wall, while a matching wingback
chair sat casually off to one side.

Walter McFadden's parking place wasn't the
only thing Dick Voland had appropriated for himself. Next to the chair was a freestanding ashtray,
filled to overflowing with the smelly leavings of
several potent cigars. The fine grains of the cherrywood desk and matching credenza were difficult
to see beneath a hodgepodge of jumbled papers
frosted by a shaky layer of opened newspapers.
Beside the credenza, a stack of unused Al Freeman
yard signs leaned conspicuously against the far
wall.

Joanna stood in the center of the room and piv-
oted slowly, examining everything around her
while Voland stood apprehensively beside the
desk. "Good," she said when she finished her 360-
degree turn. "That's all I wanted to know for
now."

Without waiting to be escorted from the room
and ignoring both Kristin and Voland, Joanna
stalked across the reception area, down the hallway, and let herself back out into the public
lobby area.

She had come to the sheriff's office that morning
with nothing at all in mind other than signing that
damn statement. By being there, however, by
seeing it in person, she had learned things that

were far more important—important and disturbing.

Predictably, the typed statement still wasn't ready to be signed. Employee productivity was yet another thorny departmental issue. For now, it was Dick Voland's problem. Eventually, it would be Joanna's.

Eighteen

WHEN SHE left the justice complex, Joanna drove straight to the new county administration offices on Melody Lane. Her arrival there was much different from that at the Sheriff's Department.

Although Joanna Brady arrived at the county manager's reception desk without an officially scheduled appointment, Norbert DeLeon himself hurried out from his inner office as soon as his secretary announced Joanna's name over the intercom. A warm, cordial smile beamed across Norbert's face as he held out his hand in welcome.

"I believe congratulations are in order," he said, ushering Joanna into his office. "Can I get you a cup of coffee?"

"No, thanks. I've had enough caffeine already this morning."

"What can I do for you then?" he asked, easing himself down behind his desk—a light oak-veneer affair that didn't come close in quality to the genuine cherrywood desk that graced Sheriff McFadden's former office.

"I came to ask you to either verify or squelch a rumor I've heard."

A concerned frown creased Norbert's face.

"We've had lots of rumors around here in the last few months. I hope it's nothing bad."

"Someone mentioned last night that since the position of sheriff is vacant, the board of supervisors was considering filling that office as soon after the election as possible."

"Oh, that," Norbert DeLeon said, dismissively. "Well, there had been some talk, but now that the election is over, no one wants to push you too hard. We're all well aware of what you've been through these past few months. The final consensus was that we should give you a chance to rest up, give you a bit of a breather before you take on your new duties in January."

"In other words, if Al Freeman or Frank Montoya had won the election, the board would have gone ahead and sworn in either one of them right away. But since I won, they won't?"

DeLeon nodded. "I guess that's about right."

"Does that seem discriminatory to you?"

The county manager looked shocked. "Well," he faltered, "I suppose it could be interpreted that way, but believe me, no one meant any harm. They were all looking out for you. I mean, you've had such a difficult time with Andy's death and all. . . ."

"Norbert," Joanna interrupted firmly. "The supervisors may have my best interests at heart, but I doubt that decision is necessarily beneficial to the people of Cochise County."

"What are you saying?" he asked.

"I was elected sheriff to solve the problems that currently exist in the Sheriff's Department. That's exactly what I intend to do, and I'd like to get started as soon as possible."

DeLeon steepled his fingers under his chin and regarded her appraisingly. "When would you like to go to work?"

"The sooner, the better."

"I see. Today?"

"Suits me."

"But what about Milo Davis? You've worked for him a long time. Won't you have to give him some kind of notice?"

"Milo's already been working on a contingency plan," Joanna replied. "Believe me, that won't be a problem."

"All right then," Norbert said, nodding and reaching at once for his telephone. "Hold on here a minute, Joanna. I'll make a few calls and see what I can do."

As a result of those phone calls, Joanna Lee Lathrop Brady was sworn into office as the first female sheriff of Cochise County at two o'clock that afternoon: Wednesday, November 7, one day after her election.

The hastily organized ceremony was held in the chambers of Superior Court Judge Cameron Moore, with Jennifer Ann Brady holding her mother's worn Bible. Joanna, dressed in a well-worn navy-blue blazer, was surprised to see tears in her mother's eyes as Eleanor pinned Hank Lathrop's old but newly polished badge over Joanna's left breast pocket.

Eleanor was disappointed that no Tucson television stations or newspapers sent reporters to

Bisbee to cover the event. Joanna didn't mind at all. By then the purplish bruise under her eye had turned a full-fledged black.

After the swearing-in, the whole crew—minus Judge Moore—trooped down to the Davis Insurance Agency in Warren to celebrate. There they sipped champagne and devoured a special, hastily decorated-to-order cake topped with an artfully designed chocolate-frosting sheriff's badge.

A beaming Milo Davis proposed the first toast. "All I can say is," he said, raising his glass, "I sure know how to pick a winner."

Joanna gazed around the crowded rooms. Winning was fine, but the prospect of leaving the homey office saddened her somehow. This was a place where she had grown to adulthood, advanced from a giddy high school part-timer to a responsible and self-assured businesswoman. With Milo's help and support, she had worked for him all the while she commuted the hundred miles back and forth to the university in Tucson to earn her B.A.

The happy crew of supporters, jammed together wall-to-wall, consisted of both family and friends—Eleanor Lathrop and Jenny, Marianne Maculyea and Jeff Daniels, Eva Lou and Jim Bob Brady, Angie Kellogg, Milo Davis, and Lisa Connors. Despite her overnight stay in the hospital, Marianne seemed none the worse for wear. Unlike Joanna, she wasn't sporting a black eye.

Acting as unofficial master of ceremonies, Milo went around the room asking for comments. He even cajoled Eleanor Lathrop into letting down her hair far enough to drink a second half-glass of champagne. Jenny, sitting cross-legged a little apart from the others and sipping sparkling cider in a champagne flute, was the last person Milo called on to speak.

"What about you, Jenny?" he asked. "Care to propose a toast?"

Struck suddenly shy, Jennifer rose to her feet and raised her glass the way she had seen the others do. "Even if you are sheriff," she said, "I'm glad you're still my mom."

People smiled and laughed and said, "Here, here!" while Joanna fought to swallow enough of the lump in her throat so she could take the expected sip of champagne.

"Thank you, Jenny," she murmured.

When post-champagne cleanup started, Joanna retreated to her desk and began the process of clearing and emptying. As she sorted and packed, Joanna was struck by the oddball bits of memorabilia that had somehow wormed their way into her work space, each bringing with it a separate and sometimes bittersweet echo from the past.

Why, for instance, had she kept Jenny's orange-and-green kindergarten-sized handprint on the credenza behind her desk? Why was that tiny plaster-of-paris plaque from Jenny's Daily Vacation Bible School more important to her mother, more worthy of display, than one of Jenny's more recent school pictures?

And what about the worn buffalo-head nickel Andy had playfully dropped down her bra the night of their first date? Always lurking in the top right-hand corner of her pencil drawer, the nickel served as a talisman, one she picked up and rubbed from time to time. By now the surface designs were worn sufficiently thin that they were only vaguely visible.

And then there was the Montblanc fountain pen Milo Davis had presented to her last summer on the tenth anniversary of the day she went to work for him. When he gave it to her, she had expected to work for the Davis Insurance Agency as long as there *was* a Davis Insurance Agency. But then, between last summer and now, Joanna's entire life had been thrown into a Waring blender.

She glanced up as Jim Bob Brady hobbled back to her desk and sank gratefully into a chair. "These dogs are killing me," he said. "Mind if I set a spell and kick off my shoes?"

"Go right ahead. You do look tired."

Her father-in-law nodded. "I'm not nearly as young as I used to be. Just that piddly-assed little bit of tramping around out in them hills this afternoon was enough to wear me out. Used to be I could go all day and not think twice about it."

"Still nothing on Harold?"

"Not by the time I left," Jim Bob replied. "We mostly worked the lower pastures because that's where Ivy said she thought he'd most likely be, repairing fences and such. Tomorrow, I guess, if he's still missing, they'll head on up toward Juniper Flats. Don't think I'll go on that one. Terrain's too rough. Besides, if they haven't found him by now . . ."

Jim Bob Brady left off without finishing the sentence. He leaned forward in the chair and began massaging his feet.

"You think Harold Patterson is dead then?" Joanna asked.

"Don't you?"

Joanna nodded. "I guess so. With the weather as cold as it's been, if he's been out in it all this time, I suppose he's done for."

"Yup," Jim Bob agreed. "Like as not he had himself a heart attack or a stroke out there in a pasture somewhere. And if it was me, I couldn't think of a better way to go. Given my druthers, I'd do the same damn thing. Die with my boots on.

"I keep telling Eva Lou I don't want none of those doctors to get hold of me and keep me hanging on with all those goldurned tubes and machines when it's time for me to go and meet my Maker."

Abruptly straightening up, Jim Bob Brady peered sharply at Joanna over the top of his wire-rimmed glasses. "How are you doing, Joanna? You holding up all right?"

"I'm fine, Daddy Jim," she said. "Tired. And a little apprehensive."

"How come?"

She shrugged. "I had planned to take the next two months to study policies and procedures so I could hit the ground running. Instead, I had to go shoot off my mouth. Now I'm caught flat-footed, wearing a badge two months too early."

"It's not too early. You'll be fine. Just take it as it comes, one thing at a time. And don't let the turkeys get you down."

"I'll do my best," she answered.

It was six by the time Joanna and Jenny stowed all the packed boxes in the back of the Eagle for the drive back home to the High Lonesome. During the campaign, an elderly neighbor named Clayton Rhodes had become the ranch's self-appointed man of all work, dropping by the place both mornings and evenings to see what needed doing and picking up the slack wherever there was some. After much badgering on Joanna's part, Clayton had finally agreed to accept some token payment for his work.

When Joanna and Jenny arrived at the turnoff to the ranch, Clayton's rattletrap Ford pickup was just clattering over the cattle guard. Never one to indulge in unnecessary conversation, the old man raised the brim of his cowboy hat with one finger, nodded in their direction, and kept right on driving.

They made their way up to and into the house through a melee of ecstatic doggy greetings. While Jenny gamboled on the floor with the two dogs, Joanna checked the answering machine. A series of blinking lights told her there were numerous messages. Joanna tried counting them but lost track after eight. She gave up and punched the Playback button.

The messages were mostly congratulatory calls, some from high-school acquaintances she hadn't talked to since graduation. Mercifully, most required no call back.

One did. It came from Adam York, the DEA agent in charge of the Tucson office. Although

York had, at one time, suspected Joanna of illicit connections to a South American drug dealer, they were now on good terms. In fact, Adam York had been one of the first people to encourage Joanna to campaign for the office of sheriff in Andy Brady's place. She was gratified to know that he had phoned her, but she waited until after Jenny was in bed and asleep before returning his call.

"Congratulations," Adam York said, sounding the now-familiar refrain. "Good going."

"Thank you," she responded. "I think," she added a little lamely.

"You think? What's this? I've been watching the newspaper reports. You ran a good strong campaign, and you wound up garnering yourself a good solid base of support. I also heard they might go ahead and swear you in prior to January."

"You heard right," Joanna said, "but you're behind times. It's a done deal. I'm a sworn officer as of two o'clock this afternoon."

"So why this distinct lack of enthusiasm? Nerves?"

Joanna laughed. "How'd you guess? That's one of the reasons I'm calling you back so late tonight. I waited until after Jenny went to sleep. She's really worried about me, Adam, afraid something's going to happen to me just like it did to her father. So I'm calling to ask what you think."

"On what subject?"

"I helped you put a major crimp in a big-time drug dealer's way of doing business. I was elected to office on the premise that I continue that process.

What are the chances of his sending one of his hit men after me?"

The phone line was quiet for so long that Joanna thought the line had gone dead. "Adam?"

"Just a minute. I'm here. Let me ask you a question in return. What are the chances of someone being hit by lightning?"

"Not that good, but it happens. Depends on where a person is standing when the storm hits. If he's out in the open with nothing much around him, or if he's wearing or holding something that's a natural conductor, then he could be in big trouble."

"Exactly," Adam York agreed.

"What do you mean—'exactly'?"

"As of right now, you are standing in the middle of an open field. A hell of a storm is blowing up all around you, and that badge they handed you today is nothing if not a goddamn lightning rod."

"Oh," Joanna breathed. "I see. Any suggestions?"

"APOA, for one thing."

The Arizona Police Officers Academy in the Phoenix suburb of Peoria was a mutually sponsored training program for officers from many different jurisdictions throughout Arizona. The six-week-long program of formal classroom lectures, lab work, and role-play provided general basic training for police recruits from all over the state, after which they returned to their separate departments for more in-depth and jurisdiction-specific instruction.

"You mean sign up for that course and take it just like I'm a new hire?"

"Aren't you?" Adam York asked pointedly.

Joanna didn't answer. "What else?"

"Target practice," Adam York returned. "Lots of it. From what I know about you, you're already a fair shot, but target practice never hurt anybody. And a Kevlar vest. Get one that's properly fitted and wear the damn thing."

"You sound serious."

"I have never been more serious in my life," Adam York asserted.

"If it really is this bad, how come you called to congratulate me?"

"Because congratulations are in order. What you did was amazing, and I'm not just talking about winning the election, either. You flat out saved that woman's life."

"If Jenny heard you sounding like this, it would scare the daylights out of her. You act as though I'm suffering from some kind of death wish."

"What I'm telling you is strictly common sense. Any other cop would say exactly the same thing. People on the outside may make fun of the 'war on drugs.' They may claim it's just so much political propaganda and bullshit. But you and I both know it's a war—a real one with real guns and live ammunition where real people get killed. I've seen you in action, Sheriff Joanna Brady. In this man's war, you're one soldier I'm very happy to have on my side."

"Thank you," Joanna said.

"Think nothing of it. By the way, I've got a catalog from a specialty shop in California. It's where some of the female federal agents get street-clothes-type equipment, vests included. I'll send a copy your way tomorrow. And there's another book you should have as well. Where do you want me to send them?"

"To the Cochise County Criminal Justice Complex, Highway Eighty, Bisbee, Arizona. I should get moved into my office sometime tomorrow morning."

"Good," Adam York told her. "It's too late to make it in tomorrow's mail, but you should have it the day after at the latest."

"Thanks, Adam," she said gratefully. "Thanks a bunch."

She went to bed and tried to sleep, but her mind wouldn't let her. At last she crawled out of bed, turned on the light, and reached for the phone book.

Bisbee had come so far into the modern era that after generations of five-number dialing, telephone users now had to use all seven numbers to make a local call, which seemed like an unnecessary and cumbersome waste of time. But some small-town practices persisted. Alvin Bernard, Bisbee's chief of police, still had his home telephone number listed in the directory, and Joanna decided it wasn't too late to call.

Back when Alvin graduated from high school, he had flunked the company physical and had missed being hired by P.D. When he went to work as a cop for the city of Bisbee, his former classmates had looked down their noses at him. They were somewhat more respectful and envious, both, now that their high-paying copper-mining jobs had disappeared and Alvin's hadn't. Not only was he still employed by his original employer, attrition and two key heart attacks had bounced him all the way up to chief.

"Congrats, Joanna," he enthused. "Welcome aboard and all that shit. Excuse me, all that crap. What can I do for you?"

"I was calling for some information about that hit-and-run incident last night."

"Ask away. We've got letters of mutual aid out the kazoo. What do you need?"

"Can you tell me what's happening on that case?"

"Sure thing. My guys talked to Holly Patterson's sleazebag lawyer. He says it's nothing. That her foot slipped on the accelerator or some such thing, and that by the time Holly had the car back under control, she was too upset to come back."

"Right."

"That's what I say. But we picked up another angle on it from someone else. One of my officers' aunts, Isobel Gonzales, and her husband work at *Casa Vieja*. She's the cook, and he's the gardener, for the new owner.

"Isobel told her sister that Holly Patterson has really been going downhill ever since she got back home. Sounds almost like a rerun of what happened to her mother. From what I've been able to pick up, Burton expected Harold Patterson to offer Holly some kind of settlement yesterday. Harold stopped by to see her, but when they couldn't come to terms, Holly went ballistic. She blames her cousin, Burton Kimball, for talking her father out of settling."

"What does Burton say?"

"He flat out denies it. He says he tried to talk Harold out of it but that he didn't get to first base. He did succeed in talking old Judge Moore into granting a continuance when Harold didn't show up in court this morning. I guess the out-of-town lawyer was screaming like a scalded Indian."

Joanna thought about all that for a minute. "I'll bet he was. So one person says Harold was going to settle, the other says he wasn't. Who's right? What do you think is going on?"

"Well," Alvin Bernard replied cheerfully, "I'd have to say somebody's lying through his teeth. It's just too damned soon to tell which is which. But then, that's what you and I get paid for, isn't it—to find out who's lying?"

"Yes," Joanna Brady answered. "I suppose it is."

Nineteen

JOANNA EXPECTED to toss and turn after those two disquieting phone calls. Instead, she fell asleep the moment her head hit the pillow; her eyes closed, and she fell into a heavy, dreamless sleep. Toward morning, though, she drifted into a dream—an unusually happy one at first, a dream about the old days, about when Andy was still alive.

Joanna and Jenny were sitting in the back of a moving pickup. Jenny was holding an old wicker picnic basket, and the two of them were laughing and singing songs at the top of their lungs.

They were driving down a bumpy dirt road. It took some time before Joanna realized they were in Hank Lathrop's old Chevrolet pickup—the venerable old half-ton truck her father had promised would be Joanna's someday when she had her license, the truck her mother had sold to a farmer from out in the Sulphur Springs Valley the week after Hank's funeral.

The time frame of the dream was disjointed and confusing. Details were disturbingly out of synch. There were two dogs riding along in the pickup, but not Liz and Pearl, Hank Lathrop's two old black-and-tans, but Joanna's present-day Sadie and Tigger.

Eventually, Joanna turned around to look in the cab and see who was driving. She was startled to find that the driver was none other than Hank Lathrop himself, while Andrew Brady rode shotgun in the passenger seat. The two of them were talking and laughing, enjoying some private joke.

Like the time-warped dogs, that part of the dream could never have happened in real life, either. D. H. Lathrop might have known Andy Brady as a child by name or reputation, but certainly not as Joanna's future husband—as Hank Lathrop's future son-in-law. By the time Andy came home from the service and he and Joanna became a hot item, Joanna's father was already dead.

But this was a dream. In the dreamscape, those things were possible, and both men were together. And the Joanna Lathrop Brady who was riding in the back of that silver Cheyenne was overjoyed to see them. She tapped on the window, wanting to catch their attention. Since there was plenty of room in the front, she wanted to ride up there with them, to join in the stories and jokes, but they were too busy laughing and having a good time to hear her. She tapped on the window again and again. Still they didn't notice.

Suddenly, a cloud seemed to pass in front of the sun, darkening the sky overhead. Joanna looked up and saw a rainstorm marching across the valley toward them. It was one of those fierce summer storms, the kind that kicks up clouds of swirling dirt and sends those out as reconnaissance troops in advance of the driving rain. Not wanting to be soaked, she turned back to the cab and pounded on the window again, only now no one was there.

The truck was still barreling down the road, but the cab was empty. The doors were open. Both her father and Andy had disappeared. No one was holding on to the steering wheel, which twisted wildly from side to side while the truck careened drunkenly down the narrow track, picking up speed as it went.

Joanna woke up slick with sweat. She fought her way out from under the covers and then lay there with her heart hammering in her chest, waiting for the fright to pass.

Gradually, her heartbeat slowed to normal, and a sort of calm numbness spread over her. You don't need a Ph.D. in dream interpretation to understand what that one meant, she thought. In the dream—as in life—both Andy and her father had bailed out on her, abandoning her to fight the good fight alone, leaving her stuck in the bed of the moving pickup of life with no way for her to reach either the steering wheel or the brakes.

As she knew it would, eventually the clarity of the dream grew fuzzy and disappeared, taking with it both the terrifying end as well as the pleasant, carefree beginning. That was the problem with dreams. In order to shake off the bad parts, you usually had to let go of the good ones as well.

Joanna glanced at the bedside clock—4:45—too late to go back to sleep but still far too early to get up. That's when she noticed where she was lying.

Ten years of habit are hard to break. Even after almost two full months, her sleeping body had yet to adjust to the changed circumstances of her life. When autumn chill penetrated the bedroom or when late-night dreams changed to terrifying nightmares, force of habit still sent Joanna scurrying toward Andy's side of the bed. Her cold or frightened body still sought comfort and refuge in the spot where his fading scent lingered in the lumpy down of what had once been his pillow.

With a sigh, and knowing now she wouldn't go back to sleep, Joanna crawled out of bed. She pulled on her heavy terry-cloth robe and went out to the kitchen, where she heated water and made herself a cup of instant cocoa. Not the old-fashioned made-from-scratch kind that Jim Bob Brady favored, but a close enough substitute to help shake off the chill.

Carrying the steaming mug with her, Joanna made her way into the darkened living room. It wasn't necessary to turn on any lights. She knew the way.

Sitting down on the couch, she dragged one of Eva Lou's heavy, hand-crocheted afghans over her icy feet. Moments later, Sadie, the big bluetick hound, emerged from Jenny's bedroom and thrust her warm, smooth muzzle into Joanna's lap.

"I didn't mean to wake you, girl," Joanna apologized, patting the dog's seemingly hollow head.

It no longer disturbed her to find herself speaking aloud to the dog. In the preceding weeks, Sadie had given more than her share of late-night comfort to a grieving Joanna Brady. Tigger—an ugly and improbable mixture of pit bull and golden retriever—had been adopted by Jenny in the aftermath of his previous owner's death. Tigger stuck with Jenny no matter what, while Sadie was more evenhanded about sharing herself. Even pawed, Joanna thought, smiling at the self-correction.

With a sigh, Sadie flopped down on the floor near Joanna's feet, and the woman was grateful for the creature's company. It made the early-morning house seem less silent and alien. In the old days, she might have turned on the radio, tuned in some far-off country-western station. She didn't do that anymore, didn't make that mistake. Those songs were all about couples, about relationships. The words always hurt too much and made her own loneliness that much worse.

So Joanna sat listening to her empty house, grateful for Sadie's jowl-flapping snores. No matter how hard she tried, Joanna couldn't escape the sense that the house was practically empty. And it wasn't just because of Jenny's continuing subdued silences, either. The small house seemed deserted and eerily abandoned because Andrew Brady wasn't in it. And would never be again.

When he was alive, there had been times when he had been away overnight, either at work or out of town on a trip. Occasionally, he had been gone for several days at a time. Joanna and Jenny had stayed on High Lonesome Ranch by themselves back then, but it hadn't been a problem. In those days, the ranch hadn't lived up to its name. It had never seemed lonesome or empty because always there was the expectation that Andy would come back eventually, and the house would once more ring with noise and laughter.

But now, with no such expectation, the High Lonesome was lonesome indeed. At times Joanna considered locking the front and back doors, slapping a For Sale sign on the front gate, and simply walking away. For good. After all, she and Andy had bought the house expecting to be there together, not alone.

She thought about leaving, but she didn't do it. Of course, the scavengers had come out in force. Two different real estate agents from Tucson— sleazy developer types who were evidently both avid followers of the obituary pages—had showed up on her doorstep within minutes of the funeral, offering to buy the High Lonesome for some ridiculously low figure.

From what they said about "taking the place off your hands" it was clear neither one of them had any idea that the insurance she and Andy had purchased over the years had left her with the mortgage paid in full and with a good deal of financial security besides. Joanna Brady sure as hell didn't have to *give* High Lonesome Ranch away, but she wasn't at all certain she wanted to keep it, either.

For one thing, located seven miles from town and two miles off the nearest paved road, the house on High Lonesome Ranch was, as one might expect, very isolated. Clayton Rhodes, her nearest neighbor, was a toothless, hard-of-hearing octogenarian who lived a good mile away. Bill and Charlene Harris were another mile beyond the Rhodes' place. If there was trouble—if lightning ever did strike—a mile or two was a long way to go for help. What happened to Andy had already proved that.

When that thought crossed her mind, Joanna's first instinct was to turn on the light, pick up the phone, and call Adam York back that very minute to see if he had anything to add to the advice he had given her the night before. She was tempted to call again, but she didn't.

What stopped her was the vision of herself—of Joanna Brady, the candidate—stomping all over hell and gone, asking the eighty thousand residents of Cochise County to vote for her. She had won the election, by God. More people had written her name in the blank for sheriff than had chosen Frank Montoya and Al Freeman put together.

Those people hadn't all voted for her because she was Hank Lathrop's poor orphaned daughter or because she was Deputy Andrew Brady's poor shattered widow, either. Sympathy stretched only so far. Voters had chosen Joanna Brady because they thought she was the right person for the job. And now, as the duly sworn sheriff of the whole damn county, she'd better not go ducking for cover at the first sign of trouble. Besides, Adam York had already told her what to do.

Joanna got up from the couch then, once more disturbing the sleeping Sadie. Leaving the dog behind, she again made her way through the house in the dark, returning this time to her bedroom, where she switched on the light. She made straight for Andy's rolltop desk and unlocked the drawer where she kept her new 9-mm Colt 2000 semi-automatic, one she had bought for herself from part of Andy's life-insurance proceeds. She had told herself at the time that she was buying it for protection; that living alone as she did, she needed the weapon regardless of whether or not she won the election. But now that she had won . . .

Handling the gun with the kind of careful respect it deserved, she carried it out to the kitchen. There, after mixing herself yet another cup of cocoa, she took a seat at the breakfast nook. Meticulously, she dismantled the weapon, cleaned it, and painstakingly put it back together. She had splurged and allowed herself the luxury of the wooden-handled First Edition model because she liked the smooth feel of it in her hand. The gun was new, and it was hers. It wasn't something that had been handed down to her by either her father or her husband.

Finished with the cleaning, Joanna dressed warmly and went outside into the cold November morning. If the cattle were surprised to be awakened and fed long before daybreak, they voiced no objection. By the time the shadowy tops of the Chiricahua Mountains to the east were dusted with a soft lavender glow, all ten head of cattle were in the corral contentedly munching hay. That was when Joanna took her holstered Colt and retreated to the back pasture for a session of target practice.

Joanna Brady had owned the semi-automatic for

less than two weeks, so it was still somewhat new and unfamiliar. Even without Adam York's advice, she had been doing target practice on her own, as much as time permitted. Every session, she pinned a black-and-white man-sized, man-shaped target to a hay bale and fired away at it.

She continued to have some difficulty in mastering the sweeping trigger-finger motion required to fire the next round, but each subsequent practice showed some slight improvement. And each succeeding target came down from the bale with the bullet holes grouped more tightly in the desired deadly patterns. She didn't have to wonder what kind of damage those kinds of groupings could do to a human body. She already knew about that. On a firsthand basis.

At ten to seven, chilled to the bone, she took off her protective ear covering and heard the shrill, sharp blasts of the soccer-referee whistle she and Jenny used to summon each other when the distances on the ranch were too great for shouts to carry.

The high-pitched blasts had a disturbingly frantic quality to them. Joanna holstered the gun and hurried back to the house with a sense of dread walking beside her. She was relieved to see Jenny and the dogs waiting for her on the back porch.

As soon as she was close enough to see her, Joanna could tell from the look on Jennifer's face that something was terribly wrong. The child's face was pasty white, her thin lips drawn together in a grim, straight line.

"What's the matter?" Joanna asked, hurrying to Jenny's side.

"Marianne called," Jenny said. "She wants you to call her back right away."

"Why? What happened?"

"She says they found Mr. Patterson. He's dead!"

And with that, Jennifer Ann Brady threw both small arms around her mother's neck and sobbed her heart out, the racking sobs shaking her whole body. It was as though she had somehow slipped through the protective cocoon of childhood into the terrible world of adulthood, of life and death.

Joanna took Jenny in her arms and held her close, murmuring what words of comfort she could summon. But the child's frantic grief, her overriding anguish, went far beyond the reach of her mother's puny words. Or of Marianne's phone call, either.

Jenny wasn't crying about Harold Patterson, an old man she barely knew. No, she was crying for her father.

Damn Tony Vargas anyway! Joanna thought, remembering the man who had murdered Jenny's father. Damn him straight to everlasting hell!

Twenty

WHEN JENNY finally calmed down enough to go shower, Joanna headed for the telephone. There were three new messages on the machine—from three different reporters—all wanting to schedule interviews, but no one from the Cochise County Sheriff's Department had bothered to dial up the new sheriff to let her know what was going on out at the Rocking P Ranch. If there was some kind of official-notification system within the department, Sheriff Joanna Brady's name was not yet included on the list.

She was tempted to call Dispatch and demand to know what the hell was going on, but she squelched that idea. Going off half-cocked would be stupid. Before she did anything at all, she needed some real knowledge of the situation from a reliable source. Instead of calling the department, she dialed Marianne Maculyea's number.

"What's up?" she asked Jeff Daniels when he answered the phone.

"Marianne's in the shower. She told me to tell you she's heading out to the ranch as soon as she gets dressed. Ivy called a few minutes ago. They found her father in a glory hole up on Juniper Flats. Harold Patterson is dead."

"Heart attack?"

"No. Hit on the head with a rock. At least that's what Ivy said. The sides must have caved in on him. Ivy was hysterical on the phone. Marianne's out of the shower now. Do you want to talk to her?"

"There's no need. Tell her thanks for letting me know, and that I'm on my way, too. I'll be there as soon as I can."

Jenny came out of the shower wrapped in a towel. "Be where?" she asked.

"At the Patterson ranch. Hurry and get dressed," Joanna told her. "We'll have to leave early. I'll check with Grandma Brady to see if you can have breakfast with her."

After making hasty arrangements with Eva Lou, Joanna dialed the Sheriff's Department and asked to speak to Dispatch.

"This is Joanna Brady," she said when a youthful-sounding operator came on the phone. "I want to speak to a dispatch supervisor."

"Who did you say this is?"

"Sheriff Joanna Brady," she said firmly. "Who are you?"

"Larry. Larry Kendrick. But I thought . . ."

"What did you think?"

"Excuse me, ma'am. You just got elected the other day. How can you be sheriff already?"

"It happens, Larry, and you should have been briefed. I still need to speak to a supervisor."

"There isn't one available at the moment. She's

down the hall. Is anything wrong? Something I can help you with?''

"When did the call come in about Harold Patterson?'' Joanna asked.

"About an hour ago.''

"Who took the call?''

"Tica Romero.''

"And who called it in?''

"Let me check.'' There was a slight delay before he answered. "Ivy Patterson. I believe she's one of Harold's daughters.''

"And who responded?''

"Deputy Dave Hollicker. His car was closest to the scene at the time. As far as I know, he's still there. After Hollicker's initial survey, he called for backup. Dick Voland and Ernie Carpenter both headed out there on the double.''

Ernie Carpenter was Cochise County's lead homicide investigator, but his being called in didn't necessarily mean murder. He was usually summoned to the site of any unexplained death, where the first order of business was to determine whether the person had died of natural or unnatural causes. As acting sheriff, Dick Voland naturally would have responded as well. The problem was, Dick Voland was no longer acting sheriff. And no one had bothered to call the real one. The new one.

"I see,'' Joanna said, keeping her voice free of any trace of rancor.

It was highly possible that Tica Romero and Larry Kendrick were doing things exactly as they had been told. Joanna's swearing-in, the official changing of the guard, should have been top priority at all duty briefings as officers came on shift, but clearly few, if any, had been told. Joanna suspected that fault for that oversight lay fairly high up in the chain of command. If Joanna was going to make an issue of it, she had to make sure she was dealing with the responsible party.

"Kristin Marsten isn't in yet, is she?"

"No, ma'am. She doesn't come in until eight or so."

"Leave word with her that I'm out at the Rocking P and won't be in until later. And from now on, Larry, things are going to be different. If there's a dead body found anywhere in this county, I want to know about it. Any time of the day or night. Once you dispatch duty officers and emergency personnel to a scene, I'm to be called next. Is that clear?"

"Yes, ma'am. Absolutely."

"Good."

"And Sheriff Brady?"

"Yes?"

"Is it okay if I say congratulations?"

"It's fine."

Once off the phone, Joanna hurried into the bedroom to grab a quick shower and get ready herself. Standing under the steaming water, she felt dumb washing her hair just to go out and tramp around a crime scene, but she did it anyway. The shower was fine, but she didn't hassle with makeup. Her shiner would just have to shine.

Once again the real question was what to wear.

Did men have this problem? Certainly not in the same way women did. No matter what she wore, it made a statement one way or the other. And given that Joanna was operating in what was perceived as a male venue, she was subject to intense scrutiny every time she poked her head outside the house.

By the time she was standing in front of the closet in her underwear, Joanna had nixed the idea of either a dress or a skirt. For working in Milo's office, the choices had been relatively simple—heels, panty hose, skirts, blouses, and blazers. But none of those made sense for a glory hole on Juniper Flats.

Finally, she settled on the much-used jeans and hiking boots she had worn for target practice earlier that morning, but she passed on the shirt. Her worn plaid flannel shirt, the comfortable one with patches on both elbows, would never do. Overcoming her natural reluctance, she turned at last to Andy's end of the closet.

All through the campaign, she had put off sorting Andy's things, telling herself that painful job, along with designating possible guardians, could wait until after the election, until she felt stronger. The Ladies' Auxiliary at Canyon Methodist had started a clothing bank, and Joanna had planned to take most of Andy's clothes there.

She rummaged around on the top shelf until she located the extra Kevlar vest Andy had kept there, the one he had insisted was too small and uncomfortable to wear. As soon as she tried strapping it on over her bra, she could certainly believe the lack of comfort. Nothing about the bulletproof vest took the specifics of female anatomy into consideration. The vest was surprisingly heavy, and it chafed the skin under her arms.

For a moment, she considered not wearing it at all. But then she thought about Adam York and the wise counsel he had been kind enough to offer—lifesaving advice it didn't make sense to disregard. Joanna was sure that in Adam York's book, even an ill-fitting vest would be preferable to none at all.

With a sigh, she undid the vest and added one of Andy's undershirts to the mix before trying again. The extra layer of material did seem to help. Next she buttoned on one of Andy's khaki uniform shirts, rolling the sleeves up far enough so her hands showed beneath the cuffs. Over the breast pocket where Andy had worn his badge, Joanna pinned the one her mother had given her. Hank Lathrop's badge. Hers now.

Once the badge was in place, she paused and studied it for a moment before pulling on jeans and boots. Next she belted the holstered semi-automatic into position and was relieved to know that at least one thing she wore actually belonged to her. She finished off the outfit with Andy's heavy denim jacket—the fleece-lined one with the single .44 caliber bullet hole in the pocket. From the inside out. She herself had pulled the trigger of that pocketed gun. She had pulled it with the intent to kill and she had done exactly that.

Finally dressed, Joanna once again examined her costume in the mirror. And it *was* a costume, she decided critically. She looked like a little girl dressed up in her father's oversized clothes and about to go out trick-or-treating. The ill-fitting, pasted-together ensemble would never pass inspection with Eleanor Lathrop. For that reason alone, Joanna found herself almost liking it.

She was still standing in front of the mirror when Jenny came into the room. Except for slightly puffy eyes, all trace of her previous outburst had been seemingly scrubbed away.

Joanna spun around, giving Jenny the full effect of her outfit. "Well," she asked, "what do you think?"

Jennifer wrinkled her nose and shook her head. "Daddy's clothes are way too big for you," she said.

Joanna shrugged off her daughter's confidence-sapping comment. "Someday soon," she said, "I guess we'll have to go shopping for some clothes of my own. Are you ready to go? Did you feed and water the dogs?"

Stopping in front of the Bradys' duplex a few minutes later, Joanna shifted into Park, set the emergency brake, and got out of the car. Meanwhile, Jenny was already on her way up the brick walkway.

"Hey, wait a minute here, Jennifer Ann Brady," Joanna said severely. "Since when don't I get a hug?"

Dejected and dragging her feet, Jenny turned and came back. When Joanna hugged her, the child's head thumped solidly against the hard surface of the Kevlar vest. Andy Brady had worn a vest like that to work for as long as Jennifer remembered. Recognizing the vest for what it was as soon as she bumped against it, the child stiffened and drew away.

"Wearing one of those didn't help Daddy," she said disparagingly. With that, Jenny darted up the walkway.

Dismayed, Joanna climbed back into the idling Eagle. This wasn't at all how she had imagined her first day as sheriff of Cochise County. Rather than savoring triumph, she seemed to be losing ground at every turn. If winning could be this bad, losing must be hell.

And it didn't get any better. When Joanna reached the turnoff to the Rocking P Ranch, a Cochise County Sheriff's Department patrol car was parked sideways just inside the cattle guard, totally blocking the entrance. Marianne Maculyea's sea-foam VW Bug was stopped on the shoulder of the highway. Reverend Maculyea herself, agitated and gesturing wildly, stood arguing with an impassive deputy, one Joanna didn't instantly recognize, but from Dispatch's information she guessed this to be Deputy Hollicker.

Joanna parked behind the VW and was surprised to hear Marianne's usually calm voice rise to the level of shrill outrage. "What do you mean, no one's allowed in? Ivy Patterson called me. She specifically asked me to come! I'm her pastor. I'm sure she called because she wants help making funeral arrangements."

Hurrying to join the fray, Joanna heard the deputy's dispassionate response. "Sorry, lady. Orders are orders."

"Whose orders?" Joanna asked.

Together, both Marianne and the deputy turned toward Joanna. She had known Marianne Maculyea for years without ever seeing the woman this angry. Two vivid red splotches colored her cheeks, while her dark eyes crackled with emotion.

"He says no one's allowed up at the house," Marianne complained. "Can you believe it?"

The deputy's glance took in Joanna's appearance in one quick appraisal before settling warily on her holstered Colt, the nose of which peeked out from under the hem of her jacket.

"Who are you?" he demanded. "What are you doing here?"

They eyed one another, giving Joanna a chance to verify the name.

"Does the name Joanna Brady ring a bell, Deputy Hollicker?" she asked, pulling aside the jacket enough so the badge showed. "The last time I heard, someone told me I was the new sheriff in this jurisdiction."

Hollicker's jaw dropped. "Oh, yes," he said, relaxing his stance. "I believe something about that just came over the radio."

Joanna smiled, but without humor. "I wouldn't be surprised. Now, what's this about orders?"

"They came straight from Dick Voland, the chief deputy. He said not to allow anyone at all past this gate."

"I see," Joanna said. "Under the circumstances, it's a perfectly understandable order, but for now

I'm countermanding it. Please move your vehicle aside so Reverend Maculyea and I can drive through. You're more than welcome to keep everyone else out after that."

"Okay," Deputy Hollicker said uncertainly, moving at once to comply. "Sure thing."

Marianne and Joanna started back toward their respective vehicles. Reverend Maculyea was still steaming. "What's the matter with that guy? He sounded as though your being sheriff was a total surprise to him, like he just found out about you a few minutes ago."

"It did sound that way," Joanna agreed. "I may be the sheriff, but someone seems to be trying to keep that fact a secret."

"You mean if they don't see you, maybe you'll go away?"

"Nice try, but no time," Joanna answered grimly in time-honored rodeo lingo. "They'll have to do better than that."

Dave Hollicker started up his Ford Taurus patrol car and drove it out of the way long enough for Joanna and Marianne to cross the cattle guard; then he moved it back into its original position, once more blocking the gate.

Marianne continued on up the road toward the Rocking P's ranch house, but Joanna stopped the car and went back to the Taurus, where Dave Hollicker was speaking animatedly into his handheld microphone. When he saw Joanna peering in the window at him, he hurriedly switched off the microphone and rolled down his window.

"Did you need something else?" he asked.

"Yes. Where is this glory hole? How do I get there?"

"Chief Voland said for you to wait right here. He'll come down and get you."

"Deputy Hollicker, I don't believe you understood what I said to you back there. I'm issuing orders, not taking them. And I have no intention of standing here waiting for *Deputy* Voland to come get me. Is that clear?"

Even as she said it, Joanna realized it wasn't fair to put Dave Hollicker in the middle of a power play between Dick Voland and herself, but something definitive had to happen to get the chief deputy's attention.

Hollicker waffled only a few seconds longer before making up his mind. "Drive just like you're going to the house," he directed. "When you reach the corrals, instead of turning in, go straight on past. About a half-mile farther on, you'll come to a gate. Go through that, then take the left-hand fork. Whenever you can after that, bear left. It's three miles, give or take."

"Thank you." Joanna turned and started back toward her Eagle.

"It's a pretty rough road," he called after her. "That's why Chief Deputy Voland wanted you to wait here. He said he'd come get you in his Blazer."

"Radio back and tell him not to bother," Joanna said over her shoulder. "My four-wheel-drive Eagle can make it anywhere Dick Voland's Blazer can."

"Oh," Dave Hollicker mumbled into the cloud of dust that billowed in her wake. "I'll be sure to tell him that. He'll love hearing it. And then he'll chew my ass."

Twenty-One

EVEN WITHOUT directions, Joanna would have had
no trouble finding her way. Much of the road was
over coarse, trackless shale, but here and there—
in still-muddy low spots or in patches of dry,
dusty dirt—a collection of freshly laid tire indenta-
tions left their separate marks. Wherever visible
tracks remained in the roadway, Joanna was careful to drive around them.

She followed the ever-narrowing trail, through a
scrub-oak-dotted landscape toward the rockbound
red cliffs that crowned the mountain. As she drove
through the ranch where Harold Patterson had
lived all his life, Joanna allowed herself a moment
of private grief. She hadn't thought about that part
of the job, about investigating the death of someone she knew and cared for. But Cochise County
was a relatively small community. Some of the
people whose deaths came under investigation
were bound to be acquaintances if not friends.

Looking around her, she hoped Jim Bob was
right; that Harold had "died with his boots on,"
doing the work he loved. But there was something
worrisome in the back of her mind, a stray thought

that wouldn't disappear no matter how much she wanted to stifle it.

The last time Joanna had seen Harold Patterson was two days ago, when he came to Milo's office. He had seemed anxious and upset when he came looking for those change-of-beneficiary forms. He had talked about wanting to change the provisions of his policies from Ivy alone to someone else. Those are the kinds of changes people don't undertake without some reason prodding them to do so—a marriage, a death, or, in this case, what seemed to be a change of heart.

Taken together, Harold Patterson's policies didn't add up to a huge fortune, but a cool quarter of a million dollars—or even half that much—couldn't be overlooked as a possible motive for murder. *If* Harold Patterson had, in fact, been murdered.

Joanna racked her brain trying to remember the old man's exact words. He had told her a story, a parable about his daughters, comparing them to two dogs pulling apart an old saddle blanket rather than sharing it. Did that mean Harold intended to split the proceeds of his policies fifty-fifty? It would be important for the investigators to learn whether or not those beneficiary forms had been properly signed and witnessed and where they were right now.

A single phone call to Milo Davis or Lisa would have answered that question in a minute, but Joanna was in her own car, with no radio and no kind of communications capability. How long would it take, Joanna wondered, for the new sheriff to have an official, properly equipped vehicle of her own? And how did she go about requesting one?

Deputy Hollicker had told her three miles. Dick Voland's Blazer blocked the path at 2.5 in a spot where the road wound between two immense boulders. When Voland stepped up to the side of her car, he leaned down as if expecting her to roll down the window so he could speak to her. Instead, she turned off the ignition, opened the door, and stepped out of the car.

"What's going on here?" she demanded.

Voland shrugged and glowered meaningfully at Joanna's Eagle. "Nothing much," he replied sarcastically. "Ernie Carpenter asked me to limit access to the area until he can have casts made of all the tire tracks. As you can see, we've been driving on the hump in the middle of the road and on the shoulder to avoid messing up anything important."

"So have I," she answered crisply. "I do know how plaster casts work."

A shadow of disappointment crossed Dick Voland's face so fleetingly that Joanna almost missed it. Clearly the chief deputy had fully expected her to screw up her first time out, but she had managed to outmaneuver him. So much for Round One.

"Why wasn't I notified when Harold Patterson's body was found?" she asked, taking the offensive. "Why wasn't I called?"

"The man was already dead," Voland answered. "Deputy Hollicker, Detective Carpenter, and I had the situation well in hand through the regular chain of command."

"Mr. Voland, are you or are you not aware that I was sworn into office as of two o'clock yesterday afternoon?"

"I knew about that," he answered reluctantly, "but I saw no reason to drag you out of bed. It didn't seem like that big a deal."

"For your information, I was already up and working at the time the call came in. I haven't yet had time enough to study all the policies and procedures, but tell me something. How would a situation like this have been handled under Walter McFadden's administration? Chain of command be damned, would he or would he not have been notified?"

"Would have," Voland conceded grudgingly. "Out of courtesy."

"Then I expect the same courtesy."

"But surely . . ." Voland started, then stopped abruptly.

"But surely what?"

"You don't want to be called and dragged out of bed to every crime scene?"

"I didn't run for office to be nothing but a glorified bureaucrat," Joanna told him. "Did you think I broke my neck the last two months for the dubious privilege of overseeing departmental budgets and vacation schedules? I'm here to be a full-fledged officer of the law. Possibly my presence won't be necessary at every unlawful death scene in the county, but for right now I intend to make up my mind on a case-by-case basis. Do I make myself clear?"

"Perfectly." Voland's reply was curt and sullen. "Is there anything else?"

"I came to see the glory hole," Joanna said.

The chief deputy spun on his heel and started back up the mountain. "This way," he grunted. "We walk from here. Stick to the shoulder."

"So what's the status?"

"Ernie's about finished with what he can do up top. He's rigging a rope to the come-along on his winch so we can lower him down into the hole itself. He wants to take pictures and gather evidence before calling in a stretcher and sling to drag Old Man Patterson's body out."

"What happened?"

"You'll have to talk to Ernie. He's not big on talking about what he's finding. He's his own one-man show."

"Who found the body?"

"Ivy, I guess."

"How'd she do it? This is a long way from the house."

"Like I said," Dick Voland groused. "Talk to Ernie."

At five-thousand-some-odd feet of elevation, the steep path soon took its toll on Richard Voland's more-than-ample frame. Exertion made it difficult for the chief deputy to walk and talk at the same time, and Joanna soon regretted her own double layers of clothing. Removing her jacket, she slung it over her shoulder as she trudged along behind him on the rocky verge of the road.

TOMBSTONE COURAGE

They crested the top of a steep rise and entered a small basin. A fenced-off area in the middle surrounded the glory hole's mound of tailings. Parked nearby was Ernie Carpenter's crew-cab pickup and Harold Patterson's much-used International Scout. Off to one side was a vintage decommissioned fire truck—a pumper—semipermanently positioned next to a metal stock tank. A length of hose led from a spigot on the truck's tank to the one on the ground. Joanna surmised the truck was used to haul water to thirsty stock in the Rocking P's upper pastures whenever necessary. From the desiccated cow pies littering the area, Joanna knew this section of pasture wasn't currently in use.

Seated on the running board of the old truck was the red-haired, red-bearded giant Joanna recognized as Yuri Malakov. Two weeks earlier, he had come to church with Ivy. Joanna had seen him and assumed from things Marianne had told her that's who the huge stranger had to be. But that Sunday had been right toward the end of the campaign. Instead of staying for after-church coffee and socializing, Joanna had rushed off to give a speech in Double Adobe.

Seeing him at first glance when they topped the rise, Joanna assumed the Russian was wearing a blue work shirt. As she came closer, however, she realized he was naked from the waist up. What she had thought to be blue cloth was actually ink. Above a wide silver-and-turquoise belt buckle, Yuri's massive chest was covered by a wild assortment of tattoos.

He was leaning against the side of the truck with his eyes closed, dozing. Joanna had never seen such a display of tattoo art. For several long moments, she studied the amazingly detailed patterns that had been inked into his skin.

Most of the pictures were surprisingly well crafted and artistically done, but the subject matter was anything but Russian. The picture covering most of the man's chest showed a complicated bucking bronco complete with cowboy flailing a Stetson. Beneath that tattoo, lettered in English, was the caption COWBOY SAM.

Two distinct versions of coiled rattlesnakes were inked onto the bunched muscles of his biceps. One forearm featured a hangman's noose, while the other pictured a single long-stemmed rose. Beneath the rose were the letters "Yellow Rose of Texas."

Despite brilliant blue skies, native Arizonans still regard November as winter. For them, it's no time to be lounging out in the sun, soaking up rays, but Yuri Malakov came from another climate entirely. What his new neighbors experienced as cold, he considered balmy.

Although Joanna was unaware of making a sound, Yuri's eyes suddenly blinked open. As soon as he saw her standing a few feet away, he grabbed for his shirt and hurriedly pulled it on, scrambling to his feet and blushing in confusion.

"So sorry," he mumbled, in his severely broken English, clumsily fastening buttons as fast as he could. "So very sorry. I did not think woman would be here. Please excuse."

"It's all right, Yuri. They say Ivy is the one who found Mr. Patterson?"

"No. Yes. But she tell me to come here to look while she stays at ranch, at house. Later she ask me to bring police here."

"She knew where to look without actually coming here?" Joanna asked. "How did she do that?"

"Those," he said, jerking his head skyward. "She say go follow those birds. There also we find father."

Joanna glanced in the direction indicated. Far overhead, three huge buzzards, harbingers of death, circled the mountaintop in long, lazy circles. But they might just as easily have been circling over a road-killed rabbit or coyote rather than over the body of Ivy Patterson's father.

"What time did you call in the report?"

Yuri shrugged. "Early," he said. "Five or maybe four."

"Early-bird buzzards," Joanna said. "They must have been out looking for worms."

Yuri looked at her with a puzzled frown. "Excuse?" he asked.

Joanna shook her head. "It's nothing," she said. "An old joke."

The hair prickled warningly on the back of Joanna's neck. There was no reason to tell Yuri Malakov that she knew either he was lying or else Ivy was. Even if the vultures had been up and circling overhead that early in the morning, they wouldn't have been visible in the dark, not to someone three miles away, down in a valley.

Joanna glanced toward the glory hole. While Joanna and Yuri had been talking, she had watched while Dick Voland used a winch and leather harness to lower Ernie down into the hole. Now, with Ernie back on the surface, the two men were earnestly conferring in tones hushed enough that none of the words carried as far as the fire truck.

"Wait here," Joanna said to Yuri. She walked to the glory-hole fence, eased her way through the strands of barbed wire, and joined the two men on the little mound of rock-chip tailings. "What's going on?" she asked.

"We've got a problem," Ernie said slowly.

"Accident or not?" Joanna asked, abandoning all hope that Harold Patterson had died of natural causes.

"It's no accident," Ernie said firmly. "And no cave-in, either. Somebody bashed his skull in with a five-pound river rock."

"River rock?" Joanna repeated, looking around at the shards of brick-red shale that littered the basin. "There's no river rock around here."

"That's right. The closest place to get it would be the last crossing of Mule Mountain Creek at least half a mile away," Ernie answered. "But that's not the major problem."

"What is?"

"Come look," he said.

Together, the three of them walked to the edge of the glory hole and looked down. The ugly stench of not-yet-disinfected death wicked up from the hole into Joanna's face. The odor that had attracted vultures from miles around sickened her, causing a bubble of nausea to rise in her throat. She held her breath to contain it.

"Here," Ernie said, taking out a flashlight and handing it to her. "Use this."

Fighting back nausea and battling dizziness as well, Joanna moved forward and aimed the flashlight into the pitch-black hole. It was some time before her eyes adjusted to the gloom; before she could see anything at all in the glow of that frail artificial light.

At last, though, the pale yellow beam illuminated something—Harold Patterson's open, blankly staring eyes.

"What about it?" Joanna asked, still not sure what she was supposed to be seeing.

"Look under his shoulder," Ernie Carpenter said. "Under his right shoulder."

By now Joanna could see well enough that she noticed river rocks scattered here and there on the floor of the hole. At first the white bulge sticking out from under Harold Patterson's shoulder seemed like one of the same.

"It's just another rock, isn't it?" she asked, keeping her voice controlled and steady.

"I wish it were," Ernie Carpenter said softly. "I wish to God it were. It's a skull, Sheriff Brady. A human skull. It looks as though the rest of the skeleton is under Harold. It's somebody who's been down in that hole a hell of a lot longer than Harold Patterson has."

"But who?" Joanna asked.

"I guess we'll just have to find out, now, won't we?" Dick Voland said.

Joanna could have been mistaken, but it seemed as though the chief deputy was smiling to himself when he said it. But the meaningful look that passed between the two men required no interpretation.

Federal EEOC guidelines notwithstanding, both Ernie Carpenter and Dick Voland regarded crime-scene investigation as an all-male preserve. They had expected Dave Hollicker's roadblock to function as a No-Girls-Allowed notice, but she had ignored the warning.

It would have been easy for Joanna to take the easy way out. For her to stagger away, grope her way over to the fire truck, collapse on the running board, and wait for her head to stop swimming. Instead, steeling herself against the fainthearted impulse, she stayed where she was and kept her eyes focused full on Harold Patterson's face.

"Yes, *we* will," she said softly, underscoring the word "we." "Now how about telling me exactly how you propose to go about it?"

Twenty-Two

JOANNA WALKED back to where Yuri Malakov was sitting on the running board of the decommissioned fire truck. He moved aside far enough to make room for her. Sinking down beside him, she wiped her clammy forehead with the sleeve of her jacket and closed her eyes, trying to shut out the memory of Harold Patterson's eerily blank eyes. She wanted to forget how they had caught the glow of Ernie Carpenter's flashlight and stared dully back up at her through the darkness.

Yuri glanced at Joanna with some sympathy, and he seemed in tune with her reaction. "Is bad thing," he muttered. "Very bad thing."

Joanna studied his broad face. Thick eyebrows hunched over heavily lidded eyes. Although from a distance he had appeared to be relaxed and snoozing, she realized now that his carefully hooded eyes were observing everything about him with intense interest.

Ernie Carpenter, leaving the glory hole for the moment, carted a cumbersome suitcase of equipment from his traveling crime-lab van to a newly dried puddle in the road. There, on hands and knees, he was attempting to make plaster casts of the tire tracks left in crusted mud. Meanwhile, Dick Voland stood beside Ernie's van, speaking into the radio microphone and gesturing with his other hand.

"Detective Voland is trying to locate a sump pump," Joanna explained.

"A what?"

"An emergency pump and a generator to run it. They need to empty the water out of the bottom of the hole before they attempt to bring up either body, Patterson or the other one."

Suddenly, Yuri Malakov was no longer lounging against the side of the truck. He loomed over Voland and Joanna, dwarfing them both. "Two peoples?" he demanded, his smoldering dark eyes boring into Joanna's. "More than one? More than Mr. Patterson?"

Joanna realized at once that she had blundered and spoken out of turn. That kind of information about an ongoing investigation shouldn't have been casually mentioned to a passing acquaintance who happened to appear at the crime scene. But it was too late to take it back, and there didn't seem to be any justification in lying about it.

She nodded. "Detective Carpenter seems to have found another body, a skeleton, under Harold Patterson. He had fallen directly on top of it."

"Who?" Yuri asked.

"We don't know that," Joanna answered. "The other victim has been dead for a long time—years, most likely. Until they can search the glory hole for evidence, there's no way to tell."

Yuri Malakov lurched to his feet. "Ivy must know about this," he declared.

"No," Joanna objected. "That kind of news should come from one of the investigating officers, from someone official."

Yuri shook his shaggy head impatiently. "Investigators busy. I am not busy. I tell her."

With that, Yuri stomped away toward the Scout, leaving Joanna no choice but to trail along after him. He was a huge man. The idea of her physically restraining someone his size was laughable. Joanna glanced back toward Dick Voland, who was still talking on the radio. He would be of no help. Besides, she didn't want to tell him about this. She didn't want to admit to blabbing out of turn.

"Wait," Joanna said. "If you'll give me a ride back down to my car, I'll come with you and tell Ivy myself."

Yuri stopped next to the Scout with one hand possessively on the door latch. "Okay," he agreed readily. "I drive. You tell."

As they maneuvered past the spot in the road where Ernie Carpenter was working on the plaster casts, Joanna directed Yuri to stop. "I need to tell Detective Carpenter where I'm going."

As if that was necessary, she thought afterward. Ernie barely glanced up when she spoke to him, acknowledging their departure with an inattentive frown. By then the homicide detective was totally focused on the solitary pursuit of obtaining evidence. Anything that removed distracting onlookers was to be regarded as a help, not a hindrance.

"That's fine," he said, waving them away. "Tell the people down at the house to stay out of Harold's room. That goes for everyone there. Tell them to leave it alone until I have a chance to go through it."

"Right," Joanna said. "I'll tell them."

At the point in the road where Dick Voland's Blazer still blocked the way, they had to abandon the Scout in favor of Joanna's Eagle. The hulking Russian had to scrunch his broad shoulders and duck his head in order to cram himself into the passenger's seat, but he did so without complaint.

While Joanna drove, he sat with his arms folded stubbornly across his massive chest, frowning and looking straight ahead, saying nothing. She looked at him from time to time and tried to decipher the troubled expression on his face.

She was surprised at the complete change in Yuri Malakov's demeanor. His appearance now was a complete 180 degrees from the way he had looked earlier, sitting relaxed and supposedly dozing on the running board of the pumper. And the change had been instantaneous rather than gradual. It happened the moment she had mentioned existence of that second body. The news had seemed to distress him in a way that went far beyond his supposedly slight connection to the Patterson clan and their troubles.

"What's the matter?" Joanna asked. "Is something bothering you?"

Yuri glanced at her suspiciously. "What means 'bother'?"

"Bother is like worry," Joanna explained. "Is something worrying you?"

"Nyet," he answered. "Nothing."

But Yuri Malakov, silent and brooding, certainly didn't look worry-free.

Thinking about his situation, Joanna realized it had to be dismaying to be thrown into a crisis—especially a crisis involving a murder investigation—in a place where the entire legal system was completely foreign. Not only that, he was having to sort through all the strange customs through a veil of stilted, inflexible classroom English.

Joanna's own four years of classroom Spanish—two in high school and two in college—had been difficult enough and barely qualified her to speak "menu Spanish" in unfamiliar Stateside Mexican restaurants. Had she been foolish enough to head for Spain or the interior of Mexico with only that rudimentary background, she could probably survive—order food and make her most basic needs known—but she had no illusions about her ability to communicate or to be understood. Complex ideas would have been far beyond her.

But here was Yuri Malakov, a grown man able to communicate only basic messages. No doubt he had taken a good deal of classroom instruction in English years earlier—his formal, nonidiomatic way of speaking indicated as much. But still, it had to be terribly difficult to be living and coping with complex day-to-day issues in a foreign country where virtually no one other than perhaps a few second-generation Slavic miners spoke some version of his native tongue.

As someone who had lived in one small Arizona town all her life, Joanna found the very idea of Yuri Malakov fascinating. What would drive a man to turn his back on everything familiar? To leave behind all family and friends? What kind of work had he done before coming here, and what career path had he abandoned in order to work as a hired hand for strangers on an isolated Arizona ranch? And what would possess a man, somewhere in his mid-forties, to set himself the task of grasping the intricacies of a whole new culture?

Maybe that was it, Joanna theorized. Perhaps Yuri's concern for Ivy Patterson was based primarily on her helping him make that difficult transition; gratitude for the invaluable role she was playing in his life as his English-language tutor. For a few moments, Joanna considered asking him, but then she let the idea go. He sat staring out the window, effectively shutting out any more questions. Besides, it didn't seem worthwhile to fight her way through the difficulties of the communication barrier in order to discuss something as esoteric as motivation. Instead, they rode the rest of the way to the Rocking P ranch house in silence.

As they entered the yard, the place looked positively idyllic. With a plume of inviting smoke curling out the chimney, the house and surrounding ranch seemed an improbable setting for two unexplained deaths. Several loose chickens scratched lazily in the dirt, and a fully adorned watchdog peacock strutted his stuff in the clear November sunlight. Marianne's VW was still parked beside the gate, as was Ivy Patterson's Chevy Luv.

The ranch house was surrounded by a white picket fence that set off the yard proper with its blanket of winter-yellowed Bermuda grass from the rest of the grounds. The house was an early-twentieth-century period piece—a single story of living space topped by a steeply pitched tin roof. The metal roof shone with a coat of freshly applied paint as did the wooden siding, shutters, and trim. Everything about the place looked neat and properly maintained.

A wide covered porch ran the entire length of each outside wall, creating a good eight feet of extra overhang and shade to help cool the house's interior from Arizona's scorching summer heat. Although the porch had to be close to ninety years old, none of the flooring sagged. Not a single spindly rail was missing or broken from the long span of banister. If some pieces of woodwork were no longer original, it didn't show. They had been replaced and repaired so carefully that it was impossible to tell old millwork from new.

Two massive wisteria vines, thick-trunked with age, stood guard on either side of the front entrance, sending out a tangle of naked gray branches that clung tenaciously along the front lip and gutters of the overhang. In the spring, the porch would be all but obscured by a curtain of lush greenery and cascading lavender flowers.

Joanna was quick to note that the grounds of the Rocking P were surprisingly clear of junk. The outbuildings were all fully upright and freshly painted. No hulks of dead cars or rusting farm equipment had been left to crumble within sight of the house. Joanna's High Lonesome suffered terribly in comparison.

The wheels on the Eagle had not yet come to a complete stop before Yuri Malakov had the door open. He would have leaped out and been long gone if Joanna hadn't stopped him. "Let me tell her," she said. "It'll be better if I do it."

Yuri glowered at her, but he subsided in the seat. "You do it then," he said.

As if on cue, the front door of the house opened. Ivy Patterson and Marianne Maculyea appeared on the porch together. Not surprisingly, Ivy's usually cheerful face was shrouded in grief, but even Marianne's features were frozen in an atypically grim mask.

Joanna opened the gate and started up the walkway. To her surprise, Ivy left Marianne on the porch and came running forward. Instead of stopping when she reached Joanna, Ivy darted past and threw herself sobbing against Yuri Malakov's massive chest. He reached down, folded her in his arms, and touched his chin to her hair.

Yuri clicked his tongue soothingly. "Is okay. Yuri is here."

That small series of loving gestures turned all of Joanna's previous conjecture on its ear. Yuri and Ivy might have known each other for only a matter of weeks, but clearly they meant far more to one another than simple teacher and pupil. They were in love. Even the desolation of her grief didn't entirely obscure the glow on Ivy's face as she abandoned herself to the comfort of Yuri's encircling arms.

Joanna cleared her throat. "Excuse me, Ivy, but I need to talk to you. There's something you need to know."

Instead of looking at Joanna, Ivy stared up at Yuri's stolid face, as if whatever she needed to know would be clearly written on his broad features. He shook his head. "She tells," he said, nodding in Joanna's direction.

"Tell me what?" Ivy asked. "What's wrong now?"

This was Joanna's first experience at delivering bad news in some kind of official capacity. Like a child thrust suddenly into the spotlight of a Sunday-school Christmas pageant, she was instantly out of her depth, stymied about what to say or where to begin.

"Maybe we should go inside and sit down," she suggested lamely.

Glaring at her but holding tightly to Ivy's hand, Yuri strode up onto the porch and inside the house. "What about me?" Marianne asked, as Joanna started by.

"Come ahead if you want to," Joanna said.

By the time Joanna and Marianne entered the living room, Ivy and Yuri were already seated side by side on an old-fashioned, faded leather couch. They sat close to one another, with Yuri's long arm sprawled intimately across Ivy's shoulder. A good-sized woman in her own right, Ivy Patterson seemed dwarfed and diminutive beside the hulking Russian. The fiercely protective look on his face was out of place—unless he and Ivy knew more about how Harold Patterson had come to be in the glory hole than Yuri had so far admitted.

But still, Joanna's first order of business was to inform Ivy of the presence of that second body. The cozy fireplace-warmed living room now seemed as bad a place to deliver that kind of news as the front porch had moments earlier.

"What is it?" Ivy asked.

Feeling every bit the unwelcome interloper, Joanna stumbled her way into a chair. For a few moments, she almost wished she were a man, wearing the lawman's stereotypical Stetson. At least that way she would have had something to take off and put in her lap, some tangible object to use as a physical buffer between Ivy Patterson's already significant pain and the news Joanna was about to add to it.

"I'm so sorry about your father," she began haltingly. "Harold Patterson was a wonderful man, and he's going to be greatly missed."

Ivy Patterson nodded. Tears threatened, but she held them in check. "Thank you," she murmured.

"As you know, Yuri and I have just come down from up on the mountain," Joanna continued. "From up at the glory hole. Did he have a chance to tell about what's going on up there?"

"Just that they wouldn't let him bring Dad's Scout back down the mountain."

Joanna nodded. "There's a roadblock near the top, and the Scout is stuck on the wrong side of it."

Ivy shrugged. "That doesn't matter. I suppose we can go up later and get it back. That's how we brought it home from the convention center yesterday. Is that what you came to tell me?"

"No," Joanna said. "There's something else." She paused for a moment, searching for the right words. "I was up there with Dick Voland and Ernie Carpenter, the homicide investigator."

"Homicide," Ivy repeated. "As in murder? You mean my dad didn't just fall in? It wasn't an accident?"

"No," Joanna said. "I'm afraid it doesn't look like accident. In the meantime, that's not all. There's something else you need to know."

"What else?" Ivy demanded impatiently, sitting forward on the couch. "What more could there be?"

Joanna took a deep breath. "Your father's isn't the only body down in that hole, Ivy," she said. "Ernie Carpenter found a human skeleton down there with him, someone who's been in the glory hole for a very long time. For years."

Ivy Patterson's eyes grew wide with shock. Her hand flew to her mouth. "Oh, my God!" she exclaimed. "It's true then!"

"What's true?" Joanna asked.

Suddenly, a fresh torrent of tears coursed down Ivy Patterson's cheeks. All color drained from her cheeks. She buried her face in her hands; while her whole body convulsed with sobs. For a moment, there was no sound in the room except Ivy's desperate weeping and the crackles and pops from the mesquite log fire. No one else had anything to say.

Eventually, Ivy drew herself erect, but the look

on her face was far more dismayed than grief-stricken. "Mother always said there was a body in that hole," she said softly. "She always said so, and I never believed her."

Joanna felt her own jolt of shock. "You mean to say your mother knew something about this?"

Ivy nodded. "I'm sure of it."

"What about your father?"

A strange look washed over Ivy's face. Her flesh seemed to harden. Her jawline froze with visible anger. "That son of a bitch," she murmured. "That rotten, low-down son of a bitch. He must have known it was true the whole time."

"Who must have known what was true?" Joanna asked, confused by the sudden shift in Ivy Patterson's demeanor.

"My father. That there was a body. When Mother told me that, he insisted she was crazy. Every time she brought it up, he claimed she was talking out of her head. That was about the time he started having someone watch her constantly—every minute, day and night. He said that if she was capable of making up such bizarre stories and of getting people to believe her, we'd have to be careful or they'd haul her away to Phoenix and lock her up in the state hospital."

"Wait a minute," Marianne said. "If your mother was telling the truth, if the body was really there the whole time, then maybe she wasn't so crazy after all."

"That's right, maybe she wasn't," Ivy added grimly, with a ferocity that was chilling to hear. "At least not at first, but she was later. And why not? Dad started locking her in her room at night. He stopped trusting her, and she went downhill fast. Before long, he wouldn't even let her out of his sight. Or mine. She did go crazy then, and maybe it happened because he drove her to it. Damn him anyway! How could he do that to her? How could he?''

Ivy collapsed against Yuri's shoulder, her whole body convulsed by a new paroxysm of broken-hearted sobs.

Sitting there, Joanna sensed something odd. Before Ivy Patterson had learned about the second body, her reaction to her father's death had been completely appropriate and understandable. But this new storm of tears was something else.

The woman weeping inconsolably on Yuri Malakov's massive shoulder wasn't simply Harold Patterson's grieving daughter. She was instead the betrayed child of a betrayed mother, a child who now—perhaps for the first time—finally was forced into seeing her once-trusted father through new eyes. Joanna's revelation had coerced Ivy into holding Harold responsible for any number of past sins—either real or imagined.

And Ivy's betrayal, her profound distress, clearly stemmed from the fact that two bodies had been found in the glory hole up on Juniper Flats. Two bodies, not one.

But there's far more to it than that, Joanna thought uneasily, as she waited for Ivy Patterson's spate of wild tears to subside.

If Harold Patterson had betrayed his own wife and daughter, if he had somehow tricked them into believing he was something he wasn't, then what had he done to the rest of the world?

After all, a man capable of deceiving his family was more than smart enough to trick a mere insurance agent.

Or a brand-new sheriff.

Twenty-Three

WITH SOME effort, Ivy pulled herself together and leveled her gaze on Marianne. "That settles it then," she said. "I've changed my mind. I want to go through with it after all, just the way I talked about in the first place."

"But, Ivy . . ." Marianne protested.

"No," Ivy interrupted forcefully, "I've had it. I'm not going to change my mind again. I've spent my whole life looking out for everybody else. I'm not going to do that anymore."

At that juncture, the front door slammed open, and Burton Kimball rushed uninvited into the room. "Is it true?" he demanded. "Did they find him? Is he dead?"

Beyond tears, Ivy's eyes suddenly glimmered with cold fury. "He's dead all right," she said.

Burton Kimball closed his eyes and shook his head. "Ivy," he said, "I'm so sorry. But these things happen. It'll be all right. You'll see."

"It is not all right!" Ivy insisted. "It'll never be all right. Don't you understand? Dad lied to me."

A stricken look washed across Burton Kimball's face. "If it's about the will, Ivy, there shouldn't be any problem. He said he was going to change it, he may have wanted to change it, but I wouldn't do it for him. Not the day he asked about it. And I doubt he found anyone else to do it on such short notice. You should still end up with the ranch. That's the way we set it up originally. And even if Holly were to attempt to go against the will or try to continue the lawsuit against his estate, I don't see how she'd win."

"I'm not talking about Dad's will," Ivy cut in icily. "It's worse than that. Way worse. Mother was right all along, Burtie. About the glory hole. They just found another body in it."

Dismayed, Burton Kimball stopped short. "What do you mean, another body?"

"Just what I said. Somebody else is dead and down in the glory hole with Dad," she answered.

Stricken, Burton Kimball staggered toward a chair. "How can that be? It's crazy."

"That's what Dad always told Mother, too—that it wasn't possible for a body to be down there, that she was crazy for saying so, remember? Dad used us, Burtie," she added bitterly. "He used us both, to spy on her and keep her in line, when the whole time she was telling the truth. It must have been true all along."

With every word, Ivy's voice had risen both in pitch and outrage. Yuri soothingly rubbed her upper arm. "Be still," he murmured. "Do not be so upset."

Ivy burrowed under Yuri's arm not so much like a lost wild thing seeking the warmth of its nest, but more like an angry wounded bear retreating to her cave. As she rested against him, Burton shot

Yuri Malakov a single scathing and questioning glance, but his full attention soon settled back on Ivy.

"Who is this other body?" he asked. "Does anyone know?"

"There's no way to tell who it is until we can raise it out of the hole," Joanna said. "From the looks of it, it's not so much a body as it is a skeleton. It's been down there a long time."

"Do you hear that, Burtie?" Ivy demanded. "Don't you remember? Mother made us both promise never to go near that place. She even made me swear that, on the family Bible."

Burton Kimball nodded. "Until after your father was dead," he added. "I do remember that much. At the time, I thought it was just more of her ranting and raving. In fact, it was one of the things that helped convince me Uncle Harold was right, that Aunt Emily was really completely around the bend. She would go on and on about that glory hole for hours on end, insisting it would be the death of your father someday."

"She was right," Ivy Patterson said shortly. "Now it is."

She took a deep breath. "I kept my promise to her," Ivy added. "I stayed away right up until last night."

Yuri pulled Ivy close in what seemed a warning for her to drop the subject, but Joanna had already caught the small discrepancy in their story.

"You went up there last night?" she asked, glancing meaningfully at Yuri Malakov, wanting him to understand that she knew he had lied to her earlier about the way he had found the body. "So the part about seeing the buzzards wasn't true?"

"It's true," Ivy said. "I saw them late yesterday afternoon, just as the search party was giving up and shutting down for the night. I wanted to go see for myself. I went up and checked as soon as I could."

"You're saying you found him yesterday afternoon then?"

Ivy nodded. "Just before sundown."

"But you didn't report it until this morning. Why not?"

"Because I didn't feel like it. There was something I had to do first," Ivy Patterson answered. "Something important."

"What?"

Ivy's hand sought the top of Yuri Malakov's knee and rested there lightly. As she answered the question, though, her eyes were defiant and focused full on Joanna's face.

"Yuri and I spent the night on an air mattress in the back of the Scout. It wasn't very romantic, but it was okay."

"You did what?" Burton exploded.

Ivy looked at him. "You heard me."

"But why on earth would you pull a crazy stunt like that?"

"To prove I could," she said defiantly. "Because I wanted to. And why not? Dad turned against me, and don't try to tell me he didn't. In my book, turnabout is fair play. I did it to get even. I did it to prove a point. I did it because it was the closest

I could come to dancing on my father's grave. Mother's grave is next to his down at Evergreen Cemetery. I couldn't do it there."

Burton Kimball was clearly thunderstruck.

"You mean to tell me, you and this ... this ... jerk"—he finally spit out the word with a heartfelt glare in Yuri's direction—"spent the night together next to a glory hole with your father's body in it, and you didn't even bother to report it until this morning? What kind of craziness is that, Ivy? What in the world's gotten into you?"

"You think it's crazy, do you? Well, maybe it is. Maybe craziness runs in our family. I think I finally just got sick and tired of being the good girl, of doing my duty and getting shit on for it, of having other people tell me what to do."

Burton Kimball held up both his hands as though trying to see through the blaze of Ivy's anger to some kind of reasonableness. "Wait a minute here," he said. "Let's try to think straight for a change. This is a tough time for all of us, Ivy. I only came by because I heard from Marliss Shackleford up at the *Bisbee Bee* that something was up. I came to see if there was anything at all Linda and I could do to help.

"Do you want me to call Norm Higgins for you? I could start working on funeral arrangements, calling relatives, that sort of thing. What exactly do you need? I guess the first thing is to find out when the body will be released and go from there." He looked at Joanna. "Any idea, Sheriff Brady?"

"That's entirely up to Ernie Carpenter," Joanna

answered. "He's the one handling the investigation. He'll be the one making that call."

"How soon can I check with him?"

"Maybe later this afternoon."

Burton turned back to Ivy. "Would you like me to call Norm then and see if he can come out here for a consultation? Maybe later on this evening—say, around eight o'clock."

"No," Ivy Patterson said decisively, answering her cousin but with her eyes focused on Marianne Maculyea's face. "Not tonight. I'm busy tonight. Yuri and I are getting married. At seven o'clock."

Kimball's jaw dropped. "You're doing what?"

"Getting married. In the Canyon Methodist parsonage, at seven o'clock."

Burton looked at Marianne Maculyea. "Surely, this is some kind of joke," he asked helplessly.

Marianne shook her head. "It's no joke. I spent all morning trying to talk her out of it, but she changed her mind back to going ahead with it just a few minutes ago."

"But with your father not even . . ."

"Don't tell me one more word about my father," Ivy Patterson warned. "I don't want to hear any more. You already told me enough, the other day."

"Ivy, I've already told you how sorry I am about that. I was drunk and way out of line. Shooting off my mouth like that was a terrible breach of ethics. I never should have mentioned a word about it."

"But the point is, you did. I figured if Dad was going to give away half of what I'd worked for, then I wasn't going to wait around any longer. Yuri and I started making plans right then. That very day. On such short notice, we haven't found anyone to come look after the stock, so we're going to spend the night in Tombstone. The motel will probably have a banner over the door—Welcome Old Maids of America. Besides, you don't need me to talk to Norm Higgins. You can do it yourself, or Holly can."

"But, Ivy," Burton argued. "Getting married like this isn't right. It's not . . . seemly. Think what people will say."

"I don't give a damn what they say. They can say whatever they like."

"But your father just died. People around here, especially those who knew Uncle Harold, aren't going to like it. It shows a terrible lack of respect, of propriety."

"You expect me to respect the man?" Ivy raged. "After everything he did? Forget it. I did respect him for forty years, and you can see how far that got me. When he decided to throw me to the wolves in favor of divvying this place up between Holly and me, he didn't hesitate, not for a minute. Maybe he didn't change his will, but only because he ran out of time. He didn't give a damn about all the years I worked here. I poured my whole life into this place. If Holly's portion and mine are exactly the same, then what I did for him and with him all those years didn't mean a thing."

"Ivy, you're being too hard on the man."

"Hard? No I'm not. Not only did he turn on me, he destroyed Mother, Burton. Maybe you don't see it the same way I do. I was here every day taking care of her. He even made me help him do it to her, dammit. That's something I'll never forgive. Never."

She paused long enough to take a ragged breath, and then a strange look passed over Ivy's face, a look of terrible comprehension. "That's it, isn't it?"

"What now?" Burton asked wearily, as though he were too exasperated to care anymore.

"Don't you see? That must be why he swore she was lying and why she insisted that we stay away from the glory hole."

"What are you talking about, Ivy?"

"The other body. The skeleton. I know now who killed that other person."

"Who?" Joanna asked.

"My father, of course," Ivy Patterson said matter-of-factly. "Don't you see? Why else would he have covered it up all these years?"

Why else? Joanna thought with her own heart constricting in her breast. Why else indeed?

Ivy cut off all further discussion by getting up, taking Yuri's hand to pull him off the couch, and leading him out the door. The other three people were left in the living room, trapped in their own stunned silence.

"I don't understand what's going on with that woman," Burton grumbled as the front door closed behind Yuri and Ivy. "Who the hell is that guy? Where's he from?"

"Yuri Malakov," Marianne answered. "He's from someplace in Russia, of course. Or from someplace in what used to be Russia. You mean you don't know him?"

"I've never laid eyes on the man, and yet Ivy says they're engaged? They're getting married? What kind of craziness is this?"

"From the way Ivy brought it up to me this morning, she sounded as though it was all decided long ago. I would have thought for sure you'd know all about it."

"Well I don't. Not a word," Burton said. He shook his head. "What did he say his name is? Malakov? What kind of name is that and what's he doing in this country? How'd he get here? And how did he meet up with Ivy?"

"He's an immigrant," Marianne explained. "And a very nice man. It's part of our national church mission to help newcomers to this country. Jeff and I actually helped him find sponsors. Hale and Natasha Robertson, from just up the road."

"You and your husband helped bring him here?" Burton asked reproachfully.

Marianne nodded. "Jeff's actually more involved with that part of our outreach program than I am. You've met Natasha Robertson, haven't you?"

Burton nodded. "Years ago. I remember when Hale brought her home as a G.I. bride right after World War II. They moved into a place a few miles down the road."

"Hale's in a wheelchair now," Marianne continued. "He was in a car accident years ago. He's turned himself into an accountant, keeping books for various ranchers. For a long time, Natasha looked after their place all by herself, but she's getting up in years now, too. It finally got to be more than she could handle. Jeff was the one who came up with the idea of putting them together with Yuri. And it's a perfect match. Natasha speaks Russian and needed somebody to help her with chores. Yuri needed a job and a place to stay, and he didn't speak much English. It seemed like a match made in heaven."

"You still haven't told me how he and Ivy got together," Burton Kimball objected. "And just what kind of man is he? You can sit there and blithely tell me what a nice man he is, but for all you know he may be taking Ivy for all she's worth."

"It's nothing like that," Marianne assured him. "Yuri Malakov is totally on the up-and-up. Ivy started out tutoring him in English. The two of them just hit it off. Right from the start. Actually," she added, "I like seeing them together. I think it's sweet."

"I hope you're happy then," Burton said sarcastically. "I suppose holding the wedding tonight was your idea?"

"Absolutely not. Having the wedding now is a terrible idea. I already told you I tried my best to talk Ivy out of it, but, as you can see, her mind's made up."

"And what was that I saw peeking out from under Lothario's shirt?"

"His shirt?" Marianne asked. "What are you talking about?"

"The top button of his shirt was open. I saw something that looked a whole lot like a tattoo."

Marianne looked puzzled. "I wouldn't have any idea about that."

"I would," Joanna said. "It was a tattoo. Why?"

"Joanna," Marianne said, "how did you . . . ?"

"I've read about Russians with tattoos," Burton Kimball went on. "In *The Wall Street Journal*."

"What about them?" Joanna asked.

"It was in an article about Russian prisons. It talked about how Russian prisoners cover themselves with tattoos as a way of showing defiance of authority. Any kind of authority. It's a variation on a theme of *The Red Badge of Courage*."

With rising excitement, Burton Kimball sat up straighter and continued. "What if this man is an ex-con? Or maybe he's an escaped criminal or a member of the Russian mafia. I've read about them, too. They're all over here in the States these days. They're into everything from drugs, to money laundering, to arms smuggling. What if Ivy's being dragged into something like that?"

Kimball got up and started toward the door.

"Wait a minute, Burton," Marianne said. "You're being ridiculous, jumping to all kinds of crazy conclusions."

Burton paused at the door. "Maybe I am," he said. "But you don't know Ivy the way I do. She's totally naïve. He probably . . . Wait a minute. Maybe that's what happened."

"What?" Joanna asked.

"Maybe Yuri was here when I called to tell Ivy about what was going on with Harold. Maybe she told him what was going on, and he decided to do something about it."

"What exactly did you tell Ivy?"

Burton shrugged. "That Uncle Harold had decided to settle Holly's lawsuit out of court. He told me that morning that he was going to give Holly everything she wanted. I was worried Ivy would be left out in the cold, with very little to show for all her hard work and with no one to take care of her. It makes perfect sense now. That gold-digging bastard was worried about the same thing, so he killed Uncle Harold before he had a chance to change the provisions of his will."

"No way," Marianne objected. "I'm sure you've got it all wrong. These are two fine, upstanding, honorable people."

But Burton Kimball was on a roll. "Oh, yeah?" he snarled back at her. "What do you know about him, really? About where he comes from, about what kind of background he has? If you ask me, he's nothing but a glorified wetback. Everybody knows getting married is a surefire way of turning a green card into U.S. citizenship. With what she was due to receive from Uncle Harold, Ivy must have looked like a sure thing."

By then, Marianne Maculyea was as outraged as Burton was. "I'm telling you you're wrong about Yuri, Mr. Kimball," she insisted. "I will personally vouch for him. He's a fine man who will make Ivy Patterson very happy."

"Like hell he will!" Harold returned. "You goddamned preachers are all alike. Little Miss Goody Two-shoes. You ought to come down off your high horse and your pulpit and grub around in the real world for a while. Come on up to the courthouse someday and just hang around, Reverend Maculyea. Maybe you can afford the luxury of taking everyone at face value, but the rest of the world can't. I can't. And I'm going to do my best to talk Ivy out of marrying him until we can find out more about him."

With that, Burton Kimball stormed out of the house. Left alone in someone else's living room, Joanna Brady and Marianne Maculyea stared at one another in subdued silence.

"I guess I'd better go," Marianne said. "If Jeff and I are having a wedding at the parsonage tonight, he may need help getting the place ready. It's a good thing I vacuumed before you conked me on the head."

Joanna ignored Marianne's small attempt at humor.

"Doesn't it seem odd to you?" Joanna asked. "For Ivy to be getting married like that, in such a rush?"

Marianne stopped to consider the question. "Actually, the older I get, more and more strange stuff is starting to seem normal."

"Is that because the world is getting weird, or because we are?"

"Maybe both," Marianne replied. "Most likely both."

They stepped outside onto the porch in time to witness the end of a fierce shouting match between Burton Kimball and Ivy Patterson. Finally, Burton slammed himself into his Jeep Cherokee and raced out of the yard, sending Ivy Patterson's normally placid flock of chickens and peacocks scattering in all directions.

"It looks to me," Marianne observed, "that the voice of sweet reason didn't prevail, and the Wedding March marches on."

Joanna shook her head. "Maybe the whole clan has flipped out. Actually, speaking of that, do you know if anyone's called Holly to tell her what's happened? She's also Harold's daughter, you know. She has as much right to be notified as anyone else."

"I don't remember anyone mentioning it to me," Marianne returned.

Joanna shook her head. "Then maybe I'd better take a crack at that one, too. Better me than Marliss Shackleford."

"By all means," Marianne agreed, "but you'd best get a move on. If I know Marliss, she won't miss a trick. In fact, she may already be there by now."

Twenty-Four

As JOANNA drove toward *Casa Vieja*, she was once more conscious of her hopelessly ill-fitting clothing. What worked for a crime scene wasn't appropriate for paying an official call. Her mother would have had a fit to think her daughter would show up at a place like *Casa Vieja* dressed as she was.

Of all the houses in town, the venerable old mansion at the top of Vista Park was by far the most ostentatious. Two stories tall and massively built, the place was constructed out of thick brown stucco and accented by decorative strips of hand-carved wood moldings. The yard was surrounded by a low-slung stucco wall backed up by an interior barrier of fifteen-foot-high oleanders, giving the place an impenetrable, secretive look.

Definitely out of my league, Joanna thought, driving up to the gate in her Eagle.

It hadn't always been that way. For instance, during the time *Casa Vieja* was carved up into apartments, Joanna's favorite high school phys-ed teacher had lived there. In fact, her sophomore year, she had even attended a tennis-club barbecue that had been held on the wide veranda overlooking Vista Park.

But that was long before *Casa Vieja* had been made over once again. According to Eleanor Lathrop, very few locals, even upscale neighbors from the immediate area, had been invited inside the refurbished place since its purchase by either the former owners—purported drug dealers—or this new one, who was supposedly someone important out in Hollywood. That stray thought caused Joanna to smile. By her mother's lights, everyone in Hollywood—no matter how obscure—was important.

Joanna pushed the bell fastened on the gatepost. "Who is it?" a disembodied voice asked.

"Joanna Brady," she answered. "Sheriff Joanna Brady to see Holly Patterson."

For an answer, the wrought-iron gate swung smoothly open, and Joanna drove in. Toward the back of the building was a garage where two open doors revealed both the fender-damaged red Allanté and a stretch limo. The thought crossed Joanna's mind that at least one Patterson girl seemed to have done all right for herself. A red Allanté was a long way from Ivy's battered Chevy Luv.

Several parking places had been marked on the pavement on the west side of the building. Joanna pulled into one of them. Before she had time to consider what entrance to use, a door on the side of the house opened, and an older Hispanic woman stepped out onto a small utility porch and began vigorously shaking a dust mop. Joanna walked several steps toward her before recognizing Isobel Gonzales, the grandmother of one of Jenny's classmates.

"Why, hello, Mrs. Gonzales," Joanna said, "I had heard you were working here."

The woman smiled and nodded. "Me and my husband both. He retired from P.D. up in Morenci. We came home to Bisbee, but he was driving me crazy at home all day. Now we're both working again, and it's better."

"You're lucky to have him around to drive you crazy," Joanna said, hoping the twinge of envy she felt didn't come across as bitterness.

"I know," Isobel said, nodding and leaning on her dust-free mop. "That's what I keep telling myself. Miss Baxter is out front."

Joanna hurried the way she'd been directed. The sunny front patio, warm and sheltered from the wind, was far different from the way she remembered it. For one thing, it seemed smaller, but better, too. The once-bare edges of the terrace were lined with huge pots filled with exotic and unidentifiable growing things, plants Joanna had never seen before and whose origins she could only guess. The rough-hewn picnic tables and homegrown barbecue were gone, replaced by patio furniture that looked too expensive to leave out in the weather.

A woman with a short-cropped pageboy under a large straw hat sat at the table reading a book.

"Miss Baxter?" Joanna asked.

The woman looked up without closing her book. "That's right. Amy Baxter," she said curtly. "I must inform you, Sheriff Brady, that Holly's attor-

ney has been called out of town again this morning. Since he won't be able to be in attendance,
I'm afraid you won't be able to see Holly. It simply
wouldn't be responsible of me to let you talk to
her under those circumstances."

"May I sit down?" Joanna asked, letting her
hand fall on the back of one of the chairs.

"Certainly. Excuse me. I didn't mean to seem
rude. Can I get you something—coffee, tea?"

"I'm fine, thank you. What circumstances do
you mean, Miss Baxter? What exactly did you
think I wanted to see Holly Patterson about?"

"The other night, naturally. I read the article in
the paper, so I'm well aware of the part you
played in averting a terrible tragedy, but still, with
the possibility of litigation . . ."

"I'm not here about the other night," Joanna interrupted. "I came to talk to Holly about her father. Harold Lamm Patterson has been found."

Amy Baxter breathed a sigh of relief. "Really.
You can't imagine how happy I am to hear that.
Holly's been in a state of perpetual crisis ever
since he turned up missing."

"I'm afraid it's not good news," Joanna hastened to add. "He's dead. I'm here to give her the
benefit of an official next-of-kin notification."

Amy Baxter's face fell. "Oh, my God. That's terrible. She'll be devastated. She's held herself somehow responsible for his disappearance; now I'm
afraid . . . What happened? Was it an accident? A
heart attack? What?"

"If I could just speak to Holly, please."

"Of course. I'll go get her right away." Amy

Baxter started toward the house. "Actually, if you don't mind, it might be better if we went up to her room. She's somewhat unstable at the moment, and I'm afraid . . ."

"I don't mind," Joanna said.

Amy Baxter stood up. "This way," she said.

The interior of the house was magnificent. Outside of pictures in home-decorating magazine articles, Joanna had never seen a more beautiful home—polished hardwood floors, covered here and there by deeply luxurious Oriental rugs. The supple leather furniture blended subtly with the Mission-style interior details into a combination that was both elegant and comfortably inviting. Discreet track lighting on the twelve-foot ceilings accented huge oil canvasses of boldly painted flowers, many of which resembled the plants growing in the pots outside on the patio.

"Pauli's really very good, isn't he?" Amy Baxter said, as Joanna admired a particularly vivid piece at the top of the winding staircase.

"Pauli?" Joanna repeated stupidly, thinking that must be the name of some artist or school of artists well known enough that she should have recognized the name on hearing it.

Amy laughed. "Paul Enders, the painter. He's a costumer really; he only paints for a hobby. We all call him Pauli. This is his house," she continued. "He's letting us stay here until this situation gets straightened out. As you'll soon see, the privacy we've enjoyed here has been a real blessing."

At the top of the stairs, Amy Baxter turned to

the right and led the way down a long corridor to the back of the house.

"There are better rooms, and Holly could have had any one of them," Amy said apologetically, "but for some strange reason, this is the one she wanted." Amy stopped in front of a closed door and knocked. "Holly," she called. "Are you in there? May we come in?"

Joanna heard no answering response, but Amy went ahead and tentatively twisted the old-fashioned knob on the door. The knob turned in her hand, and the door shifted open without protest.

The interior of the room was dark and stiflingly hot compared to the rest of the house, with the look and smell of a sickroom. In the far corner, near tall, drapery-shrouded windows, sat a high-backed rocking chair, creaking slowly back and forth.

"Holly," Amy said tentatively. "There's someone here to see you."

"Tell them to go away," Holly muttered. "I don't want to see anybody. Leave me alone."

"It's Sheriff Brady," Amy explained. "She came to talk to you about your father."

The rocking ceased abruptly. Suddenly, Holly lurched to her feet. Out of a stark, pale face two deeply troubled eyes stared at Joanna. "Where is he?" Holly demanded. "Tell me where he is. I have to see him. He was supposed to make arrangements for a settlement. He promised. But then he disappeared. No one knows where he is."

"I'm afraid your father won't be able to carry through on any promises," Joanna said quietly.

"He's dead. He died sometime between Tuesday night and now. They'll be able to fix the time better once they do the autopsy."

"My father dead?" Holly Patterson repeated slowly, sinking back into the chair as though her legs no longer had the capability of supporting her. "He's dead?"

"Yes, you see . . ."

Holly Patterson doubled over, as with a sudden attack of appendicitis, clutching her abdomen and sobbing. "Nooooooo. He can't be dead. I won't let him. I never wanted him dead. Never!"

Amy Baxter moved forward quickly and knelt beside the chair. "It's okay, Holly. Hush now. Everyone knows it's not your fault."

"Oh, but it is," Holly groaned. "Don't you understand? It is my fault. All of it. I didn't want him dead. I just wanted him to tell me to my face that he was sorry for what he did to me. That's all. I never should have come back to this terrible place. Never!"

"Please, Holly," Amy begged, "don't take it all on yourself. You didn't do it."

"How did he die?" Holly was asking, her mouth still muffled by her hand. "Please don't tell me he committed suicide. I can stand anything but that."

Joanna could see no sense in pulling punches. Better to let all the bad news out at once and give her a chance to start assimilating it while she had someone like Amy Baxter there to help as needed.

"We're investigating his death as a possible homicide," Joanna answered carefully. "I wanted you to hear that from someone in an official capacity. . . ."

"You mean he didn't kill himself then?" Holly asked, suddenly sitting up straight and pulling her hand away from her face. "You mean someone else did it?"

"That's the way it looks. . . ."

Holly Patterson let out a long sigh. "Thank God. I couldn't have stood it if he had done it himself. It would have driven me crazy, but if somebody else did it . . ."

"Good girl," Amy said, rubbing the back of Holly's neck as if to remove some of the tension. "Let it go. Don't hold on to it."

Holly Patterson closed her eyes and leaned back into the neck rub. "I should go see Mother about this," she whispered softly. "Mother will know what to do."

Amy caught Joanna's eye, shook her head, and held the fingers of one hand to her lips while she continued massaging Holly's neck with the other.

"You can't go see your mother, Holly. I've already explained that to you. Your mother is dead, remember? She died five years ago. We've been over to the cemetery and seen her grave."

"But I saw her. The other day in town, remember?"

"That was your sister, Ivy. She looks just like your mother used to look when you last remember her."

"That can't be my sister. Ivy's a little girl. She's a baby."

"Of course she is," Amy said soothingly. "A

little baby. Why don't you rest awhile now, Holly? When you wake up later, maybe we can make better sense of this."

Holly nodded but said nothing. There was a minute or so of silence. By the end of it Holly was sound asleep.

Amy turned to Joanna. "I could call Mrs. Gonzales, but if you don't mind, would you help me get her back into the bed? She hasn't been eating right, and she's barely been sleeping at all during the night. After something like this during the day, though, she'll nap for hours."

Holding Holly Patterson between them, Amy and Joanna wrestled the dozing woman from the chair to the bed, then Joanna followed Amy down both the hall and stairs.

"What's wrong with her?" Joanna asked.

"What isn't wrong with her is probably a better question," Amy Baxter said. "It's just what I was afraid of. Being here has been way too hard on her. You're looking at a textbook case. Start with a dash of incest, add in a mostly dysfunctional family, stir in some recreational drug use and a fistful of self-loathing, and you end up with a very troubled woman."

"Ernie Carpenter is the homicide detective on her father's case. He may need to talk to her. Do you think she'll be able to handle answering questions?"

Amy shrugged. "That's anybody's guess. He's more than welcome to try, but I don't know how much good it will do. Sometimes she's better than others. Have him call first to see what kind of shape she's in."

"She acts like she's on drugs," Joanna observed thoughtfully.

Amy Baxter answered with a nod. "Not recently, though. She still suffers from flashbacks, occasional echoes of LSD from her misspent youth."

Amy Baxter and Joanna were standing at the bottom of the stairway with Amy Baxter's hand still on the polished mahogany banister.

"Thanks for all the help," she said.

"It was no trouble," Joanna returned.

"I hope you won't think me too ungrateful, but I hope you never find out who did it. I'm glad that asshole father of hers is dead, and I'm hoping that whoever killed him gets away scot-free, because, whatever Harold Patterson got, that dirty old man *deserved* it!"

"What exactly did he do to her?" Joanna asked reflexively.

Amy Baxter had no business answering, but she did. "He raped her," she answered, her words as brittle as shards of ice. "He raped his own daughter from the time she was two years old. So whatever happened to Harold Patterson is fine with me. He may be dead and out of the picture now, but you saw Holly upstairs. She's an emotional cripple, and she'll live with the damage he did to her for the rest of her life."

Leaving the sheriff to find her own way out, Amy turned and hurried back up the stairs. As Joanna drove out through *Casa Vieja*'s swinging iron gates, she was thinking about what Amy had said concerning Holly's past drug use.

Was Holly Patterson really having drug-related flashbacks, or were her mental problems something else entirely, something more closely related to what had gone haywire with her mother years ago? Had Emily Patterson's mental instability passed genetically from mother to daughter?

Actually, from what Joanna personally had seen and heard during the course of the last few days, all the Patterson women seemed to be several bubbles out of plumb.

It was only after she had started down Cole Avenue toward the Warren Cutoff that Joanna remembered what she had forgotten to mention. Holly Patterson had been so upset by the news about her father that Joanna had failed to bring up the existence of that other victim.

What exactly was the connection between those two bodies? Joanna wondered. Surely, more than sheer coincidence had caused both corpses to turn up in the same glory hole. But in order to discover the connection between them, it was necessary to understand the relationship between all the other pieces on the board.

Joanna could have just left it alone. After all, it was Ernie Carpenter's case. She could either go sit in her corner office and begin trying to understand next year's budget, or she could try sticking her nose in where it didn't necessarily belong.

At the intersection of Cole Avenue and Arizona Street, it was decision time. If she drove down the Warren Cutoff, when she reached Highway 80, she could either go home or head back to the office. Or she could go straight up Cole Avenue and keep right on not minding her own business.

After only a moment's hesitation, she switched off her left-turn blinker and headed for Eleanor Lathrop's favorite haven, Helene's Salon of Hair and Beauty.

Twenty-Five

WHEN JOANNA entered the beauty shop, Helen Barco stood stolidly behind the shop's single chair twisting pink plastic permanent-wave curlers into a client's hair while the woman handed her individual pieces of tissue-paper wrappers. Both women glanced up in surprise as Joanna made her entrance.

"My land, girl!" Helen exclaimed. "Whatever did you do to your face?"

In her hurry to dress that morning, Joanna had barely glanced in her own mirror. Now, seeing her battered reflection in Helen Barco's brightly lit vanity, she was startled to see how readily apparent the damage was. Put simply, Sheriff Joanna Brady looked like hell.

"It's nothing much," she said with a shrug. "Just a black eye."

"You call that nothing much?" Helen rolled her eyes. "People straight out of the emergency room look better than that. I know you don't have an appointment, but if you can wait around a few minutes, maybe I could squeeze you in between Mrs. Owens here and my next lady. We should certainly do something about that eye of yours. What would your mother say?"

"Thanks anyway, Helen," Joanna answered, biting back a comment that was sure to go straight to her mother. "I really don't have time today. I came by to ask a favor."

"What kind of favor? I've already donated a permanent and manicure to the senior citizen's auction, if that's what you're here asking about."

"No. It's nothing like that. You do get *People* magazine here, don't you?"

Helen nodded. "*People, Good Housekeeping*, and *Ladies' Home Journal*. I tried that *New Woman* for a few months, but my ladies didn't like it very much. They're mostly older, you know, and don't take to some of these newfangled ideas."

"Do you keep any of the back issues?"

"Some. Why?"

"Do you still happen to have the one with the article about Holly Patterson in it?"

"Absolutely!" Helen answered. "I wouldn't let that one out of my sight. It's not every day that Bisbee gets that kind of coverage, thank the good Lord. Naturally, all the dealers in town sold out every last one of their copies. I was really lucky I had my subscription."

"Could I maybe borrow it from you?" Joanna asked. "I never had a chance to read it, and now I think I ought to."

"Sure," Helen said. "As long as you promise to bring it right back. But how come you need to read it now? That was weeks ago. What's going on?"

Joanna knew from things her mother had told her over the years that Helene's was a place where beauty often took a backseat to small-town gossip. It wouldn't hurt Helen to have a real scoop for a change. It was possible that the useful flow of information might travel in more than one direction. Besides, the next-of-kin notifications had already been completed.

"We found Harold Patterson," Joanna said. "He's dead."

"No. Heart attack? Stroke?"

"We're not releasing any information on cause of death at the moment," Joanna replied in what she knew Helen would consider a deliciously tantalizing nonanswer.

Helen's eyes widened. "Really? Why, forevermore! Who would have thought it! The strain musta been too much for the old duffer's ticker for him to just up and keel over like that. You wait right here, Joanna. I'll go get you that magazine."

Because flat lots are at a premium in Bisbee, Helen Barco's house was built on a hill. The shop, built in what was formerly the garage, was in the basement, while the living quarters were upstairs. Huffing and out of breath from climbing stairs, Helen returned to the shop a few moments later and handed Joanna the dog-eared issue of the magazine. Written across the front cover in red Magic Marker were the words DO NOT REMOVE.

"You're sure you don't mind if I take this?" Joanna asked.

"Like I told you before, Joanna, honey," Helen said. "You can take it wherever you like, just so long as you bring it back. I mean, after all, you're the sheriff, aren't you? If you can't trust the sheriff . . ."

Helen broke off in sudden confusion, thinking, no doubt, of Walter V. McFadden who hadn't been nearly as trustworthy as he appeared.

"Well, anyway," she continued. "I'd sure like to have it back when you finish with it. That issue could end up being a collector's item someday. You're positive you won't let me do something about that face of yours?"

"No," Joanna said, heading for the door. "Not today. I'm in too much of a rush."

It was well after one by then, and Joanna's growling stomach was complaining too much to be ignored. She resisted the temptation to go straight back to the department. After all, even the sheriff deserved a lunch break. With as much haste as the posted limits allowed, she hurried out to the High Lonesome, stripped out of her clothing, grabbed one of the world's shortest showers, and gulped down a peanut-butter-and-jelly sandwich. Still eating the last half of the sandwich, she headed for the Cochise County Justice Center dressed in some of her old insurance-agency work clothes.

This business of what to wear and what not to wear was fast becoming a pain in the neck.

Once at the Sheriff's Department, she noticed that several news vehicles were parked in front of the building. Driving around back, she pulled into the reserved parking spot marked SHERIFF. It was empty and waiting for her Eagle.

It would have been nice to use her own private entryway, but no one had as yet given her the push-button code. Instead, she had to buzz before she could be allowed in through the common entryway marked EMPLOYEES ONLY. She walked into the reception area of the back suite of offices just in time to catch Dick Voland railing at the unfortunate Kristin.

"Don't ask me what to do with all those reporters out in the lobby. It's not my problem anymore. Ask Sheriff Brady."

"Ask me what?"

Voland turned the focus of his irritation on her. "We've got a swarm of killer-bee media out there in the lobby, all of 'em wanting to know what the hell's going on. Somebody should have called a press conference."

"What a good idea," Joanna said amiably. "Why don't you go ahead and do it?"

"Me?" Dick Voland objected. "Why me?"

"Why not you? Didn't you handle media relations back when Walter McFadden was in charge?"

"Yes, but . . ."

"And you can do it again," Joanna interjected. "With a major story like this, we're a lot better off having someone experienced controlling that aspect of things. Kristin, call out front. Have them tell the reporters there'll be a press conference in fifteen minutes. By the way, where's Ernie? Is he back yet?"

"He's in his office," Kristin put in. "He said he

wasn't to be disturbed. I think he's working on his paper."

"Tell Ernie to come to my office anyway. It won't take long, but I want to see him before Chief Deputy Voland's press conference. I want you there as well, Dick. Before you talk to those reporters, the three of us need to put our heads together."

Without waiting for either a reply or an argument, Joanna headed for the private corner office, the one she knew belonged to the sheriff. She more than half expected to find it still occupied by Dick Voland's messy paraphernalia, but she was wrong.

Overnight the piles of stacked papers and accumulated junk had entirely disappeared. Even the collection of Al Freeman yard signs was gone. The wooden surfaces of the desk, credenza, and coffee table were all polished to a high gloss. The overflowing, freestanding ashtray had been replaced by a heavy, velvet-bottomed marble one that sat in clean and solitary splendor on the upper right-hand corner of the desk.

Joanna paused in the doorway and then turned back to the receptionist's desk where both Dick Voland and Kristin Marsten still stood motionless as if frozen in place.

"And, Kristin," Joanna added, "after you give Ernie my message, I need a supply of yellow pads, pens, and pencils in here."

Joanna waited long enough to see whether or not the young woman would move. With a defiant scowl and an extra toss of her big hair, Kristin turned and bent over to use her telephone. "Detective Carpenter," Joanna heard her say a moment later. "The sheriff wants to see you in her office. Right away."

Leaving the door open behind her, Joanna walked over to the desk and sat down in the massive leather chair behind it. The outsized chair was far too big for her. The tall back made her feel dwarfed and inconsequential. The office had the expectant, empty feel of a vacant apartment, but now was no time for Joanna to bring in her meager box of possessions or to think about putting her own personal stamp on the place. That would have to wait.

Moments later the miniskirted Kristin flounced into Joanna's office and unceremoniously dumped a stack of legal pads and three pens on the desk. "We're out of pencils," she mumbled through a mouthful of gum.

"Who's in charge of ordering supplies?" Joanna asked.

"I am."

"Well, order some then. I want pencils."

"Anything else?"

"Yes. I want you to have whoever is in charge of Motor Pool to make arrangements for me to have a vehicle, one with a radio."

"What else?"

Joanna studied the young receptionist. Twenty-two or twenty-three at the most, Kristin Marsten bristled with ill-disguised hostility. Up to a point, Joanna understood that. It was a necessary part of the way politics worked. When someone new won an election and took over the helm of an elected office there was always a period of adjustment with the staff, a time when, although loyalties were shifting, the work still had to be done.

"Have you ever worked for a woman before?" Joanna asked.

Startled, Kristin lowered her eyes and shifted on her feet. "Not really. Why?"

"I was just wondering," Joanna said. "You enjoyed working for Mr. Voland, didn't you?"

"Yes," Kristin said. "Very much."

"Let me ask you a question. When he was in this office, did you ever bring him coffee?"

"Yes. Sometimes. He likes his black."

"And Ernie Carpenter?"

"He takes his black, too."

"I see," Joanna said, leaning back in the chair. "That makes three of us. All black. We'll just continue the tradition then, if you don't mind. And since the three of us have already had a very long morning, why don't you bring in three cups of black coffee as soon as Ernie and Dick get here."

Kristin started toward the door. "Is that all?"

"One more question. Why exactly did you come to work here?"

Kristin shrugged. "It was a job, I guess. But I kinda thought it would be interesting, being in law enforcement."

"And is it?"

"Yes."

"Have you ever thought about doing anything more around here rather than just working as a receptionist? Have you thought about maybe being a deputy or doing something in Dispatch?

Something responsible that would give you a chance at better pay?"

Kristin shook her mane of hair. "I don't think so," she said. "I mean, being a dispatcher is really serious stuff. Nobody ever takes me seriously. I'm not really an airhead, but you know all those blonde jokes, and I . . ."

"It's difficult for men to take you seriously when they're spending all their time trying to look down your blouse or up your skirt," Joanna returned. "By the way, that's a very nice set of underwear you have on today. I particularly like that shade of turquoise, especially for a bra and matching panties. I'm sure the guys around here like them, too. I've noticed several of them looking. It's possible, though, if you want the men to take you seriously, that a longer skirt would help."

Shocked, Kristin opened her mouth, but no words came out. Blushing furiously, she spun around and nearly ran over Dick Voland in her rush to escape Joanna's office and her steady, appraising gaze.

"What's the matter with Kristin?" Dick asked, as he shambled in and sank down into one of the side chairs.

"I believe it's called culture shock," Joanna replied. "Where's Ernie?"

"He'll be here in a minute."

"Thanks for having the office ready for me to move into, Dick," Joanna said. "That was thoughtful of you. I don't know when you had time."

The chief deputy shrugged grudgingly. "No big thing," he said. Although Joanna knew it was.

Ernie appeared moments later. The man may have spent the entire morning grubbing around at a crime scene in a pair of much-used sweats and tennies, but by the time he appeared in Joanna's office, he was wearing a well-pressed suit, a tie, and a stiffly starched white shirt, to say nothing of highly polished wing tips. Looking at him, Joanna was glad she'd taken the time to go home and clean up.

"What's going on?" he asked irritably. "I'm busy as hell."

"I'm sure you are, but we've got a press conference coming up in a few minutes," Joanna told him.

"Since when?"

"Since I called it. This is a big case, and we're going to handle it in a way that won't have the press tearing us apart. Dick will be running the show, but I want a united front on what he says and what he doesn't."

Kristin walked in right then, bringing the three cups of coffee. Wordlessly, she delivered Joanna's cup to the desk. When she turned back to the two men, she paused for a moment in front of the coffee table, struggling to find a way to deposit the cups on the low surface of the table without having to bend over to do it. She finally solved the problem by passing the cups directly to their hands.

"So where do we stand?" Joanna asked, once Kristin left the room.

"Two stiffs for the price of one," Ernie Carpenter replied. "I've got Harold Patterson's body pulled up to the surface. The coroner has taken charge of him, and we've packed out most of the skeleton in a body bag. The sump pump is doing the job, but it's still too wet down there to finish searching the bottom of the glory hole."

"Any possible I.D. on the skeleton?"

"None."

"Cause of death?"

"Looks like a rock to the head to me, but that's just a wild guess."

"Do you have any leads on either case?"

"Not really. But how could I? For Pete's sake, I've been down in that damn hole mucking around in the mud all morning long."

Joanna turned from Ernie Carpenter to the chief deputy. "All right then, Dick. That's what you tell the press."

"What?"

"Two separate homicides. One positive I.D., one John Doe. No specific leads in either case at this time."

"That's all? You call a press conference and just give 'em that little snippet of information? They'll tear me apart."

"Some information is better than no information," Joanna countered. "They'll have to make do. Tell them when we know more, they'll know more."

Shaking his head, a disgruntled Dick Voland took his coffee and headed out of the office. Ernie Carpenter made as if to follow, but Joanna stopped him. "Wait a minute, Ernie."

Ernie sighed and reluctantly sat back down. "What now?"

"I picked up a few tidbits of information out at the Rocking P this morning," she told him.

"Tidbits?" he asked with a disinterested shrug. "Like what?"

Joanna got up from behind her desk, walked over to the door and closed it. "Like who might have killed Harold Patterson," she answered firmly. "And why."

Twenty-Six

ERNIE CARPENTER stayed in Joanna's office for more than an hour. Once she started relating all she had learned out at the Patterson place and during her stop at *Casa Vieja*, Ernie appropriated one of Joanna's legal pads and pens and began scribbling notes.

When she finished telling him everything she could remember, Ernie studied his notes in silence for several moments. "You know," he said thoughtfully, chewing one end of the pen, "what you've told me tallies with some of the things I picked up."

"For instance?"

"For instance," he replied, "near as I can tell, there were several sets of tire tracks in and out of that place for days. The only trouble is, they're all from the same vehicle."

"Which one?"

"Harold Patterson's Scout."

"That stands to reason."

"But only up to a point," Ernie said. "He could have driven it in one last time, but he sure as hell didn't drive it out. According to the coroner's preliminary look-see, he guesstimates time of death as sometime Tuesday or Wednesday, but Burton Kimball says he came to the Election Night party looking for his uncle because he saw his car in the convention-center parking lot."

"So the question is, how did it get from the glory hole to the parking lot?"

"No way to tell, but presumably the killer drove it there."

Ernie shook his head thoughtfully. "The part about all this that doesn't add up is Ivy and her boyfriend spending the night in the Scout with Harold lying there dead a matter of a few feet away. That one just flat-out takes the cake!"

"It's sick, all right," Joanna agreed.

"And they're getting married tonight?"

Joanna nodded. "That's what they said. Seven o'clock at the Canyon Methodist parsonage. Marianne Maculyea is officiating."

"I call that really rushing it," Ernie said, frowning. "I mean, the old guy's not even cold yet, and his daughter's out banging her boyfriend in Daddy's car. Next thing you know, she's getting married. Couldn't she hold off the celebration at least until after the funeral? And you say Burton Kimball didn't know anything at all about the wedding until today?"

"That's how it sounded—as though he'd never even heard of Yuri Malakov," Joanna told him.

"So the Russian and Ivy were already engaged, but maybe no one in the family knew anything about it, including the old man."

"Why keep your engagement a secret?" Joanna asked.

"Because you figure someone's going to object," Ernie answered. "So the next question has to be why there'd be an objection in the first place."

Joanna nodded thoughtfully. "According to Marianne, Yuri is applying for U.S. citizenship. Wouldn't Immigration have an application with fingerprints on it?"

"And with any criminal record as well," Ernie said.

"Can we get a copy?"

Ernie laughed. "Supposedly, but nobody rushes those guys down at INS. I've gone to them for records before. Just getting an answer to a simple question could take months, even with the MJ boys working on it."

The Multi-Jurisdictional Force was a recently created task force designed to counter criminal activity along the Mexican border, including unlawful enterprises that often crossed jurisdictional boundaries. One MJ squad was based out of the Cochise County Justice Center. Joanna knew about it, but only distantly. It was one of those aspects of her new job that she had expected to have time to research between Election Night and being sworn in sometime in January.

"Maybe you can get someone from there to pull a string or two," she suggested.

"Don't hold your breath," Ernie said sourly, getting up. "But I'll give it a whirl."

He was already at the door when Joanna remembered the magazine. "You don't read *People* by any chance, do you?"

Ernie shook his head. "Not me. I'm more into

Smithsonian and *Home Mechanix*," he answered. "Last month they had a great article on building decks. Why do you ask?"

Joanna leaned down, reached into her purse, and was about to haul out Helen Barco's dog-eared magazine when she thought better of it.

"Never mind," she said. "There's an article in one of them I thought you should read, but you already have enough to do. I'll try to scan it sometime tonight. If it looks as though it has any bearing on the case, I'll get it to you first thing in the morning."

"Good," Ernie said, heading out the door. "What I don't need is one more thing that has to be done tonight."

The intercom on Joanna's desk buzzed loudly. Without having been given proper operating instructions, Joanna wasn't able to figure out how to make it work. Giving up, she finally walked over to the door and threw it open.

"Yes?"

"There's someone out here waiting to see you."

"Who?"

Before Kristin could answer, a young woman rose from one of the chairs across the room and hurried forward, hand extended. Short, stocky, well dressed, and very businesslike, she seemed vaguely familiar, although Joanna couldn't quite place her.

"Sue Rolles," the woman said with a winning smile. "I'm a reporter for the *Arizona Daily Sun*."

"A reporter. I'm afraid you need to talk to Chief

Deputy Voland. He's the one handling the press on today's glory-hole cases."

"This isn't about those," Sue Rolles said. "It's something else entirely."

Joanna led the way back into her office and motioned the visitor into a chair. "Have we met before?" Joanna asked. "You look familiar."

"We didn't exactly meet," Sue Rolles replied. "We ran into one another back in September in the lobby at University Hospital in Tucson. But we were never properly introduced. Since then, I've spent a good deal of time here in Cochise County working on a special assignment."

"What kind of assignment?"

"The sheriff's race."

Joanna Brady had been in office for only one day, but she had been around law enforcement long enough to suspect ambush journalism. "That's funny," she said. "I don't remember your ever asking for an interview with me."

"It's not that kind of article," Sue Rolles said quickly.

"I see. Exactly what kind is it then?"

Sue Rolles shrugged. "You know how it is. People are free to say things before elections that they can't or won't say afterward. My editors wanted me to survey some of the people who work here to get an insider's view of how people would react depending on which of the three candidates was actually elected."

"In other words," Joanna interjected without humor, "you've been out stirring up a hornet's nest in advance of my taking office."

"Oh, no. Not at all."

"What, then?"

"Since you're the first woman to hold this office in the state of Arizona, there's a good deal of interest, especially since most of the officers who will be reporting to you are men."

"So?" Joanna asked warily.

"Do you see a problem with that?"

"Not particularly. I've addressed that question on numerous occasions during my election campaign. Crime is the problem. Gender is not the problem."

"Even though some of your officers might be vocally critical of your ... law-enforcement abilities?"

"The voters of this county didn't expect me to know everything the first day I walked into this office," Joanna countered. "You and I both know there's a learning curve on any new job. I believe the people who elected me were bargaining for a hard worker. They want me to uncover any problems that may exist in this agency and to find solutions to them. That's what the people wanted, and it's what I expect to give them."

"Do you think your election combined with what happened to the previous sheriff will make for a continuing morale problem in the department?"

Joanna Brady wasn't eager to discuss Walter V. McFadden or the role she herself had played in his death.

"Any change of administration or supervision always comes with the potential for 'morale' problems. That goes for the private sector every bit as much as it does for governmental agencies. I didn't come in here expecting to do a wholesale housecleaning. My intention is to give officers under me a fair crack at showing me what they can do. I assume they will grant me the same courtesy."

"You know about Martin Sanders' resignation then?"

Martin Sanders, deputy for administration, was Dick Voland's counterpart on the administrative side. He had always been a background player. While Dick had been out actively campaigning for Al Freeman, Martin Sanders had been at work minding the store. He was someone Joanna naturally would have expected to meet during the course of her first full day in office had two separate homicides not taken precedence.

"He resigned?" Joanna demanded in surprise. "Since when?"

Sue Rolles looked startled as well. "I thought you knew all about that. My understanding was that he turned in his letter of resignation sometime early this morning. I wonder if it would be fair to characterize his action as a vote of no confidence."

Joanna could barely contain her irritation. "Since I haven't seen the letter yet," she snapped, "I don't believe it's fair to characterize it one way or the other. My answer on that issue is no comment. Period!"

"What about Chief Deputy Richard Voland?"

"What about him?"

"Do you have anyone in mind as his replacement?"

"Replacement? Who says he's leaving?"

Sue Rolles shrugged. "Well," she said disingenuously, "both he and Martin are political appointees, patronage workers who serve at the discretion of the sheriff. And since Voland actively supported your opponent . . ."

Joanna cut the reporter off in midsentence. "Ms. Rolles," she said, "did you attend Dick Voland's press conference earlier this afternoon?"

"Yes, but . . ."

"Then you are well aware that this agency is currently in the midst of coping with not one but two separate homicides in addition to handling the regular workload of calls."

"Yes."

"From the tenor of your questions, it appears to me this interview is heading in a direction I don't especially like. I believe it's designed to undermine my new administration, to create ill will and disharmony at a time when we all need to pull together to get the job done. With that in mind, I have nothing more to say at this time."

"But . . ."

Impatiently, Joanna punched a button on the intercom. Luckily, it was the right one, and Kristin answered. "Yes?"

"Miss Marsten," Joanna said. "Ms. Rolles is just leaving. Would you please show her out? And would you mind bringing in my mail? I've been told there are some items lurking in there that require my immediate attention."

While she waited for Sue Rolles to leave and for Kristin to bring in the mail, Joanna turned and looked out her window. Not that many offices in the building boasted private windows.

It was after four. Already the late fall sun was fast disappearing behind the Mule Mountains to the west. The hillside outside her window was spiked with gray sticks of spindly, thorny ocotillo branches. At first glance, the ghostly clumps of twigs seemed dead or dying, but the slanting afternoon sunlight revealed a faint tinge of green outlining the stalks. Even though winter weather was fast approaching, pale new leaves sprouted among the spiny thorns.

In order to survive in the harsh desert climate, ocotillos spend most of the year looking parched and barren. But whenever the shallow roots are blessed with rain, short-lived leaves appear on seemingly dead branches. New crops of leaves can come and go several times in the course of a single year.

Why couldn't people be more like ocotillos? Joanna wondered, envying the hardy desert candlewood its natural resilience. Humans didn't necessarily have that same kind of toughness, the same ability to withstand and recover from terrible dry spells.

Holly Patterson had gone off to Hollywood and created a career for herself, but the pain of what had happened to her as a child had somehow robbed her of all ability to enjoy it. She sat in a darkened room, rocking back and forth, hating her father and yet blaming herself for his death.

Ivy Patterson, too, had been damaged by the family troubles. Her once seemingly placid existence of faithful daughterly duty had erupted in a geyser of anger that made murder possible. Her late-blooming rebellion against her father made even the natural and mundane acts of falling in love and getting married take on sinister and unnatural overtones.

And before you go throwing too many stones, Joanna Brady thought to herself, what about you?

With Andy gone, she didn't expect the branches of her own heart ever again to leaf out in full springtime glory.

Toward evening Isobel Gonzales went into the darkened bedroom to collect the dinner tray and straighten the tangled covers on the bed. Holly Patterson was back in her chair, rocking back and forth and staring out through a space between the curtains at the towering black shadow of the dump.

"What's up there?" she asked.

Isobel almost jumped out of her skin. For days she had come to this room—dropping off food trays, taking them away, making the bed—while the room's sole occupant seldom spoke or even acknowledged her existence.

"Up where?" Isobel asked.

"On the dump. Is it smooth? Is it lumpy?"

Isobel walked over to the window and held the curtain aside. Eventually, the moon would come up, and the few hardy mesquite and scrub oak that had managed to scrabble up through the barren waste would show up as shadows against the lighter shades of rock and dirt. For now the whole thing was still an ink-black man-made mesa.

"That's funny," Isobel said. "For years, when we were first married, my husband, Jaime, drove a dump truck out there. I always worried about him, driving down into the pit, loading up the back of the truck with all those huge boulders, and then driving out here on the dump. I was always afraid he'd back up too close to the edge and fall off. He never did, though. He drove a truck like that for years, but I never asked him what was up there. Maybe I didn't want to know."

Holly turned her gaunt face away from the window for once and studied the older woman's sturdy features. "Wouldn't you like to know what's up there now?" she asked.

Isobel Gonzales smiled wisely and shook her head. "Jaime doesn't drive dump trucks anymore," she said. "And if it wasn't so important to me back then, it sure isn't now. Are you done with your tray? You must not like my cooking. You've barely touched it."

"I'm done with it," Holly Patterson said. "Your cooking's fine. I'm just not hungry."

Twenty-Seven

KRISTIN DUMPED Joanna's mail unceremoniously on her desk. "There's someone else here to see you," she said.

With all these interruptions, how the hell did anyone ever get any work done? Joanna wondered. "Who is it this time?" she asked.

"Linda Somebody-or-other," Kristin answered.

Obviously still offended by the bra-and-panties discussion, Kristin was doing her best to get even. Joanna knew how that game worked. In office politics, passing along incomplete or inaccurate information to the boss constitutes one of the milder forms of a surly receptionist's catalog of revenge.

"Linda who?" Joanna pressed.

"I don't know." Kristin shrugged petulantly. "She didn't say."

Joanna counted to ten. "Kristin," she said, "regardless of whether or not the visitor volunteers the information, it's the receptionist's job to find out who wants to be admitted to my office. You're to tell me who's waiting out there in the lobby, and I decide whether or not I want to see them. Is that clear?"

"What do you want me to do?"

"Go find out who it is. Ask her."

The testy Kristin dragged her feet leaving Joanna's office. The intercom buzzed angrily moments later. "Linda Kimball to see you, Sheriff Brady," Kristin announced with ice crystals dripping from every word.

"Thank you very much, Kristin. Send her right in."

The door opened seconds later, and a plain-Jane Linda Kimball bustled into the room. Heavyset and not worried about it, Burton Kimball's wife had a comfortable, down-home, no-nonsense way about her from her ironclad support panty hose to her naturally graying French twist. Some of the other legal-beagle wives in town tended to dress in designer jeans and play endless games of bridge, all the while holding themselves apart from those they considered lesser beings. Inelegant Linda Kimball, on the other hand, was known and appreciated throughout the community for her boundless energy and tireless work on behalf of those less fortunate than herself.

She routinely volunteered as an aide at the community hospital, and she had served as the money-raising spark plug to keep the local Meals-on-Wheels program under way while daily serving her own family well-balanced, home-cooked meals. Her two children were well mannered and smart. And each fall the vegetables Linda Kimball raised in her backyard garden walked away with a collection of red and blue ribbons from the Cochise County Fair in Douglas.

In addition to all that, Burton Kimball's wife had

a reputation for being virtually unflappable. As she hurried into Joanna's office that afternoon, however, her arm was in a sling and distress was written large across her troubled face. But Linda wasn't there to discuss her injured arm.

"I wanted to talk to Ernie Carpenter, but they told me he's been called out of the office. I hope you don't mind my dropping in like this."

"Not at all, Linda. What can I do for you?"

"I'm in sort of a rush because I left the kids up in Old Bisbee for their piano lessons. I have to be back uptown to pick them up in another half hour, but I needed to talk to someone about what happened out on the ranch today."

"What's that?"

Linda Kimball dropped heavily into one of the visitor chairs and took a deep breath. "Burton called me at lunchtime to tell me all about it. I suppose I should have told him what I thought right then, but he was so upset, I just couldn't bring myself to do it."

"What you thought about what?" Joanna asked.

Linda's double chin quivered. "What I thought about the skeleton," she answered doggedly. "About who I think it is. Or, rather, who it was."

"You mean you know?" Joanna demanded, leaning forward in her chair.

Linda nodded miserably. "Yes, I do," she answered. "At least I have a theory about it."

"Tell me," Joanna urged.

Linda sighed as if not knowing where to start. "Burton said the one body has been there for a very long time."

"That's right. Skeletal remains only."

"Do you know anything at all about my husband?" Linda Kimball asked. "About his history, I mean?"

Joanna considered for a moment. With only six thousand people in town, residents of Bisbee tended to have some knowledge of one another's general histories, even for those people they didn't necessarily know well.

"Some, I guess," she answered. "Wasn't he raised by the Pattersons? I seem to remember something about that."

Linda nodded. "Harold Patterson was Burt's uncle, his mother's older brother. When Thornton, Burt's dad, was discharged from the service after World War II, he and his wife, Bonnie, stayed out on the Rocking P for a while. When Bonnie turned up pregnant, Thornton left her with her brother while he went off to California looking for work. He was supposed to send for her as soon as he found a job and a place to live, but he never did. No one ever heard from him again, and Bonnie Patterson Kimball died in childbirth a few months later. Aunt Emily and Uncle Harold took care of Burton from the time he was born."

Linda broke off, as though just relating her husband's painful history hurt her as well.

"It sounds like a pretty rough thing all the way around," Joanna offered by way of encouragement. "He was lucky there was someone to look after him."

Linda nodded and continued. "They were wonderful to him; treated him just like one of their own. All that ancient family history still bothers my husband, even though it isn't something he talks about. I mean, being abandoned like that does some damage, leaves scars, although, since it happened before he was born, it isn't something he personally remembers."

Joanna was puzzled about where all this was going, but she knew enough to shut up and let Linda tell the story her way.

"It's one of the reasons family is so important to him," Linda continued. "And it's why that terrible business between Uncle Harold and Holly upset him so. Burton would never say so, but he loved that crotchety old man just as much as if Uncle Harold had been his natural father. It tore him to pieces to think that Holly would come out of nowhere, armed with her high-priced lawyer and her therapist and all those horrendous stories."

Linda paused and almost stopped, as though her talking engine were running low on steam. "That's also why he's always been so concerned about Ivy," she added.

"Burton's worried about Ivy?" Joanna asked.

"Wouldn't you be?" Linda countered. "It sounds to me as though she's really gone off the deep end. The idea that she's getting married within hours of her father's death and without even mentioning it to Burton ... It's breaking his heart. Not that we would have gone, but she didn't even bother to invite him to the wedding."

"Why is Burton so upset?" Joanna asked. "I

know Ivy's timing is a little unorthodox and could raise a few eyebrows, but I'd think he'd be happy that she's finally found someone after all this time."

"You don't understand," Linda said. "Back when those three kids were growing up, Burton always considered Ivy his baby sister. All his life, he's tried to look out for her best interests the way a big brother should. Maybe even more than he should."

Linda paused as if uncertain what to say next. Stifling her inclination to rush her, Joanna kept quiet.

"Getting back to this family stuff. I knew from the beginning that family connections bothered him. I had both my parents—still do—while his natural parents were both gone. For a long time, we didn't even discuss the subject. Later on, though, when he finally could tell me about it, he admitted that he'd always hoped that someday he'd have a chance to meet his father. He said he wanted to ask Thornton Kimball why he left town. Why he ran away and never came back. Why he never even acknowledged his son's birth. That dream of someday meeting his father is one he's carried around in his heart from the time he was just a little kid. When he told me about it, I thought my heart would break just listening to him. It was so sad, so unfair."

Linda took another breath. "I love him, you see, and I finally had to do something about it."

"About what?"

"About making that dream come true. I decided to try finding Thornton Kimball on my own, without telling Burt what I was up to. I wanted to surprise him. I thought that if he finally had the chance to meet and talk to his natural father, it might help him put some of his own personal demons to rest. He's spent a lifetime blaming himself, you know, not only for his mother's death, but also for his father's desertion."

"Any luck finding his father?"

"No," Linda answered. "None. I've checked everywhere—the Salvation Army, the V.A., the genealogical library up in Salt Lake. Everywhere I go, I keep running into blank walls. It was as though Thornton Kimball left the Rocking P one day and vanished into thin air."

Feeling like some dimwitted comic-strip character, Joanna felt the light bulb switch on over her head when she finally made the connection. "You believe the other body in the glory hole might be Thornton Kimball's?"

Linda nodded. "As soon as Burt told me about the skeleton, this terrible feeling of certainty washed over me. I can't explain it. I don't know where it came from, but as far as I can tell, from the time he left here in 1945, no one ever heard a single word from Thornton Kimball. And maybe that's why—because he never really left."

Joanna felt a swift rush of rising excitement. Linda Kimball's theory made good sense. She reached for the phone. "I'll pass this information along to Ernie Carpenter right away."

"Wait," Linda said. "Don't call him yet."

"Why not?" Joanna said. "With this information, maybe we can get some help from the state crime laboratory—utilize some of their new DNA technology."

"I don't think you'll have to do that," Linda Kimball said quietly.

Joanna put down the phone. "Why not?"

Linda shifted uneasily in her chair. "Promise me you won't tell Burton how you found out. It's embarrassing. He'd be so angry if he ever found out about it."

Joanna thought she had been following all the nuances of the twisting story line, but now she was suddenly lost. "If he found out about what?" she asked.

Linda Kimball bit her lower lip while a pair of fat tears squeezed out of her eyes and ran down both cheeks, leaving behind twin tracks of dark-brown mascara. One-handed, Linda fumbled in her massive purse long enough to extract a packet of tissues. After dabbing her eyes and blowing her nose, she forged ahead.

"Do you ever go to yard sales?" she asked.

"Not often," Joanna answered. "I usually don't have either the time or the money."

"I shouldn't go to them myself, but I do," Linda said. "It's one of those things that drives Burton crazy. He really disapproves. He says it's not dignified for people in our position to go around buying other people's cast-off junk, but I can't help it. One of my hobbies is refinishing antiques, and going to those private sales is how I've found some of my very best pieces. Do you remember when Grace Luther died?"

Joanna nodded. At the time ninety-six-year-old Grace Luther passed away, her death had been the talk of the town. Since it happened while Hank Lathrop was still sheriff, Joanna knew more of the gory details than she probably should have. Everyone in town had thought Grace was up in Tucson visiting her niece, but it turned out the niece had brought her back to Bisbee and left her off at home. Somehow word of her return didn't get passed along to Grace's at-home caregiver.

While everyone in Bisbee continued to believe that Grace was out of town, the old lady was actually dead as could be, lying flat on her back in her own bed with the thermostat cranked up to eighty-some degrees. The corpse was three weeks old and pretty well cooked by the time people realized something was wrong and broke into the house. It wasn't a pretty sight. Or smell. After investigating the scene, Hank Lathrop had come home and burned all the clothes he had been wearing.

Afterward, there was a protracted battle among a bunch of feuding heirs, including the scatter-brained niece who had dropped the old lady off at home without letting anyone know. For years, while lawyers battled back and forth, the house sat vacant—boarded up but crammed full of a century's worth of junk.

"I went to that estate sale," Linda Kimball continued. "The house was a shambles—stacked with trash from floor to ceiling. But there were some treasures buried in there as well. In fact, I found that wonderful ivory-inlay table I still have in my living room. And down in the basement, I found everything from her husband's office."

"That's right," Joanna said. "I remember that, too. Wasn't Dr. Luther a dentist with an office somewhere in Upper Lowell?"

Linda nodded. "Right where the open-pit mine is now. Doc Luther was already dead in the early fifties when they tore the building down to make way for Lavender Pit. Grace had Phelps Dodge haul all her husband's equipment and everything else from his office down to her house in Warren. They loaded it into her garage and basement—chairs, drills, and everything—and there it stayed. I don't think that woman ever in her life threw anything away."

Once again Linda Kimball reached for her purse. This time she extracted a small white envelope.

"This is the part that's so embarrassing," she said. "I still can't believe I did it. Promise me you won't tell Burton. He'd have a fit."

"Tell him what?"

"While I was down in the basement that day—the day of the sale—I was rummaging around looking for antiques when I came across a huge stack of Dr. Luther's old files that had been dumped out of a file cabinet. I knew he was the dentist Burton had gone to as a young child. I thought it might be fun to have his earliest dental records, just as sort of a keepsake. But while I was looking, I found this—and I stole it."

With visibly trembling fingers, Linda Kimball handed the envelope over to Joanna, who hesitated only a second before ripping it open. Inside was a yellowed three-by-five card. The cardboard was stiff and brittle and turning brown around the edges. Printed on both sides were old-fashioned dental records, complete with predrawn diagrams of human teeth. Handwritten comments as well as arrows pointing to fillings and cavities had been added to the margins.

As she looked at the diagram, it was a moment before Joanna noticed the name written at the top of the card.

"Thornton W. Kimball's dental records!" Joanna exclaimed.

"I know it's not like modern X rays or anything," Linda Kimball was saying, almost apologetically, "but I thought it might help."

"It'll help, all right. If you don't mind, I'll go to work on it right away." Joanna reached out and punched the button on her intercom.

"Yes?" Kristin was still all ice.

"Have Dispatch raise Ernie Carpenter on the radio. Find out where he is and tell him to stay there. Tell him I'm bringing him something important."

Even though Joanna considered the interview over, when she looked back at Linda Kimball, the other woman had not yet moved.

"Is there something else?" Joanna asked.

Linda nodded. "I've tried all afternoon to put myself in Burton's shoes. Which do you think is worse?" she asked.

"Which what?" Joanna returned.

"Knowing or not knowing? Is he better off thinking his father is still alive somewhere and that he deserted his wife and his unborn son? Or is he better off knowing for sure his father is dead? That he left and didn't come back because he didn't have a choice, because he was lying dead in a glory hole on Harold Patterson's ranch?"

Joanna pondered carefully before she answered. "That's a tough call," she said finally, "but I think most people would rather know the truth, however painful it might be."

Linda Kimball groped for her purse and hefted it into her lap. "That's what I decided, too," she said. "This afternoon. But that's why I wanted to bring the envelope today. I wanted someone else to have it, before I had a chance to change my mind."

As Linda left the room, the intercom buzzed. "Ernie's down working in the glory hole on the Patterson ranch. He wants to know can it wait?"

"It can't wait. Tell him to keep on doing what he's doing. I'll come find him. What about a car, Kristin? Did you get one for me?"

"All that's available today is a five-year-old Blazer. Body's good; engine's a little rough. That's what Danny from Motor Pool says."

"I only want to know two things. Does it run, and is it equipped with a working radio?"

"Danny says yes."

"Good. Tell him to bring it around as soon as he can. I'd like to have it here in under five minutes, with the engine running and a full tank of gas. And, Kristin?"

"Yes."

"Thanks for taking care of the car," Joanna said "Good job."

Twenty-Eight

WHEN JOANNA rushed out of the office in search of Ernie Carpenter, she grabbed the stack of unopened mail and took it along with her. The Blazer with the Sheriff's Department insignia on the door was a long way from new, but that didn't bother her. After all, it was several years newer than her old Eagle.

Once on the Rocking P, she drove straight to the glory hole without turning off at the house. As she went past, though, she caught a glimpse of Ivy's Luv parked by the front gate. Seeing it made her wonder if Ivy would really go through with her hasty wedding plans. By getting married within days of her father's death, Ivy would be committing one of those breaches of small-town etiquette that would expand into legend with countless retellings.

Where hasty marriages were concerned, Joanna Brady was one of the few people in town prepared to give the benefit of the doubt to Yuri Malakov and Ivy Patterson's late-blooming, whirlwind romance. After all, Joanna and Andy had raised gossiping eyebrows years earlier with their own

293

rushed wedding. That union had certainly worked
out fine in the long run.

A rushed marriage was probably fine, but the
possibility of murder was not. Personally, Joanna
wanted to believe in the idea of two people living
happily ever after, but a determination on whether
or not the newlyweds would ride off into the sun-
set on a honeymoon or end up in prison at Flor-
ence would have to be left in Ernie Carpenter's
capable hands. It was up to him and to a judge
and jury.

This time when Joanna arrived at the glory hole,
there was a whole collection of vehicles parked
around it. She had to leave the Blazer a fair distance away and then tiptoe over the rocky ground
in her city-slicker black pumps. High heels that
were only marginally safe on flat sidewalk surfaces were downright dangerous on the splintery
shale.

Three young deputies lounged around the hole.
Ostensibly, they were running spotlights and lug-
ging equipment, but mostly they leaned on fence
posts with their hands in their pockets and chewed
the fat. As soon as Joanna drove up, they all made
an obvious pretense of looking busy.

"Hey, Detective Carpenter," one of them called
down into the hole. "Sheriff Brady's here."

"What are you waiting for then?" Ernie grumbled back. "Winch me up so I can talk to her and
get it over with."

While Joanna watched, a filthy, mud-caked spec-
ter rose up out of the glory hole. The bandbox
detective who had sat taking notes in her office

only hours earlier now looked and smelled like a battle-weary infantryman in night camouflage. Once out of the harness, he strode over to the van where a makeshift washbasin had been set up on the tailgate. Cursing her wretched shoes, Joanna tripped after him.

"How do you do it?" she asked irritably.

"Do what?" he asked, bending over and carefully soaping his hands, then sloshing the dirt off his grubby face.

"One minute you look like you just stepped out of *Gentlemen's Quarterly*. The next you look like you haven't changed clothes in years."

"Oh, that," Ernie Carpenter said with a short laugh. "It's a trick I learned from my wife. Whenever she was expecting, she always kept a packed suitcase by the front door. I keep two changes of clothes in my car at all times, because in this line of work, you never know what's going to turn up. Speaking of which, I take it something did."

Joanna nodded and pulled the white envelope out of her pocket. "Look what someone brought to my office earlier this afternoon. I thought you'd want to see it."

Drying his hands on a paper towel, Ernie took the offered envelope, opened it, and removed the three-by-five card. He read it without comment, then slipped the card back in the envelope.

"That's fine," he said without showing more than minimal interest. "It's bound to make the coroner's identification job that much easier."

"You think it's him then?" Joanna asked, disappointed that Ernie's level of excitement didn't match her own.

"I'm sure of it," he answered, opening a nylon fanny-pack that was strapped around his waist. "As soon as I saw these, I was pretty sure that's who it was."

He removed something from the bag, dunked it in the water, and then dried it with a towel. "Look at this," he said.

Joanna held out her hand, and Ernie dropped something into it. At first she thought it was the beaded brass pull chain from some old light fixture. Despite the rinsing it was still green and crusted over with muck. Eventually, she realized it was actually two chains, a larger one and a smaller, with the small one strung through the larger. Each chain held a single rectangular piece of metal. A sharp notch had been cut in the long side of one of the pieces.

"What is it?" Joanna asked.

"Look closer," Ernie said.

Holding the tarnished metal up to her eyes, Joanna was barely able to make out the faint letters that had been etched into the metal: THORNTON WILLIAM KIMBALL along with a series of numbers.

"His World War II military dog tags?" Joanna asked.

She looked down at the muddy pieces of metal in her hand. Sadly, she rubbed one finger along the sharp notch that, in wartime, would have been jammed between a dead soldier's lower front teeth to serve as identification. Just as Linda Kimball feared, this was the pitiful ending of Burton Kimball's long-cherished dream of one day being re-united with his runaway father.

"What are you going to do about it?" she asked.

Ernie rubbed his chin thoughtfully. "Conceiv-ably, somebody else could have been wearing Thornton Kimball's dog tags, but I doubt it. And with those dental records, it'll be a piece of cake to confirm."

He glanced back toward the glory hole where his assistants were beginning to dismantle the winch and lights. "I'm about done here," Ernie continued. "After I clean myself up, do you want me to notify Burton Kimball about what's going on, or would you rather do it?"

Joanna's energies were stretched thin. Too much had happened in too short a time. "No," she said, "you do it." Feeling suddenly tired, she started back toward the Blazer.

"By the way," Ernie called after her. "I did what you suggested. I tried running Yuri Malakov past the Multi-Jurisdiction guys and INS with their fancy-schmancy computer."

"Did they have any information?"

"Yes, evidently, but it's off-limits. I found that very interesting."

"What do you mean, 'interesting?' "

"It means Yuri Malakov is in their goddamned database for some reason or another, but nobody's allowed to ask about him. Or, if they do, they're not to be given a straight answer."

Joanna frowned. "That doesn't make sense. Aren't we all working the same side of the fence?"

Ernie Carpenter looked down on her and shook his head sadly, as if surprised by her naïveté.

"No ma'am," he said. "I wouldn't go so far as to say that. As a matter of fact, I'd say we haven't even gotten around to agreeing on a survey for the fence line, to say nothing of building the damn thing and settling which side everybody's on."

Joanna wasn't sure if Ernie's round-about answer was simply patronizing or if it was meant to make fun of her. Either choice made her hackles rise.

"Get to the point," she snapped irritably.

"The point is," Ernie answered, "if Yuri Malakov's name is punched into that computer but nobody's willing to talk about him or say why he's in there, then I sure as hell wouldn't want *my* daughter to marry the sonofabitch, and I'll bet money Harold Patterson didn't want Ivy to tie the knot with him, either."

Burton Kimball sat brooding in his darkened and deserted office. Everyone else had gone home. Even the ever-loyal, ever-vigilant Maxine had finally abandoned ship at six o'clock. Linda had called twice to check on him and to ask when he was coming home. He kept telling her soon now, that he was working on an important project that had to be finished before court the next day.

That was an outright lie. The surface of his desk was empty except for a sheen of blank despair.

Burton felt as though his life was whirling out of control. As the gold hands on his watch edged closer to seven, his depression deepened. He had deliberately stayed around the office all afternoon, hoping Ivy would call, hoping she would relent and invite him to the wedding. But she hadn't and it was too late now.

In a few minutes Ivy Patterson would marry that Russian nobody, and Burton Kimball wouldn't even be there to see it.

How do you go about losing your best friend? he wondered. Things had changed once he and Linda had married and come back to Bisbee to live and establish his practice. Aunt Emily was already a total invalid by then, and Ivy had been charged with her mother's day-to-day care. He and Linda had tried to help out, but there wasn't that much they could do. The old, loving Aunt Emily had been replaced by a stranger, an irascible tyrant who yelled orders from her hospital bed. She hurled insults as well as physical objects— vases; books; glasses—at anyone foolish enough to venture near her.

Ivy had carried that whole burden and it had worn her down, changed her, aged her. And today Burton was feeling the weight of his own responsibility in that regard. He should have done more to help; should have paid more attention.

Burton had grieved over Aunt Emily during her illness and rejoiced at her death, when she was finally released from her dreadful physical and mental incapacities. And he had thought somehow, that after it was all over, he and Ivy would go back to being best friends, the way they had been before. That hadn't happened. They had drifted along for years, still all right, not quarreling but not as close as they had once been, either. All that had changed once Holly Patterson had reappeared on the scene.

Somehow, logically or not, Ivy seemed to hold Burton responsible for her sister's sudden return. At first Ivy and Burton had been united once again, going nose-to-nose with Harold over how best to handle the complexities of the Holly situation. Ivy had seemed satisfied with Burton's strategy until two days earlier when the whole thing had blown up in his face and Harold had gone off to make his fateful offer. Burton now felt that Ivy was holding him entirely responsible. For everything.

A discreet knock on Burton's outside window made him jump. Looking through the darkened glass, he saw Ernie Carpenter standing there, motioning to be let into the building.

"What's going on?" Burton asked, as he opened the entryway door.

"I just talked to your wife," Ernie explained. "She said you were working late. I hope you don't mind the interruption."

Burton led Ernie back to his private office. Switching on the light revealed his damningly empty desktop. It was clear Burton wasn't really working and that he hadn't been.

"I was actually just finishing up and about to go home," he said lamely, going over to his door and making a show of taking his jacket off the hanger. He draped his tie around the back of his neck. "I have a few minutes. What can I do for you?"

"Sheriff Brady told me you were out at the Rocking P earlier today," Ernie said.

Burton nodded. "That's right. Why?"

"You already know about the other body in the glory hole?"

"Yes. Unfortunately, I do. I think the shock of finding out about that pretty much unhinged Ivy. It's probably some poor old wetback who fell into the hole before Uncle Harold got around to fencing it up."

"I doubt it's a wetback," Ernie Carpenter said firmly. "In fact, I expect to have a positive I.D. within days."

Burton Kimball's eyes blinked in surprise. "No kidding. Good work. Anyone I might know?"

Refusing to accept Burton's hints about leaving, Ernie Carpenter settled into a chair. "How old were you when your father left home?" he asked.

Kimball seemed more than a little taken aback by the detective's blunt question. A pained expression flashed across his face. "Me? I wasn't even born yet. My mother was pregnant with me when my father went off to California looking for a job and never came back."

"Who told you that story? That your father went to California, I mean."

"Uncle Harold and Aunt Emily, I suppose. I don't understand. Why are you asking about my father? What's going on?" Dropping his jacket onto the surface of the desk, Burton Kimball sank back down in his chair.

"I'm afraid I have some bad news for you, Burt," Ernie said kindly. "Your father never made it to California. Or, if he did, he must have come back home sometime later on."

"He came back? . . ." Burton began, but then comprehension slowly dawned. "You can't mean it! Surely, you're not saying it's him! The skeleton in the glory hole is my father?"

Ernie Carpenter nodded. "I'm sorry to have to break it to you like this."

Burton's ruddy complexion paled. "But how can you know that? How can you tell for sure?"

Ernie reached in his pocket and pulled out the newly cleaned dog tags, which he dropped lightly on the desk in front of Burton Kimball. For a moment, the other man stared at them without moving. Then, carefully, gingerly, as though the metal might be red-hot, he picked up the chain and held it up to the light.

"We also have dental records to go by," Ernie said. "Those should cinch it. I thought you'd want to know."

Abruptly, Burton spun his chair around. He sat with his back turned to Ernie Carpenter. Staring up at the soothing water-color garden scene Linda had given him last Christmas to hang on the blank wall behind his desk, he tried unsuccessfully to blink back tears. Ernie waited through the silence.

"I always secretly hoped he was dead," Burton Kimball croaked at last. "As a little kid, that was the only way I could cope. His being dead was the only reason I knew that justified his going off and leaving me alone like that. I wondered what was wrong with me that he'd do a thing like that.

And how could he tell something was wrong with me before I was even born?"

"Burton," Ernie began.

But the younger man continued, ignoring the interruption. "And late at night I'd tell myself stories about him, about how he'd been run down by a train somewhere or how he'd drowned in the ocean and been washed out to sea. But deep inside, I always figured he was alive somewhere, living with a beautiful new wife and new children. I always hoped he'd come back for me someday, like a knight on a white charger, and that he'd take me to live with them. He never did."

Burton Kimball fell silent. It was a long time before Ernie Carpenter spoke again. "Was there any bad blood between your father and your uncle Harold?"

"Bad blood?" Burton repeated. "What's that supposed to mean? And why would there be? Uncle Harold was my mother's brother. After my mother died, from the time I was a baby, he and Aunt Emily took care of me. As far as I know, that's all there was to it."

Burton turned back around and faced the detective, a concerned frown etching his face. "Why are you asking?"

"Because," Ernie answered simply, "they both ended up in the same place, dead in the bottom of a glory hole. From what I saw today, I'd say they were both murdered. Fifty years apart, but the same way. The killer or killers heaved rocks down at them from above."

"That doesn't make any sense," Burton Kimball said. "What would the connection be?"

The room grew very still. "You," Ernie Carpenter said softly.

"Me!"

"I've heard from several people that you and your uncle quarreled shortly before noon on Tuesday. I understand you stormed out of your office that afternoon and didn't show up again until you came to the Election Night party looking for Harold Patterson."

"That's right. I saw his car in the parking lot and . . ."

"Where did you go when you first left your office?"

Burton Kimball stiffened under Ernie Carpenter's suddenly chilly gaze. "Why do you want to know?"

"Just answer the question."

"I went drinking."

"Where?"

"Up the Gulch. The Blue Moon."

"How long did you stay there?"

"Awhile. I don't know exactly. I don't remember."

"And where did you go after that?"

As soon as Burton Kimball realized he was actually under suspicion, he snapped. "That's none of your damn business, Ernie. Now get the hell out of here. And the next time you open your big mouth around me, you'd better either be apologizing or reading me my damn rights. Understand?"

Without another word, Ernie Carpenter scooped

up the dog tags and beat it for the door. Burton sat frozen at his desk until the heavy outside door slammed shut behind the retreating detective. Only after it closed did Burton get up. He staggered around the desk and pushed the knob that locked his office door from the inside.

Then, like a dazed sleepwalker, he groped his way blindly back to his desk. He dropped heavily into the chair and sat there, staring straight ahead while his fingers clung desperately to the polished edge of his desk. It was almost as if his white-knuckled grip was all that was keeping him from being flung far into lifeless, timeless space.

Eventually, the all-enveloping, childlike whimper he had been trying so desperately to suppress managed to work its way to the surface. Forty-five years after the fact, the little boy who had never once cried aloud over his father's desertion or his mother's death put his arms on the desk, laid his head on his arms, and sobbed.

Afterward, he just sat there, dry-eyed and without moving, totally unaware of the passage of time. Finally, an unexpected knock on the door startled him out of his painful reverie.

"Go away, Maxine," he growled. "I don't want to talk to anybody."

"It's me," Linda Kimball replied tentatively. "Maxine called to see if you'd come home yet. She said she thought something was wrong. I decided to come see for myself. Can I come in?"

"Come ahead."

"I can't. The door's locked."

Burton got up and stumbled around the desk.

Even though he hadn't had a drop of liquor since Tuesday at the Blue Moon, he felt as though he'd been drinking. As though he were drunk.

When Linda Kimball saw her husband's ravaged face, she put her hand to her mouth. "Burton!" she exclaimed. "What is it? What's wrong?"

Burton shook his head and blundered back to his desk. "You won't believe it," he said. "Never in a million years."

"Yes, I will," Linda insisted. "Tell me."

Twenty-Nine

JOANNA PICKED up Jenny from the Bradys' house at six and drove straight home. She couldn't wait to strip out of her good clothes and the cumbersome bulletproof vest that had rubbed the skin under her arms until it was raw.

While Jenny went to her room to do homework, her mother set about cooking dinner. It seemed strange to look forward to an entire evening at home—an evening with no speeches to write or give, no campaign strategy meetings to oversee. The sudden sense of decompression was almost palpable. For the first time in months, Joanna Brady had only one job to do instead of two.

While searching the refrigerator for leftover vegetables to put in the roast-beef hash, she discovered two forgotten Tupperware containers shoved into the far back corner of the bottom shelf. One contained a few desiccated and no-longer-green peas. The second, filled with some kind of mystery food, sported a brilliant layer of fuchsia-colored mold and exuded a powerful odor that somehow reminded her of the glory hole. And at that moment she didn't want to think about the glory hole or Harold Patterson or Thornton Kimball.

Firmly shutting the lids on the two containers, Joanna tossed them into the sink, promising to clean both them and the refrigerator right after dinner. It was time to start paying attention to the little things again, to catch up on some of the domestic housekeeping chores that—in the aftermath of Andy's death—had been allowed to fall victim to disinterest and neglect.

Jenny came to dinner promptly when called and slipped silently into her usual place in the breakfast nook. "How was school today?" Joanna asked cheerfully, trying to bridge mealtime's now-customary silence as she filled Jenny's plate.

"Okay, I guess," the child answered, ducking her chin and not meeting her mother's questioning gaze. "How was work?"

What should she answer? Joanna wondered. Should she talk about finding Harold Patterson's body? Should she tell Jenny the old man had possibly been murdered or protect her from that knowledge? Harold had always been one of the kind old men who bought Girl Scout cookies from Jenny's makeshift stand in front of the post office. He wouldn't be doing that anymore. Ever. Was Jennifer Brady tough enough to deal with the awful details of one more violent death in her small circle of acquaintances?

"It was okay, too," Joanna answered finally, choking on the distancing words and pained by the strained formality between them. Would she and her daughter ever be easy with one another again?

They both picked at their food. The hash had

smelled so enticing to Joanna as she cooked it, but in her mouth the food turned to tasteless sand. Finally, giving up, she put down her fork. "I've been thinking about what you said," Joanna ventured tentatively. "About what would happen to you if something happened to me."

Jenny, too, put down her fork and regarded her mother through unblinking china-blue eyes. "You mean if you died?" she asked.

Joanna, dismayed by the child's directness, struggled on.

"If a man has two eyes, he doesn't have to worry that much about going blind. If he loses one, then he starts worrying about losing the other as well. If he worries about it too much; if he lets that fear of going blind become the whole focus of his life, he may stop enjoying the things he can still see with that one good eye. He ends up forgetting that even if the worst happens, even if he loses the sight in that second eye, it doesn't mean his life is over."

"He could always get a guide dog," Jenny suggested helpfully. "Erin Wallace, one of the girls in my class, is training one of those. A golden-retriever puppy. It's her 4-H project."

Joanna smiled. "It's the same thing with us," she continued. "You're so scared about what might happen next, about what might happen to me, that it's keeping you from enjoying life around you. I don't think you'd be nearly as worried about me and my new job if you still had both parents. But you don't. You only have one. It's a problem, isn't it?"

"Yes," Jenny agreed, almost in a whisper.

"So, I've been trying to find a solution; a way so that if something really did happen to me, you'd have a place to go and someone dependable to take care of you."

"Not Grandma Lathrop," Jenny protested at once, giving her long blond hair a defiant toss. "She treats me like a baby. She still thinks I should be in bed by seven o'clock."

"And not Grandma and Grandpa Brady, either," Joanna added. "They're wonderful, and they love you. But they've already raised one child, and that's enough. They shouldn't have to raise another. It's a lot of work."

Jenny nodded in agreement, chiming in with another surprisingly apt observation. "They're nice, but they're too old."

"What would you think about Jeff and Marianne?" Joanna asked carefully. "I haven't spoken to them about it yet, because I wanted to check with you first, to see what you thought of the idea."

"Do Jeff and Marianne even want kids?" Jenny asked.

"I'm sure they do."

"Why don't they have any, then?"

"Maybe they can't," Joanna replied, knowing from things Marianne had told her in confidence that it was the truth. "Maybe they've tried, and they just aren't able to."

"You could ask them," Jenny suggested.

"No, that's private, something to be discussed just between them."

Jenny picked up her fork and began drawing aimless lines through the remaining hash that was turning to a ketchup-laden crust on her plate. For once, Joanna managed to stifle the overwhelming urge to tell Jenny not to play with her food.

"So what do you think of the idea?" Joanna asked. "Of asking Jeff and Marianne?"

"Would they let me keep my dogs?"

"I don't know. That would be up to them when the time came, something you three would have to talk over and decide on."

For some time, Jenny sat thinking. Finally, she shrugged. "I guess it would be okay. That way, I'd have parents to take care of me, and they'd have a child, even if I wasn't their very own. We'd be like each other's guide dog, right?"

"Right." Joanna nodded.

Just then Sadie, the bluetick, sprang to her feet and hurried to the door, growling low in her throat while the hackles rose on the back of her neck. Tigger, the pit bull, whose hearing wasn't as keen, quickly followed suit. It was several minutes before the vehicle Sadie had evidently heard crossing the cattle guard bounced into the yard.

Joanna was waiting on the back porch when Linda Kimball's Jeep Cherokee stopped in front of the gate. Dressed in high heels, Linda climbed down and made her way over the uneven sidewalk to where Joanna was standing.

"I apologize for just showing up like this, but I couldn't call before I left home," Linda said as Joanna ushered her inside. "I told Burt I was going to a PTA officer's planning meeting."

It was one of the ironies of Joanna's Craftsman home that most guests, even strangers, arrived through the side yard and back door while the front porch and official entryway remained virtually unused. Embarrassed by piles of unwashed laundry, Joanna led her visitor through the laundry room and kitchen and on into the living room.

"Can I get you anything?" Joanna asked. "Coffee, tea?"

"You wouldn't happen to have any Postum, would you?"

"No."

"Well, nothing then. I just need to talk to you. I need to talk to somebody."

"What about?"

"About Burton. Do you have any idea what's going on?"

"What do you mean?"

"Ernie Carpenter came by the office and showed Burton his father's dog tags. Said they'd found those with the skeleton up in the glory hole. Ernie mentioned the dental records, I guess, but he didn't talk about them very much."

"What's the problem then?" Joanna asked. "I thought that's what you wanted, for someone to figure out for sure whether or not the body belonged to Burton's father and to tell Burton without letting on that some of the information came from you."

"That's true, but it's not all," Linda said. She sat down on the couch but remained stiffly upright, nervously running her good hand back and forth across the already smooth material of her skirt.

"What else?" Joanna asked.

Linda Kimball took a deep breath. "Ernie Carpenter seems to think Burt may have had something to do with Uncle Harold's death. He asked Burt where he was on Tuesday afternoon. They had a big fight, you know."

"Who did?"

"Burt and Uncle Harold. Earlier in the day. Over Uncle Harold's proposed settlement with Holly."

"So where was Burt? Did he tell you?"

Linda sighed. "He went to a bar. He hasn't done that in years, not since the night before we got married. He says he stayed there most of the afternoon."

"Which bar?"

"The Blue Moon. Up the Gulch. But now you're asking about it, too. I'm telling you, Burton Kimball didn't kill his uncle Harold. Surely, you believe that, don't you?"

"Linda," Joanna cautioned, "what I believe and what I don't believe aren't important. Homicide detectives like Ernie always ask questions. It's their job. The mere fact that they're asking someone questions doesn't necessarily mean they think that person is guilty of any crime. By talking to lots of people, interviewing them and asking questions, they get to the bottom of what really happened."

"That's exactly what I want Ernie to do," Linda Kimball declared. "I want him to get to the bottom of it and find out what really happened, because if he doesn't . . ."

Sobbing, she broke off. Unable to continue, she

went searching in her purse for that same thin packet of tissues, just as she had done earlier that same afternoon.

"Linda," Joanna said kindly. "I don't understand. What's wrong?"

Linda shook her head. "I've been married to Burton Kimball for a long time. I know him almost as well as I know myself, but I've never seen him the way he was tonight. I can't stand seeing him like that."

"Like what?"

"Afraid."

"Afraid of what?"

"Of himself," Linda answered. "He's afraid he did it."

"Did what?"

"He thinks he murdered Uncle Harold and that he doesn't remember it because he was drunk. Of course, that's just ridiculous. Burton would never do such a thing. He's the kindest man in the world. I can't stand seeing him so upset."

"Upset about his father? Upset about being a possible suspect in a homicide investigation?"

"Both, I'm sure," Linda assented. "Finding out about his father has been a terrible shock, but I don't think that's the real problem."

"What is?"

Linda Kimball's double chins trembled dangerously. "I'm afraid he's making this whole thing up, building a case and blaming himself in order to save Ivy."

"How and why would he do that?" Joanna asked.

The other woman stared vacantly off into space for several long seconds. "We met while Burt was in law school, and I was still an undergraduate. Burt refused to get married until after he was out of law school and on his way to having a practice. We've had a very good marriage, but I've always known about the competition."

"Competition?" Joanna frowned, offended by the idea that someone as seemingly upstanding as Burton Kimball might be two-timing his wife.

"Ivy," Linda Kimball answered simply. "He's always worried about her more than anyone else in the whole world. He's always tried to take care of her, to protect her."

"You don't mean . . . ?"

"Oh, no," Linda answered quickly. "Nothing nasty or improper—nothing like that. If he hadn't cared about her so much, I'm sure he wouldn't have blabbed to her about Harold wanting to make a settlement. And then, abracadabra, before Harold can make good on what he said, before he can change any of his other arrangements, Harold Patterson is murdered. And who benefits from those changes not being made? Ivy, that's who! No one but Ivy."

"You think your husband is lying about what happened? You think he's deliberately shifting blame to himself in order to protect her?"

"No," Linda Kimball returned somberly. "I think he really believes he did it. He was drunk and doesn't remember, so now he thinks he was functioning in a blackout. No, he's absolutely convinced of his own guilt. If I'd been smarter, I would have seen it coming a long time ago."

"Seen what coming?" Joanna asked, still in the dark.

"Don't you understand?" Linda Kimball pleaded, her voice cracking with suppressed emotion. "I'm afraid. Scared to death. And I don't know what to do."

"Please, Linda," Joanna said, shaking her head. "You must be leaving something out. I don't understand what you're talking about, what you're afraid of."

"That if it comes to a choice between Ivy and me, he'll choose her."

"Come on, be serious. That's ridiculous. You're married to the man, for God's sake. You're the mother of his children. Ivy is just Burt's cousin. How could he possibly choose her over you?"

"If Ernie arrests him, if Burt . . . How is it they say that on TV? Fall? Rap? That's it, the rap. If Burt takes the rap, Ivy is home free. And if it came to that, I don't think Burt would lift a finger to help himself. He as good as told me so tonight in his office. And what happens then? Whoever really murdered Harold Patterson gets away with it, and all because Burton is looking out for his precious Ivy!"

"Linda," Joanna began, "believe me, that's not going to happen."

"Oh, yeah? I can even tell you how. Burton says that since he was blind drunk at the time it happened, the worst any judge in the state would give him is probably second degree. He's sure he'll be able to plea-bargain that down to simple manslaughter."

"You're serious about this, then, aren't you?" Joanna said, with sudden understanding.

Linda nodded. "I'm serious all right, and so is Burt. He loves the kids and me, I'm sure of it. Being abandoned when he was a baby. Feeling like, except for Ivy Patterson, he was all alone in the world. Those things that happened to him when he was a child still have a powerful hold on him. I'm afraid he'd sacrifice Chris and Kim and me in a minute to save her. We wouldn't starve, I suppose. I could always go back to teaching school, and the church would help us. But still . . ."

They sat quietly for a few moments while the draining dishwasher whirred noisily in the kitchen. Jennifer had long since loaded the dishes and disappeared into her own room.

"Why did you come to me with this?" Joanna asked finally. "Ernie Carpenter is the detective on the case. Why didn't you go straight to him?"

Linda shrugged. "I don't know. I already talked to you about it this afternoon. It just seemed easier. I thought maybe another woman would understand better. A man might jump to the wrong conclusion. He might think something awful was going on between Ivy and Burton. It's just not like that. My husband is a very honorable man. After what's happened with Uncle Harold with Holly, it would kill Burton to have people thinking those same kinds of thoughts about him."

Linda glanced at her watch, then hurriedly rose

to her feet. "I'd better get going," she said. "Those meetings hardly ever last much over an hour. I don't want him being suspicious."

"You still haven't said what you expect me to do."

"I thought if I could get you to see through to what's really going on, then maybe you could help keep Ernie on track. I wonder if maybe that boyfriend of Ivy's has anything to do with it. Maybe they're getting married in such a hurry so they can't be forced to testify against one another."

"I hadn't thought of that," Joanna said.

"Well, I did," Linda Kimball returned grimly. "And I'll be damned if I'm going to stand still and let them get away with it."

"Ernie Carpenter's a pro," Joanna said reassuringly. "A real pro. If anyone can find out what really happened, Ernie can do it."

Linda Kimball straightened her shoulders. "Good," she said, sounding somewhat heartened. "I'd better be going then."

After Linda left, Joanna forgot her intention to clean the refrigerator. Instead, she returned to the living room, where she sat alone for some time, wondering about the complicated relationship between Burton Kimball and his cousin Ivy. What was the tie between them that would make Linda afraid her husband would sacrifice his whole life— his career and his family—to protect Ivy Patterson? Was it nothing more than an innocent, brotherly-type love, or was it something much more malignant?

Around nine Jenny slipped out of her room and

sat down on the couch next to her mother. The child was wearing her flannel nightgown, one Grandma Brady had made for her at Christmas the previous year. At the time the gown was new, it had been so long that the hem had skimmed the floor with every step. Now it barely covered the child's bony ankles. It was a shock for Joanna to realize how much her daughter had grown in such a short time.

For the first time in weeks, Jenny snuggled close and let her mother wrap one arm around her.

"Who was that lady?" she asked.

"A woman from town," Joanna answered, pulling Jenny closer. "Her name is Linda Kimball."

"What did she want?"

"She's worried about her husband. She's afraid he's going to say he did something he didn't do, just to keep someone else from getting in trouble."

"But why did she come here?" Jenny asked.

"I guess she came to talk to me because she didn't want to talk to Ernie Carpenter. There were things she had to say that were upsetting to her; things she wanted to talk over with another woman instead of with a man."

"She wanted a woman detective instead of a man?" Jenny asked.

Joanna smiled. "So far Cochise County doesn't have any women detectives."

"But they do have a woman sheriff," Jenny commented thoughtfully.

"That's right," Joanna agreed. "Cochise County does have one of those."

Jenny nodded and then got up. "It's late. I'd

better go to bed. Good night, Mom." Jenny leaned over and kissed her mother on the cheek.

"Sleep tight," Joanna managed to reply.

She was glad Jenny didn't turn and look back at her from the bedroom door, glad she didn't see that her mother's eyes had filled with tears—tears of gratitude.

Which were very nice for a change.

Thirty

IT WAS ten o'clock before Joanna sat down at the dining room table to look at the stack of mail Kristin Marsten had dumped on her desk early that afternoon.

One of the first pieces of paper Joanna picked up happened to be her own typed statement—the one concerning the election-night traffic incident, the one she had gone to the Justice Center to sign on Wednesday morning. That seemed so long ago now—so much had happened in between—as to be almost ancient history. To say nothing of unnecessary.

Alvin Bernard, Bisbee's chief of police, had left Joanna a message earlier that afternoon telling her that a decision had been made to cite Holly Patterson for driving without a license and negligent driving rather than vehicular assault. Joanna didn't care to contemplate why the decision had been made that particular way, or how it could have been made at all in view of the fact that her own statement had never been taken into consideration by the investigators, but she decided that wasn't her problem. She tossed the statement aside and went back to the mail.

As Sue Rolles had indicated, Martin Sanders' letter of resignation was concealed in among all the rest, sandwiched between an inner-office memo listing the jail menus for the following week and a notice of the next board of supervisors' meeting, which, as a county administrator, Joanna would now be required to attend. She read through the letter of resignation twice. It said very little, only that for personal reasons he was resigning immediately. For the next week and a half, he would be taking the remainder of his accrued vacation.

"Thanks a lot, Martin," she muttered, "maybe I can do you a favor sometime."

She took out her calendar and made a note of the supervisors' meeting. On the bottom of that notice, someone had hand-changed the routing, crossing out *R. Voland* and replacing his name with *J. Brady*.

At the very bottom of the stack was one of those eagle-decorated overnight mail packages that bore a Washington, D.C., postmark and no return address. Joanna tore it open.

Inside she found a full-color catalog called *Women Officers' Mandatory Accessories and Notions of Santa Monica, California*. WOMAN. Cute. In it she found pictures of stunning women with no subcutaneous fat and flawless teeth and nails. They looked as though they had never done a day's work in their lives, but they were all outfitted in everything from female-proportioned Kevlar vests to lightweight weapons and listening devices. Most of the latter seemed designed to be

concealed and carried on various female foundation garments. None of the price tags could be
considered cheap, but Joanna conceded that the
possibility of a comfortable Kevlar vest might be
an important, life-saving investment.

In addition to the catalog, Adam York's CARE
package contained two other items. One was a
well-worn, dog-eared copy of a clearly outdated
book. Entitled *Officer Down, Code Three* and written
by someone named Pierce Brooks, the blue volume
wasn't a book Joanna had ever seen or heard of
before. The ragged dustcover, complete with a picture of 1970s-era cops, showed its age, as did the
original publication date of 1975.

Puzzled as to why Adam York had sent her the
book, but putting it aside for a moment, Joanna
picked up the last item—Adam York's DEA business card with a hand-scrawled note of congratulations on the back. She dialed the number listed
on the card. After a strange series of clicks, the
phone finally rang, and Adam York himself
answered.

"At this hour of the night, I was expecting an
answering machine," Joanna said with a laugh.

"You got lucky. Through the wonders of phone-
factory engineers, you can dial me in Tucson and
speak to me in D.C. Isn't technology wonderful?"

"D.C.," Joanna echoed. "That's East Coast time,
so it really is late. Sorry."

"Time's relative. What's up?"

"I called to thank you for the package. I can see
that a proportioned-to-fit vest is definitely in
order. The one I wore today is way too long for

my ribs. It rubs me raw in all the wrong places. But why the book?"

"It's used as a manual in police-officer-safety courses. Before you go take that class in Peoria, I want you to sit down and read the whole thing from cover to cover. It's important."

"All right. I'll do it, just as soon as things settle down a little bit here."

"Do it sooner than that," Adam York growled. "Until you get some training, you're an accident waiting to happen. Now, how was your first full day?"

"Let's see now, two homicides—one old, one new—and one of my chief supervisors gave notice, but he's on vacation for the duration. Other than that, I guess it was a pretty normal day."

"They didn't give you much time to get your sea legs, did they?"

"I'll manage," Joanna said, "but I do have a question for you. What, if anything, do you know about ex-cons from Russia?"

Adam York's voice suddenly turned serious. "Me, personally? Not that much. What do you want to know?"

"I've evidently got one living right here in Cochise County," Joanna said. "His name is Yuri Malakov. He's been here for some time as an apparently law-abiding citizen, but he's romantically involved with the daughter of one of my two victims."

"What makes you think he's a Russian ex-con?"

"He is from Russia, for one thing. I already knew that about him, but this morning I happened to see him without his shirt. He has tattoos all over his upper body, mostly a cowboys-and-Indians motif. 'Cowboy Sam' is the only thing on it that's written in English well enough so I could make it out."

"What else?"

"What do you mean, what else?"

"I mean what else can you remember about the tattoos?"

"There were a couple of rattlesnakes, a hangman's noose, a rodeo rider, and, I think, a rose. There may have been some other things, but I don't necessarily remember them. Why? What's so important about that?"

"With all the problems we've been having with the Russian mafia, somebody over at the FBI is a known expert at decoding Russian prison tattoos," Adam York answered shortly. "Let me check this out with him and see what he has to say. I'll also get in touch with some guys I know at INS."

"I don't think that'll work," Joanna said. "My guys already tried it that way from this end and were told hands off. So if you nose around about him, don't say I sent you."

"And don't you go wandering into any dark alleys with this character," Adam York warned. "Those Russian *mafiosi* are dangerous as hell. And if he's walking around wearing a hangman's noose on his chest, you can pretty well figure he didn't get sent up for stealing chicken feed."

When Joanna got off the phone, she retreated to her bedroom, taking both *Officer Down* and the *People* magazine along with her. She glanced at the book but put it aside. She was too tired for anything but the most mindless of articles.

After hearing all the local fuss about the *People* story, Joanna was disappointed when she finally read it. There was some discussion of Holly Patterson, but the article focused more on Hollywood hypnotherapist Amy Baxter and several of her clients, all of whom had taken on their once abusive parents with sometimes greater and sometimes lesser degrees of financial success.

Joanna's last thought, as she put the magazine down and drifted off to sleep, was that some career choices were stranger than others.

In the morning, she overslept. She was still sawing logs at seven when Jenny tapped on her bedroom door, poked her head inside, and said, "Mom, aren't you awake yet? It's late."

In a mad scramble, Joanna raced outside to feed and water the animals, then dived into the shower. She was still drying her hair when Jenny came back into the bathroom.

"Do you want me to ride my bike down to catch the bus this morning?"

"That would be a big help," Joanna said. "It's not going to look good if the new boss starts out by coming to work late."

Once again she wore one of Andy's old T-shirts under the bulletproof vest. Then, expecting to spend most of the day in her office, she did pull on Eleanor Lathrop's favorite, the pearl-gray skirt and blazer. The outfit gave her a dignified, businesslike look, and the blazer was roomy enough that both the Kevlar vest and Andy's shoulder holster disappeared beneath it.

Careful not to speed, Joanna drove to the Cochise County Justice Center and parked in her own designated spot. Armed with a newly assigned, push-button door code she had unearthed in the mail, she let herself into her office through the private back entrance. Propping the outside door open, she went back to the Eagle and retrieved her box of treasured office mementos. She had barely started unpacking them when the door to the reception area opened, and Dick Voland entered her office.

Startled, he stopped short when he saw her. "I didn't know you were here," he said.

"I came in the back way and decided to unpack," she explained, holding Jenny's Bible-school handprint plaque up to the light and rubbing some accumulated dust out of the ends of the tiny finger impressions. "What can I do for you?"

Voland had lumbered into the room carrying an envelope, which he now attempted to shove into his shirt pocket. Pausing in the doorway, he seemed embarrassed, unsure of what to do next.

"Did you need something?" Joanna prodded.

He fumbled the envelope back out of his pocket and handed it over to Joanna. Her name was the only thing typewritten on the outside. "What is it?" she asked.

"My letter of resignation," Dick Voland answered. "Effective immediately."

Without opening it, Joanna dropped the envelope onto her desk. Stunned, she backed up far enough to find her way into the leather chair behind her. "Why?" she asked.

"Have you read your mail yet?"

Joanna glanced at the new stack of mail Kristin had placed on her desk. "Not yet. I wanted to unpack first. Why? What's in there now that I should have read?"

Voland reached out, pawed through the pile on her desk, pulled out a newspaper, and tossed it down in front of her. "You probably ought to read this," he said gruffly.

Joanna glanced down at a copy of that day's *Arizona Sun*. "The whole paper?" she asked. "Or some article in particular?"

He thumbed the paper open to the second section, the one that focused on statewide news. With the paper folded in half, Joanna could only see the bottom half of the page. Just below the fold was a two-column wide, two-line headline that read, OLD COPS VS. NEW SHERIFF/NO CONFIDENCE, by *Arizona Sun* staff writer Sue Rolles.

Joanna quickly scanned the article: "The people of Cochise County may have elected Arizona's first-ever female sheriff on Election Day last Tuesday, but that doesn't mean long-time law-enforcement veterans of the County Sheriff's Department are happy with the outcome.

"In a move many regard as a vote of no confidence for incoming sheriff Joanna Brady, Martin Sanders, Cochise County's deputy for administration, yesterday submitted his resignation amid widespread speculation that other well-respected and long-term departmental employees may soon follow suit.

"Although Sanders was a political appointee who served at the pleasure of the sheriff, he had nonetheless functioned in that capacity for two separate administrations and had been expected to play a pivotal part in the orderly transition to the administration of the new sheriff who was elected this week.

"One departmental employee who spoke only on condition of anonymity said, 'I'm afraid a woman is just going to cave in under the pressure. I mean, she's been in office two days, and already we have two homicides.' (See above article.)"

Joanna turned the paper over enough to see that the headline at the top of the page dealt with the two separate Cochise County slayings. But that wasn't the article Dick Voland had handed her, so she turned back to the other one and resumed reading.

"Chief Deputy Richard Voland, another political appointee, actively campaigned for Al Freeman, the former chief of police from Sierra Vista who also ran for the position of sheriff. Citing Joanna Brady's lack of law-enforcement experience, Voland emphasized that the county needed a professional law-enforcement officer to take charge of the Sheriff's Department.

" 'Joanna Brady's a nice lady,' Voland says, 'but she's never been a cop. And that's what this county needs more than anything right now— someone who knows the score.' "

Joanna glanced at Dick Voland over the top of

the newspaper and found him regarding her anxiously. "That quote's from one of your campaign speeches, isn't it? The one about me not being a cop?"

Dick Voland nodded glumly. "That's right," he said, "but the woman who wrote the article makes it sound as though I said it yesterday, as though I'm out on the streets right this minute trying to undermine you."

Without reading any more, Joanna closed the paper, folded it back up, and placed it on her desk. She left the unopened envelope lying where it fell.

"Mr. Voland," she said, "I think it's only fair for you to know that this article is written by Sue Rolles, a reporter I personally threw out of my office late yesterday afternoon. Now tell me why you're leaving. Are you really convinced that I'll never be able to hack it in this job?"

"No. That's not it at all."

"What is it then?"

"With this kind of crap showing up in the media, I'm worried about a total breakdown in the chain of command, and that could put officers' lives in jeopardy. It seems to me you might be better off with a slate of people of your own choosing. Out with the old, in with the new."

"Are you saying you don't think you can work with me?"

"No, but that may be the public perception. Especially after people read this. And anything that causes confusion; anything that makes one officer second-guess another, undermines the efficiency as well as the safety of the department."

Joanna considered what he was saying. "Let me ask you a question, Dick. Considering I'm a rookie, was there anything about my behavior at the crime scene yesterday that was out of order?"

"No, you did fine, but . . ."

"But if there had been, would you have let it pass, or would you have pointed it out to me so I wouldn't look quite so dumb the next time?"

Dick Voland met Joanna's searching gaze and didn't look away. "If something had been way out of line, I believe I would have told you."

"Good." Joanna picked up the envelope, tapped the edge of it on the desktop, but still made no move to open it. "I'll take this matter under advisement," she said. "I'll give it some thought, but for the time being, you need to understand that I have not yet accepted your resignation. Is that clear?"

"Yes."

"Good. Now, then, aren't I supposed to have some kind of early-morning briefing about what went on in the county overnight?"

"Two brothers got all drunked up at a birthday party over in Kansas Settlement and beat the crap out of one another with wooden baseball bats. One of them is in the county hospital down in Douglas. There were two domestics in the county overnight, one out in Elfrida and the other in Miracle Valley. Three DWIs, one runaway juvenile from Pirtleville, and a carload of illegals who ran out of gas between Tombstone and St. David. The deputy held them long enough for the Border Patrol to show up and take them into custody."

"That's all?"

"Isn't that enough?" Voland replied.

"What about Ernie Carpenter? Any developments there?"

"Nothing new overnight that I know of, except that Ivy Patterson and that Russian of hers did go ahead and tie the knot. I can tell you that one's raised a few eyebrows around town. Other than that, things are pretty quiet."

Voland headed for the door. "Wait, Dick," Joanna said. "There's one other thing."

"What's that?"

"Do you have any suggestions about who to get to fill Martin Sanders' position?"

Voland shook his head. "Not right offhand. It's a funny situation, neither fish nor fowl. It would be a big promotion for most of the guys out on patrol, but that person essentially functions in a staff capacity, totally cut off from any direct contact with the public.

"Not only that, it's a paper-intensive job. The person who takes it is agreeing to serve as point man for every ugly can of worms that walks in the door—from police-brutality complaints to wrangling with the board of supervisors over budget cuts."

"You're saying most of the people currently in the department would take one look at the job description and run like hell in the opposite direction?"

"That's right."

"Including you, I presume?" Joanna asked.

"Most definitely," Voland answered. "I wouldn't have that job on a bet."

He left then. For some time afterward, Joanna stared at the closed door, then she went back to the newspaper article. This time she read it all the way through. Going over the story, she realized why it was Sue Rolles had seemed so familiar to her. She didn't remember her from any kind of meeting at the hospital in Tucson the day Andy died. She could barely remember anything at all about that awful day. But she had seen Sue Rolles here and there as she traveled the campaign trail around the county, attending various civic meetings in advance of the election.

Sue Rolles must have been following every twist and turn of the campaign for months. Reading the article carefully, Joanna could tell that some of the quotes from disgruntled departmental employees were new and legitimate. There were bound to be others besides Kristin Marsten who were actively provoked at having a new female boss. But most of the quotes attributed to Richard Voland were fragments of things she recognized as campaign rhetoric, sound bites taken out of context and edited to seem like up-to-the-minute, post-election gritching.

It was easy to see now how the pieces fit together. Joanna realized that the article might have had an entirely different slant and focus if she hadn't summarily thrown Sue Rolles out of her office. The reporter was plainly pissed, and she was seeing to it that Joanna Brady paid dearly for her little tactical error.

From out of her past, she could almost hear D. H. Lathrop's New Mexican drawl telling Joanna and her mother, "Newspaper reporters are just like rattlesnakes. You're better off keeping them out in the open where you can see what they're doing."

Live and learn, Joanna told herself, and don't make the same mistake twice.

Thirty-One

JOANNA SPENT the next half hour studying every word of the articles in the *Sun* that had anything to do with her department, including the one that dealt with the two Cochise County homicides.

That story was primarily a harmless recitation of the facts as they were known and disseminated at the time of Dick Voland's early-afternoon press conference. News about the tentative identification of Thornton Kimball's remains hadn't made it into Tucson prior to press time.

One for them, one for us, Joanna thought.

She turned then to the rest of the mail. There, among that day's collection of memoranda and bulletins, she found a copy of that morning's *Bisbee Bee*. That one did contain news of the Thornton Kimball I.D. Not only that, some enterprising reporter had managed to track down copies of old Bisbee High School yearbooks. Pictures of Harold Patterson and Thornton Kimball, both as much younger men and both dressed formally in white shirts, jackets, and ties, stared out from the front page of the newspaper.

Seeing them together like that, dressed in the outdated attire of an earlier era, it was interesting to note how much Burton Kimball took after his mother's side of the family. He looked far more like a much younger version of Harold Patterson than he did his own father.

"Miss Kellogg to see you," an abrupt Kristin announced over the intercom.

When Angie sauntered into Joanna's office, she headed straight over to the window where she stood looking out. "You need to put a bird feeder in that mesquite tree and a ground feeder for the quail underneath," she said.

In two short months, Angie's knowledge of and devotion to Bisbee's native wild-bird population had become encyclopedic. The yard of her tiny house in Bisbee's Galena neighborhood had become a bird-feeding emporium and looked to outsiders like an aviary. Armed with her treasured copy of *Birds of North America*, she spent her time off work happily watching and cataloging her feathered visitors.

"I haven't exactly had time to think about birds," Joanna replied with a laugh. "What brings you here?"

Angie turned toward Joanna, her face suddenly somber. "I almost didn't come at all," Angie said. "I wanted to, but when I got as far as the parking lot, I almost chickened out and didn't come inside. My whole body started to shake. I've never walked into a place like this on my own before or without having my hands cuffed behind my back. It brought back lots of bad memories."

"I'm sure it did," Joanna said.

Angie left the window and stood briefly behind

one of the chairs as if still too nervous to sit down. "The girls in L.A. would never believe it. I can hardly believe it myself."

The fact that Angie could number a county sheriff and a Methodist minister among her friends was, in a word, unbelievable. Nothing in Angie's troubled past as a runaway teenager who survived by her own wits would have pointed toward that possibility.

"I came to show you something," she said. Reaching into the back pocket of her pants, she pulled out a credit-card-sized piece of plastic. "Here," she said, handing it over. "Look at this."

The plastic card was an Arizona driver's license—Angie Kellogg's first driver's license ever—complete with one of the best-looking driver's I.D. photos Joanna had ever seen.

"You passed," she said. "Congratulations, and it's a good picture, too. Must be beginner's luck."

Angie smiled smugly. "And I passed on the first try," she said. "In fact, I just came from there. I was afraid I might end up having to take the driving part more than once, but the guy who rode with me was great."

Looking at the lush, blond Angie, Joanna thought it wasn't surprising to think that a driving examiner might have somehow overlooked a minor miscue or two. An early loss of innocence had robbed Angie of the ability to see her own physical beauty. What was lost on her most likely hadn't been missed by the male licensing official.

Joanna was often perplexed by Angie's odd mixture of toughness and naïveté. She was at once both young and old; innocent and jaded. How could someone who had made her living by prostitution be so seemingly unaware of her own beauty and of the physical impact she made on those who met her?

Angie was experiencing some difficulty in making the transition from an economy in which her body had been the sole medium of exchange to one in which her paycheck paid the bills. With help from people like Bobo Jenkins and Jeff Daniels, she was only now learning that it was possible to have male friendships that didn't automatically lead to sex, and that real freedom existed in the privilege of saying no.

"So would you like to go for a ride? Maybe have lunch?" Angie asked, her face alive with disarming enthusiasm. "Today's my morning off. I don't have to be at work until six."

It was still early. With two homicides hanging over her head, Joanna felt as though there was something she should be doing besides going to lunch. The only trouble was, right that minute she had no idea what it was. In the end, she went.

With considerable pride, Angie escorted Joanna outside to where her cream-colored 1981 Oldsmobile Omega was parked in front of the building. They ate an early lunch at Daisy's, leaving well before the noontime crowd started arriving. Afterward, Joanna asked Angie to help her ferry the Eagle back home to the ranch so she'd have only one vehicle parked at the office rather than two. Angie was glad to help out. They stopped by the Justice Center long enough to pick up the car.

The trip out to the ranch didn't take more than twenty minutes—ten in one direction and ten back, although to a white-knuckled passenger, the ride back seemed much longer. Angie might have passed her driving exam with flying colors, but she was still a very inexperienced driver. The Omega tended to first cling to the shoulder of the highway as she met approaching vehicles and then to meander back to ride the centerline as soon as the road ahead was clear.

Joanna gripped the armrest and tried to keep her mouth shut. She remembered all too well how much she had resented Eleanor's backseat driving, but after years in the insurance business, she also understood why it is that inexperienced drivers have to pay much higher premiums for auto insurance.

"So how's it going?" Angie asked suddenly. "Is being sheriff what you thought it would be?"

If Angie Kellogg had ever given much thought to possible career choices, a position in law enforcement would never have crossed her mind.

"It's hard work," Joanna said. "With two homicides on the books since Tuesday night, I could do with a whole lot less excitement."

"I heard about those," Angie said. "The people in the bar hardly talk about anything else."

"By the way, has Detective Carpenter been by to talk with you about those?" Joanna asked.

Startled, Angie turned to stare at her passenger. During the momentary lapse of attention, the wheels on the rider's side of the Olds veered off the road. As a cloud of rock and gravel spewed up behind them, she managed to wrestle the car back onto the pavement.

"About the murders?" she managed, while the color drained from her face. "I don't like detectives. Why would one of them want to talk to me?"

Clearly Angie's old life carried some bad experiences into her new one. Joanna hastened to reassure her.

"You haven't done anything wrong," Joanna said. "It's just that a person of interest in one of the murders supposedly spent the better part of Tuesday afternoon in the Blue Moon. I know you were scheduled to work on Tuesday, so I thought you might have seen him."

"One of my customers is a suspect?" Angie asked, still bewildered. "Which one?"

"I didn't say that. He's just someone we need to check on. His name is Burton Kimball," Joanna went on. "He's a lawyer."

"Oh, him," Angie said suddenly contemptuous as she switched on the turn signal to turn into the Justice Complex. "What about him?"

"His uncle was murdered sometime that afternoon or evening. Burton Kimball isn't known to be that much of a drinker, but he evidently got himself plastered on Tuesday. In a murder case, you always look at people close to the victim and note anything unusual, including uncharacteristic behavior."

"You're right," Angie agreed. "He's not much of a drinker. That's why it was so easy to get him drunk. Couldn't hold his liquor worth a damn."

"You got him drunk? On purpose?"

"You bet."

"Why?"

"Because I wanted him so smashed that he wouldn't be able to drag his ass out of bed the next day to go defend that dirty old man of an uncle of his."

"Wait a minute here, Angie. How do you know Burton Kimball? For that matter, what makes you think Harold Patterson was a dirty old man? Did you even know him?"

"I know about him," Angie replied. "I know enough. He was a child molester, wasn't he? One of those creeps who fucks his own kids. Those guys always find some slick lawyer to get them off!"

Angie's voice trembled with suppressed rage. "You're damn right I got him drunk, and I'd do it again in a minute. I wanted the son of a bitch so blind drunk that he wouldn't be able to hold his head up, but he left too soon. Just got up and walked out."

"You're lucky he wasn't involved in an accident, Angie," Joanna said. "Bartenders can be held accountable, you know. You could have lost your job."

"I didn't think about that," Angie insisted stubbornly. "Still I'd do it again if I had a chance."

By then the Omega was parked and idling in the front parking lot of the Justice Center, sitting astraddle a white line, occupying half of two full spaces.

"But why would you do such a thing?" Joanna asked. "Why run that kind of risk?"

Angie sat with her hands gripping the wheel and with her eyes focused on some invisible middle distance. She didn't answer for such a long time that Joanna wondered if she'd even heard the question.

"How could a man defend someone like that?" Angie asked at last. "How could he try to get him off? As far as I'm concerned, that makes the lawyer as bad as the father. Maybe even worse. The father could be sick or crazy, but the lawyer is just doing it for money, working for the person who has all the cards. The little girls are the ones who have nothing, no one to turn to. They're the ones who need someone to defend them, to help them."

As Joanna watched in dismay, Angie Kellogg's face seemed to splinter into a thousand pieces. The words she had never been able to muster in her own behalf had suddenly erupted in defense of someone she didn't even know, in defense of Holly Patterson.

While Angie sobbed brokenly beside her, Joanna finally recognized the linchpin of Angie's past, a piece that had, until that very moment, eluded her.

"Oh, my God," she whispered, horrified. "The same thing happened to you, didn't it?"

Angie nodded. "And my mother wouldn't even help me. Maybe she didn't know at first, although she must have. But even when I told her, she didn't lift a finger, didn't make him stop."

Since mid-September, Joanna had struggled to pull together the stray pieces of Angie's history.

There had been a blank spot. She could never understand what had forced Angie out onto the streets from the time she was a child only a few years older than Jenny was now. And now that Joanna knew, now that she understood, she almost wished she hadn't.

"Are you going to be all right?" she asked, reaching out to touch the distraught young woman's arm.

Gradually, Angie regained her composure. The sobs diminished to hiccups and sniffles. "I'll be okay," she managed.

"Are you sure?"

"I'm sure."

"Angie," Joanna said awkwardly, "I'm so sorry. I had no idea."

Angie looked at Joanna with a questioning, sidelong glance. "You mean you believe me?"

"Well, of course I believe you," Joanna replied indignantly. "Why wouldn't I?"

"Because," Angie said in a hushed, hesitant way. "The only other person I ever told was my mother and she called me a liar. Said I made the whole thing up. But I didn't, I swear to God. And that woman whose father is dead, she probably didn't make it up, either. I wanted her to win in court, that's all. That's why I got the lawyer drunk. You do understand that, don't you, Joanna?"

"Yes," Joanna said quietly, getting out of Angie's car. "I believe I do."

Thirty-Two

BURTON KIMBALL came to work that morning out of habit, because he had no idea what else to do with himself. He sat numbly in his office with the door closed, staring without comprehension at the stack of routine correspondence Maxine had left on his desk. No matter how long he looked at the top letter on the pile, he was unable to make sense of a single paragraph. It could just as well have been written in a foreign language.

It was as though the connections in Burton's brain had been short-circuited by the knowledge that his father was dead, that he had been dead all Burton's life. The whole time, the forty-odd years Burton had been waiting for his father to show up, longing for him to come home and reclaim his son, Thornton Kimball had been within ten miles of him, lying dead in the bottom of a hole with his skull crushed to pieces by a chunk of eon-smoothed creek-bed rock.

Burton was living through his first morning without the comfort of his cherished childhood illusion. Burton Kimball was an orphan, had always been an orphan, but with the unveiling of that long-skeletonized corpse, his loss and grief were as new as if his father had died yesterday. In Burton Kimball's heart, that was the truth.

It should have fallen to him, as the closest surviving kin, to plan whatever funeral service Norm Higgins deemed appropriate, but Burton was too emotionally paralyzed. He simply couldn't cope. Instead, he turned the whole thorny issue of arrangements over to Linda and fled to his office, where he sat in his chair and hid out.

Other things that should have commanded his attention barely seeped into his consciousness. The fact that Ernie Carpenter had dared question him with regard to Harold Patterson's murder was driving Linda crazy, but it hardly mattered to Burton.

He was sorry about the death of Harold Patterson, the only "father" he had ever known. But what he was shaken by today was the sudden loss of that second, unknown father. He was amazed by the depth of the grief he felt. How could that old, scarred-over wound hurt so much?

When the phone on his desk rang, Burton jumped as though someone had just lobbed a rock through the window beside his desk. With a suddenly trembling hand, he picked up the receiver.

"Yes?" he said uncertainly, aware of the sudden catch in his throat.

"Sorry to disturb you," Maxine Smith said solicitously, "but Rex Rogers is on the phone. He insists on speaking to you personally."

"Rex Rogers. What does he want?"

"He didn't say. Do you want me to put him through or take a message?"

"Take a message. I don't want to talk to anybody this morning, especially not Rex Rogers."

"You want me to hold all your calls?"

"Please."

A few moments later, Maxine tapped on Burton's door. "What did he say?" Burton growled.

"He wanted to let you know that they'll be filing a brief to amend the suit so it goes against Mr. Patterson's estate. That is, unless Ivy is interested in negotiating a settlement now, without any more courtroom proceedings whatsoever."

Burton buried his face in his hands. "I should have known," he said. "That's Holly through and through—always more than happy to kick somebody when they're down."

He got up and took his coat off the hanger.

"Where are you going?" Maxine demanded.

"To see my client."

"I thought your client was dead."

"I've got a new one now," he answered grimly. "She may not realize she needs me yet, but she does. How are the gossip mills working around town?"

"Fine, I suppose. Why?"

"Does anyone know where the honeymooners spent the night?"

"I suppose if anyone did, Helen Barco would be the one."

"I'm going down the hall to wash my face. Get on the horn and see if you can find out where Ivy and her groom spent the night. It'll be a whole lot easier to track them down if I have some idea where I'm going."

As usual, the fact that something threatened Ivy was enough to jar Burton Kimball out of his funk. The same kind of lifetime habit that had brought him to his office that morning now propelled him to action. If Ivy was threatened, he had to do something about it.

Even as she dialed Helen Barco's number, Maxine didn't understand what had gotten into him all of a sudden. Linda Kimball would have understood, if she had known about it. Her husband was like that where Ivy Patterson was concerned—always had been.

When Isobel Gonzales finished dusting and straightening the living room, she took the morning's paper out to the kitchen, where she sat down long enough to drink a cup of coffee and read the *Bisbee Bee*.

Isobel had lived a quiet and fairly sheltered life. This was the first time a violent death of any kind had touched her life so closely. She tried to imagine how she would feel that morning if she were Holly Patterson.

It was bad enough for Holly to come back home after all those years to bring such awful charges against her own father. Isobel had no idea what had gone on during that stormy afternoon session in the library on Tuesday. Isobel herself had ushered Harold Patterson into the room for the scheduled conference while Miss Baxter and Miss Patterson were still upstairs. She supposed they were some of the last people to see the old man

alive. That saddened her, made her feel somehow responsible.

Mr. Patterson had been sitting there waiting
when Holly came into the room, accompanied by
Amy Baxter. Isobel had closed the door behind
them and had gone on about her business, doing
her best not to eavesdrop, but even in that huge
house, she hadn't been able to avoid the sound of
raised and angry voices. When you're used to a
house being peaceful and quiet, it's hard not to
notice when people are yelling.

Isobel had prepared a casserole and a salad for
dinner, and she had left the house early—
promptly at five-thirty—so she and Jaime could
go vote. She had no idea how the library battle
had ended, and she hadn't seen Holly make off
with Mr. Rogers' fancy red car either. But she had
certainly witnessed the awful aftermath.

Holly's appetite had been bad before. After the
incident with the car, it was almost nonexistent.
She had virtually quit eating altogether. Sometimes she drank something, but the food on the
trays remained almost untouched. Isobel worried
about it, but she didn't mention it to either Miss
Baxter or Mr. Rogers. As a Mexican-American
housekeeper, Isobel Gonzales knew her place. She
kept her mouth shut and tried not to listen to the
noise of the rocker creaking away in Holly's room
directly over the kitchen.

Someone would have to be crazy to rock that
much, Isobel thought, to sit there rocking and staring out the window at nothing but the dump for
hour after hour after hour. Of course, Miss Baxter

would never use the word "crazy" or even "*loco*." She said Miss Patterson had "emotional problems." Poor thing.

And then, just as those thoughts ran through her head, Isobel realized she was no longer hearing the rocker. Moments later, the kitchen door swung open, and a disheveled Holly Patterson stood there in her robe, leaning weakly against the doorjamb. "I want some more coffee," she said.

Isobel Gonzales had cared for a number of invalids in her time—people who were ill enough to require looking after, but not sick enough to need a nurse. She knew that after even a few days of bed rest, the transition from bed to walking around is a tricky one that requires careful negotiation.

"You should sit down," she said, hurrying to Holly's side. "You shouldn't be up walking like this."

Holly waved her away. "I'm fine," she announced. "I'm really fine." Nevertheless, she did totter over to the table and chairs just inside the door.

While Isobel hurried to pour a cup of coffee from a fresh pot, Holly sank down at the kitchen table. Her eyes were drawn at once to the pictures on the front page of the paper that was lying there in front of her.

The moment she saw the picture, a lifetime's worth of forgotten memories boiled to the surface, threatening to drown her in a head-crushing wave.

The hours of careful probing sessions with Amy, the hazy, hypnotic, dreamlike questions and answers, had never come near this terrible, searing pain, had never cast a light on Holly Patterson's interior darkness. Or her horror.

She grabbed the newspaper and stuffed it into the pocket of her robe, thinking that perhaps if she could no longer see that smiling face, the pain would diminish enough so she could at least breathe. But even with his visage squashed in her hand like an unwary cockroach, she could still see his face. She could still remember.

And then, in a moment of terrifying clarity, she caught a single glimpse of her own danger. Bolting upright, she knocked over the kitchen chair behind her.

Isobel started at the sound of the falling chair. Thinking Holly had fainted, she spun around, almost spilling the full cup of coffee she had just poured. When she caught sight of Holly's stricken face, she nearly dropped it altogether.

Was the woman having some kind of seizure— a heart attack perhaps? Her mouth gaped open. She seemed to be trying to speak, or maybe even scream, but no sound came out of her open mouth.

Slamming the cup back down on the counter, Isobel hurried to Holly's side. "Miss Patterson," she said. She pulled out one of the remaining chairs and pushed it in Holly's direction. "What's the matter? Sit down. Sit down right here. You look like you're going to faint."

"She's going to kill me!" Holly whispered hoarsely.

"Miss Patterson, please. No one's going to kill

anybody. You're imagining things. Please sit down."

With surprising agility, Holly Patterson dodged out of Isobel's reach and made for the stairway. Isobel stood there listening as heavy feet pounded down the long overhead corridor that led back to her room.

Isobel's first impulse was to follow the woman. It was clearer to her now than ever before that Miss Baxter was right. In Isobel's world, Holly Patterson's "emotional problems" meant the woman was crazy as she could be. Upstairs, the bedroom door slammed shut, and Isobel breathed a sigh of relief. If Miss Patterson had tried to go outside or run away, she would have been far more worried. Instead, she had gone back to her room, back to where she was supposed to be.

As soon as Miss Baxter and Mr. Rogers came back from their ride, Isobel would have to report the incident, although she still wasn't entirely sure what had happened.

Miss Patterson had been looking at the paper. Whatever she saw there, it had upset her terribly at a time when she had already been through too much. Remembering the look on the fleeing woman's face, Isobel knew she had gone over the edge.

Isobel stood waiting, expecting to hear the sound of the rocking chair resume, and finally it did.

Isobel crossed herself and breathed a small prayer. "Let the poor soul alone," she said to herself. "Just let her be."

*   *   *

Burton was less surprised by the fact that Maxine had been able to locate Ivy and Yuri Malakov than he was by where they were found. They had stayed at the Geronimo Lodge, a grade-B motel on the far side of Tombstone.

The very look of the place offended him. Certainly, Ivy deserved a better honeymoon suite than this. He called their room from a house phone in the lobby. It was almost noon, but when Ivy answered, she sounded as though the phone had awakened her out of a sound sleep.

"You're where?" Ivy demanded, finally coming to her senses.

"I'm in the lobby. I've got to talk to you, to both you and ... Yuri. It's important."

"Burt, I'm on my honeymoon. I've waited for it for forty years, and this is the only one I'll ever have. Whatever you need, it can wait until tonight. We have to come back to the ranch then to do the chores. We'll take on the funeral arrangements this evening."

"This isn't about your father," Burton said. "It's about Holly."

"What about her?"

"Her attorney called my office just a little while ago."

"Why?"

"She intends to continue to fight you, Ivy, to file against the estate unless you want to negotiate now. Her lawyer will go to Judge Moore and amend the suit."

There was a long pause. "Holly can't do that, can she?"

"Yes."

"What do we do about it?"

"That's what I need to talk to you about."

There was a pause. "All right," Ivy said finally. "Wait there in the coffee shop. We'll be down in a few minutes."

Burton went into the coffee shop, sank into a booth, and ordered himself a cup of coffee. He noticed Dave Hollicker come in a few minutes later, and Burton casually waved at the deputy as he went by.

It didn't occur to Burton Kimball that Dave's appearance had anything to do with him, or that by interrupting his cousin's honeymoon, he might be adding fuel to the fire of Ernie Carpenter's growing conspiracy theory. Because by then, the Cochise County homicide detective was hot on the trail of the possibility that Burton Kimball, Ivy Patterson, and Yuri Malakov might all be in it together.

Detective Carpenter was growing more and more convinced that the three of them, acting in concert, had murdered Harold Lamm Patterson.

Thirty-Three

FOR A while after she went back up to her room, Holly sat on the bed barely allowing herself to breathe. No wonder people thought she was crazy. She really was crazy. In her mind's eye, it was as though two parallel videotapes were running in tandem, the one from long ago and the other from Tuesday. The old one was horrifying and real. Although the colors had turned to sepia like the rusty shades of old pictures in a museum collection, the faces were still recognizable. Holly knew now who those people were. All of them.

The other was in living color, although the clouds overhead had covered the dark red cliffs of Juniper Flats in a misty gray wool blanket. First there was her father telling her the real story, while from deep inside her came the first faint rustlings of recognition and remembrance. And then the tape ended, abruptly, as though cut off in midscene. After that vivid mountaintop scene there was nothing but the warm, sweet, comfortable oblivion of forgetting. After that came an unreasoning anger that her father hadn't come as he had said he would, that he had once again betrayed her.

But that was silly. This time, she realized he hadn't let her down at all. He had been there in the library, just as he had said he would be. He had offered to make amends, to make things right. And she had forgotten it somehow. That was the part that didn't make any sense unless she had been made to forget it.

As she sat there, she tried her best to convince herself that she was wrong, that the sudden shock of panic that had overwhelmed her in the kitchen had to be some kind of horrible mistake. But it wasn't. As much as it hurt, it was no mistake.

She knew now that no chance meeting had caused Holly and hypnotherapist Amy Baxter to stumble across one another's paths months earlier. Amy must have targeted her, come looking for her deliberately. Holly's fall from grace as well as her intermittent drug-use woes had been well publicized among Hollywood insiders. Amy's offer of help and much-needed counseling had been a precious lifeline to someone whose telephone calls were no longer returned and whose longtime agent had just cut her loose.

And after hearing about Holly's rocky relationship with her family, after learning about the Rocking P, Amy had been only too eager to put Holly in touch with Rex Rogers. Of course, those two weren't exactly mere nodding acquaintances. As the *People* article had pointed out, they had worked together on several separate cases and won monetary settlements in most of them.

When she had first seen the magazine piece, Holly had been naïvely proud that Amy and Rex had been able to find so many other people to help—other people just like her. She had thought that, with Amy as a partner and with the Rocking P as the site for a treatment center, she, too, would be able to make a contribution to their pioneering work.

But now, for the first time, she saw it for what it really was—a scam. How many of the families mentioned in the article had paid damages for something that wasn't necessarily true? How many of the supposed memories were being artificially augmented, Holly wondered, and how much had each of their families ponied up to rebury the past?

Amy Baxter may have started out in life as a scholarship/charity case from the wrong side of the tracks, but she was well on her way toward amassing a fortune from a very lucrative practice, especially with Rex as her sidekick. If she happened to turn up a family with enough money to make it worthwhile, some of that money was bound to find its way to their treatment center; she and Rex could soon settle into partnership with a self-sustaining cottage industry of counseling the victims and suing the perpetrators.

The silence of the house nudged its way through Holly's solitary musings. Rex and Amy must still be out somewhere, maybe together, maybe separately. But when one or the other of them came back, Isobel was bound to tell them what had happened in the kitchen. If Amy once realized Holly knew the truth . . .

The sense of her own danger came back again,

as strong or stronger than when it first struck her in the kitchen. But if her friend Amy was really the enemy, where in God's name could Holly turn for help?

In the end, she was forced to beg for aid from the least likely of sources—her cousin Burton Kimball. Maybe he was a wimp, but she didn't know anyone else to ask.

Standing by the old-fashioned dial-type phone on the table in *Casa Vieja*'s upstairs corridor, and keeping her voice low lest she be overheard, Holly tried calling Burton's office. His secretary told her he was out, most likely for the rest of the afternoon. Could she take a message? No, no message.

Even more frightened, Holly tried to think of another solution. Was it possible, with everything that was going on, that Burton might have taken the day off? Pulling open the drawer in the table, she searched through the phone book until her trembling fingers finally located the Kimball's home number. A woman answered after only one ring.

"Who is this?" Holly asked.

"Linda Kimball. Who's this?"

Holly had never met the woman Burton had married, but this was bound to be Burton's wife. "Is your husband there?" Holly asked, rushing on in a strangled whisper.

"Ivy?" Linda said. "Is that you? Are you all right? You sound strange."

Ivy! Holly had both envied and hated Ivy all her life. Ivy was the good girl, the favorite, the one who never got her clothes dirty; who never made mud pies out of eggs from the henhouse; who never thought up practical jokes to pull on other people. And yet, until Linda Kimball mistook Holly's voice for Ivy's, it had never dawned on Holly how much they were alike, how much they sounded alike.

"I'm not Ivy; I'm Holly," she managed. "I've got to talk to your husband. Right away."

"What about?"

"About his father; about mine."

"Burton isn't home," Linda said, her voice suddenly closed and flat. "He isn't here, and I have no idea when he'll be back."

"Where did he go? I've got to see him now. It's important."

"As soon as he gets back, I'll have him call you."

"Don't do that. He can't call here."

"How can he get back in touch with you then?"

"I don't think he can," Holly Patterson said, "because by then it'll be too late. By then I'll be dead."

With that, she hung up the phone. She looked up and down the hall. The house was still unnaturally silent, but even then she heard the crunch of tires on the gravel drive outside.

Panicked, Holly knew she had to get out. Now. That was the only way to save herself. Holding her breath, she crept back down the stairs, grateful for the strip of carpeting that covered the hardwood risers.

Pausing on the ground floor, she heard Isobel working industriously in the kitchen, chopping something, singing under her breath, but there were voices outside. Rex and Amy were walking up to the back door from the garage. They'd be there any moment.

Still wearing her nightgown, robe, and fur-lined bedroom slippers, Holly tiptoed across the slate entryway and let herself out the front door. She walked bent over, hoping that, by staying close to the ground, she could avoid being seen by anyone, including Isobel's gardener husband. She crept around the far side of the building and made for the ivy-covered terraces at the back of the house where she had once tried to seduce poor Bobby Corbett.

Without looking back, she scrambled down the four-foot drops between levels of terrace. At every step, the thick, straggly vines reached out to entangle her feet and send her tumbling, but she kept on. At last she came to the far end of the property, where a barbed-wire fence barred her way. Beyond that lay the first few far-flung boulders— massive hunks of rock waste that had bounced high and fallen wide as they tumbled down the steeply angled flanks of the dump.

As Holly tried to wiggle through the fence, sharp wire barbs caught on threads of her terry-cloth robe. Unable to free it at once and intent only on reaching the dump, Holly slipped out of the robe and went on, leaving the white cloth dangling on the fence behind her like a June bug's discarded shell.

It was desperately cold that day, but even with nothing on but her nightgown, Holly didn't notice.

She had eyes only for the massive multicolored dump with the achingly blue sky arching far above it. All her life, that dump had exerted a strange, inexplicable pull on Holly Patterson. When she reached the bottom, she hesitated, but only for a moment. For all her life, she had wondered what was on top of that dump. Today, to save her life, she was going to find out.

She was halfway up when Amy's voice found her. "Holly! What are you doing? Come down. Come down right now before you hurt yourself."

Holly closed her eyes, trying to resist the inescapable pull of that beckoning voice.

"Come . . . down . . . right . . . now!"

Holly wanted desperately not to hear that voice, not to respond, but she did. Without even having to leave the bottom level of the terrace, Amy began to count.

"Ten," her voice called out in that powerfully soothing cadence. "Nine, eight, seven . . ."

Slowly, the numbers worked their inevitable way down to zero. They burrowed their way deep into Holly's consciousness like so many writhing worms, devouring both her will and her newfound memories.

When Amy's commanding voice stopped Holly's ascent, she had been near the lip of the two-hundred-foot-high dump, climbing fearlessly. Halfway down, she happened to glance at the desert floor one hundred feet below her. She gasped with shock to see how high she was, how far she had climbed. Trembling with fear in every limb, she had all she could do to continue down.

Somehow, for a few moments at least, Holly Patterson had forgotten that she was desperately afraid of heights.

Joanna came back from lunch to a world of pandemonium. The two brothers from Kansas Settlement who had tried to murder one another with baseball bats the night before were once again on a friendly basis. Despite the fact that one of the two was still hospitalized with injuries, they were ready to be ruled by brotherly love. Their mother, who had not attended the birthday fracas, had negotiated a peace treaty and hired a lawyer.

When Joanna picked up her messages, one was from a Willcox attorney letting her know that his Kansas Settlement clients were prepared to sue the county and the two deputies who had arrested them with false arrest and police brutality. A second message, from the county attorney, related to that same issue.

"What am I supposed to do about this?" Joanna asked.

Kristin shrugged.

"Who usually handles this kind of thing?"

"Mr. Sanders, usually. But he's on vacation," Kristin added with only the smallest of smirks.

"Who takes care of those problems when Mr. Sanders isn't available?"

"Nobody else that I know of. He's been doing it ever since I got here. He also usually attends the Multi-Jurisdictional meetings, and there's one of those starting at two. Are you going?"

"There isn't a note about that MJ meeting on

my calendar," Joanna said, pointing to the laminated wall calendar she had posted in order to keep track of where she was supposed to be and when. There was no Magic Marker notation in the afternoon slot.

"I must've forgotten," Kristin said. "Sorry."

"Like hell you did," Joanna muttered to herself after the door closed. It was going to take time to either shape Kristin up or get rid of her, but Joanna couldn't afford to launch into something like that when she was already up to her neck in current-crisis management.

Sitting back in the chair, Joanna closed her eyes for a moment. She felt isolated and alone. It was fine to go have lunch with Angie or Marianne, but within the department she was on her own. It was hard not to envision that she had stumbled into a den of vipers, all of them waiting for her to make the smallest misstep.

She realized that having Martin Sanders leave without even bothering to discuss the situation constituted a real blow to her credibility. She had tried to talk Dick Voland into staying, because, with one supervisor out the door, she realized the need of maintaining experienced officers around her to give the department the appearance of continuity. But she also needed an ally, someone on her side who wasn't going to be eagerly awaiting or even engineering her first public tumble.

The only problem was, she couldn't think of anywhere to turn for help. Voland would work with her, but only grudgingly, and only so long as he perceived her to be holding up under pressure. At the first sign of weakness, he'd be all over her like flies on crap. The same held true for Ernie Carpenter.

For right now, her only choice was to trudge along as best she could. Until she could forge some in-house alliances, it was important to cover all the necessary bases, wear all the hats.

She picked up the intercom and buzzed Kristin. "Call the MJ folks and let them know I've changed my mind. I'll be sitting in on their Multi-Jurisdictional meeting after all."

Without complaint, Linda Kimball had spent all morning doing what she regarded as her wifely duty. That was her job. She made one phone call after another, working her way through the confounding layers of bureaucracy, finding out when the two bodies were likely to be released for burial, making arrangements with Norm Higgins for a private service for Thornton Kimball, and politely dodging Norm's questions about services for Uncle Harold.

Norm Higgins had hinted that it would be a lot simpler for all concerned and a lot less expensive to have one joint service for both men, but Linda had nixed that harebrained idea. The funeral for Thornton Kimball would be absolutely private— for family members only. Anyone who tried to turn her husband's grief into some kind of participatory spectacle would have Linda herself to deal with. As for questions about Uncle Harold's service, she told Norm, in no uncertain terms, that she was sure Ivy would be in touch to take care of those matters just as soon as she possibly could. If Norm Higgins knew about Ivy's inappropriate wedding arrangements, he had the good sense not to broach that touchy subject with Linda Kimball.

When the phone rang between calls, Linda was taken aback to find Holly Patterson on the line. In fact, once she realized who it was, Linda's first instinct was to hang up. After all, hadn't Holly Patterson already caused enough trouble for everyone concerned? But Linda's overall courtesy and good nature won out. Instead of hanging up, she listened.

When the call was over, she stood with her hand on the receiver for only a moment or two while she made up her mind. A sincere request for help was something Linda Kimball was almost physically incapable of ignoring.

Without giving herself a chance to change her mind or back out, she combed her hair, put on lipstick and a jacket, and headed for *Casa Vieja*. She presented herself at the front door at precisely half-past two and smiled pleasantly at the uniformed Mexican woman who opened the door.

"Why, Isobel Gonzales. I haven't seen you since your mother passed away in the hospital three years ago. I had no idea you worked here."

Isobel nodded. "For almost a year now. Jaime and me both. It's a good job."

"I'm looking for Holly Patterson. Is she here?"

Another woman appeared over Isobel Gonzales' shoulder. "Who is it, Isobel?"

"Mrs. Kimball," Isobel answered. "To see Miss Patterson."

"I'm Holly's therapist, Amy Baxter," the other woman said, moving fully into Linda's view and easing Isobel aside. "Is there something I can do for you?"

"I came to see Holly."

"I'm afraid Holly isn't up to seeing anyone just now. She hasn't been feeling well, with what happened to her father and all. I've prescribed total bed rest."

"But she called me," Linda Kimball protested. "She called earlier this afternoon and asked me to stop by."

A look of seeming dismay flickered briefly across Amy Baxter's countenance and then disappeared, replaced by a determined shake of her head. "That can't be," Amy said.

"But it is," Linda returned civilly. "I came as soon as I could."

"I'm afraid you don't understand, Mrs. Kimball. The woman is seriously ill. It simply isn't possible for her to see you or anybody else."

Linda Kimball was an experienced mother whose finely honed instincts warned her whenever one or both of her children was even tempted to tell a lie. Although the reason for it eluded her, she nonetheless sensed the lie behind Amy Baxter's bland words and felt the blind panic Linda's unexpected appearance at the door of *Casa Vieja* had engendered in the other woman's supposedly composed expression.

What's going on? Linda wondered.

"I'll be dead by then." That's what Holly Patterson had said on the phone—not threateningly, as if dying were something within her own power. She wasn't crying out with the plaintive voice of someone contemplating suicide and hoping for a last-minute rescue. No, she spoke with the fatalistic, matter-of-fact despair of someone caught in the middle of a railroad trestle with an oncoming train speeding toward her.

This was Bisbee, a small and supposedly safe community, a town where general wisdom assumed that murders weren't supposed to happen. But murders do happen here, Linda thought grimly, more often than she liked to believe possible.

Astute enough to realize that forcing her way into the house would do nothing to help the situation, Linda backed off at once. She donned her best hospital-volunteer mask—the one she used to comfort the grieving relatives and friends she often found huddled outside sickrooms in the polished corridors of Copper Queen Hospital.

"Just let Holly know I stopped by to see her, would you?" Linda said with a sincerely concerned smile. "I'll be glad to drop by later on this evening if she's feeling up to it by then."

"I'll do that," Amy Baxter said.

With her knees knocking under her, Linda Kimball marched back to the car. She was frightened. Without knowing quite what it was, she realized she had uncovered something important. Whom should she tell about all this? she wondered. She had to tell someone.

TOMBSTONE COURAGE

As soon as she was outside the swinging electronic gates of *Casa Vieja*, instead of going home, she turned right and headed straight for the sheriff's office out on Highway 80.

Thirty-Four

THE MJ meeting was dull as watching grass grow. Max Foster, a vice detective from the Pima County Sheriff's Department, was the ranking officer for the Cochise County Multi-Jurisdictional Unit. Foster might have been a fine detective, but he was an incredibly poor public speaker. The meeting droned on and on. Even though the information was vitally important, Joanna wasn't the only one fighting to stay awake. She was relieved when Kristin poked her head in the door and crooked a finger at her.

Probably the Kansas Settlement boys acting up again, Joanna thought, as she gathered her notepad and followed Kristin out the door.

"What is it?" she asked, as soon as they were in the corridor.

"Linda Kimball to see you," Kristin said. "Again."

Linda was waiting and pacing the confines of the reception area. "I'm doing it again." She smiled apologetically. "You're probably getting pretty tired of me by now."

"Come on in," Joanna said, gesturing Linda into

her corner office. "What seems to be the problem?"

Linda barely waited for the door to finish closing behind them. "I've just come from *Casa Vieja*," she said, "and I have a funny feeling something isn't right over there. Something's the matter with my husband's cousin Holly."

Joanna suppressed a smile. "Considering what all's gone on this past week," she replied, "the idea that something's the matter with Holly Patterson is hardly news."

But by the time an anxious Linda Kimball finished recounting her story, even Joanna had to agree that what was happening at *Casa Vieja* sounded disturbing.

"Someone should look into this, all right," Joanna agreed. "If for no other reason but to ask a few questions."

"Maybe it's nothing," Linda said. "Burton always says I'm forever jumping to conclusions, but the whole thing gave me a very bad feeling, an edgy feeling. What my mother used to call the willies."

"Don't worry," Joanna said. "I'll have someone check it out."

When Linda left her office, Joanna went looking for both Richard Voland and Ernie Carpenter. Voland was in Willcox talking to the two deputies involved in the Kansas Settlement problem. Carpenter had gone to Sierra Vista to make arrangements for shipping evidence off to the state crime lab for processing.

So much for delegating tasks to her second- and

third-in-command, Joanna thought. She briefly considered sending one of the deputies by to check on Holly Patterson, but she thought better of it. A deputy would need to have some idea what to look for, what questions to ask. Unfortunately, Joanna had no idea what directions to give to anyone else. In the end, she decided, like the Little Red Hen, to do it herself.

Picking up the intercom, Joanna buzzed Kristin. "I'll be out for a while," she said. "If you hear from either Dick Voland or Ernie Carpenter, tell them I went to *Casa Vieja* to see Holly Patterson. Leave a message for both of them to get in touch with me as soon as they get back to town."

It pleased her to be able to go in and out of her office by way of her own private entrance. Climbing into the county-owned Blazer, she felt as though she was beginning to have a handle on the scope of the job, both the pitfalls and the responsibilities. There was plenty of hard work ahead and lots to learn, but she was a quick study. In her third full day on the job, Joanna Brady was actually beginning to feel like a sheriff.

She turned into the gates at *Casa Vieja*, buzzed for admittance, and then parked outside. This time she went directly to the front entryway and rang the bell. Amy Baxter herself came to the door. "Why, Sheriff Brady," she said, "I don't believe we were expecting you."

"Actually, I came to see Holly Patterson," Joanna responded.

"Holly is resting right now," Amy said, smiling

and cordial, but firm. "She really isn't in any condition to entertain visitors."

"I'd still like to see her. I understand she seems to think herself in some kind of danger."

"Holly in danger? Here? That's absurd! She's up in her room, safe as can be."

"Let me see her then, just to set my mind at ease."

Amy sighed and looked exasperated. "Well, I don't suppose it can hurt anything, but I'm afraid Rex will insist on being in attendance. Wait here."

"That's fine," Joanna said.

Moments later, she was led up to the second floor and back to Holly Patterson's room, where a man who introduced himself as Rex Rogers was waiting in the hallway. He led her inside.

Once more the heavy curtains were pulled almost shut, and once again the room was shrouded in drapery gloom. Dressed in a sweat suit and bedroom slippers, Holly sat rocking back and forth in her old-fashioned rocking chair. Her hands rested limp and open in her lap. Her face was lax and expressionless.

"Holly," Rex Rogers said, gently shaking her shoulder. "There's someone here to see you."

As if she were waking from a drug-induced stupor, Holly Patterson's eyes fluttered open. "What?" she asked vaguely.

"Someone to see you," Rogers repeated. "The sheriff. I believe she wants to ask you some questions."

"How are you?" Joanna asked. "I heard you were under the weather."

"I'm fine," Holly answered unconvincingly.

"What happened to your hands?"

Holly looked down at the hands that lay in her lap. Joanna had noticed the heel of the palm on both hands was badly skinned, as though she had taken a bad fall and had used her hands to cushion herself. The damage was new enough that the abrasions were still leaking fluid, but Holly looked down at the injuries with surprised dismay.

"I don't know," she said tentatively. "They hurt, but I don't know what happened to them."

"She fell down," Rex supplied brusquely. "Holly's always falling down like that. She's easily distracted."

"Where did she fall?"

"Outside," Rex answered again. "Off one of the terraces."

"Isn't she capable of answering questions on her own?" Joanna asked. "Where did you fall, Holly? How did it happen?"

Rex Rogers grimaced with annoyance while Holly Patterson looked at Joanna with strangely vacant eyes. "I don't know," she said, without ever stopping rocking. "I don't remember."

"But it happened just a little while ago," Joanna insisted. "Look. Your hands are still bleeding."

"I don't know," Holly repeated hopelessly. "I just don't know."

Joanna turned back to Rex Rogers. "What kinds of medication is this woman on?" she asked.

"How should I know?" Rex Rogers answered sharply. "I'm her lawyer, not her doctor."

"What seems to be the problem?" Amy Baxter asked from the doorway of the room.

"Holly has hurt herself," Joanna answered. "Recently enough that the palm of her hands are still seeping serum, but she can't remember how it happened. Is she on medication of some kind, or has she maybe suffered an injury, a concussion perhaps?"

"I tried to tell you downstairs that she wasn't in any condition to receive visitors. You were the one who insisted"—the phone rang out in the hall, interrupting her statement—"on seeing her."

"I believe she should be examined by a physician," Joanna said.

"That's ridiculous. I'm telling you she's fine."

Isobel Gonzales appeared behind Amy Baxter in the corridor. "The phone's for you, Mr. Rogers," she said. "Burton Kimball."

Amy nodded to Rex. "You take care of that; I'll handle this."

Rex Rogers dodged out of the room, leaving the three women there together. For some time, the only sound was the creaking of Holly's rocker on the polished hardwood floor.

"Is she being held here against her will?" Joanna asked suddenly.

"Against her will? Of course not! What kind of preposterous idea is that?"

Joanna bent her head close to Holly's. "Look at your hands," she said kindly. "You've hurt yourself. Don't you think you ought to see a doctor about them?"

She held Holly's limp hands up in the air. In

the dim light, Holly examined them as though they were strange appendages having nothing at all to do with her own body.

"How did I hurt my hands, Amy?" Holly asked in a strangely disembodied voice. "Do you know?"

"You fell, Holly," Amy answered firmly. "You fell down outside, just a little while ago."

"Why can't I remember then?" Holly asked, still studying her hands. "It's weird not to be able to remember."

"Maybe you hit your head when you fell, and that's why you can't remember," Joanna suggested. "The hospital is only a few blocks away. It wouldn't be any trouble at all for me to take you there and have a doctor take a look at you."

"Oh, go if you want to," Amy said with sudden irritation. "I won't stand in your way."

"No," Holly said, doubtfully at first but then with stronger conviction. "I think I'm okay. It's okay. I'll just stay here."

Amy Baxter smiled at Joanna in triumph. "See there?" she said.

Joanna reached in the pocket of her blazer and located a business card, one of her old ones from the Davis Insurance Agency. On the back of it, she scrawled her home phone number as well as the word "sheriff."

"Feel free to call me anytime," she said.

Holly Patterson took the card but dropped it into her lap without even glancing at it.

"Is that all, Sheriff Brady?" Amy Baxter prompted.

Joanna nodded. "Yes," she said. "For the time being."

"Good," Amy said, settling onto the edge of Holly's bed. "Mrs. Gonzales can show you out."

Isobel, waiting in the hall, led the way down the stairs. "What's going on up there?" Joanna asked.

The Hispanic woman shook her head. "I don't know. If it had been up to me, I would have let her go. She only wanted to see what was up on the dump. She's been sitting in her room staring at it and worrying herself sick about it for days. She was already that far. What would it have hurt to let her go the rest of the way?"

"Holly wanted to see what was on top of the dump?" Joanna asked. "Why?"

"Who knows? She keeps on asking me about it. What's up there? What's it like? I told her I didn't know."

"But she climbed up it?"

"Yes."

By then they were outside the house. "Where?"

Isobel walked far enough to see the dump around the corner of the house. "There," she said, pointing. "She was almost up at the top, just above that little mesquite halfway up."

Joanna shaded her eyes, but she saw nothing. The dump was a dangerous and barren wasteland that had barely changed for as long as she could remember. Why would Holly Patterson want to climb it?

"What's wrong with her, Isobel?" Joanna asked.

Isobel Gonzales shook her head. "She's been bad all along, ever since she's been here; not eating very much; barely sleeping. All she does is sit in that chair of hers, rocking and rocking. But she's been worse these last few days, ever since her dad came to see her."

"Harold Patterson came here?" Joanna demanded. "When?"

"Tuesday afternoon," Isobel answered. "He got here just before I left to go vote."

Joanna instantly recognized the discrepancy. Holly's lawyer had claimed she tried to kill Burton because he had talked Harold out of settling and out of keeping the scheduled appointment with Holly. But the old man had kept that appointment after all.

"Did Ernie Carpenter ever talk to you about that? Does he know Harold Patterson stopped by here that day?"

"Nobody's talked to me about it at all."

He should have, Joanna thought. "But go on with your story," she said.

"Well, this morning I thought things were better. Miss Patterson even came down to the kitchen for coffee. But as soon as she saw the paper, she fell all to pieces. I thought for a minute she was having a heart attack. It scared me to death. You saw her. Now she's back to rocking again."

"You said something about a paper," Joanna said. "What paper?"

"Today's *Bisbee Bee*," Isobel answered.

"What happened then?"

Isobel shrugged. "She looked at the paper, and then she went all weird. After a minute, she went running back upstairs. I thought she was fine. I went back to work. A few minutes later, Mr. Rogers and Miss Baxter came back from lunch. I told Miss Baxter what happened. She went up to talk to Miss Patterson. A few minutes later, I heard the commotion outside. I saw it all from the kitchen window. Miss Patterson was up on the dump, and Miss Baxter was trying to get her to come down. That's when she fell. I was afraid she'd break her neck, but I guess she only skinned her hands."

"Where exactly did she fall?"

"When she was climbing back down the dump. A rock must have slipped out from under her foot."

"She fell on the dump, not the terraces?"

"She wasn't anywhere near the terraces."

Joanna felt the skin prickle on the back of her neck. For a long moment, she stood looking at the somber brown facade of *Casa Vieja*. Linda Kimball was right. Something was definitely wrong inside those brown stuccoed walls, and Holly Patterson was in danger.

"Isobel," Joanna said, "I need to drive out of here because they're expecting me to leave. But if I came back on foot, could you let me in and get me up to Holly's room without anyone seeing me?"

"Sure," Isobel answered. "Why don't you park down by my house? Take that little dirt road just outside the gate. It goes around the wall to the back. Park down there and then come up the stairs through the terraces. That's the way I come to work. I'll meet you at the basement door and take you up the inside back stairway."

Joanna nodded. "Good," she said. "I'll be right back. Don't tell anyone I'm coming."

"Oh, no," Isobel Gonzales agreed. "I wouldn't think of it."

Thirty-Five

By the time Joanna parked the Blazer on the far side of the *Casa Vieja* caretaker's cottage, she had reached only one firm decision—she would attempt to lure Holly Patterson out of the house so she could talk to her. If Holly was in mortal danger, as she had hinted to Linda Kimball, then the source of that danger had to be the people who were there in the house with her.

Other than the fact they were liars, Joanna had no other concrete charges to lay at the door of either Amy Baxter or Rex Rogers, but Rex's lie about Holly falling off the terrace had been a direct falsehood.

Amy's was more subtle. She had simply gone along with the idea that Harold Patterson had never showed up for his scheduled appointment with Holly when in fact he had. Both times. Holly's attempt at vehicular manslaughter—regardless of whether or not the city of Bisbee called it negligent driving—had been based on that erroneous premise, Holly's mistaken belief that her father had once again let her down.

Halfway up the cracked flagstone steps that led through the terraced backyard, Joanna pulled off her pumps and stuck them in the pockets of her blazer. Within three steps, she felt the distinctive crackle of a run that started at the back of her heel and stopped somewhere midthigh. So much for the brand-new pair of panty hose she had put on that morning.

She could see now the very real wisdom behind Ernie Carpenter's system of stashing a selection of extra clothing wherever it might be needed. As soon as she had a chance—and as soon as she had that many extra clothes—she'd have to follow his example with a suitcase of her own.

When Joanna reached the highest level of terraces, she saw Isobel standing beside what was evidently a basement door, beckoning her to hurry. "This way," she mouthed.

"They're in the front room talking," she whispered, as soon as Joanna was close enough. "Arguing, really. If we go up this back way, they won't hear a thing."

The back stairs were long, steep, and uncarpeted. They had to walk close to the ends of the risers in order to keep the boards from squeaking noisily underfoot. At the second landing, Isobel paused to catch her breath. In the otherwise-silent house, the only sound was an eerie rhythmic creaking, a sound Joanna eventually recognized as coming from Holly's rocking chair. It was there in the background, like the steady but annoying drip of a constantly leaking faucet.

"I'm glad someone is helping Miss Patterson," Isobel Gonzales gasped between breaths. "I feel sorry for her."

"Why?"

The older woman shrugged. "I don't know," she said. "It's like something is weighing her down and crushing the life out of her."

"Maybe it is," Joanna replied.

They climbed on then, coming out through a door in the upper corridor just across from Holly Patterson's room. "I can handle it from here," Joanna said. "You go on back downstairs. Hopefully, they won't know you helped me."

Isobel nodded and started back down at once. She didn't care much for either Rex Rogers or Amy Baxter, but it would be a shame if she and Jaime lost their jobs with that nice Mr. Enders. *Casa Vieja* provided them both with a living wage as well as a free place to live. In a one-horse town like Bisbee, where mining had disappeared and jobs were scarce as hen's teeth, that wasn't something to throw away lightly.

Unsure how Holly would react to her sudden reappearance, Joanna waited several minutes before she emerged from the landing and crossed the hallway. She wanted to give Isobel plenty of time to distance herself from any difficulty that might arise.

And all the time she stood there waiting, the eerie rocking continued. Finally, after checking the corridor, Joanna darted across the hallway. To her surprise, when she tried turning the knob, she found the door was locked. That gave some validity to the theory that Holly Patterson was indeed being held against her will.

A skeleton key lay on a nearby oak hall table.

Joanna tried it, and the door swung open, revealing a room in which nothing had changed. Joanna's business card still lay exactly where it had fallen. Holly hadn't moved at all. Her two scraped hands still lay hopelessly in her lap, while her vacant eyes stared through the small opening in the otherwise-drawn drapes.

"Holly," Joanna said softly, her voice barely rising above the incessant racket of the rocker.

Slowly, like a television camera doing a gradual pan around a room, Holly Patterson's face and eyes swung away from the window. Her questioning gaze settled on Joanna's face with a puzzled frown. "Who are you?" she asked.

The question startled Joanna. She had been in that very room scant minutes earlier, speaking to this same woman, asking her questions. But now Holly obviously had no memory of it. Joanna was as much a stranger as if she had never laid eyes on her. Joanna felt with rising certainty that chemicals of some kind were responsible for Holly Patterson's faulty memory.

"I'm Joanna Brady," she answered, speaking calmly, trying to instill confidence. "I'm the new sheriff. I came to talk to you, to see if there was anything I could do to help. Would you like to go for a walk?"

"A walk? No!" Holly shook her head vigorously. "Amy wouldn't want me to do that. She doesn't like it when I go for walks."

"Amy wouldn't have to know," Joanna said conspiratorially. "We could just walk down the back stairs and out the door. She wouldn't have any idea we were gone."

"No, I'd better not. I'd get in trouble."

Holly's voice was plaintive, like that of a child who, while already being punished for one misdeed, fears the additional retribution of another. As Joanna watched, two tears squeezed out of the corners of Holly Patterson's eyes and ran down her sunken cheeks. There is something seriously out of whack here, Joanna told herself, but she still couldn't quite put her finger on what it was.

There were no visible restraints on the rocking chair, but there could just as well have been. Holly refused to budge, but her tearful refusal did nothing but strengthen Joanna's determination to somehow entice Holly out of the house.

Suddenly, she remembered what Isobel had told her earlier, about Holly wanting to see the top of the dump. Maybe that would serve as enough of a temptation. "Would you like to go up on the dump?" Joanna asked.

Joanna's educated guess was right on the money. Holly's rocking ceased abruptly. A look of heartbreaking eagerness settled over her face. "You could take me up there? Really?"

"Yes. And you wouldn't have to climb, either," Joanna answered quickly. "That's too dangerous. I could take you in my car, in my Blazer. I'm sure, if I called ahead and asked, the P.D. watchman would give us a tour."

"Yes, please," Holly Patterson said avidly, staggering to her feet and then swaying back and forth as though about to black out from the sudden effort. "I'd like that very much."

"Then we have to move quickly," Joanna cautioned. "Down the back stairs. I'll lead the way. Follow me, and stay close to the wall so the stairs don't creak so much."

Once Holly was out of the room, Joanna relocked the door and returned the key to its place on the table while Holly stood in the middle of the hallway, watching her in a state of confused bewilderment.

"This way," Joanna said, taking her by the arm. "Hurry."

As they started down the stairs, Joanna realized the whole house now echoed with sudden, deafening silence. The ever-present sound of the rocker was stilled. In its absence, the creaking floors, many times amplified, seemed to echo off the walls and ceilings.

What if we're caught? Joanna wondered worriedly. It was bad enough to have two of her deputies charged with false arrest in the Kansas Settlement case. It would be far worse to have the new sheriff herself up on similar charges.

When they stepped outside, Joanna was shocked by how cold it seemed. Running up and down the stairs had left her overheated and winded, but she at least had the wool blazer. Holly had been sitting in a very warm room, and she was wearing nothing but loose-fitting sweats and a pair of bedroom slippers. They were barely out the door when Holly shivered and hunched her thin shoulders against the cold.

"Here," Joanna said, shrugging off her blazer. "Put this on. The car's this way."

But instead of heading in the way Joanna pointed, Holly Patterson set off determinedly in the other direction, winding her way down through the terrace, heading toward the towering dump, gliding along like a sleepwalker, drawn forward by some invisible and inexplicable force. Joanna darted after her. "The car's over here," she insisted.

When Holly still ignored her, Joanna grasped her arm and tried to turn her bodily in the right direction. It was no use. Holly Patterson, headed straight for the dump, was as unstoppable as a loaded freight train on rails. She shook off Joanna's grasp and continued forward with single-minded focus.

"Where are you going?" Joanna asked.

"I've got to see if he's up there," Holly answered with surprising animation. "I've got to know."

"If who's up there?" Joanna demanded.

Behind them, a door to the house slammed open, then closed. "Hey!" Amy Baxter shouted. "What the hell do you think you're doing? Come back."

The sound of that distinctive voice seemed to galvanize Holly Patterson. Her eyes widened. She leaped forward like a startled hare. Joanna was momentarily left behind by Holly's first sudden burst of speed.

Part of Joanna's difficulty lay in her bare feet. Holly Patterson's house slippers, poor as they were, gave her somewhat better mobility and traction. Joanna's feet were cold and bleeding. The rough surface of every bit of gravel cut painfully into her soles. She whimpered with every step. She considered stopping and giving up, but Holly Patterson was still hurrying forward, and Amy Baxter was coming across the backyard toward them at a dead run.

Joanna turned and limped after Holly. She caught her when they reached the tightly strung fence at the bottom of the dump. Holly stood there, tugging desperately on what seemed to be a bathrobe that had somehow become entangled in the tightly strung wire.

"Go on through," Joanna urged. "Hurry. If you want the robe, I'll bring it."

With the familiarity of a country-raised child, Holly wiggled through the fence. Naturally, one barb caught on Joanna's blazer and left a jagged rip down the center of the back, but that barely slowed Holly's forward motion. And as Joanna wormed her way through the fence, she tore her own blouse in the process. As promised, she wrenched the robe loose from the fence and pulled it on over her shoulders, grateful for some covering to ward off the bone-chilling cold.

By the time Joanna reached the bottom of the dump, Holly was already scrambling up the steep incline. Conscious once more of her painful, bleeding feet, Joanna paused, but only for a moment before she, too, began the difficult ascent.

"Holly!" Amy Baxter's voice commanded from

behind them, from the other side of the fence. "Come back!"

Joanna saw it happen. It was as though an invisible choke chain were being pulled taut around Holly's neck. She slowed her desperate flight. Slowed first, and then stopped.

"Come back down!"

Joanna had been scrabbling along behind Holly, picking her way as best she could over and around the huge boulders, trying not to dislodge anything, and trying not to think about what would happen if one of those huge stones came loose and rolled back down the steeply angled incline.

They were only a third of the way up the slope now. Joanna had seen no sign of a weapon on Amy Baxter's person, but Holly's fear was palpable—absolutely real and overwhelmingly contagious. Joanna didn't have to see a gun to understand they were both in terrible danger, that they had to get away.

"Come on, Holly," Joanna urged, overtaking the no-longer-moving woman. "Don't stop now." But Holly was already making the first hesitant motions toward retracing her steps.

"Don't you want to see what's up here?" Joanna taunted, trying her best to counter the almost magnetic effect Amy Baxter's voice seemed to have on Holly Patterson.

"She already kept you from doing this once," Joanna continued. "You're not going to let her take it away from you again, are you? Not when you're this close."

Holly looked at Joanna, as though trying to

make sense of what she was saying, but now she stopped and didn't move in either direction. Joanna dared to look back down, wondering why Amy's shouting had suddenly stopped. On the far side of the fence, Amy Baxter and Rex Rogers seemed to be standing and arguing.

"Come on, Holly," Joanna urged again, knowing the respite wouldn't last long. "Why won't she let you climb up here? What's Amy Baxter afraid of?"

And then, miraculously, Holly was moving in the right direction again, climbing slowly uphill with Joanna scrambling along at her side. Off in the distance, she could hear the sound of a wailing siren, of some siren, but Joanna didn't know the sounds well enough to differentiate between one emergency vehicle and another. She couldn't tell whether what was coming was a police car of some kind or one of Bisbee's fire trucks.

And even if it was a police vehicle, Joanna thought despairingly, it wouldn't be coming for her. How could it? She had told Kristin where she was going, but she hadn't expected this kind of difficulty.

"Holly!" Amy was shouting again. "Are you listening to me?"

Joanna looked down. Rex Rogers was no longer visible, but Amy was. She had crawled through the fence and even now was at the base of the dump and starting to climb.

"Holly," she ordered. "I told you to stop! Come back! I want to talk to you."

Holly slowed once more. "Don't listen to her," Joanna urged. "Shut her out! Sing something."

Already, Holly's eyes were starting to glaze over. The pull of Amy Baxter's voice was so strong as to be almost irresistible. In desperation, Joanna Brady began to sing the only song she could remember at a moment's notice. A hiking song, from her days in the Girl Scouts. She sang it at the top of her panting, air-starved lungs.

> *"Ninety-nine bottles of beer on the wall,*
> *Ninety-nine bottles of beer.*
> *You take one down and pass it around,*
> *Ninety-eight bottles of beer on the wall."*

And to her amazement, Holly Patterson miraculously began to climb once more.

By then Joanna was slightly in the lead, and by then the top of the dump was only a few feet away. Joanna was first over the top, pulling herself up over a steep lip and then falling down the far side into what was evidently a rough roadway. On the other side of the road was a raised ridge, a berm, that formed an inner boundary along the entire length of road as far as the eye could see.

Staying low and slipping her automatic out of the shoulder holster, Joanna belly-crawled back to the edge and looked down. Holly had stopped again, cowering in an eroded dip behind a precariously perched boulder only inches from the top. Below them Amy Baxter was climbing steadily.

"Come on down, Holly," Amy was grunting between breaths. "I won't hurt you."

"She's lying," Joanna yelled. "Don't listen to her. Come on! Up here!"

But once more Holly seemed frozen, unable to move.

"Give me your hand!" Joanna ordered. "Now!"

When Holly failed to budge, Joanna reached down and grasped Holly's wrist. With a surge of strength Joanna had no idea she possessed, she hauled Holly up and over the edge. She tumbled down the lip and landed with a breathless thump. Joanna tumbled after her and lifted the fallen woman to her feet.

"Go," Joanna urged, pointing toward the ridge and drawing the Colt. She wasn't sure whether or not Amy was armed but if there was a possibility weapons would be involved, Joanna wanted Holly behind her, out of the line of fire. The ridge on the other side of the road seemed to offer the only possible cover. But Holly seemed incapable of independent action. She stared at Joanna uncomprehendingly and didn't move.

"Come on, then," Joanna said, grabbing Holly's hand again and dragging her forward. As they started up and over the side of the berm, there was a clatter of dislodged rock from the side of the dump. At that critical instant, Joanna glanced back over her shoulder.

Rather than being just a berm, the ridge was actually the outside of a retaining wall for one of the series of rectangular copper leaching ponds that covered most of the surface of the dump. On the outside, the retaining wall was simply a rocky ridge, but the inside was covered with a slick layer of slimy, greaselike silt.

In desperation to reach safety and to protect the seemingly helpless woman who was now in her charge, Joanna had been moving as fast as possible. Now, as they topped the berm, there was nothing at all to break their forward momentum. Staggering like a pair of inept skiers, they skidded down the slippery bank and into the water, where they landed, floundering and sputtering, in the chemically saturated water of a Phelps Dodge leaching pond.

Thirty-Six

THE FIRST shock of landing in frigid water took Joanna's breath away. For a moment, she was too stunned to move. When she tried, her hands and knees slipped and slid on the oozy, slime-covered bottom. Finally, though, she managed to pull herself out of the evil-smelling water and back up onto the berm.

Grabbing Holly's arm, she dragged her out as well and up onto the bank where they both lay, gasping and spent. As soon as her head cleared, she realized her gun was gone. Her brand-new First Edition Colt 2000 was lost somewhere in the whitish slime at the bottom of the coppery-colored pool.

If Joanna had paused long enough to think about how cold the water was or how filled with God-knows-what kinds of chemicals, she never would have plunged back into the pond. But the semi-automatic was essential. Without a backup coming, she had to have a weapon.

Holding her breath against the assault of cold, Joanna plowed back into the icy water, splashing through the mud in her numbed bare feet, using them to dredge through the thick sludge on the murky bottom. The harsh leaching chemicals burned fiercely in the lacerations on the bottoms of her bleeding feet, but she was grateful for the burning sensation. At least she could feel her feet again, and she used them to good advantage—dragging them through the water.

Although it seemed much longer, it was only a matter of seconds before she smashed the end of her big toe on the grip of the missing weapon, and once she had it in her hand, it was all she could do to hold on to the slippery, slime-covered metal. With fingers stiff and awkward with cold, she pulled the relatively clean tail of her blouse free of her skirt and used that to wipe off the muck from the Colt.

Her hands were shaking violently with the cold. How long before hypothermia sets in? she wondered.

"Where are you, Holly?" Amy Baxter's voice came again, calling from much closer now, from somewhere on the other side of the berm.

At the sound of her voice, Holly moaned like someone in desperate pain. She dropped to the ground and didn't move.

"Come here," Amy continued. "I only want to talk to you."

"What's going on?" Joanna demanded, falling down on the berm beside Holly, forcing the woman to lower her head so it would be out of sight. "Why was she keeping you locked up? Why doesn't she want you to get away?"

But Holly didn't answer. She huddled next to Joanna, quaking with cold and saying nothing.

"Holly," Joanna snapped. "Answer the damn question!"

"This has to be where it was," Holly muttered through chattering teeth. "Right here. Below where we are right now."

"What was here?" Joanna asked, raising her head an inch or so, trying to peer over the top of the berm without being seen herself.

"His house," Holly answered. "Not a house really. Just a Quonset hut with a bare concrete floor. I remember that now. I remember seeing the green trees of *Casa Vieja* from there, the trees and the terraces."

"Holly," Amy's disembodied voice called. "Where are you? Come out so I can see you, so we can talk." She spoke her words slowly, putting a peculiar weight behind each and every syllable. "Come here."

At once Holly's eyes began to glaze, and she started to rise to her feet. With a grunt of effort, Joanna jerked her back down.

"I've got to go," Holly said. "Amy wants me."

"Why?" Joanna demanded. "Just tell me why."

"I don't know." Holly began sobbing. "She sounds mad at me. I must have done something wrong."

It was becoming more and more clear to Joanna that the sound of Amy's voice exerted some kind of hypnotic mental hold on Holly, and the only way to counter it was to keep her too occupied to fall under Amy's spell. Joanna moved closer to the weeping woman, until their faces were mere inches apart.

"You haven't done anything wrong, Holly. They had you locked in your room. Getting away from people like that isn't bad, believe me. Why didn't they want you to come up here?"

"They were afraid I'd remember."

"Remember what?"

"His face," Holly whispered. "I saw it for a while. I think I saw it on a piece of paper, but it went away again, and now I can't remember."

"Holly," Amy Baxter said. "Where are you? We have to talk."

"Whose face?" Joanna asked. "I don't understand."

"The man's face ... the man who ..." Holly's voice faded into nothing.

"The man who what?" Joanna demanded.

"The man who hurt me. A long time ago."

Joanna remembered Isobel talking about Holly looking at the paper, the *Bisbee Bee*. She had seen a copy of the paper that morning herself. There had been two pictures on the front page: Harold Lamm Patterson's and Thornton Kimball's.

"You saw the man's face in the newspaper?"

"Yes."

"Your father?"

"No, not him. The other one."

"It was, too, your father," Amy Baxter said, appearing over the ridge of the berm. "You're confused, Holly. You're making things up."

There was no sign of a weapon on Amy's person, but with that voice of hers, she was nonetheless armed. Joanna held up the Colt. "Stay where you are, Amy. Don't come any closer. This is loaded. I'll use it if I have to."

"Don't threaten me. You can see I'm not armed. I came to get Holly and take her back to bed before she freezes to death. You had no business bringing an invalid out into weather like this. You're soaked, Holly. Come along."

"She's staying with me until I get to the bottom of all this," Joanna countered. "Why did you have her locked in her room?"

"Isn't that obvious?" Amy asked. "Twice, now, so far today, she's taken off on her own and run to this dump. She could fall and hurt herself. Or worse."

"What's here on the dump?" Joanna demanded. "Or else under it. She said something about a house, a Quonset hut."

"There's nothing here."

"Yes, there was." Holly insisted suddenly. "Don't you remember, Amy? My father told us all about it. About where Uncle Thorny and Aunt Bonnie were staying when it happened. When it happened the first time."

"Be quiet, Holly," Amy ordered sharply. "You're confused and making things up. He didn't say any such thing."

Slowly, the picture was beginning to shift into focus. Of course. Uncle Thorny. Thornton Kimball. The other picture in the paper along with Harold Patterson's.

"Is Uncle Thorny the one who hurt you when you were little?"

Holly didn't answer. Instead she collapsed face-down on the berm, weeping.

"Look what you've done," Amy Baxter said, taking a step toward them.

"I said don't move, and I meant it!" Joanna ordered through chattering teeth. She was so cold now, she wasn't sure she could pull the trigger if she had to, but Amy Baxter took her at her word and stayed where she was.

"That's it, isn't it?" Joanna said. "You fingered the wrong man."

"I don't know what you're talking about," Amy returned.

"Yes, you do. I know about you and your forgotten-memory program. I read the article in *People*. You correctly identified Holly as someone who had been molested as a child, but when you went through the forgotten-memory process, you dredged up the wrong man, didn't you?"

Amy Baxter's face grew stony. "Come on, Holly. It's time to go. We'll go back down to the house and put you to bed."

"Why?" Joanna taunted. "So you can make her remember what you want her to remember and forget what you want her to forget?"

"Holly, come!"

But the cord had frayed too much. The choke chain of Amy's voice didn't work as it must have in the past. Holly Patterson didn't move.

"She's not a dog, Amy," Joanna said. "She doesn't have to obey you just because you issue an order. What else have you made her forget?"

"I remember the rocks," Holly said softly, almost to herself. "Rocks that were so big, I could barely lift them."

"Holly!" Amy warned, but her voice had no effect.

"I carried them for her one at a time. Carried the rocks over to the hole. I could hear him the whole time. He was down there in the hole, crying and begging her to stop, please stop. But she wouldn't. Mother kept right on throwing the rocks down there. . . ."

"Holly . . ."

The tears had stopped. Holly's voice had taken on a strange, dreamlike quality. It was as though she wasn't telling a story that had happened almost half a century ago but reporting something she was watching right then, the action being replayed on the indelible screen of a much younger mind.

". . . and crying and saying he'd never do it again. He'd never hurt anyone ever, ever again. And then Father was there. He grabbed her by the arms. He held her and made her stop. I remember now. He held us both. And he said it was going to be okay."

The whole time Holly was speaking, Joanna never took her eyes off Amy. For some time after Holly finished, they were all three quiet.

"You're finished, aren't you?" Joanna said at last to Amy Baxter. "This shoots your credibility right down the toilet."

"You think someone's going to believe her?" Amy said contemptuously. "If she remembered one thing wrong, the rest of it may be wrong as well. People will just call her a liar."

"I'm not lying!" Holly said. "I'm telling the truth. Why did you do it?"

Amy shook her head. "This is stupid. It's too cold to stand outside arguing like this. I'm leaving."

She turned and started back toward the edge of the dump. If she was walking away with no further threat, it seemed as though the confrontation was over. In the sudden quiet, Joanna could hear sirens now. A whole flock of them, so perhaps backup help was on its way.

Meanwhile Holly was pulling herself up onto her hands and knees. "Why did you?" she said again. "Why did you make me throw those rocks again, just like I did before. You said it was Uncle Thorny and that I was finally going to get rid of him. But it wasn't. It was my father. My God, Amy! I killed him, didn't I? You made me kill my own father!"

As she spoke, Holly's voice keened up in pitch, rising on the cold air like the howl of a wounded wild thing. And the sound of that desperate voice acted like a string on her body, pulling her collapsed form up from the ground the way a puppeteer gives life to a limp marionette.

Amy didn't pause or look back. Holly, on her feet now, lurched after Amy.

Joanna, watching Amy over the top of the berm, making sure she intended no further harm, saw too late that Holly was flailing after Amy.

Afterward, there was never any clear way to tell exactly what happened—whether Holly Patterson reached out for Amy to grab her and stop her or whether she pushed her over the edge. For a moment, the two of them grappled there together—tottering on the brink, hanging in space. And then they both disappeared.

Two separate and distinct screams floated back up to the top of the dump. Joanna Brady heard them both, heard the clatter of falling rocks and boulders that were jarred loose as they fell. And then there was silence.

A moment later, Dick Voland's voice floated up to her. "Sheriff Brady," he shouted. "Sheriff Joanna Brady! Where the hell are you?"

"Here," she called back. "Up here on top!"

Huffing and puffing, out of breath from a mad scramble up the side of the dump, Chief Deputy Dick Voland was the first person to reach Joanna's side.

"Are you all right?" he demanded, throwing his own jacket around her quaking shoulders.

"I'm okay."

"The hell you are." He stomped away from her to the top of the berm. "We need another ambulance up here," he shouted. "Now! And blankets. On the double!"

Voland came back. Somehow Joanna's legs gave way, and she sank back to the ground. Dick Voland knelt beside her. "The city ambulance is down below. I've got cars and an ambulance coming here, but they'll have to come by way of the main gate with a P.D. watchman escort."

Joanna nodded through chattering teeth that made speech impossible.

"Lie down," Dick Voland urged. "Lie down before you fall down!"

Joanna did her best to obey. The two hands that eased her down to the ground were both strong and amazingly gentle.

"Are you hurt?"

She shook her head. "Just . . . co . . . co . . . cold!"

Two deputies and a pair of emergency medical technicians scrambled over the top of the berm. Blankets appeared out of nowhere. One of the EMTs slapped a blood-pressure cuff around Joanna's arm, while the other helped wrap her in the blanket. "How are the other two?" Voland asked. The EMT shook his head and didn't answer. Which, in itself, was answer enough.

Voland knelt in front of Joanna and examined her stained and bleeding feet, watching her face anxiously while the medics went to work. As it became clear Joanna wasn't badly injured his anxiety turned to anger.

"If you were one of my deputies," he growled, "I'd fire your ass in a minute! What the hell do you mean trying to pull some kind of rescue stunt without a damn word? If that lawyer hadn't lost his nerve and yelled for help, it could have been much worse."

Joanna tried to answer but couldn't. Right then talking was out of the question.

"Forget it!" Voland barked. "And by the way, forget about that letter I gave you. If you want to fire me, fine. But if you're going to pull this kind of damn-fool stunt, you need me too damned bad for me to quit."

Thirty-Seven

THINGS BECAME hazy after that. Gradually, Joanna realized there were emergency lights coming toward them on the road that ran along the outside edge of the dump. The ambulance that arrived was an old one that Phelps Dodge still maintained on its own property.

The next thing Joanna remembered was arriving at the hospital. An emergency-room nurse approached the gurney. Brandishing a pair of scissors in one hand, she had a determined businesslike look on her face, but she spoke like an effusive kindergarten teacher.

"I'll just help you out of those wet things," she said, starting to peel off the wet layers. "We'll get you wrapped up in some nice warm blankets."

Joanna looked down at what was left of her torn blouse and once-good wool skirt. The material on both was a yellow, mottled brown. "Don't cut off my clothes," Joanna said. "I can take them off myself. This is an almost new outfit. I'll have it cleaned."

"Forget it, honey," the nurse told her. "What ails these clothes no dry cleaner in the world is going to fix."

With that, she started with what was left of Joanna's panty hose and began working her way up. Only when she got as far as the bulletproof vest and shoulder holster, was the nurse stymied enough to let Joanna remove them under her own steam.

Jenny arrived at the emergency room, big-eyed and frightened, as the doctor finished cleaning and bandaging Joanna's stained and lacerated feet.

"Mom, are you okay? What happened?"

Two more people were dead—Amy Baxter and Holly in addition to Harold Patterson. Joanna was struggling to figure what part of the responsibility for those two additional deaths was hers alone.

"It's a new job," Joanna said. "I think it's going to take a while to learn how to do it."

Eva Lou Brady appeared and said she was taking Jenny home with her and that she'd make sure the dogs got fed. "Thank you," Joanna told her.

The phone in Joanna's room rang almost before the nurses lifted her off the gurney and loaded her into the bed. "How long are you in for?" Adam York asked.

"Just overnight I think. How did you know to call me here?"

"I tried to call you about Yuri Malakov's prints. He checks out, by the way. According to my sources, there's nothing to worry about as far as he's concerned. When I called your office to let you know, they told me there'd been a problem with you. What the hell happened?"

Joanna told him.

"Tombstone Courage," he said when she fin-

J. A. Jance

ished. "Not a fatal case, at least not for you, but Tombstone Courage all the same."

"What's that?"

"Have you started reading that book I sent you?"

"No. Not yet."

"Where is it?"

"Out at the house."

"Have someone go get it and bring it to you. You read every word of that book before you leave that hospital. Understand?"

"Yes, sir."

Marianne Maculyea brought the book to the hospital later that evening along with a suitcase of toiletries. Despite the disapproval of the nurses, Joanna read *Officer Down* all the way through. It was an awful book. An appalling book. One at a time, it listed and gave horrifying examples of the ten fatal errors police officers make.

Number eight was Tombstone Courage. Failure to call for backup. Adam York was right. Sheriff Joanna Brady had been guilty as charged.

It was Wednesday of the following week when Joanna had her appointment with Burton Kimball to make arrangements to draw up the guardianship. Once she had asked Jeff and Marianne and they had agreed to serve, she didn't want any time to pass before getting the details ironed out. Joanna knew now that lightning did strike the same place on occasion, and she wanted to be prepared. She was due to leave for Peoria the following Monday to take her six-week county-paid training

404

course, and she didn't want Jennifer's guardianship hanging fire while she was gone.

When Joanna looked up from signing the last documents, she caught Burton Kimball staring at her. "I'm glad you weren't hurt worse than you were," he said.

Joanna blushed and looked down at her feet. She was still clunking around with bandages covered by rubber-soled splints.

"I never saw Holly going after Amy Baxter until it was too late. If I had seen her in time, maybe I could have stopped her."

"No," Burton said. "Don't blame yourself. It wasn't your fault, any more than it was anyone else's. Everyone did the best they could under terrible circumstances."

"Was it deliberate, do you think?" Joanna asked. "Or was it an accident?"

"It doesn't really matter, does it?" Burton Kimball said. "What does matter now is that it's over."

"Is a tragedy like that ever over?" Too many people were dead, Joanna thought. Too many lives were changed.

Burton Kimball sighed and opened his desk drawer. "I think such things can come to an end," he said. "Ivy gave me this. It's a letter she found in Uncle Harold's safety-deposit box. She told me it was up to me whether or not I showed it to you."

He put it on the desk, but Joanna made no effort to pick it up. "What is it?" she asked.

"It's Aunt Emily's confession," he said. "To my father's murder. She didn't want anyone else to be

405

blamed. She caught my father . . ." He broke off and couldn't continue.

Joanna picked the letter up and read it. Afterward she gazed thoughtfully out Burton Kimball's window at the gray mountainside. Finally she put the letter back in the envelope.

"I don't think anyone else needs to see that letter, Burton," she said quietly. "You never mentioned it, and I never saw it. Understand?"

He nodded. "Thank you," he said, and put the letter away.

"How is Ivy, by the way?" Joanna asked.

For the first time, the somber look on Burton Kimball's face lightened. "She's having a hell of a time with morning sickness. Linda says it'll most likely be a boy. She says morning sickness is always worse with boys."

Joanna was genuinely surprised. "I don't believe it. Ivy Patterson pregnant? I thought she was tutoring Yuri in *English*!"

Burton grinned. "It is something, isn't it?" he said. "You'd think someone her age would know better than to let that happen, wouldn't you? But I guess she just got carried away. Sowing her wild oats, as they say. Uncle Harold would be thrilled if he knew it. In fact, if it is a boy, I hope they name it after him."

"So do I," Joanna said.

The following Friday morning, Frank Montoya, formerly the Willcox city marshal and now the newly appointed chief deputy for administration, was present for his first-ever Cochise County Sheriff's Department briefing.

With Joanna going off to class for six weeks the following Monday morning, she had wanted to fill that position as soon as possible. She wanted someone who was on her side keeping an eye on things in her absence.

She knew now that she could pull her own weight around the department, but in choosing a right-hand man, she had decided on Frank Montoya, her old opponent.

When Dick Voland and Ernie Carpenter left Joanna's office after the briefing, Frank stayed on for a few minutes. "Are you sure Dick Voland won't shoot me in the back while you're gone?" Frank asked with a grin.

"As long as you don't do anything stupid," she told him. "Both Dick Voland and Ernie Carpenter are real hard on stupidity. That's why those two guys have been around so long. That's why we need them."

"Whatever you say, Chief," Frank said.

He went out and closed the door. Joanna leaned back in her chair and closed her eyes for a moment. Then she opened them and looked down at the worn buffalo-head nickel she was holding in her hand.

All during the meeting, she'd been holding Andy's nickel concealed in the palm of her hand, holding it for luck.

After a moment, she opened her top desk drawer and dropped the nickel back inside. She wasn't going to take that to Peoria to class with her. She'd leave it there in Bisbee in the sheriff's cherrywood desk.

She'd leave it where it belonged.

At the beginning of *Desert Heat* Joanna Brady
was the happy young wife of an ambitious deputy
who was running for sheriff of Cochise County
in an attempt to create reforms that would control
the increasing lawlessness associated with the drug
trade. A successful insurance worker, the daughter
of a previous county sheriff, and the mother of a
nine-year-old daughter, she was looking forward
to supporting her husband's campaign.

When he was gunned down by an assassin sent
to town by a drug lord and then framed for murder and drug-running, Joanna felt compelled to
take a hand in rescuing his reputation and assum-
ing his candidacy for sheriff.

As you've just finished reading in the second
book, *Tombstone Courage*, Joanna successfully runs
for sheriff, encounters entrenched opposition
within her own department, and manages to solve
a major and complicated murder case, but only by
foolishly risking her life in a way that no properly-
trained officer would imagine doing.

J. A. Jance

Realizing that she must learn the basics of law enforcement in a hurry in order to effectively run and lead her department, Joanna has made the difficult decision to leave her daughter and the department for a five-week session at the Arizona Police Officers' Academy school in a suburb of Phoenix. Inevitably she becomes embroiled in complications both personal and professional. The following excerpt from *Shoot, Don't Shoot* simultaneously illustrates Joanna's strengths and weaknesses and should be a tantalizing look into the latest Brady adventure which will be available in hardcover from William Morrow in summer 1995.

Within minutes of the beginning of Dave Thompson's opening classroom lecture, Joanna was ready to pack her bags and go back home to Bisbee. Her first encounter with the bull-necked Thompson hadn't left a very good impression. The lecture made his stock go down even further.

Listening to him talk, Joanna could close her eyes and imagine that she was listening to her chief deputy for operations, Dick Voland. The words used, the opinions voiced, were almost the same. Why should she bother to travel four hundred miles round trip and spend the better part of six weeks locked up in a classroom when she could have the same kind of aggravation for free at home just by going into the office? The only difference between listening to Dave Thompson and being lectured to by Dick Voland lay in the fact that after a day of wrangling with Voland, Joanna could at least go home to her own bed at night. As far as beds were concerned, the ones in the APOA dormitory weren't worth a damn.

The man droned on and on. Joanna had to fight to stay awake while Dave Thompson paced back and forth in front of the class. Joanna had spent years listening to Jim Bob Brady's warm Southern drawl. Thompson's down-home manner of speech sounded put-on and gratingly phony. Waving an old-fashioned pointer for emphasis, he delivered a drill instructor–style diatribe meant to scare off all but the most serious-minded of the assembled students.

"Look around you," he urged, waggling the pointer until it encompassed all the people in the room. "There'll be some faces missing by the time we get to the end of this course. We generally expect a washout rate of between forty and fifty percent, and that's in a good class."

Joanna raised her eyebrows at that. The night before Thompson had said this was a good class. This morning it wasn't. What had changed his mind?

"You may have noticed that there aren't any television sets in these rooms of yours," Thompson continued. "No swimming pool or tennis courts, either. This ain't no paid vacation, my friends. You're here to work, plain and simple. You'd by God better get that straight from the get-go.

"There may be a few party animals in the crowd. If you think you can party all night long and then drag your ass in here the next morning and sleep through the lectures, think again. Days are for class work, and nights are for hitting the books. Do I make myself clear?"

Careful not to move her head in any direction, Joanna kept her eyes focused on Thompson's beefy face. Peripheral vision allowed her a glimpse of movement in the front row where a young blond-haired man nodded his head in earnest agreement. The gesture of unquestioning approval was so pronounced it was a wonder his teeth didn't rattle.

"Over the next few weeks you'll be working with a staff made up from outstanding officers who have been selected from jurisdictions all over the state," Thompson was saying. "These are the guys who, along with yours truly, will be conducting most of the classroom instruction. We'll be overseeing some of the hands-on training as well as evaluating each student's individual progress. All told, the instructors here have a combined total of more than one hundred and twenty years of law enforcement experience. Try that on for size."

He paused and grinned. "You know what they say about experience and treachery, don't you? Wins out over youth and enthusiasm every time. Count on it."

The room was quiet. No doubt the comment had been meant as a joke, but no one laughed. While Thompson consulted his notes, Joanna noticed that the young guy in the front row was busily nodding once again.

"That brings us to the subject of ride-alongs," Thompson resumed. "When it comes time for those, you'll be doing them with experienced on-duty officers from one or more of the participating agencies here in the Valley. By the way, be sure to sign the ride-along waivers in your packet and return them to me by the end of the day.

"This particular class procedure is my baby. It's also the backbone of what we do here. As you all know, the academy is being funded partially by state and federal grants and partially by the tuition paid by each participating agency. Tuition doesn't come cheap. The state maybe picked up this fine facility for a song from the folks at the RTC, but we've gotta pay our way. Here's how it works, folks. Listen up.

"Each person's whole tuition and room rent is due and payable on the first day of class. In other words, today. The minute you all walked through our door this morning, that money was gone. The academy doesn't do refunds. You quit tonight, too bad. The guy who hired you—the one who sent you here in the first place—doesn't get to put that money back in his departmental budget. That means anybody who drops out turns into a regular pain in the bottom line.

"In other words, boys and girls, if you blow this chance, you end up outta here and outta law enforcement, too. Nobody in his right mind's gonna give a quitter another opportunity.

"For those of you who don't blow it, for those of you who make the grade, when you go back to your various departments, you're more than welcome to do things the way they do them there. Here at the academy, we have our own procedures, and we do things our way. The APOA way. In other words, as that great American hero

A. J. Foyt has been quoted as saying, 'my way or the highway.'

"It's like you and your ex-wife own this little dog, and the doggie spends part of the time at her house and part of the time at yours. Maybe your ex doesn't mind if the dog climbs all over her damn furniture, but you do. When the dog goes to her house, he does whatever the hell he damn well pleases, but when he's at your house, he lives by your rules. Got it?"

Joanna didn't even have to look to know that the guy in the front row was nodding once again. Disgusted by what she'd heard, and convinced the whole training experience was destined to be nothing more than five weeks of hot air, she folded her arms across her chest, sighed, and sank down in her seat. Next to her at the table sat a tall, slender young woman with hair almost as red as Joanna's.

Using one hand to shield her face from the speaker's view, the other woman grinned in Joanna's direction, then crossed both eyes. Wary that Thompson might have spotted the derogatory gesture, Joanna glanced in the speaker's direction, but he was far too busy pontificating to notice the byplay. Relieved, Joanna smiled back. Somehow that bit of schoolgirlish highjinks made Joanna feel better. If nothing else, it convinced her that she wasn't the only person in the room who regarded Dave Thompson as a loud-mouthed, overbearing jerk.

"Our mission here is to turn you people into police officers," Thompson continued. "It's not easy, and it's gonna get down and dirty at times. If you two ladies think you're going to come through this course looking like one of the sexy babes on 'L. A. Law,' you'd better think again."

The redhead at the table next to Joanna scribbled a hasty note on a yellow notepad and then pushed it close enough so Joanna could read it. "Who has time to watch TV?" the note asked.

This time Joanna had to cough in order to suppress an involuntary giggle. She had never watched the show herself, but according to Eva Lou "L. A. Law" had always been a favorite with Jim Bob Brady. Eva Lou said she thought it had something to do with the length of the women's skirts.

Thompson glowered once in Joanna's direction, but he didn't pause for breath. "Out on the streets it's gonna be a matter of life and death—your life or your partner's, or the life of some innocent bystander. Every department in the state has a mandate to bring more women and minorities on board. Cultural diversity is okay, I guess," he added, sounding unconvinced.

"It's probably even a good thing, up to a point—as long as those new hires are all fully qualified people. And that's where the APOA comes in. The buck stops here. The training we offer is supposed to help separate the men from the boys, if you will. The wheat from the chaff. The people who can handle this job from the wimps who can't. We're going to start that process here and now. Could I have a volunteer?"

Pausing momentarily, Thompson's gray eyes

scanned the room. Naturally the guy in the front row, the head-bobber, raised his hand and waved it in the air. Thompson ignored him. Tapping the end of the pointer with one hand, he allowed his gaze to come to rest on Joanna. A half smile tweaked the corners of his mouth.

"My mother always taught me that it was ladies before gentlemen. Tell the class your name."

"Joanna," she answered. "Joanna Brady."

"And where are you from?"

"Cochise County," Joanna answered.

"And how long have you been a police officer now?" he asked.

"Less than two weeks."

Thompson nodded. "That's good. We like to get our recruits in here early—before they have time to learn too many bad habits. And why, exactly, do you want to be a cop?"

Joanna wasn't sure what to say. Each student in the class wore a plastic badge that listed his or her name and home jurisdiction. The badges gave no indication of rank. Hoping to blend in with her classmates, Joanna wasn't eager to reveal that although she was as much of a rookie as any of the others, she was also a newly-elected county sheriff.

"Well?" Thompson urged impatiently.

"My father was a police officer," she said flatly. "So was my husband."

Thompson frowned. "That's right," he said. "I remember your daddy, old D. H. Lathrop. Good man. And your husband's the one who got shot in the line of duty, isn't he?"

Joanna bit her lip and nodded. Andy's death as

well as its violent aftermath had been big news back in September. Both their pictures and names had been plastered in newspapers and on television broadcasts all over Arizona.

"And unless I'm mistaken, you had something to do with the end of that case, didn't you, Mrs. Brady? Wasn't there some kind of shootout?"

"Yes," Joanna answered, recalling the charred edges of the single bullet hole that still branded the pocket of her sheepskin-lined jacket.

"So it would be safe to assume that you've used a handgun before—that you have some experience?" The rising inflection in Dave Thompson's voice made it sound as if he were asking a question, but Joanna understood that he already knew the answer.

A vivid flush crept up her neck and face. The last thing Joanna wanted was to be singled out from her classmates, the other academy attendees. Dave Thompson seemed to have other ideas. He focused on her in a way that caused all the other people in the room to recede into the background.

"Yes," she answered softly, keeping her voice level, fending off the natural urge to blink. "I suppose it would."

Thompson smiled and nodded. "Good," he said. "You come on up here then. We'll have you take the first shot, if you'll excuse the pun." Visibly appreciative of his own joke, he grinned and seemed only vaguely disappointed when Joanna didn't respond in kind.

Unsure what the joke was, Joanna rose resolutely from her chair and walked to the front of the classroom. Her hands shook, more from suppressed anger at being singled out than with any kind of nervousness or stage fright. Weeks of public speaking on the campaign trail had cured her of all fear of appearing in front of a group of strangers.

The room was arranged as a formal classroom with half a dozen rows of tables facing a front podium. Behind the podium stood several carts loaded with an assortment of audio/visual equipment. As he spoke, Thompson moved one cart holding a video console and VCR to a spot beside the podium. He knelt for a few moments in front of the cart and selected a video from a locked storage cabinet underneath. After inserting the video in the VCR, Thompson reached into another locked storage cabinet and withdrew a holstered service revolver and belt.

"Ever seen one of these before?"

The way he was holding the weapon, Joanna wasn't able to see anything about it. "I'm not sure," she said.

"For your information," Thompson returned haughtily, "it happens to be a revolver."

His contemptuous tone implied that he had misread her inability to see the weapon as total ignorance as far as guns were concerned. "It's a .38," he continued. "A Smith and Wesson Model 10 Military and Police revolver with a four-inch barrel."

He handed the belt and holstered weapon to Joanna. "Here," he said. "Take this and put it on.

Don't be afraid," he added. "It's loaded with blanks."

Removing the gun from the holster, Joanna swung open the cylinder. One by one, she checked each of the rounds, ascertaining for herself that they were indeed blanks loaded with paper wadding rather than metal bullets. Only after reinserting the rounds did she look back at Dave Thompson who was watching her with rapt interest.

"So you do know something about guns."

"A little," she returned with a grim smile. "And you're right. They are all blanks. I hope you don't mind my checking for myself. My father always taught me that when it comes to loaded weapons, I shouldn't take anybody else's word for it."

There was a rustle of appreciative chuckles from a few of Joanna's fellow classmates. Dave Thompson was not amused. "What else did your daddy teach you?" he asked.

"One or two things," Joanna answered. "Now what do you want me to do with this pistol?"

"Put it back in the holster and strap on the belt."

The belt—designed to be used on adult male bodies—was cumbersome and several sizes too large for Joanna's slender waist. Even fastened in the tightest configuration, the heavy belt slipped down until it rested on the curve of her hips rather than staying where it belonged. Convinced the low-slung gun made her look like a comic parody of some old-time gunfighter, Joanna felt ridiculous. As she struggled with the awkward belt, she barely heard what Thompson was saying.

"You ever hear of a shoot/don't shoot scenario?"

"I don't think so."

"You're about to. Here's what we're gonna do. Once you get that belt on properly, I want you to spend a few minutes practicing removing the weapon and returning it to the holster. No matter what you see on TV, cops don't spend all their time walking around holding drawn side arms in their hands. But when you need a gun, you've gotta be able to get it out in a hell of a hurry."

Joanna attempted to do as she was told. By then the belt had slipped so far down her body, she was afraid it was going to fall off altogether. Each time she tried to draw the weapon, the belt jerked up along with the gun. With the belt sliding loosely around her waist, she couldn't get enough leverage to pull the gun free of the holster. It took several bumbling tries before she finally succeeded in freeing the gun from the leather.

"Very good," Dave Thompson said at last. "Now, here's the next step. I want you to stand right here beside the VCR. The tape I just loaded is one of about a hundred or so that we use here at the academy. In each one, the camera is the cop. The lens of the camera is situated at the cop's eye level. You'll be seeing the incident unfold through the cop's eyes, through his point of view. You'll see what he sees; hear what he hears.

"Each scenario is based on a real case," he added. "You'll have the same information available to you as the cop did in the real case. At some point in the film—some critical juncture in the action—you will have to decide whether or not to draw your weapon, whether or not to fire. It's up to you. Ready?"

Joanna nodded. Aware that all eyes in the room were turned on her, she waited while Thompson checked to be sure the plug was in and then switched on the video.

For a moment the screen was covered with snow, then the room was filled with the sound of a mumbled police radio transmission. When the picture came on, Joanna was seeing the world through the front windshield of a moving patrol car, one that was following another vehicle—a Ford Taurus—down a broad city street. Moments after the tape started, the lead vehicle, carrying two visible occupants, signaled for a right hand turn and then pulled off onto a tree-lined residential side street. Seconds later the patrol car turned as well. After following the lead vehicle for a block or two, there was the brief squawk from a siren as the officer signaled for the other car to pull over.

In what seemed like slow motion, the door of the patrol car opened and the officer stepped out into the seemingly peaceful street. The camera, positioned at shoulder height, moved jerkily toward the stopped car. In the background came a steady murmur of continuing radio transmissions. Standing just to the rear of the driver's door, the camera bent down and peered inside. Two young men were seated on the front seat.

"Step out of the car please," the officer said, speaking over the sound of loud music blaring from the radio in the Taurus.

The driver hesitated for a moment then moved

to comply. As he did so, his passenger suddenly slammed open the rider's door. He leaped from the car and went racing up the toy-littered sidewalk of a nearby home. For a moment the camera didn't move away from the door of the stopped Taurus, although its focus did. The scene on the screen swung back and forth several times, darting between the passenger fleeing up the sidewalk and the driver who was already raising his hands in the air and leaning over the hood of his vehicle.

"How come you stopped us?" the driver whined. "We wasn't doin' nothin'."

By then Joanna had lost track of everything but what was happening on the screen. A sudden knot tightened in her stomach as she was sucked into the scene's unfolding drama. She felt the responding officer's momentary but agonizing indecision. His hesitation was hers as well. Should he stay with the one suspect or go pounding up the sidewalk after the other one?

Joanna's mind raced as she tried to sort things out. As the fleeing suspect ran toward the house, she had caught a glimpse of something in his right hand. Was it a stick or a tire iron? Or was it a gun? From the little she had seen, there was no way to know for sure, but if one suspect carried a gun, chances were the other one did, too.

The kid with his hands in the air couldn't have been more than sixteen or seventeen. He wasn't a total innocent. No doubt he'd been involved in previous run-ins with the law. He knew the drill. Without being ordered to do so, he had automatically raised his hands, spread his legs, and bent over the hood of the car. Most law-abiding folks don't react quite that way when stopped for a routine traffic violation. They are far more likely to start rummaging shakily through glove compartments, searching frantically for elusive insurance papers and vehicle registrations.

As the camera's focus switched once more from the driver back to the fleeing suspect, Joanna again glimpsed something in his hand. Again she couldn't identify what it was, not for certain.

"Stop, police!" the invisible officer bellowed. "Drop it!"

The shouted order came too late. Even as the voice thundered out through speakers, the fleeing suspect vaulted up the steps, bounded across the porch, flung open the screen door, and shouldered his way into the house.

At once the camera started moving forward, jerking awkwardly up and down as the cop, too, raced up the sidewalk and onto the porch. Taking a hint from what was happening on-screen, Joanna began trying to wrest the Smith and Wesson out of the holster. Once again, the gun hung up on the balky leather while the belt and holster twisted loosely around her waist. Only after three separate tries did she manage to draw the weapon.

When she was able to glance back at the screen, the cop/camera had taken up a defensive position on the porch, crouching next to the wall of the house just to the right of the screen door. "Come out," he yelled. "Come out with your hands up!"

Just then Joanna heard the sound of a woman's voice coming from inside the house. "Who are you?" the rising female voice demanded. "What are you doing in my house? What do you want? What . . ."

Suddenly her voice changed. Outrage changed in pitch and became a shriek of terror. "No. Don't do that. Don't, please! No! Oh, no! Nooooooooo!"

"Come out," the officer ordered again. "Now!"

By then Joanna had the gun firmly in hand. She spread her feet into the proper stance and raised the revolver. The Smith and Wesson seemed far heavier than the brand new Colt 2000 Joanna personally owned, the one she was accustomed to using in daily target practice. Even holding the gun with both hands, it wasn't easy to keep her aim steady.

Suddenly the screen door crashed open. The first thing that appeared beyond the edge of the door was an arm holding the unmistakable silhouette of a drawn gun followed by the dark figure of the man who was carrying it.

As the suspect burst out through the open doorway, Joanna bit her lip. Aiming high enough for a chest shot, she eased back on the trigger. At once the classroom reverberated with the roar of the blank cartridge. Immediately the room filled with the smell of burned cordite, and the video screen went blank.

Holding the VCR's remote control, smiling and nodding, Dave Thompson stood up and looked around the room. "The lady seems to know how to shoot," he said. "But the question is, did she do the right thing?"

The guy in the front row was already waving

his hand in the air. "The officer never should have left the vehicle," he announced triumphantly. "He should have stayed where he was and radioed for backup."

That same sentiment was echoed in so many words by most of the rest of the class. While debate over Joanna's handling of the incident swirled around her, she resumed her seat.

The main focus of the discussion was what the officer should have done to take better control of the situation. "He for sure should have called for backup," someone else offered. "What if the other guy was armed, too? While the officer was chasing after the one guy, the other one could have turned on him as well."

The consensus seemed to be that in the heat of the moment the officer may not have done everything in his power to avert a possible tragedy.

Finally Dave Thompson called a halt to any further discussion. "All right, boys and girls," he said. "That's enough. Now we're going to see whether or not Officer Brady's response was right or wrong."

With a flick of the remote the video came back to life. The man on the VCR stepped out from behind the screen door. His right hand was fully extended, and the gun was now completely visible. He let the door slam shut behind him and then turned directly into the lens of the camera. As soon as he did so, there was a collective gasp from the entire room.

To her horror, Joanna saw that he was holding something in his other hand, something else in addition to the gun—a baby. A screaming, diaper-clad baby was clutched in the crook of his left elbow. As he moved toward the camera, the suspect held the frightened child chest-high, using the baby as a human shield.

A wave of gooseflesh swept down Joanna's body. Sickened, she realized she had deliberately aimed for the suspect's chest when she fired off her round. Had this been a real incident—had that been a real bullet—it would have sliced through the child. The baby would have died.

From the front of the classroom Dave Thompson looked squarely at Joanna. A superior, knowing grin played around the corners of his mouth.

"I guess you lose, little lady," he said, tapping the pointer in his right hand into the palm of his left. "Better luck next time."